Anonymous

The Lives and daring Deeds of the most celebrated Pirates and Bucaneers, of all Countries

Anonymous

The Lives and daring Deeds of the most celebrated Pirates and Bucaneers, of all Countries

ISBN/EAN: 9783337191269

Printed in Europe, USA, Canada, Australia, Japan

Cover: Foto ©Raphael Reischuk / pixelio.de

More available books at **www.hansebooks.com**

THE

LIVES AND DARING DEEDS

OF

THE MOST CELEBRATED

PIRATES AND BUCCANEERS,

OF ALL COUNTRIES.

With numerous Engravings.

PHILADELPHIA:
GEO. G. EVANS, 439 CHESTNUT STREET.

CONTENTS

MEWATTIES.—BHEELS.—BAUGRIES.—MOGHIES.— GWARRIAHS.—THUGS.

THE Pindarries whose modes of life and atrocities I have endeavoured to sketch, might have been thought of themselves a curse sufficient for any country, however vast, seeing, as we have done, with what rapidity and to what immense distances they were accustomed to extend their incursions. But besides these hordes, Central India was devastated by other associations of wretches, who for the most part subsisted entirely on plunder. Some of them seem to have struck their baneful roots in the country long ago, others to have arisen under the Mahratta system, and the times of revolution and trouble, which would naturally tend to give strength to the old and birth to the new—and facilities to the execrable operations of all. Sir John Malcolm has described, in a striking manner, the desolation which ensued from letting loose a population composed of such iniquitous materials. Only those who resided in walled towns were safe from the ravages and massacres of the banditti. The state of the unprotected parts of the country near the Vindyha mountains and the river Nerbudda, where hundreds of villages were seen deserted and roofless, is described by Captain Ambrose, one of Sir John Malcolm's officers: in the year 1818, he ascertained the names, and the names of the villages they belonged to, of eighty-four individuals who had been killed by tigers; these ferocious animals having literally usurped the country and fought with the returning inhabitants for their fields. Authentic documents also testify that in the state of Holkar, in 1817, sixteen hundred and sixty-three villages were deserted, or, as the natives emphatically term it—"without a lamp," a phrase that denotes the extreme of desolation. All this ruin had been effected by the banditti of Central India, and to Britons is due the cessation of such misery, and the restoration of the country to prosperity and peace.*

To proceed with these other robbers, in the order I have set them down:

The Mewatties are, or were (for happily we can use the past tense in almost all these cases!) an ambiguous race, half Mahometan, half Hindoo, who were not only robbers and assassins, but according to Sir John Malcolm, the most desperate rogues in India. It is delightful to learn from Bishop Heber, that they were in a great measure reclaimed, even when he travelled through the scenes of their crimes, which he did with perfect safety; and to contrast this with the former state of the country, when it was as dangerous as the interior of Arabia is at this moment, and when merchants were obliged to travel in caravans, and to pay high rates for protection to every paltry plundering Raja. "This neighbourhood," says the Bishop, speaking of part of the province of Delhi, "is still but badly cultivated; but fifteen years ago it was as wild as the Terrai, as full of tigers, and with no human inhabitants but banditti. Cattle-stealing still prevails to a considerable extent, but the Mewatties are now most of them subject either to the British Government or that of Bhurtpoor, and the security of life and property afforded them by the former, has induced many of the tribes to abandon their fortresses, to seat themselves in the plain, and cultivate the ground like honest men and good subjects."

the Bheels who inhabit the wild and mountainous tracts which separate Malwa from Nemaur and Guzerat, are a totally distinct race, insulated in their abodes, and separated by their habits, usages, and forms of worship, from

---

* In 1818 the number of villages restored was two hundred and sixty-nine; in 1819, three hundred and forty-three; and in 1820, five hundred and eight; leaving only five hundred and forty-three deserted, of which the whole are long ere this repeopled. This was all done under the influence of the British, whose benefits conferred upon humanity in India, are as a thousand to one in the scale against their injustice and injuries.

all other tribes of India. According to Bishop Heber, they were unquestionably the original inhabitants of Rajpootana, and driven to their fastnesses and desperate and miserable way of life by the invasion of those tribes, wherever they may have come from, who profess the religion of Brahma. "This the Rajpoots themselves virtually allow, by admitting in their traditional history, that most of their principal cities and fortresses were founded by such or such Bheel chiefs, and conquered from them by the children of the sun."

Here we have again, as it were, the Gael retreating from the Sassenach, and indemnifying and avenging himself by foray, blood, and plunder.

Thieves and savages as they were, the British officers who conversed with Bishop Heber, thought them on the whole a better race than their conquerors. Their word is said to be more to be depended on; they are of a franker and livelier character; their women are far better treated and enjoy more influence; and though they shed blood without scruple in cases of feud, or in the regular way of a foray, they are not vindictive or inhospitable under other circumstances, and several British officers have, with perfect safety, gone hunting and fishing in their country, without escort or guide, except what these poor savages themselves cheerfully furnished for a little brandy.

"In a Sanscrit vocabulary, seven hundred or more years old, the term Bheel denotes a particular race of barbarians living on plunder; and the Mahabharat, an ancient Hindoo poem, gives the same description of them. At all times formidable, they became the general terror of Central India under the guidance of Nadir Sing. This chief committed a murder, or rather caused it to be committed. The English had now the power of administering justice, and the following instance, which occurred on the trial of Nadir Sing, is strongly characteristic of the Bheel race.

" During the examination into the guilt of Nadir, when taking the evidence of some female prisoners, it appeared hat the father and husband of one of them, a girl abou·

fourteen years of age, had been instruments in committing the murder of which Nadir was accused. She was asked if they put the deceased to death, 'Certainly they did,' was her firm reply; 'but they acted by our Dhunnee's (or Lord's) order.'

" 'That may be true,' it was remarked, 'but it does not clear them; for it was not an affray; it was a deed perpetrated in cold blood.'

" 'Still,' said the girl, 'they had the chief's order!'

" The person* conducting the examination shook his head, implying it would not be received in justification. The child, for she was hardly more, rose from the ground where she was sitting, and, pointing to two sentries who guarded them, and were standing at the door of the room, exclaimed, with all the animation of strong feeling, " These are your soldiers; you are their Dhunnee; your words are their laws; if you order them this moment to advance, and put me, my mother, and cousin, who are now before you, to death, would they hesitate in slaying three female Bheels? If we are innocent, would you be guilty of our blood, or these faithful men?' After this observation she re-seated herself, saying, 'My father and husband are Nadir's soldiers.' "

The chiefs of the Bheels, indeed, who were usually called Bhomeahs, exercised the most absolute power, and their orders to commit the most atrocious crimes were obeyed, (as among the sectaries of the Old Man of the Mountain,) by their ignorant but attached subjects, without a conception, on their part, that they had an option. But Nadir Sing was banished for the murder alluded to; his son, who had been carefully educated at Sir John Malcolm's head-quarters, succeeded to his authority; and there is now no part of the country where life and property are safer than amid the late dreaded Bheels of his father

The Bheels excite tne horror of the higher classes of Hindoos, by eating not only the flesh of buffaloes, but

---

* Sir John Malcolm himself. He was assisted on the trial by Captain D. Stuart, who noted down the girl's expressions.

of cows; an abomination which places them just above
the *Chumars*, or shoemakers, who feast on dead carcases,
and are not allowed to dwell within the precincts of the
village. The wild Bheels, who keep among the hills, are
a diminutive and wretched-looking race, but active, and
capable of great fatigue; they go armed with bows and
arrows, and are still professed robbers and thieves, lying
in wait for the weak and unprotected, while they fly from
the strong. Their excesses, however, are now chiefly
indulged in against the Hindoos. "A few months since,"
says Bishop Heber, "one of the bazaars of Neemuch was
attacked and plundered by a body of the 'hill-people;'
and there are, doubtless, even in the plains, many who
still sigh after their late anarchy, and exclaim amid the
comforts of a peaceable government,

> ' Give us our wildness and our woods,
> Our huts and caves again !'

"The son of Mr. Palmer, Chaplain of Nusseerabad,
while travelling lately with his father and mother in their
way from Mhow, observed some Bheels looking earnestly at a large drove of laden bullocks which were drinking in a ford. He asked one of the Bheels if the bullocks
belonged to him. 'No !' was the reply, ' but a good part
of them would have been ours, if it were not for you
English, who will let nobody thrive but yourselves."

(These were precisely the envyings and lamentations
of many among our own highlandmen, when their depredations were checked, and they could no longer carry on
the " honourable" calling of their forefathers.)

On first approaching the Bheel villages, the Bishop
observed a man run from the nearest hut to the top of a
hill, and give a shrill shout or scream, which he heard
repeated from the furthest hamlet in sight, and again from
two others which the Bishop could not see. " I asked
the meaning of this," he continues, " and my guards
informed me that these were their signals to give the
alarm of our coming, our numbers, and that we had
horse with us. By this means they knew at once whether
it was advisable to attack us, to fly, or to remain quiet
while, if there were any of their number who had par

ticular reasons for avoiding an interview with the troops and magistrates of the low-lands, they had thus fair warning given them to keep out of the way. This sounds like a description of Rob Roy's country, but these poor Bheels are far less formidable enemies than the Old Mac Gregors."

This ancient people are very expert in the use of the bow, and have a curious way of shooting from the long grass, where they lie concealed, holding the bow with their feet. Besides, against their prey, quadruped, biped, and winged, the Bheels use the bow and arrow against fish, which they kill in the rivers and pools with great certainty and rapidity. Their bows are of split bamboo, simple, but strong and elastic. The arrows are also of bamboo, with an iron head coarsely made, and a long single barb. Those intended for striking fish, have this head so contrived as to slip off from the shaft where the fish is struck, but to remain connected with it by a long line, on the principle of the harpoon. The shaft, in consequence, remains floating in the water, and not only contributes to weary out the animal, but shows its pursuer which way he flees, and thus enables him to seize it.

They have many curious customs that date from very remote antiquity. One of them was witnessed by Bishop Heber, and described in his usual felicitous manner.

" A number of Bheels, men and women, came to our camp, (near Jhalloda,) with bamboos in their hands, and the women with their clothes so scanty, and tucked up so high, as to leave the whole limb nearly bare. They had a drum, a horn, and some other rude minstrelsy, and said they were come to celebrate the *hoolee*.* They

---

* The Hoolee is the Hindoo carnival, during which the people of Central India more particularly indulge in all kinds of riot, drunk-enness, and festivity. The same indecency of language is permitted as among the ancient and modern inhabitants of Italy at vintage time. This is also the season in India for pelting each other with a red powder. " During this carnival," says Sir John Malcolm, " which lasts four weeks, men forget both their restraints and dis-tinctions; the poorest may cast the red powder upon his lord, the wife is freed from her habitual respect to her husband, and nothing

drew up in two parties, one men, one women, and had a mock fight, in which at first the females had much the advantage, having very slender poles, while the men had only short cudgels, with which they had some difficulty in guarding their heads. At last some of the women began to strike a little too hard, on which their antagonists lost temper, and closed with them so fiercely, that the poor females were put to the rout in real or pretended terror. They collected a little money in the camp, and then went on to another village. The Hoolee, according to the orthodox system, was over, but these games are often prolonged for several days after its conclusion.

As Bishop Heber advanced in the country infested by the Bheels, he met caravans of Brinjarrees, or carriers of grain, (a singular wandering race,*) escorted by Bheels, paid by the carriers for the purpose. They proceeded by day with an advanced and rear-guard of these naked bowmen, and at night, for security against the robbers, the honest Brinjarrees drew their corn wagons into a circle, placing their cattle in the centre, and connecting each ox with his yoke-fellow, and at length to the wain, by iron collars riveted round their necks, and fastened to an iron chain, which last is locked to the cart-wheel. It is thus extremely difficult to plunder without

---

but the song and the dance is heard. The festival extends to the lowest inhabitants, equal, if not greater enjoyments than to the higher; and for the last eight days the labourer ceases from his toil, and the cultivator quits his field, deeming it impious to attend to any thing but the voice of joy and gladness." Vol. ii. p. 195.

* The Brinjarrees pass their whole lives in carrying grain from one part of the country to the other, seldom on their own account, but as agents for others. They travel in large bodies with their wives, children, and loaded bullocks. The men are all armed as a protection against petty thieves. From the sovereigns and armies of Hindostan they have nothing to apprehend. Their calling is almost considered as sacred. Even contending armies allow them to pass and repass safely; never taking their goods without purchase, or even preventing them, if they choose, from victualling their enemy's camp: both sides wisely agreeing to respect and encourage a branch of industry, the interruption of which might be attended with fatal consequences to both. The punctuality of these corn carriers is marvellous.

awaking them; and in places of greater danger, one of the Brinjarrees always stands sentry. Still farther on, descending from the hills to the low-lands, the Bishop had himself one of these poor Bheels for a guide, who, as he trotted along the rugged road before his horse's head, with a shield and a neatly-made hatchet, and with a blanket of red baize flung over his shoulder, reminded him strongly of the pictures of a North American Indian. The dashing appearance of this man was owing to his being in the Company's pay as a policeman; but the Bheels here were generally in much better plight, and less given to robbing than in the hilly country.

After this, a strong escort of Bheels was added to the Bishop's retinue. They not only led him safely through a perilous country abounding with ravines, and broken land overgrown with brushwood, (the most favourable of places for the spring of a tiger, or the arrows of an ambushed band of robbers, where recently passengers had been plundered by Bheels, and a man carried off by a tiger from a numerous convoy of artillery, on its march to Kairah,) but they conducted him across the rapid stream of the Mhye, and on his arrival at Wasnud, acted as watchmen to his camp, where their shrill calls from one to the other, were heard all night.

"We were told," says the Bishop, "not to be surprised at this choice, since these poor thieves are, when trusted, the trustiest of men, and of all sentries, the most wakeful and indefatigable. They and the Kholees, a race almost equally wild, are uniformly preferred in Guzerat for the service of the police, and as durwans to gentlemen's houses and gardens."

When Sir John Malcolm began the work of reforma tion, the very first step he took was to raise a small corps · of Bheels, commanded by their own chiefs, and " before," says he, " these robbers had been in the service one month, I placed them as a guard over treasure, which had a surprising effect, both in elevating them in their own minds, and in those of other parts of the community." Nor did the judicious reformer stop here; he took as his constant attendants some of the most desperate of the plundering chiefs; and the good effects fully answered the expectations which he had formed, by thus inspiring confidence, and exalting bold and courageous men in their own estimation.

We have only to add in honour of this ancient robber race, that the fair sex have great influence in the society, and that in the recent reform, their women acted a prominent part, and one worthy of the feelings and character of their sex.

The very interesting work of Mr. Charles Coleman, (The Mythology of the Hindoos, with notices of various mountain and island Tribes, &c.) recently published, affords the following additional anecdotes relative to the Bheels previous to their reformation.

"An English officer, a Captain B——d, had, by interrupting and wounding a Bheel, while labouring in his vocation (of robbery,) been marked out for vengeance. In consequence of this he had a sentry to his house; but from the neighbouring bank of the river they had worked a subterraneous passage for a considerable distance, large enough for one man to crawl along, who had begun to perforate the floor of his bed-chamber when he was discovered. We had at the city where this took place nearly two thousand troops, yet it was necessary, for the officer's safety, to remove him to Bombay. A Parsee messman, who had refused to pay the usual tribute to the Bheels, was found dead in the morning in the mess-room. It was his custom to put his mat on a large wine-chest where he slept: in the morning he was found with his head placed on the mess-table, the headless body lying on the chest."

An encampment of English, surrounded by two hundred sentries, was robbed by this people:—

"When the morning broke forth, every officer had been robbed, save one, and he had a priest (Bhaut) and a Bheel guard. Nor did the poor *siphauees* escape; for when they gave the alarm of 'thief! thief!' they were sure to get a blow or wound in the leg or thigh, from a Bheel lying on the ground, or moving about on all-fours, wrapped in a bullock's hide or a sheep-skin, or carrying a bush before or over him, so that the sentries were deceived; and if they fired, they were as likely to hit some of the women or children, or the followers, or the officers, as the Bheel himself; and had they fired, the Bheel, in the dark, thus placed in a populous camp, had every advantage, his weapon making no noise, and his companions being ready to shoot the *siphauee* through the head.

"Most of the officers were up during the night, but their presence was useless. Lieutenant B—— did lay hands on a Bheel, but he literally slipped through his fingers, being naked, his body oiled all over, and his head shaved; and on giving the alarm, one or two arrows were seen to have gone through the cloths of the tent. Were it possible to retain a hold of a Bheel, your motions must be as quick as lightning; for they carry the blade of a knife, which is fastened round the neck by a string, and with which, if they find themselves in a dilemma, they will rip up the person holding them."

Captain Mundy, in his very spirited "Pen and Pencil Sketches in India," relates this personal adventure.

"I retired to my tent this evening pretty well knocked up; and during the night had an adventure, which might have terminated with more loss to myself, had I slept sounder. My bed, a low charpoy, or 'four feet,' was in one corner of the tent, close to a door, and I woke several times from a feverish doze, fancying I heard something moving in my tent; but could not discover anything, though a cherang, or little Indian lamp, was burning on the table. I therefore again wooed the balmy power, and slept. At length, just as 'the iron tongue of midnight had told twelve' (for I had looked at my watch five minutes before, and replaced it under my pillow), I was awakened by a rustling sound under my head; and, half opening my eyes, without changing my position, I saw a hideous black face within a foot of mine, and the owner of this index of a cut-throat, or, at least, cut-purse disposition, kneeling on the carpet, with one hand under my pillow, and the other grasping—not a dagger!—but the door-post. Still without moving my body, and with half-closed eyes, I gently stole my right hand to a boar-spear, which at night was always placed between my bed and the wall; and as soon as I had clutched it, made a rapid and violent movement, in order to wrench it from its place, and try the virtue of its point upon the intruder's body, but I wrenched in vain. Fortunately for the robber, my bearer, in placing the weapon in its usual recess, had forced the point into the top of the tent and the butt into the ground so firmly, that I failed to extract it at the first effort; and my visiter, alarmed by the movement, started upon his feet and rushed through the door.

had time to see that he was perfectly naked, with the xception of a black blanket twisted round his loins, and that he had already stowed away in his cloth my candlesticks and my dressing-case, which latter contained letters, keys, money, and other valuables. I had also leisure, in that brief space, to judge, from the size of the arm extended to my bed, that the bearer was more formed for activity than strength; and, by his grizzled beard, that he was rather old than young. I therefore sprang from my bed, and darting through the purdar of the inner door, seized him by the cummerbund just as he was passing the outer entrance.* The cloth, however, being loose, gave way, and ere I could confirm my grasp, he snatched it from my hand, tearing away my thumbnail down to the quick. In his anxiety to escape, he stumbled through the outer purdar, and the much-esteemed dressing-case fell out of his loosened zone. I was so close at his heels, that he could not recover it; and jumping over the tent-ropes—which, doubtless, the rogue calculated would trip me up—he ran towards the road. I was in such a fury, that, forgetting my bare feet, I gave hase, vociferating lustily, 'Choor! choor!' (thief! thief!) out was soon brought up by some sharp stones, just in time to see my rascal, by the faint light of the moon through the thick foliage overhead, jump upon a horse standing unheld near the road, and dash down the path at full speed, his black blanket flying in the wind. What

---

* The tents in India have double flies; the outer khanaut, or wall, forming a verandah, of some four feet wide, round the interior pavilion.

would I have given for my double-barrelled Joe at tha.
moment!   As he and his steed went clattering along the
rocky forest-road, I thought of the black huntsman of
the Hartz, or the erl-king!   Returning to my tent, I
solaced myself by abusing my servants, who were just
rubbing their eyes and stirring themselves, and by
threatening the terrified sepoy sentry with a court-mar-
tial.   My trunks at night were always placed outside the
tent, under the sentry's eye; the robber, therefore, must
have made his entry on the opposite side, and he must
have been an adept in his vocation, as four or five servants were sleeping between the khanauts.   The poor
devil did not get much booty for his trouble, having only
secured a razor, a pot of pomatum, (which will serve to
lubricate his person for his next exploit,)* and the candlesticks, which on closer inspection will prove to him
the truth of the axiom, that 'all is not gold that glitters,'
nor even silver. * * * The next morning, on relating
my adventure, I was told that I was fortunate in having
escaped cold steel ; and many comfortable instances were
recited, of the robbed being stabbed in attempting to
secure the robber."

Of the other professed robbers and thieves in Central
India, the two principal are the Baugries and Moghies,
both Hindoos of the lowest caste : their redeeming qualities are bravery and expertness ; they are " true to their
salt," or to those who feed them, beyond most of the
Hindoos ; and so literally do they adopt the proverb, that
they avoid tasting salt from the hands of any but their
own brethren, that they may not be fettered in their
darling pursuit of plunder.   The Gwarriahs are a tribe
who support themselves by stealing women and children
whom they sell as slaves ; but this abominable practice
has nearly been abolished wherever British influence extends.   The Thugs are the last, and worst of all.   They
are bands of mendicants, self-called pilgrims, pilferers,
robbers, and cowardly, treacherous murderers, chiefly
Brahmins, but composed of all classes, even of Mahomet-

---

* Indian thieves oil their naked bodies to render their seizure
difficult.

ans   They assume all sorts of disguises; sometimes seeking protection from travellers, at others offering it; in either case the fate of those who trust them is the same.

"The Thugs," says Sir John Malcolm, "carry concealed a long silken cord with a noose, which they throw round the necks of their heedless companions, who are strangled and plundered. Their victims, who are always selected for having property, are, when numerous or at all on their guard, lulled by every art into confidence. They are invited to feasts, where their victuals and drink are mixed with soporific and poisonous drugs, through the effects of which they fall an easy prey to these murderers and robbers, the extraordinary success of whose atrocities can only be accounted for by the condition of the countries in which they take place."

The name of these monsters—Thug, *quasi* Tug, in English, would not be altogether inapplicable as regards a principal part of their performance. "They watch their opportunity," says Bishop Heber, "to fling a rope with a slip-knot over the heads of their victims, and then they drag them from their horses and strangle them: and so nimbly and with such fatal aim are they said to do this, that they seldom miss, and leave no time to the traveller to draw a sword, or use a gun, or in any way defend or disentangle himself. The wretches who practise this are very numerous in Guzerat and Malwa, but when they occur in Hindostan, are generally from the south-eastern provinces."

At an immeasurable distance from these nations of robbers—these hosts of hereditary banditti in India, and more like our casual, lawless associations in Europe, are the Decoits, who particularly infest the neighbourhood of Calcutta, robbing on the river in boats, or plundering on shore. Their gang-robbery is said very nearly to resemble that of the Riband-men of Ireland, but unmixed with any political feeling. Five or ten peasants will meet together as soon as it is dark, to attack some neighbour's house, and not only plunder, but torture him, his wife, and children, with horrible cruelty, to make him discover his money. In the day-time these marauders follow peaceable professions, and some of them are thriving men, while the whole firm is often under the protection of a Zemindar, (a landholder, or Lord of the Manor,) who shares the booty, and does his best to bring off any of the gang who may fall into the hands of justice, by suborning witnesses to prove an alibi, bribing the inferior agents of police, or intimidating the witnesses for the prosecution. Thus, many men suspected of these practices, contrive to live on, from year to year, in tolerably good esteem with their neighbours, and completely beyond the reach of a government which requires proof ere it will punish. The evil is supposed to have increased since the number of spirit-shops has spread so rapidly in Calcutta. These fountains of mischief are thronged both by the Hindoo and Mussulman population, especially at night; and thus drunkenness on ardent spirits, and the fierce and hateful passions they engender, lead naturally to those results which night favours, at the same time that the drinking shops furnish convenient places of meeting for all men who may be banded for an illicit purpose.

AFGHAN ROBBERS.

The mountain tribes of the Afghan race who dwell in Caubul, between India and Persia, are nearly all robbers; but like the Arabs, unite pillage with pastoral or other pursuits, and commit their depredations almost exclusively on the strangers that travel through their countries. Although I am not in possession of any striking stories of their actions, there are two or three of these tribes that may claim attention from their peculiarities.

There is, for example, that of the Jadrauns, a race of goat-herds, who wander continually with their goats through the thick pine forests that cover their mountains, and are in appearance and habits of life more like mountain bears than men. They are not numerous; their wild country is never explored by travellers, and they are never by any chance met with out of their own hills. They are sometimes at war with their neighbours, and always on the look-out for travellers on the road from Caubul through Bungush, near the pass of Peiwaur, whom they invariably plunder.

More important than these bear-like robbers, are the Vizeerees, a powerful tribe, occupying an extensive country among the mountains, which are also here covered by pine forests, but contain some few cleared and cultivated spots. Their habits are almost as retiring as those of their neighbours, the Jadrauns, and Mr. Elphinstone found it impossible to meet with a Vizeeree out of his own country. Those of the tribe who are fixed, live in small hamlets of thatched and terraced houses; in some places they live in caves cut out of the rocks. Some of these rise above each other in three stories, and others are so high as to admit a camel. But most of the tribe dwell in black tents, or moveable hovels of mats, or temporary straw huts; these go up to the high mountains in spring, and stay there till the cold and snow drive them back to the low and warm hills. Their principal stock is goats; but they also breed many small but serviceable horses. They have no general government; but are divided into societies, some under powerful Khans, and others under a simple democracy; they are all most remarkable for their peaceful conduct among themselves; they have no wars between clans, and private dissension is hardly ever heard of; and yet they are all robbers!

Notorious plunderers, however, as they are, the smallest escort granted by them, secures a traveller a hospitable reception tnrough the whole tribe.

" They are particularly remarkable for their attacks on the caravans and migratory tribes to the west of the pass of Gholairee. No escorts are ever granted, or applied for there; the caravan is well guarded, and able to deter attacks or fight its way through. No quarter is given to men in these predatory wars; it is said that the Vizeerees would even kill a male child that fell into their hands; but they never molest women; and if one of

their sex wander from a caravan, they treat her with
kindness, and send guides to escort her to her tribe. Even
a man would meet with the same treatment, if he could
once make his way into the house of a Vizeeree; the
master would then be obliged to treat him with all the
attention and good will which is due to a guest. Such is
their veracity, that if there is a dispute about a stray
goat, and one party will say it is his, and confirm his
assertion by stroking his beard, the other instantly gives
it up, without suspicion of fraud."

These mountain robbers have really exalted notions of
what is due to the gentler sex. So kind to the stray
wives or daughters of others, unlike savages or semi-
barbarous men, who throw off from their own shoulders
nearly all drudgery and labour save that of the chase, or
the care of their flocks, these Vizeerees do not require
any labour from their women. But not only this; a
most extraordinary custom is said to prevail among them
—a female prerogative that has no parallel among any
other people upon earth, and that reverses what we are
in the habit of considering the natural order of things—
the women choose their husbands, and not the husbands
their wives!

"If a woman is pleased with a man, she sends the
drummer of the camp to pin a handkerchief to his cap,
with a pin which she has used to fasten her hair. The
drummer watches his opportunity, and does this in public,
naming the woman, and the man is immediately obliged
to marry her, if he can pay her price to her father."

The Sheeraunees are a tribe more important still, great
part of whose country is occupied by the lofty mountain
of Tukhti Solimaun, and the hills which surround its
base. Many parts of it are nearly inaccessible; one of
the roads is in some places cut out of the steep face of
the mountain, and in others supported by beams inserted
in the rock, and with all this labour is still impracticable
for beasts of burden.

The habits of a pastoral, wandering life, dispose to
robbery; but unlike the other tribes, the Sheeraunees are
essentially an agricultural people, keeping their valleys

in a high state of cultivation, by means of damming the hill streams to irrigate them; and yet they are, perhaps, the greatest robbers of all these Afghans.

They are governed by a chief called the Neeka, or Grandfather, who is superstitiously reverenced by them, and left in possession of an extraordinary degree of power. He commands them in their predatory expeditions, and before the men march they all pass under his turban, which is stretched out for the purpose by the Neeka and a Moolah. This, they think, secures them from wounds and death.

They respect none of the neighbouring tribes that pass through their country, in their annual pastoral migrations; they attack them all: they may, indeed, be said to be at war with all the world, since they plunder every traveller that comes within their reach. They even attack the dead!

"While I was in their neighbourhood," says Mr. Elphinstone, "they stopped the body of a Douranee of rank, which was going through their country to be buried at Candahar, and detained it till a ransom had been paid for it."

This is rather worse than a barbarous law that has lingered on even in England to our days, and allows the creditor to arrest the corpse of a debtor. These Sheeraunees, however, enjoy the reputation of unblemished good faith, and a traveller who trusts himself to them, or hires an escort from among them, may pass through their country in perfect security. Mr. Elphinstone says that these curious robbers are very punctual in their prayers, but do not appear to feel much real devotion. In confirmation of this opinion, he adds the following amusing anecdote.

"I once saw a Sheeraunee performing his Namaz, while some people in the same company were talking of hunting; the size of deer happened to be mentioned, and the Sheeraunee, in the midst of his prostrations, called out that the deer in his country were as large as little bullocks, and then went on with his devotions!"

THE BUCCANEERS OF AMERICA.

No class of robbers, always excepting the Pindarries of India, have been more conspicuous, or have operated on a grander scale, than the Buccaneers and Flibustiers of America. I remember, when a child, being horribly amused by a book that was popular at the time, as it probably still is with young people, which contained the lives of many of these notorious characters, with minute accounts of their cruelties and atrocities. The book is probably as fresh in the memory of most of my readers. It is not my intention to draw from it, or to give a ghastly interest to the present work, by quoting how the monster Morgan tortured his captives, or made them "walk the plank," or similar matters, but to give a brief sketch of these daring adventurers from Captain Burney's voluminous, but interesting and authentic work, which in itself contains a mine of geographical and various information, first collected by the Buccaneers. All the other histories of these men, and they are numerous, are, as Captain Burney remarks, "boastful compositions which have delighted in exaggeration; and what is most mischievous, they have lavished commendations upon acts which demanded reprobation, and have endeavoured to raise miscreants, notorious for their want of humanity, to the rank of heroes, lessening thereby the stain upon robbery, and the abhorrence naturally conceived against cruelty."

Captain Burney thus describes the origin of these lawless associations, which for two centuries were allowed to carry on their depredations.

"The men whose enterprises are to be related, were natives of different European nations, but chiefly of Great Britain and France, and most of them sea-faring people, who being disappointed, by accidents or the enmity of the Spaniards, in their more sober pursuits in the West Indies, and also instigated by thirst for plunder, as much as by desire for vengeance, embodied themselves

under different leaders of their own choosing, to make
predatory war upon the Spaniards. These men the
Spaniards naturally treated as pirates; but some peculiar
circumstances which provoked their first enterprises, and
a general feeling of enmity against that nation on account of her American conquests, procured them the
connivance of the rest of the maritime States of Europe,
and to be distinguished, first by the softened appellations
of freebooters and adventurers, and afterwards by that
of Buccaneers."

Spain, indeed, considered the New World as treasure
trove of which she was lawfully and exclusively the mistress. The well-known Bull of Pope Alexander VI. gave
what was then held as a sacred recognition of these ex-
clusive rights. Unaccountable as such folly may now
appear, it is an historical fact that the Spaniards at first
fancied they could keep their discovery of the West India Islands and of the American continent a secret from
the rest of the world, and prevent the ships of other nations from finding their way thither. When, in the year
1517, about twenty-five years after their first settlements,
the Spaniards found a large English ship between St.
Domingo and Porto Rico, they were overcome with rage
and astonishment; and when this ship came to the mouth
of the port of St. Domingo, and the captain sent on shore
to request permission to sell his goods, Francisco di
Tapia, the Governor of the Spanish fort, ordered the can-
nons to be fired at her, on which the English were obliged to weigh anchor and sheer off. The news of this unexpected visit, when known in Spain, caused great in-
quietude, and the Governor of the castle of St. Domingo
was reprimanded, " because he had not, instead of forcing
the English ship to depart by firing his cannon, contrived
to seize her, so that no one might have returned to teach
others of her nation the route to the Spanish Indies."

In the plenitude of her power and pretensions, however
neither the French nor the English, though when taken
they were barbarously treated as pirates, were to be deterred. According to Hakluyt, one Thomas Tyson was
sent to the West Indies in 1526, as factor to some Eng-

lish merchants, and many adventurers soon followed him. The French, who had made several voyages to the Brazils, also increased in numbers in the West Indies. All these went with the certainty that they should meet with hostility from the Spaniards, which they resolved to return with hostility. That they did not always wait for an attack, appears by an ingenious phrase of the French adventurers, who, if the first opportunity was in their favour, termed their profiting by it " *se dédommager par avance*." To repress these interlopers, the jealous Spaniards employed armed ships, or *guarda-costas*, the commanders of which were instructed to take no prisoners ! On the other hand, the intruders joined their numbers made combinations, and descended on different parts of the coast, ravaging the Spanish towns and settlements. A warfare was thus established between Europeans in the West Indies. All Europeans not Spaniards, whether there was war or peace between their respective nations in the Old World, on their meeting in the New, regarded each other as friends and allies, with the Spaniards for their common enemy, and called themselves " Brethren of the Coast."

Their principal pursuit was not of a nature to humanize these desperate adventurers, for it was hunting of cattle, the hides and suet of which they could turn to profitable account. " The time when they began to form factories," says Captain Burney, " to hunt cattle for the skins, and to cure the flesh as an article of traffic, is not certain, but it may be concluded that these occupations were begun by the crews of wrecked vessels, or by seamen who had disagreed with their commander; and that the ease, plenty, and freedom from all command and subordination enjoyed in such a life, soon drew others to quit their ships, and join in the same occupations. The ships that touched on the coast supplied the hunters with European commodities, for which they received in return, hides, tallow, and cured meat."

When the Spanish Court complained to the different Governments of Europe, of which these men were the natural subjects, it was answered: " That the people complained against, acted entirely on their own authority and responsibility, not as the subjects of any prince, and that the King of Spain was at liberty to proceed against them according to his own pleasure." But the lion-hearted Queen Bess retorted more boldly, " That the Spaniards had drawn these inconveniences upon themselves, by their severe and unjust dealings in their American commerce; for she did not understand why either her subjects, or those of any other European Prince, should be debarred from traffic in the West Indies. That as she did not acknowledge the Spaniards to have any title by the donation of the Bishop of Rome, so she knew no right they had to any places others than those they were in actual possession of; for that their having touched only here and there upon a coast, and given names to a few rivers or capes, were such insignificant things as could no ways entitle them to a propriety further than in the parts where they actually settled and continued to inhabit."

" The Brethren of the Coast" were first known by the general term of Flibustier, which is supposed to be nothing but the French sailors' corruption of our word " free-booter." The derivation of the term Buccaneer, by which they were afterwards designated, is of very curious origin.

" The flesh of the cattle killed by the hunters was cured to keep good for use, after a manner learned from the Caribbe Indians, which was as follows : the meat was laid to be dried upon a wooden grate or hurdle, which the Indians called *barbecu*, placed at a good distance over a slow fire. The meat when cured was called *boucan*, and the same name was given to the place of their cookery." From *boucan*, they made the verb *bou-caner*, which the *Dictionnaire de Trevoux* explains to be *Boucanier, quasi* Buccaneer.

This curious association, that united the calling of hunters and cruisers, was held together by a very simple code of laws and regulations. It is said that every member of it had his chosen and declared comrade, between whom property was in common while they lived together, and when one of the two died, the other succeeded to whatever he possessed. This, however, was not a compulsory regulation, for the Buccaneers were known at times to bequeath by will to their relatives or friends in Europe. There was a general right of participation insisted upon in certain things, among which was meat for present consumption and other necessaries of life. It has even been said that bolts, locks, and every kind of fastening were prohibited as implying a doubt of "the honour of their vocation." Many of respectable lineage became Buccaneers, on which it was customary for them to drop their family name, and to assume a *nom de guerre*. "Some curious anecdotes," says Captain Burney, "are produced, to show the great respect some of them entertained for religion and morality. A certain Flibustier Captain, named Daniel, shot one of his crew in the church, for behaving irreverently during the performance of mass. Raveneau de Lussan took the occupation of a Buccaneer, because he was in debt, and wished, as every honest man should do, to have wherewithal to satisfy his creditors."

In the year 1625 the English and French together took possession of the island of St. Christopher, and five years later of the small island of Tortuga, near the northwest end of Hispaniola, which continued to be for some years the head-quarters of the Buccaneers, who, whenever the countries of which they were natives were at war with Spain, obtained commissions from Europe, and acted as regular privateers in the West Indies, and on the Spanish main.

In 1638, the Spaniards in great force surprised the island of Tortuga, while most of the adventurers were absent in Hispaniola engaged in the chase of cattle, and barbarously massacred all who fell into their hands. The Spaniards did not garrison the island. Soon after their departure, the Buccaneers, to the number of three hundred, again took possession of Tortuga, and then for the first time elected a chief or commander.

As the hostility of the Buccaneers was solely directed against the Spaniards, all other Europeans in these latitudes regarded them as champions in the common cause and the severities which had been exercised against them increased the sympathy for them in the breasts of others, and inflamed their own hearts with the thirst of revenge. Their numbers were speedily recruited by English, French, and Dutch from all parts, and both the pursuits of hunting and cruising were followed with redoubled vigour. At this time, the French in particular seemed to pride themselves in the Buccaneers, whom their writers styled "*nos braves*." The English contented themselves with speaking of their " unparalleled exploits."

About the middle of the seventeenth century, the French addicted themselves almost exclusively to hunting. Hispaniola was their great resort, and as the Spaniards found they could not expel them from that island, they themselves destroyed the cattle and wild hogs, in order to render the business of hunting unproductive. This drove the French to other branches of industry, equally opposed to the inclinations of the Spaniards ; for finding the chase no longer profitable, they began to cultivate the soil and to cruise more than ever.

The extermination practised upon them by the Spaniards whenever they fell into their hands, seems to have been admitted as a standing and praiseworthy law among the latter people, while it naturally produced an equally sanguinary retaliation on the part of the adventurers. The cruelties of the Spaniards were much circulated in Europe in the form of popular stories, and produced a great effect. A Frenchman, a native of Languedoc, of the name of Montbars, on reading one of these stories conceived such an implacable hatred against the Spaniards, that he went to the West Indies, joined the Buccaneers, and pursued his vengeance with so much ardour and success, that he obtained the title of " The Exterminator."

Pierre, a native of Dieppe, whose name was graced with the adjunct of " Le Grand," was another famous French Buccaneer. In a boat with only twenty-eight men, he surprised and took the ship of the Vice-Admiral of the Spanish galleons, as she was sailing homeward with a rich freight.　He did not, however, disgrace his exploit by massacre, for he set the Spanish crew on shore at Cape Tiburon, and carried his prize safely to France.

A native of Portugal, styled Bartolomeo Portuguez, also rendered himself famous about this time for his numerous and wonderful escapes in battle and from the gallows.

"But," continues Captain Burney, "no one of the Buccaneers hitherto named, arrived at so great a degree of notoriety as a Frenchman called François L'Olonnais. This man, and Michel le Basque, at the head of 650 men, took the towns of Maracaibo and Gibraltar, in the gulf of Venezuela.　The booty they obtained by the plunder and ransom of these places was estimated at 400,000 crowns.　The barbarities practised on the prisoners could not be exceeded.　L'Olonnais was possessed with an ambition to make himself renowned for being terrible. At one time, it is said, he put the whole crew of a Spanish ship, ninety men, to death, performing himself the office of executioner, by beheading them.　He caused the crews of four other vessels to be thrown into the sea; and more than once, in his frenzies, he tore out the hearts of his victims, and devoured them!　Yet this man had his en-comiasts! so much will loose notions concerning glory, aided by a little partiality, mislead even sensible men. Père Charlevoix, (a French Priest,) says ' *Celui de tous, dont les actions illustrèrent d'avantage les premières années du gouvernement de M. d'Orgeron, fut l'Olonnais. Ses premiers succès furent suivis de quelques malheurs, qui ne servirent qu' à donner nouveau lustre à sa gloire.*' The career of this savage was terminated by the Indians of the coast of Darien, on which he had landed."

The Buccaneers now became so formidable, that several Spanish towns submitted to pay them regular contribu-tions.　They were commanded at this time by one Mans-velt, whose country is unknown, but who was followed with equal alacrity by both French and English, and who seems to have been more provident and more am-bitious than any chief who had preceded him.　He formed a plan for founding an independent Buccaneer establishment, and at the head of five hundred men took the island of Santa Katalina for that purpose from the Spaniards, and garrisoned it with one hundred Buccaneers, and all the slaves he had taken. A Welshman called Henry Morgan, was the second in command on this expedition. Mansvelt died of illness shortly after, when the garrison he had left was obliged to surrender to the Spaniards.

On the death of Mansvelt, Morgan became the chief and the most fortunate leader of the Buccaneers. A body of several hundred men placed themselves under his command, with whom he took and plundered the town of Puerto del Principe in Cuba. At this place a Frenchman was foully slain by an Englishman. All the French took to arms, but Morgan pacified them by putting the murderer in irons, and afterwards hanging him at Jamaica. Morgan, however, whom the old English author of " the Buccaneers of America" styles Sir Henry Morgan, did not respect the old proverb, of honour among thieves; in consequence of which, most of the French separated from him. Yet he was strong enough shortly after to attack Porto Bello, one of the best fortified places belonging to the Spaniards. His bravery and his wonderful address are overshadowed by the shocking cruelties he committed in this expedition. In the attack of a fort, he compelled a number of priests, monks, and nuns, his prisoners, to carry and plant the scaling ladders against the walls ; and many of these poor creatures were killed by their countrymen who defended the fort. A castle that had made a bold resistance, on surrendering, was set on fire, and burned to the ground with the garrison within it. Many prisoners died under the tortures that Morgan inflicted on them to make them discover concealed treasures which frequently had no existence, save in the cupidity of his imagination.

In the brilliancy of this success, the French forgot Morgan's peccadilloes in money matters, and joined him again in great numbers. There was one large French Buccaneer ship, the commander and crew of which refused to act with him. The crafty Welshman dissembled his rage, and pressingly invited the French captain and his officers to dine on board his own ship. These guests he made his prisoners, and in their absence easily took their ship. The men he put in charge of this prize got drunk on the occasion, and the ship was suddenly blown up; whether from the drunkenness and carelessness of the English, or the direful revenge of some Frenchmen remains matter of doubt. The number of the French prisoners is not mentioned, but, it is said, that three hundred and fifty Englishmen perished with this ship, which was the largest of the fleet.

Morgan's next operation was an attack on Maracaibo and Gibraltar, which unfortunate towns were again sacked. These merciless desperadoes were accustomed to shut up their prisoners in churches, where it was easy to keep guard over them. At Maracaibo and Gibraltar, in this instance, so little care was taken of them, that many of these unfortunate captives were actually starved to death in the churches, whilst the Buccaneers were revelling in their dwellings.

Morgan was near being destroyed on his return from these places, for the Spaniards had time to put in order a castle at the entrance of the Lagune of Maracaibo, and three large men-of-war had arrived, and stationed themselves by the castle to cut off the pirate's retreat.

But the Welshman fitted up one of his vessels as a fire-ship, in which were stuck logs of wood, dressed with hats on to look like men, and which in every thing was made to bear the appearance of a common fighting-ship. Following close in the rear of this mute crew, he saw two of the Spanish men-of-war blown up, and he took the third. He then passed the castle without loss, by means of a stratagem, by which he threw the stupid garrison off their guard. The value of the booty obtained was 250,000 pieces of eight.

The year after this expedition, (in July 1670,) a solemn treaty of peace, known in diplomacy under the name of the "Treaty of America," and made, in the view of terminating the Buccaneer warfare, and settling all disputes between the subjects of the two countries in the

Burning of the French Ship.

PIRATES AND ROBBERS.

CAPTAIN MORGAN.

Western hemisphere, was concluded between Great Britain and Spain. But the Buccaneers cared nothing for treaties, and would not be pacified. On the contrary, as soon as the news of the peace reached them, they resolved, as of one accord, to undertake some grand expedition, of which the skilful Morgan should have the command. In the beginning of December 1670, thirty-seven vessels, having on board altogether more than two thousand men, joined the Welshman at Cape Tiburon, the place of general rendezvous he had himself appointed. Lots were then cast as to which of the three places, Carthagena, Vera Cruz, and Panama, should be attacked. The lot fell upon Panama, which was believed to be the richest of the three.

Preparatory to this arduous undertaking, Morgan employed men to hunt cattle and cure meat, and sent vessels to procure maize, at the settlements on the main. For the distribution of the plunder they were to obtain, specific articles of agreement were drawn up and subscribed to. Morgan, as commander-in-chief, was to receive one hundredth part of the whole; each captain was to have eight shares; those who should be maimed and wounded were provided for, and additional rewards promised for those who should particularly distinguish themselves by their bravery and conduct. On the 16th of December, the fleet set sail, and on the 20th they retook the island of Santa Katalina, which Morgan, who had embraced the notion of Mansvelt to erect himself into the head of a free state, independent of any European nation, resolved should be the centre of his establishment and power. The Buccaneers next took the castle of San Lorenzo, at the entrance of the river Chagre, on the West-India side of the American isthmus, losing one hundred men in killed, and having seventy wounded. Of three hundred and fourteen Spaniards who composed the garrison, more than two hundred were put to death.

Morgan had now a *pied-à-terre*, and a good place of retreat on one side of the wild and perilous isthmus; he accordingly set his prisoners to work to repair and strengthen the castle of San Lorenzo, where he left five hundred men as a garrison, besides one hundred and fifty men to take care of the ships which were left in the Atlantic, while he should go to the shores of the Pacific. It was on the 18th of January 1671, that he set forward at the head of twelve hundred men for Panama. The length of the march from ocean to ocean was not long, but rendered tremendous by the nature of the intervening country and the wildness of its Indian inhabitants. One party of this pirate-army, with artillery and stores, embarked in canoes, to ascend the river Chagre, the course of which is very serpentine. At the end of the second day they were obliged to quit their canoes, for a vast number of fallen trees obstructed them, and the river was found in many places almost dry; but the way by land offered so many difficulties to the carriage of their stores, that they again resorted to their canoes, where they could —making very little way. On the sixth day, when they had nearly exhausted their travelling store of provision, and death by hunger in that horrid wilderness stared them in the face, they had the good fortune to discover a barn full of maize. The native Indians fled at their approach, and could never be caught. On the seventh day they reached a village called Cruz, which was set on fire and abandoned by its inhabitants, who fled as the Buccaneers approached. They, however, found there a sack of bread and fifteen jars of Peruvian wine. They were still eight leagues distant from Panama. On the ninth day of the journey, they saw the expanse of the South Sea before them, and around them some fields with cattle grazing. As evening approached, they came in sight of the church towers of Panama, when they halted and waited impatiently for the morrow. They had lost in their march thus far, by being fired at from concealed places, ten men; and had ten more wounded.

The city of Panama is said to have consisted at that time of seven thousand houses, many of which were edifices of considerable magnificence and built with cedar: but no regular fortifications defended the wealth and magnificence of the place. Some works had been raised, but in most parts the city lay open and was to be won and defended by plain fighting. The Buccaneers asserted that the Spaniards had a force amounting to two thousand infantry and four hundred horse; but it is supposed that this was in part made up of inhabitants and slaves.

When the Buccaneers resumed their march at an early hour next morning, the Spaniards came out to meet them, preceded by herds of wild bulls, which they drove upon the adventurers to disorder their ranks. But the Buccaneers, as hunters of these wild animals, were too well acquainted with their habits to be discomposed by them; and this attack of the van does not seem to have had much effect. The Spaniards, however, must have made an obstinate resistance, for it was night before they gave way and the Buccaneers became masters of the city. During the long battle, and, indeed, all that day and night, the Buccaneers gave no quarter. Six hundred Spaniards fell. The loss of the Buccaneers is not specified, but it appears to have been very considerable.

When master of the city, Morgan was afraid that his men might get drunk and be surprised and cut off by the Spaniards: to prevent this, he caused it to be reported that all the wine in the city had been expressly poisoned by the inhabitants. The dread of poison kept the fellows sober. But Morgan had scarcely taken up his quarters in Panama when several parts of the city burst out into flames, which, fed by the cedar-wood and other combustible materials of which the houses were chiefly built, spread so rapidly, that in a short time a great part of the city was burnt to the ground. It has been disputed whether this was done by design or accident—by the Buccaneers or the despairing Spaniards; but it appears that Morgan, who always charged it upon the Spaniards, gave all the assistance he could to such of the inhabitants as endeavoured to stop the progress of the fire, which, however, was not quite extinguished for weeks. Among the buildings destroyed, was a factory-house belonging to the Genoese, who then carried on the trade of supplying the Spaniards with slaves from Africa.

The licentiousness, rapacity, and cruelty of the Buc

caneers had no bounds. " They spared," says Exquemelin, a Dutchman and one of the party, " in these their
cruelties, no sex nor condition whatsoever. As to religious persons (monks and nuns, he means) and priests,
they granted them less quarter than others, unless they
procured a considerable sum of money for their ransom."
Detachments scoured the country to plunder and bring in
prisoners. Many of the unfortunate inhabitants escaped
with their effects by sea, and reached the islands that are
thickly clustered in the bay of Panama. But Morgan
found a large boat lying aground in the port, which he
launched and manned with a numerous crew, and sent
her to cruise among those islands. A galleon, on board
which the nuns of a convent had taken refuge, and where
much money, plate, and other effects of value had been
lodged, had a very narrow escape from these desperadoes. They took several vessels in the bay. One of
them was large and admirably adapted for cruising. This
opened a new prospect, that was brilliant and enticing;
an unexplored ocean studded with islands was before
them, and some of the Buccaneers began to consult how
they might leave their chief, Morgan, and try their fortunes on the South Sea, whence they proposed to sail,
with the plunder they should obtain, by the East Indies
to Europe. This diminution of force would have been
fatal to Morgan, who, therefore, as soon as he got a hint
of the design, cut away the masts of the ship, and burned
every boat and vessel lying at Panama that could suit
their purpose.

At length, on the 24th of February 1671, about four
weeks after the taking of Panama, Morgan and his men
departed from the still smouldering ruins of that unfortunate city, taking with them one hundred and seventy-
five mules loaded with spoil, and six hundred prisoners,
part of whom were detained to carry burdens across the
isthmus, and others for the ransom expected for their release. Among the latter were many women and children,
who were made to suffer cruel fatigue, hunger, and thirst,
and artfully made to apprehend being carried to Jamaica
and sold as slaves, that they might the more earnestly

endeavour to procure money for their ransom. When these poor creatures threw themselves on their knees, and weeping and tearing their hair, begged of Morgan to let them return to their families, his brutal answer was, that " he came not there to listen to cries and lamentations, but to seek money." This idol of his soul, indeed, he sought from his comrades as well as his captives, and in such a manner that it is astonishing they did not blow his brains out. In the middle of his march back to the fort of San Lorenzo, he drew up his men, and caused every one of them to take a solemn oath, that he had not reserved for himself or concealed any plunder, but had delivered all fairly into the common stock. (This ceremony, it appears, was not uncommon among the Buccaneers.) "But," says Exquemelin, "Captain Morgan having had experience that those loose fellows would not much stickle to swear falsely in such a case, he commanded every one to be searched; and that it might not be taken as an affront, he permitted himself to be first searched, even to the very soles of his shoes. The French Buccaneers who had engaged in this expedition with Morgan, were not well satisfied with this new custom of searching; but their number being less than that of the English, they were forced to submit."

As soon as the marauders arrived at San Lorenzo, a division was made of the booty, according to the proportions agreed upon before sailing from Hispaniola. But the narrative says, " Every person received his portion, or rather what part thereof Captain Morgan was pleased to give him. For so it was, that his companions, even those of his own nation, complained of his proceedings; for they judged it impossible that, of so many valuable robberies, no greater share should belong to them than 200 pieces of eight per head. But Captain Morgan was deaf to these, and to many other complaints of the same kind."

Morgan, however, having well filled his own purse, determined to withdraw quietly from the command: " Which he did," says the narrative of the Buccaneer, " without calling any council, or bidding any one adieu .

but went secretly on board his own ship, and put out to sea without giving any notice, being followed only by three or four vessels of the whole fleet, who it is believed went shares with him in the greatest part of the spoil."

The rest of the Buccaneer vessels left before the Castle of San Lorenzo at Chagre, soon separated. Morgan sailed straight to Jamaica, where he had begun to make fresh levies of men to accompany him to the island of St. Katalina, which he purposed to hold as his own independent state, and to make it a common place of refuge for pirates; but the arrival of a new Governor at Jamaica, Lord John Vaughan, with strict orders to enforce the late treaty with Spain, obliged him to abandon his plan.*

The Buccaneers, however, were not put down by this new Governor of Jamaica, but under different leaders continued their depredations for more than twenty years longer. Lord John Vaughan proclaimed a pardon for all piratical offences committed to that time, and promised a grant of thirty-five acres of land to every Buccaneer who should claim the benefit of the proclamation and engage

---

* This audacious and barbarous rover went to England, where he so ingratiated himself with King Charles II. or with his Ministers, that he received the honour of Knighthood and the appointment of Commissioner of the Admiralty Court in Jamaica. In 1681 the Earl of Carlisle, then Governor of that island, returned to England on the plea of bad health, and left as Deputy Governor, Morgan the Buccaneer, the plunderer of Panama, but who was now in reality Sir Henry Morgan. In his new capacity he was far from being favourable or lenient to his old associates, "some of whom suffered the extreme hardship of being tried and hanged under his authority." Morgan was certainly a villain of the first water, for when a crew of Buccaneers, most of whom were his own countrymen, fell into his hands, he delivered them over (he was strongly suspected of having sold them) to the vindictive Spaniards. His "brief authority" only lasted till the next year, when he was superseded by the arrival of a new Governor from England. He continued, however, to hold office in Jamaica during the rest of the moral reign of Charles II. though accused by the Spaniards of conniving with the Buccaneers. In the next reign the Spanish Court had influence sufficient to procure his being sent home prisoner from the West Indies. He was kept in prison three years, but no charge being brought against him, the worthy Knight was liberated.

to apply himself to planting. I am startled almost into incredulity by what follows.

"The author of the History of Jamaica says, 'This offer was intended as a lure to engage the Buccaneers to come into port with their effects, that the Governor might, and which he was directed to do, take from them the tenths and the fifteenths of their booty as the dues of the crown, and of the Colonial Government for granting them commissions.' Those who had neglected to obtain commissions would of course have to make their peace by an increased composition. In consequence of this scandalous procedure, the Jamaica Buccaneers, to avoid being so taxed, kept aloof from Jamaica, and were provoked to continue their old occupations. Most of them joined the French Flibustiers at Tortuga. Some were afterwards apprehended at Jamaica, where they were brought to trial, condemned as pirates, and executed."

A war entered into by the English and French against the Dutch, gave, for a time, employment to the Buccaneers and Flibustiers, and a short respite to the Spaniards, who, however, exercised their wonted barbarous revenge on their old enemies, whenever and in whatsoever manner they fell into their hands.

In 1673, for example, they murdered in cold blood three hundred French Flibustiers, who had been shipwrecked on their coast at Porto Rico, sparing only seventeen of their officers. These officers were put on board a vessel bound for the continent, with the intention of transporting them to Peru; but an English Buccaneer cruiser met the ship at sea, liberated the Frenchmen, and, in all probability, cut the throats of the Spaniards.

Ever since the plundering of Panama by Morgan, the imagination of the Buccaneers had been heated by the prospect of expeditions to the South Sea. This became known to the Spaniards, and gave rise to numerous forebodings and prophecies, both in Spain and in Peru, of great invasions by sea and by land.

In 1673 an Englishman of the name of Thomas Peche, who had formerly been a Buccaneer in the West Indies, fitted out a ship in England for a piratical voyage to the

South Sea against the Spaniards; and two years after, La Sound, a Frenchman, with a small body of daring adventurers, attempted to cross the isthmus, as Morgan had done, (though not by the same route), but he could not get further than the town of Cheapo, where he was driven back. These events greatly increased the alarm of the Spaniards, who, according to Dampier, prophesied with confidence "that the English privateers in the West Indies would that year (1675) open a door into the South Seas."

But it was not till five years after, or in 1680, when, having contracted friendship with the Darien Indians, and particularly with a small tribe called the Mosquitos, the English adventurers again found their way across the isthmus to those alarmed shores. Some of these Mosquito Indians, who seem to have been a noble race of savages deserving of better companions than the Buccaneers, went with this party, being animated by a deadly hatred of the Spaniards and a fervent attachment to the English.

The Buccaneers who engaged in this expedition were the crews of seven vessels, amounting altogether to three hundred and sixty-six men, of whom thirty-seven were left to guard the ships during the absence of those who went on the expedition, which was not expected to be of long continuance. There were several men of some literary talent among the marauders, who have written accounts of the proceedings, which have the most romantic interest. These were Basil Ringrose, Barty Sharp, William Dampier, who, though a common seaman, was endowed with great observation and a talent for description, and Lionel Wafer, a surgeon providentially engaged by the Buccaneers, whose "Description of the Isthmus of Darien" is one of the most instructive, and decidedly the most amusing book of travels we have in our language.

It was on the 16th of April, that the expedition passed over from Golden Island, and landed in Darien, each man provided with four cakes of bread called dough-boys, with a fusil, a pistol, and a hanger. They began their arduous march marshalled in divisions, each with its commander and distinguishing flag. Many Darien Indians came to supply them with provisions, and to keep them company as confederates; among these were two chiefs, who went by the names of Captain Andreas and Captain Antonio.

The very first day's journey discouraged four of the Buccaneers, who returned to their ships. The object of the expedition was to reach and plunder the town of Santa Maria, near the gulf of San Miguel, on the South Sea side of the isthmus; and on the afternoon of the second day they came to a river, which Captain Andreas, the Indian chief, told them, crossed the isthmus and ran by Santa Maria. On the third day they came to a house belonging to a son of Captain Andreas, who wore a wreath of gold about his head, which made the Buccaneers call him "King Golden Cap."

Wherever there were Indian habitations, they were most kindly and hospitably received. On the evening of the fourth day, they gained a point whence the river of Santa Maria was navigable, and where canoes were prepared for them. The next morning, as they were about to depart, the harmony of the party was disturbed by the quarrel of two of the Buccaneer commanders. John Coxon fired his musket at Peter Harris, which Harris was going to return, when the others interfered and effected a reconciliation. Here seventy of the Buccaneers embarked in fourteen canoes, in each of which there went two Indians to manage them, and guide them down the stream. This mode of travelling, owing to the scarcity of water and other impediments, was as wearisome as marching. After enduring tremendous fatigue, the land and water party met on the eighth day of the journey at a beachy point of land, where the river, being joined by another stream, became broad and deep. This had often been a rendezvous of the Darien Indians, when they collected for attack or defence against the Spaniards; and here the whole party now made a halt, to rest themselves, and to clean and prepare their arms.

On the ninth day, Buccaneers and Indians, in all nearly six hundred men, embarked in sixty-eight canoes, got together by the Indians, and glided pleasantly down the river. At midnight they landed within half a mile of the town of Santa Maria.   The next morning, at day-break, they heard the Spanish garrison firing muskets and beating the *réveillée*. It was seven in the morning when they came to the open ground before the fort, when the Spaniards commenced firing upon them. This fort was nothing but a stockade, which the Buccaneers took without the loss of a single man—an immunity which did not teach them mercy, for they killed twenty-six Spaniards, and wounded sixteen.

The Indians, however, were still less merciful.   After the Spaniards had surrendered, they took many of them into the adjoining woods, where they killed them with their spears, and if the Buccaneers had not prevented them, they would not have left a single Spaniard alive. The long and bloody grievances these savages had scored against their conquerors, was aggravated here by the circumstance that one of their chiefs, or, as the Buccaneers call him, the King of Darien, found in the fort his eldest daughter, who had been forced from her father's habitation by one of the Spanish garrison, and was with child by him.

The Spaniards had by some means been warned of the intended visit to Santa Maria, and had secreted or sent away almost every thing that was of value.—" Though we examined our prisoners severely," says a Buccaneer, " the whole that we could pillage, both in the town and fort, amounted only to twenty pounds weight of gold, and a small quantity of silver ; whereas three days sooner we should have found three hundred pounds weight in gold in the fort." It ought to be mentioned, that the Spaniards were in the habit of collecting considerable quantities of gold from the mountains in the neighbourhood of Santa Maria.

This disappointment was felt very severely, and whether it was previously decided, or now entered their heads to seek compensation for this disappointment, the majority of the Buccaneers resolved to proceed to the South Sea. The boldness of this resolution will be felt by reflecting, that they had only canoes to go in, and that they might meet at their very outset a lofty Spanish galleon or ship

of war, that might sink half of their frail boats at a broadside. Some of them, indeed, were deterred by this prospect. John Coxon, the commander, who had fired his
musket at Peter Harris, and who seems to have been a
contemptible bully, was for returning across the isthmus
to their ships, and so were his followers. To win him
over, those who were for the South Sea, though they had
a mean opinion of his capability, offered him the post of
General, or Commander-in-chief, which Coxon accepted,
and as it was on the condition that he and his men should
join in the scheme, all the Buccaneers went together.
The Darien chief Andreas, with his son Golden Cap, and
some followers, also continued with the rovers, but the
greater part of the Darien Indians left them at Santa Maria, and returned to their homes.

On the 17th of April, the expedition embarked, and fell
down the river to the gulf of San Miguel, which they did
not reach until the following morning, owing to a flood-
tide.

They were now fairly in the South Sea! The pro-
phecy of the Spaniards was accomplished, and the Buccaneers looked across that magnificent expanse of waters
with sanguine hope.

On the 19th of April, they entered the vast bay of
Panama, and fortunately captured at one of the islands, a
Spanish vessel of thirty tons, on board of which one hundred and thirty of the Buccaneers immediately threw
themselves, overjoyed to be relieved from the cramped
state they had endured in the canoes—though of a certainty, even now, so many men on board so small a vessel, could leave small room for comfort.

The next day, they took another small bark. On the
22d, they rendezvoused at the island of Chepillo, near the
mouth of the river Cheapo; and in the afternoon began
to row along shore from that island towards the city of
Panama. The Spaniards there had obtained intelligence
. of the Buccaneers' being in the bay, and prepared to meet
them. Eight vessels were lying in the road; three of
these they hastily equipped, manning them with the crews
of all the vessels, and with men from shore; the whole,

nowever, according to the Buccaneer accounts, not exceeding two hundred and thirty men; and of these, one-
third only were Europeans—the rest mulattoes and negroes.   The great disparity therefore was in the nature
of the vessels.—" We had sent away the Spanish barks
we had taken," says one of the Buccaneers, " to seek
fresh water, so that we had only canoes for the fight, and
in them not two hundred men."

As this fleet of canoes came in sight at daybreak on
the 23d, the three armed Spanish ships got under sail,
and stood towards them.   The conflict was severe, and
lasted the greater part of the day.   The Spanish ships
fought with great bravery, but their crews were motley
and unskilful, whilst the Buccaneers were expert seamen,
and well trained to the use of their arms.   Richard Sawkins was the hero of the day: after three repulses, he
succeeded in boarding and capturing one of the Spanish
ships, which decided the victory.   Another ship was carried by boarding soon after, and the third saved herself
by flight.   The Spanish commander fell with many of his
people.   The Buccaneers had eighteen killed, and above
thirty wounded.   Peter Harris, the captain, who had been
fired at by Coxon, was among the wounded, and died two
days after.   As for John Coxon, who was nominally
General, he showed great backwardness in the engagement, which lost him the confidence of the rovers.   The
Darien chiefs were in the heat of the battle, and behaved
bravely.

The Buccaneers, not thinking themselves strong enough
to land and attack Panama, contented themselves with
capturing the vessels that were at anchor in the road before the city.   One of these was a ship named the Trinidad, of 400 tons burden, a fast sailer and in good condition.   She had on board a cargo principally consisting of
wine, sugar, and sweetmeats; and, moreover, a considerable sum of money was found.   In the other prizes they
found flour and ammunition.   Two of these, with the
Trinidad, they fitted out for cruising.

Thus, in less than a week after their arrival on the
coast of the South Sea, they were in possession of a flee.

"The next day, they took another small bark."

Page 45.

nɔt ill-equipped, with which they formed a close blockade of Panama for the present, and for the future might scour that ocean.

Two or three days after the battle with the Spaniards, discord broke out among the Buccaneers. The taunts and reflections that fell upon the General, Coxon, and some of his followers, determined him and seventy men to return, by the way they had come, across the isthmu to the Atlantic. The Darien chiefs, Andreas and Antonio, also departed for their homes; but Andreas, to prove his good-will to the Buccaneers, who remained in the South Sea, left a son and one of his nephews with them.

Richard Sawkins, who had behaved so well in the battle, was now unanimously chosen General, or chief commander. After staying ten days before Panama, they retired to the island of Taboga, in the near neighbourhood. Here they stopped nearly a fortnight in expectation of the arrival of a rich ship from Lima. This ship came not, but several other vessels fell into their hands, by which they obtained nearly sixty thousand dollars in specie, 1200 sacks of flour, 2000 jars of wine, a quantity of brandy, sugar, sweetmeats, poultry, and other provisions, some gunpowder, shot, &c. Among their prisoners was a number of unfortunate negro slaves, which tempted the Spanish merchants of Panama to go to the Buccaneers, and to buy as many of the slaves as they were inclined to sell. These merchants paid two hundred pieces of eight for every negro, and they sold to the Buccaneers all such stores and commodities as they stood in need of.

Ringrose, one of the Buccaneers, relates that during these communications the Governor of Panama sent to demand of their leader, " Why, during a time of peace between England and Spain, Englishmen should come into those seas to commit injury ? and from whom they had their commission so to do ?" Sawkins replied, " That he and his companions came to assist their friend the King of Darien, (the said chief Andreas,) who was the rightful Lord of Panama, and all the country thereabouts. That as they had come so far, it was reasonable they should receive some satisfaction for their trouble; and if the Governor would send to them 500 pieces of eight for each man, and 1000 for each commander, and would promise not any further to annoy the Darien Indians, their allies, that then the Buccaneers would desist from hostilities, and go quietly about their business." The Governor could scarcely be expected to comply with these moderate demands.

The General Sawkins, having learned from one of the Spaniards who traded with the Buccaneers, that the Bishop of Panama was a person whom he had formerly taken prisoner in the West Indies, sent him a small present as a token of regard and old acquaintanceship: the Bishop in return sent Sawkins a gold ring!

Having consumed all the live stock within reach, and tired of waiting for the rich ship from Peru, the Buccaneers sailed on the 15th of May to the island of Otoque, where they found hogs and poultry, and rested a day. From Otoque they departed with three ships and two small barks, steering out of the bay of Panama, and then westward for the town of Pueblo Nuevo. In this short voyage a violent storm separated from the ships two of the barks, which never joined them again. One of them was taken by the Spaniards, who shot the men; and the crew of the other contrived to reach Coxon's party, and to recross the isthmus with them. On reaching Pueblo Nuevo, the Buccaneers, instead of meeting with an easy prize, sustained a complete discomfiture, and lost their brave commander Sawkins, who was shot dead by the Spaniards, as he was advancing at the head of his men towards a breastwork. " Captain Sawkins," says his comrade Ringrose, " was a valiant and generous-spirited man, and beloved more than any other we ever had among us, which he well deserved." His loss not only disheartened the whole, but induced between sixty and seventy men, and all the Darien Indians, to abandon the expedition and return to the Isthmus.

Only one hundred and forty-six Buccaneers now remained with Bartholomew Sharp, whom they had chosen commander, but who, though clerk enough to write and publish, on his return to England, a very readable account of his adventures, did not at first shine as a leader.

In their retreat from Pueblo Nuevo, they took a ship loaded with indigo, butter, and pitch, and burned two others. They lay at anchor for some time at the island of Quibo, where they pleasantly and profitably employed their time in taking " red deer, turtle, and oysters, so large that they were obliged to cut them into four quarters, each quarter being a good mouthful."

On the 6th of June, Sharp, who had boasted he would " take them a cruise, whereby he doubted not they would gain a thousand pounds per man," sailed with two ships for the coast of Peru. But on the 17th he came to anchor at the island of Gorgona, where the Buccaneers idled away their time till near the end of July, doing nothing worthy of mention, except killing " a snake eleven feet long, and fourteen inches in circumference."

On the 13th of August they got as far as the island Plata, where Sharp again came to anchor. From Plata they beat to the south, and on the 25th, when near Cape St. Elena, they captured, after a short contest, in which one Buccaneer was killed and two were wounded, a Spanish ship bound for Panama. In this prize they found 3000 dollars. The ship they sank, but it is not said what they did with the crew ; as, however, Ringrose makes particular mention that they " punished a friar and shot him upon deck, casting him overboard while he was yet alive," it is to be presumed he was the only sufferer, and that the crew were kept to work as seamen or servants, or in hopes that they might be ransomed, or merely until some convenient opportunity were found for dismissing them.

One of the two vessels in which the Buccaneers cruised, was now found to sail so badly, that she was abandoned, and they all embarked together in the Trinidad.

On the 4th of September, they took another ship bound for Lima. It appears here to have been a custom among the Buccaneers, that the first who boarded, should be allowed some extra privilege of plunder ; for Ringrose says, " we cast dice for the first entrance, and the lot fell to the larboard watch, so twenty men belonging to that watch entered her."

They took out of this prize as much of the cargo as suited them; they then put some of their prisoners in her, and dismissed her with only one mast standing and one sail.

Sharp passed Callao at a distance, fearing the Spaniards might have ships of war there. On the 26th of October, he attempted a landing at the town of Arica, but was prevented by a heavy surf, and the armed appearance of the place. This was the more mortifying, as the stock of fresh water was so reduced, that the men were only allowed half a pint a day each; and it is related, that a pint of water was sold in the ship for thirty dollars. They bore away, however, for the Island of Ilo, where they succeeded in landing, and obtained water, wine, flour, fruit, and other provisions, and did all the mischief they could to the houses and plantations, because the Spaniards refused to purchase their forbearance either with money or cattle.

From Ilo, keeping still southward, they came, on the 3d of December, to the town of La Serena, which they took without opposition. They here obtained, besides other things, five hundred pounds weight of silver, but were very near having their ship burned by a desperate Spaniard, who went by night on a float made of a horse's hide, blown up like a bladder, and crammed oakum and brimstone, and other combustible matters between the rudder and the stern-post, to which he set fire by a match, and then escaped.

From La Serena, the Buccaneers made for Juan Fernandez, at which interesting, romantic island, they arrived on Christmas-day, and remained some time. Here they again disagreed, some of them wishing to sail immediately homeward by the Strait of Magalhanes, and others desiring to try their fortune longer in the South Sea. Sharp was of the homeward party; but the majority being against him, deposed him from the command, and elected in his stead John Watling, "an old privateer, and esteemed a stout seaman." Articles between Watling

and the crew were drawn up in writing, and subscribed
in due form.

One narrative, however, says, "the true occasion of
the grudge against Sharp was, that he had got by these
adventures almost a thousand pounds, whereas many of
our men were scarce worth a groat; and good reason
there was for their poverty, for at the Isle of Plata, and
other places, they had lost all their money to their fellow
Buccaneers at dice; so that some had a great deal, and
others just nothing. Those who were thrifty, sided with
Captain Sharp, but the others, being the greatest number,
turned Sharp out of his command; and Sharp's party
were persuaded to have patience, seeing they were the
fewest, and had money to lose, which the other party had
not." But Dampier says, Sharp was dismissed the command by general consent, the Buccaneers being satisfied
neither with his courage nor his conduct.

John Watling, as Richard Sawkins before him, had a
glimmering of devotion in his composition. He began
his command by insisting on the observance of the Lord's
day by the Buccaneers. "This day, January the 9th,
1681," says Ringrose, "was the first Sunday that ever
we kept by command, since the loss and death of our
valiant commander Captain Sawkins, who once threw
the dice overboard, finding them in use on the said day."

On the 12th of January, they were scared away from
their anchorage at Juan Fernandez, by the appearance
of three sail, and left behind them on shore, William, a
Musquito Indian.

The three vessels, whose appearance had caused them
to move in such a hurry, were armed Spanish ships.
They remained in sight two days, but showed no inclination to fight. The Buccaneers had not a single great
gun in their ship, and must have trusted to their musketry
and to boarding; yet it seems they must have contemplated making an attack themselves, as they remained so
long without resigning the honour of the field to the
Spaniards. They then sailed eastward for the coast of
the continent, where they intended to attack the rich town
of Arica.

On the 26th of January, they made the small island of Yqueque, about twenty-five leagues from Arica, where they plundered an Indian village of provisions, and made prisoners of two old Spaniards and two Indians. The next day Watling examined one of the old Spaniards, concerning the force at Arica, and taking offence at his answer, ordered him to be shot—which was done! Shortly after, he took a small bark, laden with fresh water for the little island, which was destitute of it.

The next night Watling, with one hundred men, left the ship in the boats and the small bark they had taken, and rowed for Arica. They landed on the continent about five leagues to the south of Arica before it was light, and remained there all day concealed among the rocks. When the shades of night fell, they crept along the coast without being perceived, and at the next morning dawn Watling landed with ninety-two men. They were still four miles from the town, but they marched boldly and rapidly forward, and gained an entrance with the loss of three men killed and two wounded. Though in possession of the town, Watling neglected a fort or little castle, and when he had lost time and was hampered by the number of prisoners he had made for the sake of their ransom, and the inhabitants had recovered from their first panic, and had thrown themselves into the fort, he found that place too strong for him. He attacked it, however, making use of the cruel expedient of placing his prisoners in front of his own men ; but the defenders of the fort, though they might kill countrymen, friends, and relatives, were not by this deterred, but kept up a teady fire, and twice repulsed the Buccaneers. Meanwhile the Spaniards outside of the fort made head from all parts, and hemmed in the Buccaneers, who, from assailants, found themselves obliged to look for their own defence and retreat. Watling paid for his imprudence with his life, and two quarter-masters, the boatswain, and some of the best men among the rovers, fell before the fort. When the rest withdrew from the town, and made for their boats, they were harassed the whole way by a distant firing from the Spaniards, but they effected their

retreat in tolerably good order. The whole party, however, narrowly escaped destruction; for the Spaniards
had forced from the prisoners they took the signals which
had been agreed upon with the men left four miles off in
charge of the Buccaneer boats; and having made these
signals, the boats had quitted their post, to which the
rovers were now retreating, and were setting sail to run
down to the town, when the most swift of foot of the
band reached the sea-side just in time to call them back.
They embarked in the greatest hurry and ran for their
ships, too much disheartened to attempt to capture three
vessels that lay at anchor in the roads.

In this mismanaged attack on Arica, the Buccaneers
lost, between killed and taken, twenty-eight men, besides
having eighteen wounded. Among the prisoners taken
by the Spaniards, were two surgeons, to whom had been
confided the care of the wounded. "We could have
brought off our doctors," says Ringrose, "but they got
to drinking while we were assaulting the fort, and when
we called to them, they would not come. The Spaniards
gave quarter to the surgeons, they being able to do them
good service in that country; but as to the wounded men
taken prisoners, they were all knocked on the head!"

The deposed chief, Barty Sharp, was now reinstated
in the command, being esteemed a leader of safer conduct than any other. It was unanimously agreed to quit
the South Sea, which they proposed to do, not by sailing
round the American continent by the Strait of Magalhanes, but by recrossing the isthmus of Darien. They
did not, however, immediately alter their course, but still
beating to the South, landed on the 10th of March at
Guasco, whence they carried off one hundred and twenty
sheep, eighty goats, two hundred bushels of corn, and a
plentiful supply of fresh water. They then stood to the
north, and on the 27th passed Arica at a respectful distance: "our former entertainment," says one of the
Buccaneers, "having been so very bad, that we were no
ways encouraged to stop there again."

By the 16th of April, however, when they were near
the island Plata, where on a former occasion many of

them " had lost their money to their fellow Buccaneers at dice," the spirits of some of the crew had so much revived, that they were again willing to try their fortunes longer in the South Sea. But one party would not continue under Sharp, and others would not recognise a new commander. As neither party would yield, it was determined to separate, and agreed, " that which party soever upon polling should be found to have the majority should keep the ship." Sharp's party proved the most numerous, and they kept the vessel. The minority, which consisted of forty-four Europeans, two Mosquito Indians, and a Spanish Indian, took the long boat and the canoes, as had been agreed, and separating from their old comrades, proceeded to the gulf of San Miguel, where they landed, and travelled on foot over the isthmus by much the same route as they had come. From the Atlantic side of the isthmus they found their way to the West Indies. In this seceding party were the two authors, William Dampier and Lionel Wafer, the surgeon. Dampier published a brief sketch of this Expedition to the South Sea, with an account of his return across the isthmus; but of the latter, the most entertaining description was written by Wafer, who, meeting with an accident on his journey back, which disabled him from keeping pace with his countrymen, was left behind, and remained for some months the guest of the Darien Indians. Living among them as he did, he had ample opportunity of informing himself of all their manners and customs, and I know no book that gives so complete and amusing a picture of the habits of savage life, unless it be the volume on the New Zealanders.

Sharp, with his diminished crew, which must have been reduced to about seventy men, sailed with the ship northward to the gulf of Nicoya. Meeting no booty there, he returned to the is'and Plata, picking up three prizes in his way. The first was a ship called the San Pedro, with a lading of cocoa-nuts, and 21,000 pieces of eight in chests, and 16,000 in bags, besides plate. The money in bags, with all the loose plunder, was immediately divided, each man receiving 234 pieces of eight.

PIRATES AND ROBBERS.

CAPTAIN SHARP.

The money in chests was reserved for a future division. Their second prize was a packet from Panama bound to Callao, by which they learned that in Panama it was believed that all the Buccaneers had returned overland to the West Indies. The third was a ship called the San Rosario, which made a bold resistance, and did not submit until her captain was killed. She came from Callao with a cargo of wine, brandy, oil, and fruit, and had in her as much money as yielded ninety-four dollars to each Buccaneer. Through their ignorance of metals, they missed a much greater booty. There were 700 pigs of plate which they mistook for tin, on account of its not being refined and fitted for coining. They only took one of the seven hundred pigs, and two-thirds of this they melted down into bullets and otherwise squandered away. After having beaten along the coast, coming at times to anchor, making a few discoveries, and giving names to islands and bays, but taking no prizes, they sailed early in November from the shores of Patagonia. Their navigation hence, as Captain Burney remarks, was more than could be imagined; it was like the journey of travellers by night in a strange country without a guide. The weather being very stormy, they were afraid to venture through the Strait of Magalhanes, but ran to the south to go round the Tierra del Fuego. Spite of tempests, clouds, and darkness, and immense ice-bergs, they doubled in safety the redoubtable Cape Horn, nine months after their comrades, who went back by the isthmus of Darien, had left them.

On the 5th of December they made a division of such of their spoils as had been reserved. Each man's share amounted to 328 pieces of eight.

On January the 28th, 1682, they made the island of Barbadoes, where the British frigate Richmond was lying. "We having acted in all our voyage without a commission," says Ringrose, "dared not be so bold as to put in, est the said frigate should seize us for privateering, and strip us of all we had got in the whole voyage." They, therefore, sailed to Antigua. People may say what they choose about the virtues of old times! It is a notorious fact that statesmen and the servants of government were in those days corrupt, rapacious, dishonest. It seems to have been an established practice among the Buccaneers to purchase impunity by bribing our governors of the West India islands. But at Antigua, Sharp now found, as Governor, Colonel Codrington, an honest man, who would not allow his lady to accept of a present of jewels sent by the Buccaneers as a propitiatory offering, nor give the Buccaneers leave to enter the harbour. The Buccaneers then separated. Some stole into Antigua on board of other craft; Sharp and some others landed at Nevis, whence they procured a passage to England. Their ship, the Trinidad, which they had captured in the Bay of Panama, was left to seven desperadoes of the company, who having lost every thing by gaming, had no inducement to lead them to England, but remained where they were, in the hope of picking up new associates, with whom they might again try their fortunes as free rovers.

When Bartholomew Sharp arrived in England, he and a few of his men were apprehended and brought before a Court of Admiralty, where, at the instance of the Spanish ambassador, they were tried for piracies in the South Sea. One of the principal charges against them was taking the Spanish ship Rosario, and killing the Captain and one of her men; "But it was proved," says the author of an anonymous narrative, who was one of the Buccaneers tried, "that the Spaniards fired at us first, and it was judged that we ought to defend ourselves." I can hardly understand how it should have been so, but it is said, from the general defectiveness of the evidence produced, they all escaped conviction.

Three of Sharp's men were also tried at Jamaica, one of whom "being wheedled into an open confession, was condemned and hanged; the other two stood it out, and escaped for want of witnesses to prove the fact against them."

"Thus terminated," adds Captain Burney, "what may be called the First Expedition of the Buccaneers in the South Sea; the boat-excursion by Morgan's men in the Bay of Panama being of too little consequence to be so reckoned. They had now made successful experiments of the route both by sea and land; and the Spaniards in the South Sea had reason to apprehend a speedy renewal of their visit."

And indeed their visit was repeated the very next year. "On August the 23d, 1683," says William Dampier, who had not had enough of his first expedition, "we sailed from Virginia, under the command of Captain Cook, bound for the South Seas." Their adventurous, dangerous mode of life must have had strong charms for them, for besides Dampier and Cook, Lionel Wafer, Edward Davis, and Ambrose Cowley, went for the second time, and indeed nearly all of their crew, amounting to about seventy men, were old Buccaneers.

Their ship was called the Revenge, and mounted eighteen guns: an immense superiority over the craft with which they had already scoured those seas, and which had not even a single large gun on board.

Quite enough has been said to give the reader a notion of the mode of proceeding and living of these marauders. Without including an account of the discoveries they made in the South Sea, and the additions Dampier and Wafer procured to our knowledge of the natural history of those parts of the globe, and of the manners and habits of the savages who inhabited them, a continuation of the narrative of the Buccaneers would be monotonous; and to include these would occupy too much space, and not be germane to a work like the present. I will, therefore, mention only a few particulars, and hasten to the extinction of these extraordinary associations.

When the Revenge got into the South Sea, they were surprised to find another English ship there. This ship had been fitted out in the river Thames, under a pretence of trading, but with the intention of making a piratical voyage. Her commander was one John Eaton, who readily agreed to keep company with Cook. Cook died in July, just as they made Cape Blanco, and Edward Davis the second in command, was unanimously elected to succeed him. This man, though a Buccaneer, had many good and some great qualities. Humane himself, he re pressed the ferocity of his companions ; he was prudent, moderate, and steady; and such was his commanding character, and the confidence his worth and talent inspired, that no rival authority was ever set up against him, but the lawless and capricious freebooters obeyed him implicitly in all that he ordered. For a long while he maintained his sway, not only over the two ships already mentioned, but over another English vessel, and over two hundred French, and eighty English Buccaneers that crossed the isthmus of Darien, and joined him, besides other parties, that went from time to time to try their fortunes in the South Seas.

By far the most interesting incident in the history of these marauders is found in this their second expedition in the Pacific.

On their first cruise, when under the command of Watling, the Buccaneers having been suddenly scared away from the uninhabited island of Juan Fernandez by the appearance of three armed Spanish ships, left behind them one William, an Indian of the Mosquito tribe, whose attachment to the English adventurers has been mentioned. The poor fellow was absent in the woods hunting goats for food for the Buccaneers at the time of the alarm, and hey could spare no time to search after him. When this second expedition came near Juan Fernandez, on March 22d, 1684, several of the Buccaneers who had been with Watling, and were still attached to their faithful Indian comrade William, were eager to discover if any traces could be found of him on the island, and accordingly made for it in great haste in a row-boat.

In this boat was Dampier, who, marauder though he was, has described the scene with exquisite simplicity and feeling, and Robin a Mosquito Indian. As they approached the shore, to their astonishment and delight they saw William at the sea-side waiting to receive them.

" Robin, his countryman," says Dampier, " was the first who leaped ashore from the boat, and running to his brother Mosquito man, threw himself flat on his face at his feet, who helping him up and embracing him, fell flat with his face on the ground at Robin's feet, and was by him taken up also. We stood with pleasure to behold the surprise, tenderness, and solemnity of this interview, which was exceedingly affectionate on both sides; and when their ceremonies were over, we, also, that stood gazing at them, drew near, each of us embracing him we had found here, who was overjoyed to see so many of his old friends come hither, as he thought purposely to fetch him."

William had by this time lived in utter solitude for more than three years. The Spaniards knew that he had been left behind at the island, and several ships of that nation had stopped there and sent people in pursuit of him, but he, dreading they would put him to death as an ally of their persecutors, the English Buccaneers, had each time fled and succeeded in concealing himself from their search.

When his friends first sailed away and left him at Juan Fernandez, William had with him a musket, a small horn of powder, a few shot, and a knife. " When his ammunition was expended," continues Dampier, " he contrived, by notching his knife, to saw the barrel of his gun into small pieces, wherewith he made harpoons, lances, hooks, and a long knife, heating the pieces of iron first in the fire, and then hammering them out as he pleased with stones. This may seem strange to those not acquainted with the sagacity of the Indians; but it is no more than what the Mosquito men were accustomed to in their own country." He had worn out the English clothes with which he had landed, and now had no covering save a goat-skin round his waist. For fishing, he made lines from seal-skins cut into thongs. " He had built himself a hut, half a mile from the sea-shore, which he lined with goat-skins, and slept on his couch or *barbecu* of sticks raised about two feet from the ground, and spread with goats'-skins." He saw the Buccaneers' ships the day before, and with his quick sight perceived at a great distance, that from their rigging and manner of manœuvring they must be English; he therefore killed three goats, which he dressed with vegetables, and when his friends and liberators landed he had a feast ready prepared for them.

After having cruised for four years, Davis and many of his companions returned to the West Indies in 1688, in time to benefit by a proclamation offering the King's pardon to all Buccaneers who would claim it and quit their lawless way of life. "It was not," says Captain Burney, " the least of fortune's favours to this crew, that they should find it in their power, without any care or forethought of their own, to terminate a long course of piratical adventures in quietness and security."

By a short time after the return of Davis, all the Buccaneers, both French and English, had quitted the South Sea, most of them having effected a retreat across the isthmus, in which they met with some most desperate adventures. They continued their depredations for a few years longer in the West Indian seas, and on the coasts of the Spanish main, but they never returned to the Pacific.

On the accession of William III. a war between Great Britain and France, that had been an unusually long time at peace with each other, seemed inevitable. The French in the West Indies did not wait for its declaration, but attacked the English portion of St. Christopher, which island, by joint agreement, had been made the original and confederated settlement of the two nations. The English were forced to retire to the island of St. Nevis. The war between France and England, which followed, lasted till nearly the end of William's reign. The old ties of amity were rent asunder, and the Buccaneers, who had been so long leagued against the Spaniards, now carried arms against each other, the French acting as auxiliaries to the regular forces of their nation, the English fighting under the royal flag of theirs. They never again confederated in any Buccaneer cause. Had they been always united and properly headed—had conquest and not plunder been their object, they might gradually have obtained possession of a great part of the West Indies—they might at once have established an inde pendent state among the islands of the Pacific ocean.

The treaty of Ryswick, which was signed in September

1697, and the views of the English and French cabinets as regarded Spain, and then, four years later, the accession of a Bourbon prince to the Spanish throne, led to the final suppression of these marauders. Many of them turned planters or negro drivers, or followed their profession of sailors on board of merchant vessels; but others, who had good cruising ships, quitted the West Indies, separated, and went roving to different parts of the globe. "Their distinctive mark, which they undeviatingly preserved nearly two centuries, was their waging constant war against the Spaniards, and against them only."— Now this was obliterated, and they no longer existed as Buccaneers.

I conclude with the words of Captain Burney, in which will be found a melancholy truth, but which, I hope, from the amelioration of our Colonial governments and our general improvement, will soon, as regards Englishmen and present times, appear like a falsehood.

"In the history of so much robbery and outrage, the rapacity shown in some instances by the European Governments in their West Indian transactions, and by Governors of their appointment, appears in a worse light than that of the Buccaneers, from whom, they being professed ruffians, nothing better was expected. The superior attainments of Europeans, though they have done much towards their own civilization, chiefly in humanizing their institutions, have, in their dealings with the inhabitants of the rest of the globe, with few exceptions, been made the instruments of usurpation and extortion.

"After the suppression of the Buccaneers, and partly from their relics, arose a race of pirates of a more desperate cast, so rendered by the increased danger of their occupation, who for a number of years preyed upon the commerce of all nations, till they were hunted down, and, it may be said, exterminated."

I will now give a short sketch of Black Beard, one of the most notorious of the Buccaneers.

CAPTAIN TEACH, ALIAS BLACK BEARD.

EDWARD TEACH, alias Black Beard, was a native of
Bristol, and having gone to Jamaica, frequently sailed
from that port as one of the crew of a privateer during
the French war. In that station he gave frequent proofs
of his boldness and personal courage; but he was not
entrusted with any command until Captain Benjamin
Hornigold gave him the command which he had taken.

In the spring of 1717, Hornigold and Teach sailed
from Providence for the continent of America, and in
their way captured a small vessel with 120 barrels of
flour, which they put on board their own vessels. They
also seized two other vessels; from one they took some
gallons of wine, and from the other, plunder to a considerable value. After cleaning upon the coast of Virginia, they made a prize of a large French Guineaman
bound to Martinique, and Teach obtaining the command
of her, went upon a cruise. Hornigold, with the two
vessels, returned to the island of Providence, and surrendered to the king's clemency.

Teach now began to act an independent part. He
mounted his vessel with forty guns, and named her "The
Queen Anne's Revenge." Cruising near the island of St.
Vincent, he took a large ship called the Great Allan, and
after plundering her of what he deemed proper, set her on
fire. A few days after, Teach encountered the Scarbo-
rough man-of-war, and engaged her for some hours; but
perceiving his strength and resolution, she retired, and
left Teach to pursue his depredations. His next adventure was with a sloop of ten guns, commanded by Major
Bonnet, whose actions we have already related, and these
two having united their fortunes, co-operated for some
time: but Teach finding him unacquainted with naval
affairs, gave the command of Bonnet's ship to Richards,
one of his own crew, and entertained Bonnet on board his
own vessel. Watering at Turniff, they discovered a sail,
and Richards with the Revenge slipped her cable, and ran

out to meet her. Upon seeing the black flag hoisted, the vessel struck, and came-to under the stern of Teach the commodore. This was the Adventure, from Jamaica. They took the captain and his men on board the great ship, and manned his sloop for their own service.

Weighing from Turniff, where they remained during a week, and sailing to the bay, they found there a ship and four sloops. Teach hoisted his flag, and began to fire at them, upon which the captain and his men left their ship and fled to the shore. Teach burned two of these sloops, and let the other three depart.

They afterwards sailed to different places, and having taken two small vessels, anchored off the bar of Charlestown for a few days. Here they captured a ship bound for England, as she was coming out of the harbour. They next seized a vessel coming out of Charlestown, and two pinks coming into the same harbour, together with a brigantine with fourteen negroes. The audacity of these transactions, performed in sight of the town, struck the inhabitants with terror, as they had been lately visited by some other notorious pirates. Meanwhile, there were eight sail in the harbour, none of which durst set to sea for fear of falling into the hands of Teach. The trade of this place was totally interrupted, and the inhabitants were abandoned to despair. Their calamity was greatly augmented from this circumstance, that a long and desperate war had just terminated, when they began to be infested by these robbers.

Teach having detained all the persons taken in these ships as prisoners, they were soon in great want of medicines, and he had the audacity to demand a chest from the Governor. This demand was made in a manner not less daring than insolent. Teach sent Richards, the captain of the Revenge, with Mr. Marks, one of the prisoners, and several others, to present their request. Richards informed the governor, that unless their demand was granted, and he and his companions returned in safety, every prisoner on board the captured ships should instantly be slain, and the vessels consumed to ashes.

During the time that Mr. Marks was negotiating with

the governor, Richards and his associates walked the streets at pleasure, while indignation flamed from every eye against them, as the robbers of their property, and the terror of their country. Though the affront thus offered to the Government was great and most audacious, yet, to preserve the lives of so many men, they granted their request, and sent on board a chest valued at three or four hundred pounds.

Teach, as soon as he received the medicines and his fellow pirates, pillaged the ships of gold and provisions, and then dismissed the prisoners with their vessels. From the bar of Charlestown, they sailed to North Carolina. Teach now began to reflect how he could best secure the spoil, along with some of his crew who were his favourites. Accordingly, under pretence of cleaning, he ran his vessel on shore, and grounded ; then ordered the men in Hand's sloop to come to his assistance, which they endeavouring to do, also ran aground, and so they were both lost. Then Teach went into the tender with forty hands, and upon a sandy island, about a league from shore, where there was neither bird nor beast, nor herb for their subsistence, he left seventeen of his crew, who must have inevitably perished, had not Major Bonnet received intelligence of their miserable situation, and sent a long-boat for them. After this barbarous deed, Teach, with the remainder of his crew, went and surrendered to the Governor of North Carolina, retaining all the property which had been acquired by his fleet.

This temporary suspension of the depredations of Black Beard, for so he was now called, did not proceed from a conviction of his former errors, or a determination to reform, but to prepare for future and more extensive exploits. As governors are but men, and not unfrequently by no means possessed of the most virtuous principles, the gold of Black Beard rendered him comely in the governor's eyes, and, by his influence, he obtained a legal right to the great ship called " The Queen Anne's Revenge." By order of the governor, a court of vice-admiralty was held at Bath-town, and that vessel was condemned as a lawful prize which he had taken from the Spaniards, though it was a well-known fact that she belonged to English merchants. Before he entered upon his new adventures, he married a young woman of about sixteen years of age, the governor himself attending the ceremony. It was reported that this was only his fourteenth wife, about twelve of whom were yet alive; and though this woman was young and amiable, he behaved towards her in a manner so brutal, that it was shocking to all decency and propriety, even among his abandoned crew of pirates.

In his first voyage, Black Beard directed his course to the Bermudas, and meeting with two or three English vessels, emptied them of their stores and other necessaries, and allowed them to proceed. He also met with two French vessels bound for Martinique, the one light and the other laden with sugar and cocoa: he put the men on board the latter into the former, and allowed her to depart. He brought the freighted vessel into North Carolina, where the governor and Black Beard shared the prizes. Nor did their audacity and villany stop here. Teach and some of his abandoned crew waited upon his excellency, and swore that they had seized the French ship at sea, without a soul on board; therefore a court was called, and she was condemned, the honourable governor received sixty hogsheads of sugar for his share, his secretary twenty, and the pirates the remainder. But as guilt always inspires suspicion, Teach was afraid that some one might arrive in the harbour who might detect the roguery: therefore, upon pretence that she was leaky, and might sink, and so stop up the entrance to the harbour where she lay, they obtained the governor's liberty to drag her into the river, where she was set on fire and when burnt to the water, her bottom was sunk, that so she might never rise in judgment against the governor and his confederates.

Black Beard now being in the province of Friendship, passed several months in the river, giving and receiving visits from the planters; while he traded with the vessels which came to that river, sometimes in the way of lawful commerce, and sometimes in his own way. When he chose to appear the honest man, he made fair purchases on equal barter; but when this did not suit his necessities, or his humour, he would rob at pleasure, and leave them to seek their redress from the governor; and the better to cover his intrigues with his excellency, he would sometimes outbrave him to his face, and administer to him a share of that contempt and insolence which he so liberally bestowed upon the rest of the inhabitants of the province.

But there are limits to human insolence and depravity. The captains of the vessels who frequented that river, and had been so often harassed and plundered by Black Beard, secretly consulted with some of the planters what measures to pursue, in order to banish such an infamous miscreant from their coasts, and to bring him to deserved punishment. Convinced from long experience, that the governor himself, to whom it belonged, would give no redress, they presented the matter to the Governor of Virginia, and entreated that an armed force might be sent from the men-of-war lying there, either to take or to destroy those pirates who infested their coast.

Upon this representation, the Governor of Virginia consulted with the captains of the two men-of-war as to the best measures to be adopted. He was resolved that the governor should hire two small vessels, which could pursue Black Beard into all his inlets and creeks; that they should be manned from the men-of-war, and the command given to Lieutenant Maynard, an experienced and resolute officer. When all was ready for his departure, the governor called an assembly, in which it was resolved to issue a proclamation, offering a great reward to any who, within a year, should take or destroy any pirate.

Upon the 17th of November, 1717, Maynard left James's river in quest of Black Beard, and on the evening of the 21st came in sight of the pirate. This expedition was fitted out with all possible expedition and secrecy, no boat being permitted to pass that might convey any intelligence, while care was taken to discover where the pirates were lurking. His excellency the Governor of Bermuda, and his secretary, however, having obtained information of the intended expedition, the latter wrote a letter to Black Beard, intimating that he had sent him four of his men, who were all he could meet with in or about town, and so bade him be upon his guard. These men were sent from Bathtown to the place where Black Beard lay, about the distance of twenty leagues.

The hardened and infatuated pirate, having been often deceived by false intelligence, was the less attentive to this information, nor was he convinced of its accuracy until he saw the sloops sent to apprehend him. Though he had then only twenty men on board, he prepared to give battle. Lieutenant Maynard arrived with his sloops in the evening, and anchored, as he could not venture, under cloud of night, to go into the place where Black Beard lay. The latter spent the night in drinking with the master of a trading-vessel, with the same indifference as if no danger had been near. Nay, such was the desperate wickedness of this villain, that it is reported, during the carousals of that night, one of his men asked him, " In case anything should happen to him during the engagement with the two sloops which were waiting to attack him in the morning, whether his wife knew where he had buried his money?" when he impiously replied, " That nobody but himself and the devil knew where it was, and the longest liver should take all."

In the morning Maynard weighed, and sent his boat to sound, which coming near the pirate, received her fire. Maynard then hoisted royal colours, and made towards Black Beard with every sail and oar. In a little time the pirate ran aground, and so also did the king's vessels. Maynard lightened his vessel of the ballast and water, and made towards Black Beard. Upon this he hailed him in his own rude style, " D—n you for villains, who are you, and from whence come you?" The lieutenant answered, " You may see from our colours we are no pirates." Black Beard bade him send his boat on board that he might see who he was. But Maynard replied, " I cannot spare my boat, but I will come on board of you as soon as I can with my sloop." Upon this Black Beard took a glass of liquor and drank to him,

saying, "I'll give no quarter nor take any from you."
Maynard replied, " He expected no quarter from him, nor
should he give him any."

During this dialogue the pirate's ship floated, and the
sloops were rowing with all expedition towards him. As
she came near, the pirate fired a broadside, charged with
all manner of small shot, which killed or wounded
twenty men. Black Beard's ship in a little after fell
broadside to the shore; one of the sloops called the
Ranger also fell astern. But Maynard finding that his
own sloop had way, and would soon be on board of
Teach, ordered all his men down, while himself and the
man at the helm, whom he commanded to lie concealed,
were the only persons who remained on deck. He at
the same time desired them to take their pistols, cutlasses,
and swords, and be ready for action upon his call, and,
for greater expedition, two ladders were placed in the
hatchway. When the king's sloop boarded, the pirate's
case-boxes, filled with powder, small shot, slugs and
pieces of lead and iron, with a quickmatch in the mouth
of them, were thrown into Maynard's sloop. Fortunately,
however, the men being in the hold, they did small
injury on the present occasion, though they are usually
very destructive. Black Beard seeing few or no hands
upon deck, cried to his men that they were all knocked
on the head except three or four; " and therefore," said
he, " let us jump on board, and cut to pieces those that
are alive."

Upon this, during the smoke occasioned by one of
these case-boxes, Black Beard, with fourteen of his men,
entered and were not perceived until the smoke was dis-
pelled. The signal was given to Maynard's men, who
rushed up in an instant. Black Beard and the lieutenant
exchanged shots, and the pirate was wounded ; they then
engaged sword in hand, until the sword of the lieutenant
broke, but fortunately one of his men at that instant gave
Black Beard a terrible wound in the neck and throat.
The most desperate and bloody conflict ensued :—May
nard with twelve men, and Black Beard with fourteen
The sea was dyed with blood all around the vessel, and

BLACKBEARD.

uncommon bravery was displayed upon both sides. Though the pirate was wounded by the first shot from Maynard, though he had received twenty cuts, and as many shots, he fought with desperate valour; but at length, when in the act of cocking his pistol, fell down dead. By this time eight of his men had fallen, and the rest being wounded, cried out for quarter, which was granted as the ringleader was slain. The other sloop also attacked the men who remained in the pirate vessels, until they also cried out for quarter. And such was the desperation of Black Beard, that, having small hope of escaping, he had placed a negro with a match at the gunpowder-door, to blow up the ship the moment that he should have been boarded by the king's men, in order to involve the whole in general ruin. That destructive broadside at the commencement of the action, which at first appeared so unlucky, was, however, the means of their preservation from the intended destruction.

Maynard severed the pirate's head from his body, suspended it upon his bowsprit-end, and sailed to Bathtown, to obtain medical aid for his wounded men. In the pirate sloop several letters and papers were found, which Black Beard would certainly have destroyed previous to the engagement, had he not determined to blow her up upon his being taken, which disclosed the whole villainy between the honourable Governor of Bermuda and his honest secretary on the one hand, and the notorious pirate on the other, who had now suffered the just punishment of his crimes.

Scarcely was Maynard returned to Bathtown, when he boldly went and made free with the sixty hogsheads of sugar in the possession of the governor, and the twenty in that of his secretary.

After his men had been healed at Bathtown, the lieutenant proceeded to Virginia with the head of Black Beard still suspended on his bowsprit-end, as a trophy of his victory, to the great joy of all the inhabitants. The prisoners were tried, condemned, and executed; and thus all the crew of that infernal miscreant Black Beard were destroyed, except two.   One of these was taken out of a trading-vessel, only the day before the engagement, in which he received no less than seventy wounds, of all which he was cured.   The other was Israel Hands, who was master of the Queen Anne's Revenge; he was taken at Bathtown, being wounded in one of Black Beard's savage humours. One night Black Beard, drinking in his cabin with Hands, the pilot, and another man, without any pretence, took a small pair of pistols, and cocked them under the table; which being perceived by the man, he went on deck, leaving the captain, Hands, and the pilot together.   When his pistols were prepared, he extinguished the candle, crossed his arms, and fired at his company.   The one pistol did no execution, but the other wounded Hands in the knee.   Interrogated concerning the meaning of this, he answered with an imprecation, " That if he did not now and then kill one of them, they would forget who he was."   Hands was eventually tried and condemned, but as he was about to be executed, a vessel arrived with a proclamation prolonging the time of his Majesty's pardon, which Hands pleading, he was saved from a violent and shameful death.

In the commonwealth of pirates, he who goes the greatest length of wickedness, is looked upon with a kind of envy amongst them, as a person of a more extraordinary gallantry; he is therefore entitled to be distinguished by some post, and, if such a one has but courage, he must certainly be a great man.   The hero of whom we are writing was thoroughly accomplished in this way, and some of his frolics of wickedness were as extravagant as if he aimed at making his men believe he was a devil incarnate.   Being one day at sea, and a little flushed with drink : " Come," said he, " let us make a hell of our own, and try how long we can bear it."   Accordingly, he, with two or three others, went down into the hold, and, closing up all the hatches, filled several pots full of brimstone, and other combustible matter; they then set it on fire, and so continued till they were almost suffocated, when some of the men cried out for air; at length

Fight on board the Pirate.

Page 71.

he opened the hatches, not a little pleased that he had held out the longest.

Those of his crew who were taken alive, told a story which may appear a little incredible. That once, upon a cruise, they found out that they had a man on board more than their crew; such a one was seen several days amongst them, sometimes below, and sometimes upon deck, yet no man in the ship could give any account who he was, or from whence he came; but that he disappeared a little before they were cast away in their great ship, and, it seems, they verily believed it was the devil.

One would think these things should have induced them to reform their lives; but being so many reprobates together, they encouraged and spirited one another up in their wickedness, to which a continual course of drinking did not a little contribute. In Black Beard's journal, which was taken, there were several memoranda of the following nature, all written with his own hand.—" Such a day, rum all out;—our company somewhat sober;—a d—d confusion amongst us!—rogues a plotting; great talk of separation.—So I looked sharp for a prize;—such a day took one, with a great deal of liquor on board; so kept the company hot, d—d hot, then all things went well again."

We shall close the narrative of this extraordinary man's life by an account of the cause why he was denominated Black Beard. He derived this name from his long black beard, which, like a frightful meteor, covered his whole face, and terrified all America more than any comet that had ever appeared. He was accustomed to twist it with ribbon in small quantities, and turn them about his ears. In time of action he wore a sling over his shoulders with three brace of pistols. He stuck lighted matches under his hat, which appearing on both sides of his face and eyes, naturally fierce and wild, made him such a figure that the human imagination cannot form a conception of a fury more terrible and alarming; and if he had the appearance and look of a fury, his actions corresponded with that character.

Vol. II. 7

ENGLISH ROBBERS.

ROBIN HOOD.

When tradition is resorted to in default of history, it commonly happens that the latter is superseded altogether; and, indeed, when we consider the times in which our celebrated outlaw, Robin Hood, lived, and the course of adventure which it was either his fate or his inclination to pursue, and the remarkable silence or utter extinction of contemporary writers, we shall not be surprised to find that the fame or infamy of our hero has only been preserved in the slender custody of an old ballad, and committed to the tender mercies of the ingenious commentator.

Fancy, however, when it leans on fact, is in no danger of falling ; and so long as the throstle sings in " merry Sherwood," and the sun shall kindle the spires of Nottingham, will the name of Robin Hood be a household word in the mouths of the people of England.

Robin Hood was born at Locksley, in the county of Nottingham, a place no longer in existence, in the year 1160, and in the reign of King Henry II. He is commonly reputed to have been Earl of Huntingdon, a title to which, it is said, he had no small pretension. It is certain, however, that his lineage was noble, and his true name Robert Fitzooth, which a pliant commentator conjectures was *easily* corrupted by vulgar pronunciation into Robin Hood. Another avers that Hood is only a corruption of " o' th' wood," — of Sherwood; while a third supposes that it may, probably, be referred to a particular sort of hood worn by him, either by way of distinction or with a view to disguise. This last supposition is favoured by the fact, that Hugh *Capet*, the first King of France, obtained his surname from a similar circumstance ; it is, at the same time, almost set aside by the improbability of the twofold designation.

Robin Hood appears to have been in his youth of an extravagant and lawless disposition, and, having dissipated his inheritance, insomuch that it had become forfeited, and being in the predicament of outlawry for debt, he was fain to seek an asylum in the woods, and to levy contributions on the wealthy passenger who might chance to traverse his self-granted territories.

In these forests, of which he chiefly inclined to Barnsdale in Yorkshire, Sherwood in Nottinghamshire, and Plompton Park in Cumberland, he reigned for many years, with all the authority, if not in all the splendour, of a legitimate sovereign ; and his subjects, in process of time, amounted to the number of a hundred archers, " men most skilful in battle, whom four times that number of the boldest fellows durst not attack."

The royal forests at that period abounded with deer, and, consequently, afforded to Robin Hood and his retainers a sufficient supply of luxurious provender during the year; and it is apparent that there could be no lack of fuel for the purpose of dressing their venison. How their other needments were procured is equally certain. A rich bishop, a wealthy priest, or a money-laden abbot, was always to be met with in those days ; and a system of barter or exchange with the adjacent villages or great towns was easily established, more particularly among those who were not indisposed to favour the means whereby the adventurous commercial capitalist became possessed of his commodities.

Let it, however, be stated to the honour of Robin Hood, that in all his predatory exertions of power, he attacked the goods of the wealthy only—that he never killed any person, unless resisted or attacked—that he would never permit a woman to be abused or in any way maltreated, and that he never plundered the poor, but bestowed upon them the wealth he wrested from the abbots.

Robin, indeed, appears to have held all the clergy in most uncatholic abhorrence, and

> " These byshoppes and thyse archebyshoppes,
>   Ye shall them bete and bynde,

was a condition solemnly imposed upon all his adherents when they entered his service.

In spite, however, of the hatred in which he held the priesthood of all denominations, Robin Hood was, according to the convictions of that age, a man of no common piety, and retained a chaplain, Friar Tuck, for the daily ministration of divine service.

One day, while he was attending the celebration of mass, which it was his devout custom to do, he was perceived and recognised by a sheriff and his officers, who had frequently before interfered with and molested him. He was instantly apprised by certain of his men of the circumstance, and exhorted to fly, which, out of reverence for the sacrament which he was at that moment receiving, he refused to do. But, most of his men having betaken themselves to flight, Robin, "putting his trust in Him whom he worshipped," assisted by a very few of his subjects who were present, attacked his enemies, whom he vanquished, and enriched himself with their spoils and ransom.

But it is high time that we should give some account of the adventures in which our hero was engaged, and of the manner in which he betook himself, and incited others, to the commission of practices which, however indefensible they may be considered in these times, when the rights of property are better understood and maintained, are not either so monstrous or manifold as some of his enemies have delighted to describe them. It must be remembered that, in those days, an outlaw, being deprived of protection, owed no allegiance; and the better title of Richard to the throne of England was, perhaps, only a better title because it was upheld by stronger means than those wherewith Robin Hood could contrive to invest himself.

It appears, then, that the active and promising talents of Robin were so signally exhibited, on a visit to his maternal uncle Gamwell, at Christmas, that the old man conceived a strong affection for him, and, dying soon after, constituted him his sole heir. In the possession of some wealth, Robin began to display both his liberality to the poor and his hospitality to his friends, so that in a short time he became very popular in the neighbourhood. The coffers of our adventurer were, however, by these means soon emptied, and his ingenuity soon suggested an easy and agreeable method of recruiting them by the plunder of the rich; in no wise modifying his benevolent views of bestowing upon the poor the chief portion of his compulsory exactions.

One Little John (whose surname is said to have been Nailor), the son of a servant of his uncle, and subsequently his own page, now became his chief confident and companion. The first recorded exploit of these two heroes, assisted by fifteen other associates, was an attack upon the Bishop of Carlisle and his retinue. Informed that the prelate was on his way to the capital, Robin met him on the south side of Ferrybridge, Yorkshire, and, though his retinue consisted of fifty men, he attacked the prelate, took from him eight hundred marks, tied him to a tree, constrained him to say mass, untied him, placed him upon his horse with his face to the tail, and obliged him in that position to ride to London.

Though the Bishop made severe complaints to the king against the indignity which had been offered him, yet Robin and his men were resolved to be spectators of a hunting-match, at which the king and most of his courtiers were to be present. The royal train vied with each other at the shooting of the bow; until Robin, stepping forward, engaged, at the risk of a hundred marks, to single out three of his own companions who would excel any other three who should be opposed to them. The king took the wager, and the queen Eleanor, admiring he boldness of the stranger, laid one thousand gold pieces, with the king, upon his side. Her example was imitated by several of the courtiers.

Matters thus arranged, Robin drew his bow and shot almost into the centre of the clout. Little John vanquished his antagonist, and struck the black mark. Much, the miller's son, clave the pin in the centre of the black mark; and the queen and all her party shouted with joy. The king, however, some time after, obtained intelligence that

it was Robin and his men who had conquered his attendants at the bow, and he, accordingly, sent out detachments in search of them throughout the whole king
dom. Robin went from place to place to evade their
search, and at last repaired to London, until the hue-and-
cry was over. He then returned to his old haunt, to the
great joy of his companions.

Robin next resolved to undertake an excursion un-
attended by any of his men; and, deviating into a by-
path, he came to a small hut, where being admitted, he
found an old widow weeping and lamenting her hard fate.
Robin, moved with compassion, inquired into the cause
of her distress, whereupon the old woman informed him
that she was behind in her rent, and that her landlord
was about to take her all and turn her out of doors. He
desired her to be comforted, and pulling off his laced coat,
put on an old doublet given him by the widow, and took
his seat by the fire-side. The hard-hearted landlord in a
short time appeared, and urged his demand. Robin
began to intercede in her behalf, and used various arguments to gain delay. All was unavailing; he was
answered by the landlord that he must have his rent,
else he would seize her goods and turn her out of his
house.

Robin then drew out his purse, demanded the receipt,
and paid the rent, to the unspeakable joy of the poor
widow. When the landlord was about to depart, Robin
advised him, as the neighbourhood was infested by robbers, to tarry all night. The other obstinately refused,
and added that he was not afraid of being robbed by any
person. Accordingly, he set out on his journey. Robin,
having dressed himself in his laced coat, mounted his
horse and pursued him. Coming up with the landlord at
a place where he was certain that he was to pass, he requested him to deliver up his money. He was instantly
stripped of the rent, and a great deal more, whereupon
our generous hero returned to his quarters with the
widow.

He was scarcely seated, however, when the landlord
knocked at the door; the good woman knew his stern

voice, and immediately received him under her hospitable roof. He informed them that he had gone but a little way when he was robbed by a man with a laced coat Robin chid him for neglecting to follow his friendly advice, and repeated his entreaties that he would remain in the hovel for the night. The obstinate man, however, refused, and again renewed his journey with an empty purse.

The ensuing adventure of Robin was on a somewhat more magnificent scale. The king had determined to make a progress into the north of England, and Robin on learning his intention, was ambitious of joining the retinue of his majesty. He arrayed himself and about sixty of his merry men upon white horses, richly har nessed and completely armed. During that period the kings of England were not attended by a troop of horse-guards, their retinue consisting only of about thirty men. Robin Hood, who rode the foremost in his train, address-ed the king in the following manner: " My liege," said he, " by our dress we might seem to you to be persons of quality and fortune, but I must take the liberty to inform you that we are persons of a different character. I was born of honest parents, who left me a small fortune, which, and much more, I have since squandered. I reckon myself one of your countrymen, who finds him-self happy in having spent his all upon good living."— " What mean you, sir," replied the king, " by this mysterious mode of speech? Explain yourself, for I am at a loss to understand your meaning."—" Understand me!" answered Robin; " my actions are well known throughout the whole kingdom. I have only to inform your majesty, that, having exhausted all our means, these men have made me their captain, and we collect taxes upon the road, not to feed insolent ministers, as you do, but we take from the rich to give to the poor, who participate in our daily bounty. Your generosity, I hope, will deem me worthy of a little: it is your money that I want, sire, and then you may proceed on your journey." Perceiv-ing from the superiority of numbers that it was in vain to resist, the king presented him with a purse, which from its weight Robin deemed sufficient to supply his present necessities.

Robin's adventures were sometimes of a solitary as well as of a social nature. One day, happening to travel alone, he discovered a fine-looking young man, sitting pensively under a tree. He advanced towards him, and demanded the cause of his dejection. The youth replied, that he should have been married to a gentleman's daughter in the neighbourhood, but that sordid motives had induced her father to bestow her on a richer lover, who was this day to lead her to the altar. Robin bade him be of good cheer, for that he should have both his love and her fortune. He immediately took the young man along with him to his comrades, with whom he hastened to the church, where he began to converse with the bishop upon certain points in religion.

Meanwhile entered the wealthy knight and his beautiful young bride to be married. Robin remarked to the bishop, that it was matter of regret to see such a young woman married to an old man, and that she ought to espouse her lawful bridegroom; whereupon he made a signal, and the discarded lover approached, followed by twenty armed men. After some altercation, the old suitor was dismissed, and the young pair joyfully returned with the party to Sherwood to spend their honeymoon.

Robin once disguised himself in a friar's habit, and, travelling by himself, met two priests, whom he entreated to assist a brother of the holy function in distress. To this they answered, that they would most willingly have done so, but that they had been attacked by a gang of robbers, who had not left them a sixpence. Robin, suspecting their veracity, was determined to discover, by stratagem, if they really had wherewithal to meet his demand. He proposed that they should all kneel in prayer to the Virgin Mary to send them some money. After they had all devoutly prayed, he enquired what money the holy Mother had sent them. They replied that they had been unsuccessful. Upon this our adventurer fell into a prodigious passion, exclaiming, that they were all a race of imposing and deceitful rogues, for that it was not possible that the Virgin would allow them to pray for nothing. He accordingly searched their pockets and drew from thence four hundred pieces of gold. The bereaved friars were now about to depart, but Robin constrained them to stop, and to take an oath that they would not again lie to a brother friar, nor intrude upon the sacred rights of virgins or married men.

Another adventure of Robin's was with a butcher, of whom he purchased all his stock, and, going to the market, sold them at reduced prices, and also treated his customers into the bargain. The sheriff of the county hearing of this, and supposing that he was some country spark, from whom a good bargain might be obtained, intruded himself into the company, and, entering into conversation with Robin, enquired if he had any more cattle to sell. "I have," said he, "two or three hundred head at home, and a hundred acres of good land to feed them on, and if you will purchase them, you may have a good penny-worth." The squire agreed, and taking with him four hundred pounds in gold, set forward with Robin to complete the purchase. He led him into a solitary road, where the dread of meeting with robbers began to alarm the squire. He had scarcely expressed his fears, when Little John and fifty of his associates appeared. Robin desired them to take the sheriff to dinner, assuring them that he had plenty of money to pay his share. Accordingly, a collation was prepared for the sheriff, and after dinner he was led into a thick part of the wood, and stripped of his gold.

At length, after he had by these means established a species of independent sovereignty, and held at defiance kings, magistrates, and judges, a proclamation was put forth, offering a considerable reward for bringing him in dead or alive, which, however, was no more successful than the many previous endeavours to the same end which had been resorted to.

But old age was advancing upon him, and, falling sick, and desirous of being relieved by blood-letting, he betook himself to the prioress of Kirkley's nunnery, in York

shire, his relation, by whom he was cruelly and treacherously suffered to bleed to death. His decease took place
on the 18th November 1247, being the 31st year of the
reign of King Henry III. If, therefore, the date of his
birth be correct, Robin Hood was in the 87th year of his
age when his death took place. He was buried beneath
some trees at a short distance from the priory, and a
stone was laid over his grave on which was an inscription
to his memory.

Such is the celebrity of Robin Hood, and so great is
the interest with which everything relating to him is in-
vested, that we shall probably be excused if we advert to
the many traditions respecting him which are to this day
" rife and perfect in the listening ear" of the people of
our own country. There would, indeed, appear to be
something in the character of this extraordinary man, as
it is presented to us in the various ballads to which his
adventures have given birth, so thoroughly English, and
so entirely consonant to English feelings and prejudices,
that we doubt very much whether all the attempts which
have been made to represent him as a daring and un-
principled robber, have not rather tended to establish him
in the affections of his admirers than to diminish or ob-
scure the light of his unquestionable virtues. For, when
it is held in mind that the exactions of our hero were
chiefly enforced against the wealthy priesthood, and that
he only did on a small scale what the Reformation carried out to the fullest extent, we shall not be far wrong,
(however much the more philosophical reader may smile
at the designation,) if we bestow upon him the title of
" The first Church Reformer." Let it be remembered
also, that it was from the wealthy he took the spoil, and
to the poor consigned it—thus, possibly, when we consider the means by which wealth was amassed in those
days, only returning money to the pockets from which it
had been originally wrested.

From the many ballads still extant relating to Robin
Hood and his merry men, we find that his chief favour-
ites, and those in whose fidelity he mostly confided, were
Little John, William Scadlock, (Scathelock or Scarlet)·

George a Green, Pinder, or Poundkeeper, of Wakefield,
Much, a miller's son, and a certain monk, or friar, named
Tuck. It is likewise said that he was tended in his retreat by a female of whom he was enamoured, and whose
real or assumed name was Marian. There have been
many conjectures as to the identity of this lady, the most
probable of which is that she was Matilda, the daughter
of Robert Lord Fitzwater, while Robin Hood remained
in a state of outlawry. In the very old ballad, however,
of " Robin Hood's birth, breeding," &c. we read of his
courtship and marriage to Clorinda, whose first appearance to Robin is thus beautifully described—

> As that word was spoke, Clorinda came by,
>   The Queen of the Shepherds was she,
> And her gown was of velvet as green as the grass,
>   And her buskin did reach to her knee.
>
> Her gait it was graceful, her body was straight,
>   And her countenance free from pride;
> A bow in her hand, and a quiver of arrows,
>   Hung dangling by her sweet side.
>
> Her eyebrows were black, ay, and so was her hair,
>   And her skin was as smooth as glass,
> Her visage spoke wisdom and modesty too;
>   Sets with Robin Hood such a lass!

The manner in which Robin Hood recruited his company is singular, for, to use the words of an old writer,
" whersoever he hard of any that were of unusual strength
and hardines, he would disgyse himselfe, and, rather than
fayle, go lyke a beggar to become acquaynted with them;
and, after he had tryed them with fyghting, never give
them over till he had used means to draw them to lyve
after his fashion." It seems, however, that in these en-
counters, Robin had usually the worst of it,* and it was
only in the acomplishment of drawing the long-bow that

---

* We refer the curious reader to Ritson's collection of Old Ballads
relative to Robin Hood—more particularly to the three called "Robin Hood and the Beggar," "Robin Hood and the Potter," and
"Robin Hood and the Pinder of Wakefield," as examples bearing
out our assertion in the text.

Robin was pre-eminent above his fellows. His archery, both for truth of aim and distance of shot, was unparalleled, and it is recorded of Robin Hood, and of Little John also, that they have frequently shot an arrow a measured mile, or 1760 yards, which, it is supposed, no one before or since was ever able to do. Some of the stories told of the extent of these shots are marvellous enough; for instance, an ancient ballad-writer, unwilling to be outdone in drawing the long-bow, even by Robin Hood himself, tells us that

> " The father of Robin a forester was,
>   And he shot in a lusty strong bow
> *Two north country miles and an inch* at a shot,
>   As the Pinder of Wakefield does know."

That last inch is a sufficient evidence of the scrupulous accuracy of the writer! But the exploit most worthy of mention, and best showing the fatal skill of Robin Hood in archery, is to be found in the following ballad.

ROBIN HOOD'S PROGRESS TO NOTTINGHAM.

> Robin Hood he was and a tall young man,
>   *Derry derry down;*
>   And fifteen winters old,
> And Robin Hood he was a proper young man,
>   Of courage stout and bold.
>   *Hey down, derry derry down.*

> Robin hee would and to fair Nottingham
>   With the general for to dine,
> There was hee aware of fifteen forresters,
>   And a drinking beer, ale, and wine.

> " What news? what news?" said bold Robin Hood,
>   " What news fain woulds't thou know?"
> Our king hath provided a shooting match,
>   And I'm ready with my bow.

> We hold it in scorn, said the forresters,
>   That ever a boy so young
> Should bear a bow before the king
>   That 's not able to draw one string.

I 'll hold you twenty marks, said bold Robin Hood
  By the leave of Our Lady,
That I 'll hit a mark a hundred rod,
  And I'll cause a hart to dye.

We 'l hold you twenty mark, then said the forresters,
  By the leave of Our Lady,
Thou hit'st not the mark a hundred rod,
  Nor causest a hart to dye.

Robin he bent up a noble bow,
  And a broad arrow he let flye;
He hit the mark a hundred rod,
  And he caused the hart to dye.

Some say hee brake ribs one or two,
  And some say hee brake three;
The arrow within the hart would not abide,
  But it glanced in two or three.

The hart did skip and the hart did leap,
  And the hart lay on the ground;
The wager is mine, said bold Robin Hood,
  If 'twere for a thousand pound.

The wager's none of thine, then said the forresters,
  Although thou beest in haste,
Take up thy bow, and get thee hence,
  Lest we thy sides do baste.

Robin Hood he took up his noble bow,
  And his broad arrows all amain;
And Robin he laught and begun for to smile,
  And hee went over the plain.

Then Robin he bent his noble bow,
  And his broad arrows hee let flye,
Till fourteen of those fifteen forresters
  Upon the ground did lye.

He that did this quarrel first begin,
  Went tripping over the plain,
But Robin he bent his noble bow
  And hee fetcht him back again.

You said I was no archer, said Robin Hood,
  But say so now again;
With that he sent another arrow,
  That split his head in twain.

> You have found mee an archer, saith Robin **Hood,**
>   Which will make your wives for to wring,
> And wish that you had never spoke the word,
>   That I could not draw one string.
>
> The people that liv'd in fair Nottingham,
>   Came running out amain,
> Supposing to have taken bold Robin **Hood,**
>   With the forresters that were slain.
>
> Some lost legs, and some lost arms,
>   And some did lose their blood;
> But Robin hee took up his noble bow,
>   And is gone to the merry green-wood.
>
> They carried these forresters into fair Nottingham,
>   As many there did know,
> They dig'd them graves in their church-yard,
>   And they buried them all a-row.

It is a corroborating circumstance in favour of the truth of this exploit, that, in the year 1796, as some labourers were digging in a garden at Fox Cave, near Nottingham, they discovered six human skeletons entire, deposited in regular order, side by side, supposed to be part of the fifteen foresters slain by Robin Hood.

In taking our leave of this extraordinary man, we fear lest we should lie under the imputation of having been tediously prolix, at the same time that we are equally in doubt whether we have not been especially brief. But, in a work of this nature, a biographer is placed in a dilemma when he has to record the achievements of such a man as Robin Hood: he either pre-supposes, on the part of his reader, some knowledge of so well-known a character, and, accordingly, contents himself with giving the more striking and least hackneyed of his adventures; or, constraining himself to believe that his reader is profoundly ignorant, even of the name of his hero, he goes through his task with the ridiculous merit and the sorry triumph of having recited "a thrice-told tale."

We find the character of Robin Hood summed up in so admirable a manner by the acute and sagacious Ritson, that we cannot do better than close our account of him in his words :—

"With respect to his personal character, it is sufficiently evident, that he was active, brave, prudent, patient; possessed of uncommon bodily strength, and considerable military skill; just, generous, benevolent, faithful, and beloved or revered by his followers or adherents for his excellent and amiable qualities. Fordun, a priest, extols his piety; Major pronounces him the most humane, and the prince of all robbers. As proofs of his universal and singular popularity, his story and exploits have been made the subject as well of various dramatic exhibitions as of innumerable poems, rhymes, songs, and ballads; he has given rise to various proverbs; and to swear by him or some of his companions appears to have been a usual practice; his songs have been chanted on the most solemn occasions: he may be regarded as the patron of archery, and, though not actually canonized, he obtained the principal distinction of sainthood, in having a festival allotted to him, and solemn games instituted in honour of his memory, which were celebrated till the latter end of the sixteenth century; not by the populace only, but by kings, and princes, and grave magistrates; and that as well in Scotland as in England. His bow, and one of his arrows, his chair, his cap, and one of his slippers, were preserved with peculiar veneration till within the last century; and not only the places which afforded him security or amusement, but even the well at which he quenched his thirst, still retain his name—a name which, in the middle of the last century, was conferred as a singular distinction upon the prime minister to the King of Madagascar."

The company of Robin Hood was dispersed after his death; but history has not been particular in the relation of the circumstances. All that is known is, that the honour of Little John's death and burial is contended for by rival nations; that he was really buried at Hathersaye, a small village near Castleton, in Derbyshire; and that some of his descendants, surnamed Naylor, were in existence as late as the last century.

SIR GOSSELIN DENVILLE.

Sir Gosselin was descended of very honourable parents at Northallerton, in the North Riding of Yorkshire. His family came into England with William the Conqueror, who assigned them lands for their services where they lived in great repute, until the days of Sir Gosselin. His father, being of a pious turn, intended his son for the priesthood, and for this purpose sent him to college, where he prosecuted his studies with great assiduity and seeming warmth. As he was, however, the heir to a very handsome fortune, and was naturally of a vicious disposition, he merely dissembled to please his father, until he should get possession of his fortune.

He could not long restrain his natural habits, and he soon displayed his propensity to a luxurious and profligate life. So vicious was his conduct, that he broke his father's heart. Little good can be expected from such a beginning, and unless he had been naturally depraved, this might have operated somewhat to recall him to the steps of virtue. But his newly acquired wealth only gave loose to the reins which he had before held with a careless hand, and with his brother Robert he soon dissipated in licentiousness and luxury all his father had left him. They now had recourse to the highway for maintenance, and on this field were no less conspicuous. By their audacity and cruelty they became the terror of the country, and the number of their associates was so considerable as even to alarm the state. Such was the celebrity of Sir Gosselin, that Shadwell seems to have had his character in view in the plot of the Libertine, the whole of which bears a remarkable resemblance to many occurrences in the life of this knight.

The first enterprise of note which we have recorded of Sir Gosselin is one in which he was joined by Middleton and Selby, two robbers of that time, with a considerable force. Their design was to rob two Cardinals, sent into this kingdom by the Pope in the time of Edward II which they accomplished with great success. Not only travellers, but monasteries, churches, nunneries, and houses, were the objects of their attack, and they were not merely contented with booty, but barbarously murdered all who made the least opposition.

A Dominican monk, of the name of Andrew Simpson, was once met by our knight and his associates, and obliged to surrender his purse; wishing, however, to make pastime of him, they compelled him to mount a tree and preach an extempore sermon.

The monk selected for his text these words : "A certain man went down from Jerusalem to Jericho, and fell among thieves, who stripped him of his raiment and wounded him, and departed, leaving him half dead." He commenced by explaining the context, viz. that a certain lawyer came to Christ, asking what he should do to inherit eternal life. He recommended to him, love to his neighbour; and to enforce this, represented the parable, or the fact, upon which the text is founded; even that a priest and a Levite had passed by this poor man without compassion, but a Samaritan had compassion, and did what he could to heal his wounds, and to relieve his necessities.

The monk then proceeded to divide his text in the following manner; to show the danger of travelling, the persons from whom the danger arose, and the danger itself, even the probable loss of both goods and life.

In illustrating the first, he mentioned that the number of inhabitants in a town affords protection to a stranger; it is otherwise in the open country, where a man may only move a few miles from his own house when he may fall among thieves. The man mentioned in the text had only to go from Jerusalem to Jericho, which is six miles, but, having to go through a desert infested with thieves, he met with the accident related.

He, in the second place, adverted to those who exposed honest travellers upon the road; even those who abandon themselves to indolence, and follow unlawful pleasures, such as drunkenness, gaming, and other vices, and become thieves to maintain their extravagances. "And if,"

8 *

he continued, " it is evil to prevent a man from receiving an advantage, it is more criminal to take from a man what is his property : hence, both the law of God and man has made this a capital offence. There are three kinds of stealing: the taking away what is another man's ; the taking that by rapine or force and sacrilege, the taking away that which is devoted to a holy use ; of the last kind of stealing you have now been guilty.

" But you, gentlemen, are not the only thieves in the world. Princes, when they impose unnecessary taxes ; subjects, when they refuse to pay lawful taxes ; tradesmen, who give wrong measure or weight, and who neglect to pay their accounts ; masters, who delay to pay the wages of their servants ; or servants who neglect the work or interest of their masters ; physicians, apothecaries, tailors, butchers, lawyers, and a tedious catalogue, are all belonging to your fraternity. These are no better in many of their transactions than thieves, who cannot inherit the kingdom of God.

" The inference then follows, ' Thou shalt not steal.' This is a positive precept delivered by God himself, to all kinds of thieves under whatever garb and colour. They who leave the paths of honesty and commence thieves, should they not come to an untimely end by the gallows, may fall in combat, or meet with some other signal punishment from the hand of God ; and so involve themselves and their families in lasting disgrace, while they themselves are hurried away to endless torments in another world. It may be that you may live long, and frequently escape before you are apprehended ; but you cannot fly from your consciences, which will continually harass, torment, and fill you with fear. Ill-acquired wealth is more corroding than the loss of fortune ; the latter only troubles the mind once, the former continually. Gentlemen, have an eye upon the end as well as upon the beginning of things.

" Now, gentlemen, the beginning of theft is an entrance into a prison, where your companions are hunger, thirst, shackle-bolts, iron, and vermin, and the end hanging, unless you meet with an adversary as favourable as Edward the Confessor. I will relate the story for your instruction. While Edward was one morning in bed a poor courtier entered his chamber, went up to his coffer, and took away as much money as he could, and, unsatisfied, returned a second time. But, when attempting a third time, he interrupted him, saying, that if his treasurer detected him in the act he would be in danger of his life. The treasurer immediately entered the room, but the king desired him to allow the man to go, as he had more need of the money than he.

"The inference from this fact is, that persons of your profession may sometimes escape; but in a continued course you may expect also to meet with deserved punishment. The punishments of God are not always sudden but they are always certain, unless repentance ensue."

It might be imagined that this discourse would have awakened our adventurers to a better sense of their conduct; but they were too far plunged in iniquity to reform. They continued their course, and every day became more formidable, and robbed with such boldness that country-seats were forsaken and safety sought in fortified cities. They defeated forces sent out to suppress them, and were not deterred from any project, either by the magnitude of the danger, or the greatness of the individuals concerned. The king, on a tour through the north of England, was beset by the gang in priests' habits, and he and his nobles had to submit themselves to be rifled. This robbery was highly resented, and several proclamations offering great rewards were issued for the apprehension of any or every of them. The promise of the premium bred traitors among themselves, and in less than a month afterwards sixty were delivered up to justice.

The last recorded exploit of Sir Gosselin and his remaining associates was an attack which he made upon the Bishop of Durham. They rifled his palace of everything valuable, and maltreated not only himself but his servants and family. But the fortune of our knight seemed now on the wane.

His amours were many, and among them was one with the wife of a publican whose house he used to frequent, not so much for the goodness of the ale as the beauty of the hostess. The husband, however, sought his revenge in due season, and betrayed the knight and his men one evening while they were carousing in his house. The sheriff and five hundred men surrounded the party, who fought with desperation. It was not before two hundred of the besiegers had fallen, and they were completely hemmed in, that they surrendered. They were escorted under a strong guard to York, where, without the privilege of a trial, they were immediately executed, to the joy of thousands, the satisfaction of the great, and the delight of the commonalty, who waited upon them to the scaffold, triumphing in their ignominious exit.

SAWNEY BEANE.

THE following narrative presents such a picture of human barbarity, that, were it not attested by the most unquestionable historical evidence, it would be rejected as altogether fabulous and incredible.

Sawney Beane was born in the county of East Lothian, about eight miles east of Edinburgh, in the reign of James I. of Scotland. His father was a hedger and ditcher, and brought up his son to the same laborious employment. Naturally idle and vicious, he abandoned that place in company with a young woman equally idle and profligate, and retired to the deserts of Galloway, where they took up their habitation by the sea-side. The place which Sawney and his wife selected for their dwelling, was a cave of about a mile in length, and of considerable breadth, so near the sea, that the tide often penetrated into the cave about two hundred yards. The entry had many intricate windings and turnings, leading to the extremity of the subterraneous dwelling, which was literally ' the habitation of horrid cruelty."

Sawney and his wife took shelter in this cave, and

commenced their depredations. To prevent the possibility of detection, they murdered every person they robbed. Destitute also of the means of obtaining any other food, they resolved to live upon human flesh. Accordingly, when they had murdered any man, woman, or child, they carried them to their den, quartered them, salted the limbs, and dried them for food. In this manner they lived, carrying on their depredations and murder, until they had eight sons and six daughters, eighteen grand-sons and fourteen granddaughters, all the offspring of incest.

But though they soon became numerous, yet such was the multitude which fell into their hands, that they had often superabundance of provisions, and would, at a distance from their own habitation, throw legs and arms of dried human bodies into the sea by night. These were often cast out by the tide, and taken up by the country people, to the great consternation and dismay of all the surrounding inhabitants. Nor could any one discover what had befallen the many friends, relations, and neighbours who had unfortunately fallen into the hands of these merciless cannibals.

In proportion as Sawney's family increased, every one that was able acted his part in these horrid assassinations. They would sometimes attack four or six men on foot, but never more than two upon horseback. To prevent the possibility of escape, they would lie in ambush in every direction, that if they escaped those who first attacked, they might be assailed with renewed fury by another party, and inevitably murdered. By this means they always secured their prey, and prevented detection.

At last, however, the vast number who were slain raised the inhabitants of the country, and all the woods and lurking-places were carefully searched; yet, though they often passed by the mouth of the horrible den, it was never once suspected that any human being resided there. In this state of uncertainty and suspense concerning the authors of such frequent massacres, several innocent travellers and innkeepers were taken up on suspicion, be cause the persons who were missing had been seen last in their company, or had last resided in their houses. The effect of this well-meant and severe justice constrained the greater part of the innkeepers in those parts to abandon such employments, to the great inconvenience of those who travelled through that district.

Meanwhile, the country became depopulated, and the whole nation was at a loss to account for the numerous and unheard-of villanies and cruelties that were perpetrated without the slightest clue to the discovery of the abominable actors. At length Providence interposed in the following manner to terminate the horrible scene. One evening, a man and his wife were riding home upon the same horse from a fair which had been held in the neighbourhood, and being attacked, the husband made a most vigorous resistance : his wife, however, was dragged from behind him, carried to a little distance, and her entrails instantly taken out. Struck with grief and horror, the husband continued to redouble his efforts to escape, and even trod some of the assassins down under his horse's feet. Fortunately for him, and for the inhabitants of that part of the country, in the meantime, twenty or thirty in a company came riding home from the fair. Upon their approach, Sawney and his bloody crew fled into a thick wood, and hastened to their infernal den.

This man, who was the first that had ever escaped out of their hands, related to his neighbours what had happened, and showed them the mangled body of his wife lying at a distance, the blood-thirsty wretches not having time to carry it along with them. They were all struck with astonishment and horror, took him with them to Glascow, and reported the whole adventure to the chief magistrate of the city, who, upon this information, instantly wrote to the king, informing him of the matter.

In a few days, his majesty in person, accompanied by four hundred men, went in quest of the perpetrators of these horrible cruelties. The man, whose wife had been murdered before his eyes, went as their guide, with a great number of bloodhounds, that no possible means might be left unattempted to discover the haunt of such execrable villains.

They searched the woods, and traversed and examined the sea-shore; but though they passed by the entrance into their cave, they had no suspicion that any creature resided in that dark and dismal abode. Fortunately however, some of the bloodhounds entered the cave, raising an uncommon barking and noise, an indication that they were about to seize their prey. The king and his men returned, but could scarcely conceive how any human being could reside in a place of utter darkness, and where the entrance was difficult and narrow; but, as the bloodhounds increased in their vociferation, and refused to return, it occurred to all that the cave ought to be explored to the extremity. Accordingly, a sufficient number of torches was provided; the hounds were permitted to pursue their course; a great number of men penetrated through all the intricacies of the path, and at length arrived at the private residence of the horrible cannibals.

They were followed by all the band, who were shocked to behold a sight unequalled in Scotland, if not in any part of the universe. Legs, arms, thighs, hands, and feet, of men, women, and children, were suspended in rows like dried beef. Some limbs and other members were soaked in pickle; while a great mass of money, both of gold and silver, watches, rings, pistols, clothes, both linen and woollen, with an immense quantity of other articles, were either thrown together in heaps, or suspended upon the sides of the cave.

The whole cruel, brutal family, to the number former-ly mentioned, were seized; the human flesh buried in the sand of the sea-shore; the immense booty carried away, and the king marched to Edinburgh with the prisoners. This new and wretched spectacle attracted the attention of the inhabitants, who flocked from all quarters to see, as they passed along, so bloody and unnatural a family which had increased, in the space of twenty-five years, to the number of twenty-seven men and twenty-one women. Arrived in the capital, they were all confined in the Tolbooth under a strong guard, and were next day conducted to the common place of execution in Leith Walk, and executed without any formal trial, it being deemed unnecessary to try those who were avowed enemies of all mankind, and of all social order.

The enormity of their crimes dictated the severity of their death. The men had their entrails thrown into the fire, their hands and legs were severed from their bodies, and they were permitted to bleed to death. The wretched mother of the whole crew, the daughters, and grandchildren, after being spectators of the death of the men, were cast into three separate fires, and consumed to ashes. Nor did they, in general, display any signs of repentance or regret, but continued, with their last breath, to pour forth the most dreadful curses and imprecations upon all around, and upon those who were instrumental in consigning them to the hands of a tardy but a certain and inevitable justice.

THOMAS WYNNE.

THIS notorious criminal was born at Ipswich, where he continued till he was between fifteen and sixteen, and then went to sea. Nine years after, coming to London, and associating with loose company, especially with women of the most infamous character, he left no villany undone for the support of himself and them in their extravagances, till at last he became so expert in house-breaking and all sorts of theft, that he was esteemed the most remarkable villain of his time.

It was in the reign of Queen Elizabeth that our artist flourished: accordingly we find that he had the boldness to rob the royal lodgings at Whitehall Palace of plate to the amount of 400*l.* for which he was taken and committed to Newgate. But fortunately for him, her Majesty's act of grace coming out, granting a free pardon for all

offences except murder, treason, and other notorious
crimes, he was allowed the benefit of that act, and thus
obtained his liberty. But neither the royal clemency,
nor the imminent danger to which he had been exposed,
had any effect upon the obdurate heart of Wynne ; for,
pursuing his villanies, he was soon constrained to hire
himself as under servant in the kitchen, to the Earl of
Salisbury, to avoid detection. While he was in this post,
he had the audacity to make love to the Countess's wo
man, who, astonished at such insolence in a fellow of his
rank, returned his addresses with the greatest contempt
This exasperated Wynne so much, that his pretended love
turned to hatred, and he vowed revenge. He embraced
an opportunity, and used her in a very brutal manner
until she was under the necessity of calling to the other
servants for assistance. The poor woman took to her
bed, and remained very unwell for some time. The
master, informed of this shocking piece of cruelty, ordered Wynne to be whipped by the coachman, and the same
to be repeated once a week during a month. Though
Wynne was happy in having satiated his vengéance upon
the woman who had contemptuously spurned his addresses, yet he was not very much in love with the reward assigned him by his master ; therefore, robbing the
coachman of 9*l.*, borrowing 15*l.* of the master-cook, carrying off a silver cup of the master's, and all the best
clothes of the woman whom he had so greatly injured, he
went in quest of new adventures.

At that time innkeepers were not so active as now
Wynne therefore often dressed himself in the garb of a
porter, and carried off parcels consigned to carriers, and
continued undetected in this practice, until he had acquired about two hundred pounds, for which the different carriers had to pay through their neglect. Taught by experience, however, they began to look better after the
goods entrusted to their care, so that Wynne had to turn
to a new employment.

· One day, hearing a man inform his wife, as he was
going out, that it would be five or six hours before he
would return, he followed him until he saw him go into a

tavern; and, after getting acquainted with the name of the landlord, he went back to the man's neighbourhood, and discovered his name also. Having obtained this intelligence, he goes to the man's wife, and informs her that her husband is taken suddenly ill, and wishes to see her before his death. Upon this the poor woman cried bitterly, and, after giving the maid orders to take care of the house, she ran off with this pretended messenger to the place where her husband was supposed to be in the jaws of death.

They had not proceeded far, when Wynne, upon pretence of business, in a different part of the town, left her to prosecute her journey,—returned back to the house, and told the maid, that " her mistress had sent him to acquaint her, that if she did not come home by such an hour, she might go to bed, for she would not come home all night." Wynne, in the meantime, seeming out of breath with haste, the maid civilly requested him to come in and rest himself. This according with his wishes, he immediately complied, and, when the maid was going to fetch him some meat, he suddenly knocked her down, bound her hand and foot, and robbed the house of every thing he could carry off, to the amount of 200*l.*

Wynne having reigned eight years in his villanies, formed a strong desire to rob a linen-draper, who had retired from business, and with his wife was living upon the fruits of his industry. He accordingly one evening broke into their house, and, to prevent discovery, cut both their throats while they were asleep, and rifled the house to the amount of 2500*l.*; and, to prevent detection, sailed to Virginia, with his wife and four children.

The two old people not appearing in the neighbourhood next day as usual, and the doors remaining locked, the neighbours were alarmed, sent for a constable, and burst open the doors, when they found them weltering in their blood, and their house pillaged. Diligent search was made, and a poor man who begged his bread, was taken up on suspicion, because he had been seen about the doors, and sitting upon a bench belonging to the house the day before : and although nothing but circumstantial evidence appeared against him, he was condemned, tried, and executed before the door of the house, and his body hung in chains in Holloway.

Meanwhile Wynne, the murderer, was in safety in a foreign land. It also happened, that by the price of innocent blood he prospered, and his riches greatly increased. After he had resided twenty years in Virginia, where his family became numerous, and his riches great, he resolved to visit England before his death, and then to return to deposit his bones in a foreign grave. During his stay in London, he one day went into a goldsmith's shop in Cheapside, to purchase some plate that he intended to take home with him. It happened, while the goldsmith was weighing the plate which Wynne had purchased, that an uproar took place in the street, occasioned by the circumstance of a gentleman running off from certain bailiffs who were conducting him to prison. Upon this Wynne ran also out into the street, and hearing somebody behind him crying out, " Stop him! stop him!" his conscience instantly awoke, so that he stopped, and exclaimed, " I am the man!" " You the man," replied the people; " What man?" " The man," replied Wynne, " that committed such a murder in Honey-lane twenty years ago, for which a poor man was hanged wrongfully!"

, Upon this confession, he was carried before a magistrate, to whom he repeated the same acknowledgment, and was committed to Newgate, tried, condemned, and executed before the house where he perpetrated the horrid deed. In this manner the justice of Heaven pursued this guilty wretch long after he thought himself beyond the reach of punishment. Justice also overtook his family, who were privy to his guilt. Upon the intelligence of his shameful end, his wife immediately became deranged, and continued so to her death. Two of his sons were hanged in Virginia for robbery, and the whole family were soon reduced to beggary.

THOMAS WITHERINGTON.

THIS person was the son of a worthy gentleman of Carlisle, in the county of Cumberland, who possessed a considerable estate, and brought up his children suitably to his condition. Thomas, the subject of this memoir, received a liberal education, as his father intended that he should live free from the toil and hazard of business. The father dying, Thomas came into possession of the estate, which soon procured him a rich wife, who after-wards proved the chief cause of his ruin. She was loose in her conduct, and violated her matrimonial obligations, which drove him from his house to seek happiness in the tavern, or in the company of abandoned women. These by degrees perverted all the good qualities he possessed; nor was his estate less subject to ruin and decay; for the mortgages he made on it, in order to support his luxury and profusion, soon reduced his circumstances to the lowest ebb. Undisciplined in poverty, how could a man of his late affluent fortune, and unacquainted with business, procure a maintenance? He was possessed of too independent a spirit to stoop either to relations or friends for a precarious subsistence, and to solicit the benevolence of his fellow-men was what his soul abhorred. Starve he could not, and only one way of living presented itself to his choice—levying contributions on the road. This he followed for six or seven years with tolerable success, and we shall now relate a few of his most remarkable dventures.

Upon his first outset he repaired to a friend, and with a grave face lamented his late irregularities, and declared his determination to live by some honest means ; but for this purpose he required a little money to assist him in establishing himself, and hoped his friend would find it convenient to accommodate him. His friend was over-joyed at the prospect of his amendment and willingly lent him fifty pounds, with as many blessings and exhor-tations. But Witherington frustrated the expectations of his friend, and with the money bought himself a horse and other necessaries fit for his future enterprises.

One night he stopped at Keswick in Cumberland, where he met with the Dean of Carlisle. Being equally learned, they found each other's company very agreeable, and Witherington passed himself off for a gentleman who had just returned from the East Indies with a handsome competency, and was returning to his friends at Carlisle, among whom he had a rich uncle, who had lately died and left him sole heir to his estate. "True," said the Dean, "I have often heard of a relation of Mr. Witherington's being in the East Indies; but his family, I can assure you, received repeated information of his death, and what prejudice this may have done to your affairs at Carlisle, to-morrow will be the best witness." The Dean then told him his own history, and concluded with these words :—" And I am now informed that, to support his extravagance, Mr. Witherington frequents the road, and takes a purse wherever he can extort it." Our adventurer seemed greatly hurt at this account of his cousin's conduct, and thanked the Doctor for his information. Being both fond of their bottle, they spent the evening very agreeably, promising to travel together on the following day to Carlisle.

Having arrived at a wood on the road, Witherington rode close up to the Dean, and whispered into his ear, " Sir, though the place at which we now are is private enough, yet willing that what I do should be still more private, I take the liberty to acquaint you, that you have something about you that will do me an infinite piece of service."—" What's that?" answered the Doctor; " you shall have it with all my heart."—" I thank you for your civility," said Witherington. " Well then, to be plain, the money in your breeches'-pocket will be very serviceable to me at the present moment."—" Money !" rejoined the Doctor; " Sir, you cannot want money; your garb and person both tell me you are in no want."—" Ay, but I am ; for the ship in which I came over happened to be wrecked, so that I have lost all I brought from India; and I would not enter Carlisle for the whole world with-

out money in my pocket."—"Friend, I may urge the
same plea, and say I would not go into that city without
money for the world; but what then? If you are Mr.
Witherington's nephew, as you pretend to be, you would
not thus peremptorily demand money of me, for at Carlisle your friends will supply you; and if you have none
now, I will bear your expenses to that place."—"Sir,"
said Witherington, "the question is not whether I have
money or not, but concerning that which is in your
pocket; for, as you say, my cousin is obliged to take
purses on the road, and so am I; so that if I take your's,
you may ride to Carlisle, and say that Mr. Witherington
met you and demanded your charity." After a good
deal of expostulation, the Dean, terrified at the sight of a
pistol, delivered to Witherington a purse containing fifty
guineas, before he pursued his journey to Carlisle, and
our adventurer set off in search of more prey.

Witherington being at Newcastle, put up at an inn
where some commissioners were to meet that day, to
make choice of a schoolmaster for a neighbouring parish.
The salary being very handsome, many spruce young
clergymen and students appeared as competitors: and,
being possessed of sufficient qualifications, Witherington
bethought him of standing a candidate, for which purpose
he borrowed coarse plain clothes from the landlord, to
make his appearance correspond with the conduct he
meant to pursue. Repairing to the kitchen, and sitting
down by the fire, he called for a mug of ale, putting on
a very dejected countenance. One of the freeholders
who came to vote, observing him as he stood warming
himself by the fire, was taken with his countenance, and
entered into conversation with him. He very modestly
let the freeholder know that he had come with the intention of standing a candidate, but when he saw so many
gay young men as competitors, and fearing that every
thing would be carried by interest, he resolved to return
home. "Nay," replied the honest freeholder, "as long
as I have a vote, justice shall be done; and never fear,
for egad, I say, merit shall have the place, and if thou
be found the best scholar, thou shalt certainly have it

and to show you I am sincere, I now, though you are a stranger to me, promise you my vote, and my interest likewise." Witherington thanked him for his civility, and consented to wait for the trial. A keen contest took place between two of the most successful candidates, when our adventurer was introduced as a man who had so much modesty as to make him fearful of appearing before so great an assembly, but who nevertheless wished to be examined. He confronted the two opponents, and exposed their ignorance to the trustees, who were all astonished at the stranger. He showed it was not a number of Greek and Latin sentences that constituted a good scholar, but a thorough knowledge of the nature of the book which he read, and the ability to discover the design of the author. Suffice it to say, that Witherington was installed into the office with all the usual formalities.

Conducting himself with much moderation and humility, the churchwardens of the parish took a great fancy to him, and made him overseer and tax-gatherer to the parish; and the rector likewise committed to his care the collection of his rents and tithes. This friendly disposition towards Witherington extended itself over the parish, and never was a man believed to be more honest or industrious. Of the latter qualification, we must say, in this instance, he showed himself possessed; but of the former he had never any notion. His opinion had great weight with the heads of the parish, and he proposed the erection of a new school-house, and for this purpose offered, himself, to sink a year's salary towards a subscription. It was willingly agreed to, and contributions came in from all quarters, and a sum exceeding 700*l.* was speedily raised. The mind of Witherington was now big with hope, but, being discovered by two gentlemen, who had come from Carlisle, he made off with all the subscriptions and funds in his possession, leaving the parish to reflect upon the honesty of their schoolmaster and their own credulity.

He went to Buckinghamshire, and, being at an inn in the county town, fell into the company of some farmers, who, he discovered, were come to meet their landlord with their rents. They were all tenants of the same proprietor, and poured out many complaints against him for his harshness and injustice, in not allowing some deduction from their rents, or time after quarter-day, when they met with severe losses from bad weather or other causes. He learned that this landlord was very rich, and so miserly that he denied himself even the necessaries of life; our adventurer, therefore, determined, if possible, to rifle him before he parted.

The landlord soon arrived, and the company were shown into a private room; Witherington, upon pretence of being a friend of one of the farmers, and a lawyer, accompanied them. He requested a sight of the last receipts, and examined them with great care, and then addressing the landlord, "Sir," said he, "these honest men, my friends, have been your tenants for a long time, and have paid their rents very regularly; but why they should be so fond of your farms at so high a rent I am unable to comprehend, when they may get other lands much cheaper; and that you should be so unreasonable as not to allow a reduction in their rents in a season like this, when they must lose instead of gaining by their farms. It is your duty, Sir, to encourage them, and not to grind them so unmercifully, else they will soon be obliged to leave your farms altogether." The landlord endeavoured to argue the point; and the farmers seeing the drift of Witherington, refrained from interfering. "It is unnecessary," resumed Witherington, "to have more parley about it; I insist, on behalf of my friends here, that you remit them a hundred and fifty pounds of the three hundred you expect them to pay you, for I am told you have more than enough to support yourself and family." "Not a sous," replied the landlord. "We'll try that presently. But pray, Sir, take your pen, ink, and paper, in the mean time, and write out their receipts, and the money shall be forthcoming immediately." "Not a letter, till the money is in my hands." "It must be so, then," answered Witherington; "you will force a good-natured man to use extremities with you;" and so saving, he laid a brace of loaded pistols on the table. In a moment the landlord was on his knees, crying, " Oh! dear Sir, sweet Sir, kind Sir, merciful Sir, for God of Heaven's sake, Sir, don't take away the life of an innocent man, Sir, who never intended harm to any one, Sir." " Why, what harm do I intend you, friend? Cannot I lay the pistols I travel with on the table, but you must throw yourself into this unnecessary fear? Pray, proceed to the receipts, and write them in full of all demands to this time, or else,"—" Oh, God, Sir! Oh, dear Sir! you have an intention—pray, dear Sir, have no intention against my life." " To the receipts then, or by Jupiter Ammon! I'll —"—" O yes, I will, Sir." With this the old landlord wrote full receipts, and delivered them to the respective farmers.

" Come," said Witherington, " this is honest, and to show you that you have to deal with honest people, here is the hundred and fifty pounds; and I promise you, in the name of these honest men, that if things succeed well, you shall have the other half next quarter-day." The farmers paid the money, and departed astonished, and not a little afraid, at the consequences of this proceeding. Witherington ordered his horse, and enquired of the ostler the road the old gentleman had to travel, and presently took his departure.

He chose the road which the old gentleman had to travel, and soon observed him jogging away in sullen silence, with a servant behind him. When he observed our hero, he would have fled, but Witherington seized the bridle of his horse, and forced him to proceed, bantering him upon the folly of hoarding up wealth, without enjoying it himself, merely for some spendthrift son to squander after his death. " For," he continued, " money is a blessing sent us from Heaven, in order that, by its circulation, it may afford nourishment to the body politic; and if such wretches as you, by laying up thousands in your coffers to no advantage, cause a stagnation, there are thousands in the world that must feel the consequences, and I am to acquaint you of them; so that a better deed cannot be done, than to bestow what you have

about you upon me; for, to be plain with you, I am not
to be refused;" and hereupon he presented his pistol.
The old gentleman, in trepidation for his life, resigned his
purse, containing more than three hundred and fifty guineas; and Witherington, unbuckling the portmanteau
from behind the servant, placed it on his own horse, and
left the old landlord with an admonition, to be in future
affable and generous to his tenants, for they where the
persons who supported him, adding, that, if he ever again
heard complaints from them, he would visit his house,
and partake liberally of what he most coveted.

The county, after this adventure, was up in pursuit of
Witherington, and he retired to Cheshire with great expedition. The first house he put up at was an inn kept
by a young widow, noted as well for her kindness to
travellers, as her wealth and beauty. She paid our ad
venturer great attention, and invited him to be of a party,
consisting of some friends, which she was to have that
evening. He was not blind to the charms of the widow,
and gladly accepted the invitation. The company he
found to consist chiefly of gentlemen, who, he could discover, were angling for the widow's riches. Witherington gained great favour in the eyes of the lady, and she
asked him to favour the company with a song, as she
was sure, from his sweet clear voice, he could perform
well. Witherington wanting no farther importunity from
a person he had fixed his affections upon, complied with
the request, and sang an amorous ditty, very applicable
to his present situation, and, with the assistance of a side
glance and a sigh, enabled the widow to draw the most
favourable inferences. He was completely successful
and the widow evidently vanquished. Witherington was
now requested by the widow to relate some story concerning himself, " as certainly a person who could make
himself so agreeable, and make others take such an interest in his welfare, could not fail to have met with
something remarkable in his lifetime." Witherington
was all compliance, and begged leave to give a short
recital of his life; and the company were anxious that he

should proceed, expecting to be informed of something marvellous and mysterious.

He invented an artful story, the drift of which was to give the widow a high idea of himself, of the power that love had over him, and of the generosity of his own mind. His greatest misfortune, he said, was disappointment in love, the object of his choice having been stolen from him by an old rich uncle, against her inclination, and he stated that he had just left home, in order to divert his mind from the melancholy with which this had overcast him; " chance," said he, in conclusion, " has thrown me into this hospitable house, where I cannot but own I have found as much beauty as I have been unfortunately deprived of."

This story excited considerable interest throughout the company, more particularly in the breast of the widow, towards whom Witherington now evinced unequivocal marks of attention, which seemed to excite considerable jealousy in some of the gentlemen present. They all parted, however, on the most friendly terms, and our adventurer resolved to stay some time at Nantwich, in order to follow out this adventure. Next morning, Witherington renewed his assiduities, and both he and the amorous widow were equally gratified with each other's company; at length, determined to carry his point by a *coup de grace*, he declared a most ardent passion for her, which, after much prefacing and many assurances, was returned tenfold. She assured him, at the same time, that he had many rivals, but over these he had gained the pre-eminence in her estimation.

A few days after the first interview with the other suitors at the inn, Witherington's ascendancy was so evident, that a rival, who imagined he had the game within reach, was seriously alarmed, and had recourse to stratagem to free himself from such an opponent. For this purpose he sent for Witherington, and, with every appearance of disinterested friendship, informed him, that he had sent for him to caution him against further intimacy with the widow, to whom he confessed he once paid matrimonial court, but that he had thrown her completely off since he had discovered the measure of her guilt, and congratulated himself upon his escape. Expressing his detestation of the character of a defamer, and solemnly avowing the purity of his motives, he informed Witherington, that the widow was most fickle and insincere in her attachment, as any one might have discovered at the supper party ; and, in order to gratify this wavering inclination, she had poisoned her last husband. He entreated him then, as he valued his own happiness and security, to desist from prosecuting his intentions farther, and hoped Witherington would pardon the liberty he had taken ; for, hearing his acquaintance was to end in marriage, and considering the fortunate escape he had himself made, he was bound to prevent a stranger from being imposed upon.

Witherington at once saw the drift of his rival, and humoured him accordingly. He seemed shocked at the baseness of the widow, and joined the other in self-congratulation. He thanked the gentleman for his kindly warning, and told him to leave the affair to his management, and he would soon discover the depth of her guilt ; and that as they both seemed to have one object in view, namely, the possession of her money, they might then be able to make what use of the circumstances they found convenient and proper. The gentleman seemed satisfied, and they parted for the present.

Our adventurer returning to the inn, acquainted the widow with the whole conversation between him and the gentleman. She was greatly incensed, declared the world was very censorious, and vowed revenge at whatever price. Witherington judging that a rupture was about to take place, thought it high time to take advantage of the credulous woman ; so, that evening, taking her aside, he observed to her that the best way of revenging herself upon his rival would be, if she had any serious intention of marrying him, to show her inclination by some mark of her favour that might distinguish him above his rival. Glad of this opportunity, she conveyed him into a closet, where, showing him all her money and plate, she told him that all these were at his service provided he could deliver her from the importunities of the gentleman. Witherington assured her that she might depend upon him, and, taking his leave for the night, retired to his chamber. Here he wrote the following letter to the widow:

"My Dear,

"Ever mindful of what a woman says, especially one who has been pleasad to set her affections on me, I have written this letter purely to acquaint you that, being obliged to go to London, and the journey being pretty long, I could not do better than make use of the money in the closet which you were so good as to say was at my service. I was in exceeding haste when I began to write this, so that I can spare no more time than to request you to be sure of thinking of me till my return.

"T. Witherington."

After writing this he went privately into the widow's closet, and secured all her ready money, which amounted to above three hundred pounds ; then, going into the stable, saddled his horse, mounted, and rode out at the back door, leaving the family fast asleep, and the widow and the gentleman lover to prosecute their amours as they thought fit.

Witherington, not yet content with the spoil obtained from the parish and the widow, repaired to the London road, where he perpetrated a robbery between Acton and Uxbridge; after which he was detected and committed to Newgate, where he led a most profligate life till the day of his execution.

He was executed with Jonathan Woodward and James Philpot, two most notorious housebreakers, who had once before received mercy from King James I. upon his accession to the throne. One of the name of Elliot, the son of a respectable lady then living, was condemned at the same time, but afterwards pardoned. This individual, thus restored to society by the royal clemency, afterwards became a worthy citizen and a good Christian. Out of compassion for other criminals, and in acknowledgment of the king's favour, his mother, upon her death-bed, be

queathed a handsome sum to the parish of St. Sepulchre's
in London, upon the condition of finding a man who
should always, between the hours of eleven and twelve
o'clock of the night previous to the execution of any unhappy criminal, go under Newgate, and, giving notice of
his approach by the ringing of a bell, remind the prisoners of their approaching end, by repeating religious exhortations, tending to prepare them for death.   Witherington and his companions in death were the first to whom
these exhortations were given ; and as the design is truly
benevolent, and as they are often fraught with incalcula-
ble blessings to the guilty, we will gratify our readers by
the insertion of them, and with this close the life of
Witherington.

The person appointed, after inquiring of the criminals
if they are awake, and being answered in the affirmative,
proceeds thus :

" Gentlemen, I am the unwelcome messenger who
comes to inform you that to-morrow you must die. Your
time is but short, the time slides away apace, the glass
runs fast, and the last sand being now about to drop,
when you must launch out into boundless eternity, give
not yourselves to sleep, but watch and pray to gain eternal life.   Repent sooner than St. Peter, and repent before
the cock crows, for now repentance is the only road to
salvation ; be fervent in this great duty, and without doubt
you may to-morrow be with the penitent thief in Paradise.   Pray without ceasing ; quench not the spirit ; ab
stain from all appearance of evil ; as your own wicked
ness hath caused all this to fall upon you, and brough
the day of tribulation near at hand, so let goodness be
your sole comfort, that your souls may find perpetual
rest with your blessed Saviour who died for the sins of
the world ; he will wipe all tears from your eyes, remove
your sorrows, and assuage your grief, so that your sin
sick souls shall be healed for evermore.   I exhort you
earnestly not to be negligent of the work of your salvation, which depends upon your sincere devotion betwixt
this and to-morrow, when the sword of justice shall send
you out of the land of the living.   Fight the good fight

of faith, and lay hold of eternal life whilst you may, for there is no repentance in the grave. Ye have pierced yourselves with many sorrows, but a few hours will bring you to a place where you will know nothing but joy and gladness. Love righteousness and hate iniquity, then God, even your God, will anoint you with the oil of gladness above your fellows. Go now boldly to the throne of grace, that ye may obtain mercy and find grace to help in time of need. The God of peace sanctify you wholly! and I pray God, your whole spirits, and souls, and bodies, may be preserved blameless, until the meeting of your blessed Redeemer! The Lord have mercy upon you! Christ have mercy upon you! Sweet Jesus receive your souls! and to-morrow may you sup with him in Paradise! Amen! Amen."

Next day, when they were to die, the bell on the steeple was tolled, and the cart stopped under the churchyard wall at St. Sepulchre's, where the same person repeated from the wall the following additional exhortation:

"Gentlemen, consider now you are going out of this world into another, where you will live in happiness or woe for evermore. Make your peace with God Almighty, and let your whole thoughts be entirely bent upon your latter end. Cursed is he that hangeth on a tree; but it is hoped the fatal knot will bring your precious souls to an union with the great Creator of heaven and earth, to whom I recommend your souls, in this your final hour of distress. Lord have mercy upon you! Christ look down upon you and comfort you! Sweet Jesus receive your souls this day into eternal life! Amen."

JAMES BATSON.

This famous robber was born in the first year of James the First. It so happens (although perhaps the circumstance is no very satisfactory evidence of the authenticity of his adventures) that he is his own historian; we are accordingly compelled, in default of other particulars, to lay his auto-biography before our readers.

" I suppose," says he, " that, according to custom, the reader will expect some relation of my genealogy, and as I am a great admirer of fashion, I shall gratify his curiosity. My grandfather had the good fortune to marry a woman well skilled in vaulting and rope-dancing, and who could act her part uncommonly well. Though above fifty years of age, and affected with the phthisick, she died in the air. To avoid seeing other women fly as she had done, her husband would not marry again; but diverted himself with keeping a puppet-show in Moorfields, deemed the most remarkable that ever had been seen in that place. My grandfather was also so little, that the only difference between him and his puppets was, that they spoke through a trunk, and he without one. He was, however, so eloquent, and made such lively speeches, that his audience were never rendered drowsy. All the apple-women, hawkers, and fish-women, were so charmed by his wit, that they would run to hear him, and leave their goods without any guard but their own straw-hats.

" My father had two trades, or two strings to his bow; he was a painter and a gamester, and master much alike at both; for his painting could scarcely rise so high as a sign-post, and his hand at play was of such an ancient date, that it could scarcely pass. He had one misfortune, which, like original sin, he entailed upon all his children; and that was his being born a gentleman, which is as bad as being a poet, few of whom escape eternal poverty.

" My mother had the misfortune to die longing for mushrooms. Besides myself she left two daughters, both very handsome and very young; and though I was then young myself, yet I was much better skilled in sharping than my age seemed to promise. When the funeral sermon was preached, the funeral rites performed, and our tears dried up, my father returned to his daubing, my sisters to their stitching, and I was despatched to school. I had such an excellent memory, that though my dispositions were then what they have continued to be, yet I soon learned as much as might have been applied to better purposes than I have done. My tricks upon my master and my companions were so numerous

that I obtained the honourable appellation of the Little
Judas. My avaricious disposition soon appeared, and if
my covetous eyes once beheld any thing, my invention
soon put it into my possession. These, however, I could
not obtain gratis, for they cost me many a boxing bout
every day. The reports of my conduct were conveyed
home, and my eldest sister would frequently spend her
white hands upon the side of my pate; and even sometimes carried her admonitions so far, as politely to inform
me, that I would prove a disgrace to the family.

"It was my good fortune, however, not to be greatly
agitated by her remonstrances, which went in at the one
ear and out at the other. It happened, however, that my
adventures were so numerous, and daily increasing in
their magnitude, that I was dismissed the school with as
much solemnity as if it had been by beat of drum. After
giving me a complete drubbing, my father carried me to
a barber, in order to be bound as his apprentice. I was
first sent to the kitchen, where my mistress soon provided
me with employment, by showing me a parcel of dirty
clothes, informing me, that it made part of the apprentice's work to clean them: "Jemmy," says she, "mind
your heels, there's a good boy!" I hung down my head,
tumbled all the clouts into a trough, and washed them as
well as I could. I so managed the matter, that I was
soon discarded from my office, which was very fortunate
for me, for it would have put an end to Jemmy in less
than a fortnight.

"The third day of my apprenticeship, my master having just given me a note to receive money, there came
into the shop a ruffian with a pair of whiskers, and told
my master he would have them turned up. The journeyman not being at hand, my master began to turn them
up himself, and desired me to heat the irons. I complied,
and just as he had turned up one whisker, there happened
a quarrel in the street, and my master ran out to learn
the cause. The scuffle lasting long, and my master desirous to see the end as well as the beginning of the bustle,
the spark was all the time detained in the shop, with the
one whisker ornamented, and the other hanging down like

an aspen leaf. In a harsh tone he asked me, if I understood my trade; and I, thinking it derogatory to my un-
derstanding to be ignorant, boldly replied, that I did;
'Why, then,' said he, 'turn up this whisker for me, or 1
shall go into the street as I am, and kick your master.
I was unwilling to be detected in a lie, and deeming it no
difficult matter to turn up a whisker, never showed the
least concern, but took up one of the irons that had been
in the fire ever since the commencement of the street
bustle, and having nothing to try it on, and willing to
appear expeditious, I took a comb, stuck it into his bristly
bush, and clapped the iron to it: no sooner did they meet,
than there arose a smoke, as if it had been out of a chim-
ney, with a whizzing noise, and in a moment all the hair
vanished. He exclaimed furiously, 'Thou son of a thousand dogs! dost thou take me for St. Lawrence, that thou
burnest me alive!' With that he let fly such a bang at
me, that the comb dropped out of my hand, and I could
not avoid, in the fright, laying the hot iron close along
his cheek: this made him give such a shriek as shook
the whole house, and he, at the same time, drew his sword
to send me to the other world. I, however, recollecting
the proverb, 'That one pair of heels is worth two pair of
hands,' ran so nimbly into the street, and fled so quickly
from that part of the town, that though I was a good
runner, I was amazed when I found myself about a mile
from home, with the iron in my hand, and the remainder
of the whisker sticking to it. As fortune would have it,
I was near the dwelling of the person who was to pay
the note my master gave me: I went and received the
money, but deemed it proper to detain it in lieu of my
 hree days' wages.

"This money was all exhausted in one month, when I
was under the necessity of returning to my father's house.
Before arriving there, I was informed, that he was gone
to the country to receive a large sum of money which
was due to him, and therefore went boldly in, as if the
house had been my own. My grave sisters received me
very coldly, and severely blamed me for the money which
my father paid for my pranks. Maintaining, however

the honour of my birthright, I kept them at considerable
distance. The domestic war being thus prolonged, I one
day lost temper, and was resolved to make them feel the
consequences of giving me sour beer; and, though the
dinner was upon the table, I threw the dish at my eldest
sister, and the beer at the younger, overthrew the table,
and marched out of doors on a ramble. Fortunately,
however, I was interrupted in my flight by one who informed me, that my father was dead, and in his testa-
ment had very wisely left me sole heir and executor.
Upon this I returned, and soon found the tones and
tempers of my sisters changed, in consequence of the
recent news. I sold the goods, collected the debts, and
feasted all the rakes in town, until not one farthing remained.

"One evening, a party of my companions carried me
along with them, and opening the door of a certain house,
conveyed from thence some trunks, which a faithful dog
perceiving, he gave the alarm. The people of the house
attacked the robbers, who threw down their burdens to defend themselves: meanwhile, I skulked into a corner all
trembling. The watch made their appearance, and seeing
three trunks in the street, two men dangerously wounded,
and myself standing at a small distance, they seized me
as one concerned in the robbery. Next day I was ordered
to a place of confinement, and could find no friend to bail
me from thence. In ten days I was tried, and my defences
being frivolous and unsatisfactory, I was about to be hoisted up by the neck, and sent out the world in a swinging
manner, when a reprieve came, and in two months a full
pardon.

After this horrible fright, (for I was not much disposed
to visit the dwelling of my grandfather,) I commenced
travelling merchant, and according to my finances, purchased a quantity of wash-balls, tooth-picks, and tooth-
powders. Pretending that they came from Japan, Peru,
or Tartary, and extolling them to the skies, I had a good
sale, particularly among the gentry of the playhouse.
Upon a certain day, one of the actresses, a beautiful
woman of eighteen, and married to one of the actors,

addressed me, saying, ' She had taken a liking to me, because I was a confident, sharp, forward youth ; and therefore, if I would serve her, she would entertain me with all her heart ; and that, when the company were strolling, I might beat the drum and stick up the bills.' Deeming it an easier mode of moving through the world, I readily consented, only requesting two days to dispose of my stock, and to settle all my accounts.

" In my new profession my employments were various, some of which, though not very pleasant, I endeavoured to reconcile myself to, inasmuch as they were comparatively better than my former. In a little time, I became more acquainted with the tempers of my master and mistress, and became so great a favourite, that fees and bribes replenished my coffers from all expectants and authors who courted their favour. Unfortunately, however, one day, in their absence, I was invited by some of the party to take a walk, and, going into a tavern, commenced playing at cards, till my last farthing was lost.   Determined, if possible, to be revenged of my antagonist, I requested time to run home for more money : it was readily granted.   I ran and seized an article belonging to my mistress, pawned it for a small sum, which soon followed my other stores.   But evils seldom come alone : I was in this situation not only deprived of my money, but also obliged to decamp."

The next adventure of Batson was to enlist as a soldier. It happened, however, that his captain cheating him out of his pay, caused a grievous quarrel. Batson soon found that it was dangerous to reside in Rome and strive with the Pope. His captain, upon some pretence of improper conduct, had him apprehended, tried, and condemned to be hanged. The cause of this harsh treatment was a very simple one : " For," says Batson, " I was one day drinking with a soldier, and happened to fall out about a lie given. My sword unluckily running into his throat, he kicked up his heels, through his own fault, for he ran upon my point, so that he may thank his own hastiness." Upon this, our hero says, " as if it had been a thing of nothing, or as a matter of pas time, they gave sentence that I should be led in state along the streets, then mounted upon a ladder, kick up my heels before all the people, and take a swing in the open air, as if I had another life in my knapsack. A notary informed me of this sentence, who was so generous that he requested no fee, nor any expences for his trouble during the trial. The unfeeling gaoler desired me to make my peace with my Maker, without giving me one drop to cheer my desponding heart. Informed of my melancholy condition, a compassionate friar came to prepare me for another world, since the inhabitants of this were so ready to bid me farewell. When he arrived, he inquired for the condemned person. I answered, 'Father, I am the man, though you do not know me.' He said, 'Dear child, it is now time for you to think of another world, since sentence is passed, and, therefore, you must employ the short time allowed you in confessing your sins, and asking forgiveness of your offences.' I answered, ' Reverend father, in obedience to the commands of the church, I confess but once in the year, and that is in Lent ; but if, according to the human laws, I must atone with my life for the crime I have committed, your reverence, being so learned, must be truly sensible that there is no divine precept which says, ' Thou shalt not eat or drink ;' and therefore, since it is not contrary to the law of God, I desire that I may have meat and drink, and then we will discourse of what is best for us both; for I am in a Christian country, and plead the privilege of sanctuary.'

" The good friar was much moved at finding me so jocular when I ought to be so serious, and began to preach to me a loud and long sermon upon the parable of the lost sheep, and the repentance of the good thief. But the charity bells that ring when criminals are executed knolling in my ears, made a deeper impression than the loud and impressive voice of the friar. I therefore kneeled down before my ghostly father, and cleared the store-house of my sins, and poured forth a dreadful budget of iniquity. He then gave me his blessing, and poor Batson seemed prepared to take his flight from a world of misfortunes and insults.

" But, having previously presented a petition to the Marquis D'Este, then commanding officer, he at that critical moment called me before him. He, being a merciful man, respited my sentence, and sent me to the gallies for ten years. Some friends farther interfered, and informed the Marquis, that the accusation and sentence against me were effected by the malice of the captain, who was offended because I had insisted for the whole of my listing money. The result was that he ordered me to be set at liberty, to the disappointment of my captain, together with that of the multitude and the executioner.

" The deadly fright being over, and my mind restored to tranquillity, I went forth to walk, and to meditate upon what method I was now to pursue in the rugged journey of life. Every man has his own fortune, and, as good luck would have it, I again met with a recruiting officer, who enlisted me, and, from partiality, took me home to his own quarters. The cook, taking leave of the family, I was interrogated if I understood anything in that line. To this I replied as usual in the affirmative, and was accordingly installed in the important office of cook.

" In the course of a military life, my master took up his winter residence at Bavaria, in the house of one of the richest men in those parts. To save his property, however, the Bavarian pretended to be very poor, drove away all his cattle, and removed all his stores to another quarter. Informed of this, I waited upon him, and acquainted him, that, as he had a person of quality in his house, it would be necessary for him to provide liberally for him and his servants. He replied that I had only to inform him what provisions I wanted, and he would order them immediately. I then informed him, that my master always kept three tables, one for the gentlemen and pages, a second for the butler and under-officers, a third for the footmen, grooms, and other liveries; that for these tables he must supply one ox, two calves, four sheep, twelve pullets, six capons, two dozens of pigeons,

six pounds of bacon, four pounds of sugar, two of all
sorts of spice; a hundred eggs, half a dozen dishes of
fish, a pot of wine to every plate, and six hogsheads to
stand by. He blessed himself, and exclaimed, 'If all
you speak of be only for the servants' tables, the village
will not be able to furnish the master's.' To this I replied that my master was such a good-natured man, that
if he saw his servants and attendants well provided, he
was indifferent to his own table; a dish of imperia
stuffed meat, with an egg in it, would be sufficient for
him. He asked me of what that same imperial stuffed
meat was composed? I desired him to send for a grave-
digger and a cobler, and while they were at work, I
would inform him what there was wanting. They were
instantly called. I then took an egg, and putting it into
the body of a pigeon, which I had already gutted with
my knife, said to him, ' Now, sir, take notice; this egg
is in the pigeon, the pigeon is to be put into a partridge,
the partridge into a pheasant, the pheasant into a pullet,
the pullet into a turkey, the turkey into a kid, the kid
into a sheep, the sheep into a calf, the calf into a cow;
all these creatures are to be pulled, flead, and larded, ex
cept the cow, which is to have her hide on; and as they
are through one into another, like a nest of boxes, the
cobbler is to sew every one of them with an end, that
they may not slip out; and the grave-digger is to throw
up a deep trench, into which one load of coals is to be
cast, and the cow laid on the top of it, and another load
above her,—the fuel set on fire, to burn about four hours,
more or less, when the meat being taken out, is incor-
porated, and becomes such a delicious dish, that formerly the emperors used to dine upon it on their
coronation-day; for which reason, and because an egg
is the foundation of all that curious mass, it is named
the 'imperial egg-stuffed meat.' The landlord was
not a little astonished, but after some conversation we
understood each other, and my master left the matter to
my care.

" In the course of my negociations with the landlord,
I incurred the displeasure of my master, who, discovering

my policy, came into the kitchen, seized the first convenient instrument, and belaboured me most unmercifully
He was, however, punished for his rashness, by the want
of a cook for two weeks.

" The scoundrels of the French were audacious enough
to pay us a visit while we remained here. I was ordered
out with the rest, but I kept at the greatest distance, lest
any bullet should have mistaken me for some other
person. No sooner did I receive the intelligence that the
French were conquered, than I ran to the field of battle,
brandishing my sword, and cutting and slashing among
the dead men. It unfortunately happened, however, that,
as I struck one of them with my sword, he uttered a
mournful groan, and, apprehensive that he was about to
revenge the injury done to him, I ran off with full speed,
leaving my sword in his body. In passing along, I met
with another sword, which saved my honour, as I vaunt-
ed that I had seized it from one in the field of battle.

" While thus rambling through the field of blood and
danger, my master was carried home mortally wounded,
who called me a scoundrel, and cried, ' Why did not you
obey me ?' ' Lest, sir,' replied I, ' I should have been as
you now are.' The good man soon breathed his last,
leaving me a horse and fifty ducats.

" Being again emancipated from bonds of servitude, I
began to enjoy life, and continued to treat all my acquaintance so long as my money would permit. The
return of poverty, however, made me again enlist under
the banners of servitude.

" About this time a singular occurrence happened to
me. I chanced to go out into the street, when my eye-
sight was so affected, that I could not discern black from
green, nor white from grey. Observing the candles
suspended in a candle-maker's shop, and taking them for
radishes, I thought there was no great harm though I
should taste one of them. Accordingly, laying hold of
one, down fell the whole of the row, and being dashed to
pieces upon the floor, a scuffle ensued ; I was taken into
custody, and made to pay the damage, which operated to
restore my sight to its natural state.

"Not long after this adventure, I was assailed with love for the fair sex, and, after some sighs and presents, I was bound to a woman for better or for worse, and continued with her until the charms of the marriage state and the pleasures of domestic life began to pall upon me, and an ardent desire to return to my old course of adventure took possession of my mind. Towards the attainment of this desirable end, I one day kicked my wife out of doors, dressed myself, and prepared to sally forth. I had no sooner effected this liberation, than a tavern was my first resting-place to recruit my spirits and to redeem lost time.

"I at last formed the resolution of returning to my native home, and there spending the evening of my bustling life in calm repose. After travelling many a tedious mile, I got to London. Arrived in the capital, I went directly to my father's house but found it in the possession of another, and my sisters departed this life. As both of them had been married, and had left children, there was no hope of any legacy by their death: I was therefore under the necessity of doing something for a living. Finding the gout increasing upon me, I, by the advice of an acquaintance, took a public-house; and, as I understood several languages, I thought I might have many customers from among foreigners."

Batson then gravely concludes his own narrative in these words:—

"I intend to leave off my foolish pranks, and, as I have spent my juvenile years and money in keeping company, hope to find some fools as bad as myself, who delight in throwing away their estates and impairing their health."

He accordingly took a house in Smithfield, and acquired a considerable sum. But, being desirous to make a fortune with one dash, he hastened his end. Among others who put up at his house was a gentleman who had purchased a large estate in the country, and was going to deliver the cash. The ostler observed to his master, that the bags belonging to the gentleman were uncommonly heavy when he carried them into the house. 'They

mutually agreed to rob, and afterwards to murder him;
and the ostler accomplished the horrid deed. But, differ-
ing about the division of the spoil, the ostler got drunk,
and disclosed the whole matter. The house was searched,
the body of the gentleman found, and both the murderers
were seized, tried, and condemned. The ostler died before the fatal day, but Batson was executed, and, accord
ing to the Catholic faith, died a penitent, a year before
the restoration of King Charles II.

MULLED SACK, ALIAS JOHN COTTINGTON.

THIS man's father was a petty haberdasher in Cheapside, but, living above his income, he died so poor that
he was interred by the parish. He had eighteen children,
fifteen daughters and three sons. Our hero was the
youngest of the family, and at the age of eight, was bound
apprentice to a chimney-sweeper. In his first year,
deeming himself as expert at his profession as his master,
he left him, and, acting for himself, soon acquired a great
run of business.

Money now coming in upon him, he frequented the
tavern, and, disdaining to taste of any thing but mulled
sack, he acquired that appellation. One evening he there
met with a young woman, with whom he was so enamoured, that " he took her for better for worse." But, not
enjoying that degree of comfort in this union which his
imagination had painted to him, he frequented the company of other women, until it became necessary to make
public contributions to supply their pressing necessities.
His first trials were in picking pockets of watches, and
any small sum he could find. Among others, he robbed
a lady famous among the usurers, of a gold watch set
with diamonds, and another lady of a similar piece of
luxury, as she was going into church to hear a celebrated
preacher. By the aid of his accomplices, the pin was
taken out of the axle of her coach, which fell down at the

church door, and in the crowd, Mulled Sack, being dressed as a gentleman, gave her his hand, while he seized her watch. The pious lady did not discover her loss, until she wished to know the length of the sermon, when her devout meditations, excited by the consoling exhortation of the pious preacher, were sadly interrupted by the loss of her time-piece. It is related, that, upon a certain occasion, he had the boldness to attempt the pocket of Oliver Cromwell, and that the danger to which he was then exposed determined him to leave that sneaking trade, and in a genteel manner to enter upon the honourable profession of public collector on the highway.

He entered into partnership with Tom Cheney. Their first adventure was attacking Colonel Hewson, who had raised himself by his merit from a cobbler to a colonel. He was riding at some distance from his regiment upon Hounslow-heath, and, even in the sight of some of his men, these two rogues robbed him. The pursuit was keen: Tom's horse failing him, he was apprehended, but Mulled Sack escaped. The prisoner, being severely wounded, intreated that his trial might be postponed on that account. But, on the contrary, lest he should die of his wounds, he was condemned at two o'clock, and executed that evening.

One Horne was the next accomplice of Mulled Sack. His companions were, however, generally unfortunate. Upon their first attempt, Horne was pursued, taken, and executed.

Thus, twice bereft of his associates, he acted alone, but generally committed his depredations upon the republican party, who then had the wealth of the nation in their possession. Informed that the sum of four thousand pounds was on its way from London, to pay the regiments of Oxford and Gloucester, he concealed himself behind a hedge where the wagon was to pass, presented his pistols, and the guard supposing that many more must have been concealed, fled, and left him the immense prize.

There were a few passengers in the wagon, who were greatly affrighted. He, however, consoled them, assuring them that he would not injure them, saying, " This which I have taken is as much mine as theirs who own it, being all extorted from the public by the rapacious members of our commonwealth, to enrich themselves maintain their janizaries, and keep honest people in subjection, the most effectual way to do which is to keep them very poor."

When not employed as a chimney-sweep, which profession he still occasionally pursued, he dressed in high style, and is said to have received more money by robbery than any man in that age. One day, being informed that the receiver-general was to send up to London six thousand pounds, he entered his house the night before, and rendered that trouble unnecessary. Upon the noise which this notorious robbery occasioned, Mulled Sack was apprehended; but through cunning, baffling the evidence, or corrupting the jury, he was acquitted.

In a little time after, he robbed and murdered a gentleman, and for fear of detection, went to the Continent, and was introduced into the Court of Charles the Second. Upon pretence of giving information, he came home, and applied to Cromwell, confessed his crime, but proposed to purchase his life by important information. But whether he failed in his promise, or whether Cromwell thought that such a notorious offender was unworthy to live, cannot be ascertained; one thing is certain, that he was tried and executed in the forty-fifth year of his age, in the month of April 1659.

CAPTAIN JAMES HIND.

THE father of Hind was an industrious saddler, a cheerful companion, and a good Christian. He was a native of Chipping Norton, Oxfordshire, where James was born As our hero was his only son, he received a good education, and remained at school until he was fifteen years of age.

"He was unfortunately detected with a woman, who had just robbed a gentleman.   Page 125.

He was then sent as an apprentice to a butcher in that place, and continued in that employment during two years. Upon leaving his master's service, he applied to his mother for money to bear his expenses to London, complaining bitterly of the rough and quarrelsome temper of his master. The complying mother yielded, and giving him three pounds, she, with a sorrowful heart, took farewell of her beloved son.

Arrived in the capital, he soon contracted a relish fo the pleasures of the town. His bottle and a female companion became his principal delight, and occupied the greater part of his time. He was unfortunately detected one evening with a woman of the town who had just robbed a gentleman, and along with her confined until the morning. He was acquitted because no evidence appeared against him, but his fair companion was committed to Newgate.

Captain Hind, soon after this accident, became acquainted with one Allan, a famous highwayman. While partaking of a bottle, their conversation became mutually so agreeable that they consented to unite their fortunes.

Their measures being concerted, they set out in quest of plunder. They fortunately met a gentleman and his servant travelling along the road. Hind being raw and inexperienced, Allan was desirous to have a proof of his courage and address; he, therefore, remained at a distance, while Hind boldly rode up to them and took from them fifteen pounds, at the same time returning one to bear their expenses home. This he did with so much grace and pleasantry, that the gentleman vowed that he would not injure a hair of his head though it were in his power.

About this period, the unfortunate Charles I. suffered death for his political principles. Captain Hind conceived an inveterate enmity to all those who had stained their hands with their sovereign's blood, and gladly embraced every opportunity to wreak his vengeance upon them. In a short time, Allan and Hind met with the usurper, Oliver Cromwell, riding from Huntingdon to London. They attacked the coach, but Oliver, being attended by sever servants, Allan was apprehended, and it was with no small difficulty that Hind made his escape. The unfortunate Allan was soon after tried, and suffered death for his audacity. The only effect which this produced upon Hind was to render him more cautious in his future depredations. He could not, however, think of abandoning a course on which he had just entered, and which promised so many advantages.

The captain had ridden so hard to escape from Cromwell and his train that he killed his horse, and, having no money to purchase a substitute, he was under the necessity of trying his fortune upon foot, until he should find means to procure another. It was not long before he espied a horse tied to a hedge with a saddle on and a brace of pistols attached to it. He looked round and observed a gentleman on the other side of the hedge. "This is my horse," exclaimed the captain, and immediately vaulted into the saddle. The gentleman called out to him that the horse was his. "Sir," said Hind, "you may think yourself well off that I have left you all the money in your pocket to buy another, which you had best lay out before I meet you again, lest you should be worse used." So saying, he rode off in search of new booty.

There is another story of Hind's ingenious method of supplying himself with a horse upon occasion. It appears that, being upon a second extremity reduced to the humble station of a footpad, he hired a sorry nag, and proceeded on his journey. He was overtaken by a gentleman mounted on a fine hunter, with a portmanteau behind him. They entered into conversation upon such topics as are common to travellers, and Hind was very eloquent in the praise of the gentleman's horse, which inclined the other to descant upon the qualifications of the animal. There was upon one side of the road a wall, which the gentleman said his horse would leap over. Hind offered to risk a bottle on it, to which the gentleman agreed, and quickly made his horse leap over. The captain acknowledged that he had lost his wager, but requested the gentleman to let him try if he could do the same; to which he consented, and the captain, being seated in the saddle

of his companion, rode off at full speed and left him to
return the other miserable animal to its owner.

At another time the captain met the regicide Hugh
Peters in Enfield chase, and commanded him to deliver
his money. Hugh, who was not deficient in confidence,
began to combat Hind with texts of scripture, and to
cudgel our bold robber with the eighth commandment :
" It is written in the law," said he, that " Thou shalt not
steal ;" and furthermore, Solomon, who was surely a very
wise man, spoke in this manner, " Rob not the poor, because he is poor." Hind was desirous to answer him in
his own strain, and for that purpose began to rub up his
memory for some of the texts he had learned when at
school. " Verily," said Hind, " if thou hadst regarded the
divine precepts as thou oughtest to have done, thou wouldst
not have wrested them to such an abominable and wicked
sense as thou didst the words of the prophet, when he
said, ' Bind their kings with chains, and their nobles with
fetters of iron.' Didst thou not then, detestable hypocrite,
endeavour, from these words, to aggravate the misfortunes
of thy royal master, whom thy cursed republican party
unjustly murdered before the gate of his own palace ?"
Here Hugh Peters began to extenuate that proceeding,
and to allege other parts of scripture in his own defence.
" Pray, Sir," replied Hind, " make no reflections against
men of my profession, for Solomon plainly said, ' do not
despise a thief.' But it is to little purpose for us to dispute, the substance of what I have to say is this, deliver
thy money presently, or else I shall send thee out of the
world to thy master, the devil, in an instant." These terrible words of the captain's so terrified the old Presbyterian, that he forthwith gave him thirty broad pieces of
gold and then departed.

But Hind was not satisfied with allowing so bitter an
enemy to the royal cause to depart in such a manner
He accordingly rode after him at full speed, and, overtaking him, addressed him in the following language :—
" Sir, now I think of it, I am convinced this misfortune
has happened to you because you did not obey the words
of the scripture, which expressly says, ' provide neither

gold nor silver, nor brass, in your purses, for your journey, whereas it is evident that you had provided a pretty
decent quantity of gold. However, as it is now in my
power to make you fulfil another commandment, I would
by no means slip the opportunity; therefore, pray give
me your cloak." Peters was so surprised that he neither
stood still to dispute nor to examine what was the drift
of Hind's demand. But he soon made him understand
his meaning, when he added, " You know, Sir, our Saviour has commanded, that if any man take away thy
cloak, thou must not refuse thy coat also; therefore, I
cannot suppose that you will act in direct contradiction
to such an express command, especially as you cannot
pretend you have forgot it, seeing that I now remind you
of that duty." The old Puritan shrugged his shoulders
some time before he proceeded to uncase them; but Hind
told him that his delay would be of no service to him, for
he would be implicitly obeyed, because he was sure that
what he requested was entirely consonant with the scripture. He accordingly surrendered, and Hind carried off
the cloak.

The following sabbath, when Hugh ascended the pulpit,
he was inclined to pour forth an invective against stealing,
and selected for his subject these words. " I have put off
my coat, how shall I put it on?" An honest plain man,
who was present, and knew how he had been treated by
the robber, promptly cried out, " Upon my word, Sir, I
believe there is nobody here can tell you, unless Captain
Hind were here." Which ready answer to Hugh's scriptural question put the congregation into such an outrageous
fit of laughter, that the parson was made to blush, and
descended from his pulpit, without prosecuting the subject
farther.

The captain, as before mentioned, indulged a rooted
hatred against all those who were concerned in the murder of the late king; and frequently these men fell in his
way. He was one day riding on the road, when President Bradshaw, who had sat as judge upon the king, and
passed the sentence of death upon him, met with the captain. The place where they came into collision was on

the road between Sherbourne and Shaftesbury. Hind rode up to the coach, and demanded Bradshaw's money, who, supposing that his very name would convey terror along with it, informed him who he was. "Marry," cried Hind, "I neither fear you nor any king-killing villain alive. I have now as much power over you, as you lately had over the king, and I should do God and my country good service, if I made the same use of it; but live, villain, to suffer the pangs of thine own conscience, till justice shall lay her iron hand upon thee, and require an answer for thy crimes, in a way more proper for such a monster, who art unworthy to die by any hands but those of the common hangman, or at any other place than Tyburn. Nevertheless, though I spare thy life as a regicide, be assured, that unless thou deliver up thy money immediately, thou shalt die for thy obstinacy."

Bradshaw began to perceive that the case was not now with him as it was when he sat at Westminster Hall, supported by all the strength of the rebellion. A horror took possession of his soul, and discovered itself in his countenance. He put his trembling hand into his pocket, and pulled out about forty shillings in silver, which he presented to the captain, who swore he would that minute shoot him through the heart, unless he found him coin of another species. To save his life, the sergeant pulled out that which he valued next to it, and presented the captain with a purse full of Jacobuses.

But though Hind had got possession of the cash, he was inclined to detain the sergeant a little longer, and began the following eulogium upon the value of money:—

" This, sir, is the metal that wins my heart for ever! O precious gold! I admire and adore thee, as much as either Bradshaw, Prynne, or any other villain of the same stamp, who, for the sake of thee, would sell his Redeemer again, were he now upon earth. This is that incomparable medicament, which the republican phy sicians call the wonder-working plaster; it is truly catholic in operation, and somewhat of kin to the Jesuit's powder, but more effectual. The virtues of it are strange and various; it maketh justice deaf, as well as blind,

and takes out spots of the deepest treasons as easily as
Castile soap does common stains; it alters a man's con-
stitution in two or three days, more than the virtuoso's
transfusion of blood can do in seven years. It is a great
alexipharmick, and helps poisonous principles of rebellion, and those that use them; it miraculously exalts and
purifies the eye-sight, and makes traitors behold nothing
but innocence in the blackest malefactors; it is a mighty
cordial for a declining cause; it stifles faction and schism
as certainly as rats are destroyed by common arsenic;
in a word, it makes fools wise men, and wise men fools,
and both of them knaves. The very colour of this precious balm is bright and dazzling. If it be properly applied to the fist, that is, in a decent manner, and in a
competent dose, it infallibly performs all the above-mentioned cures, and many others too numerous to be here
mentioned."

The captain, having finished his panegyric upon the
virtues of the glittering metal, pulled out his pistol, and
again addressed the sergeant, saying, "You and your
infernal crew have a long while run on, like Jehu, in a
career of blood and impiety, falsely pretending that zeal
for the Lord of Hosts has been your only motive. How
long you may be suffered to continue in the same course,
God only knows. I will, however, for this time, stop
your race in a literal sense of the word." And without
farther delay, he shot all the six horses that were in the
carriage, and left Bradshaw to ponder upon the lesson
he had received.

Hind's next adventure was with a company of ladies,
in a coach upon the road between Petersfield and Portsmouth. He accosted them in a polite manner, and informed them that he was a protector of the fair sex, and
it was purely to win the favour of a hard-hearted mistress
that he had travelled the country. "But, ladies," added
he, "I am at this time reduced to the necessity of asking
relief, having nothing to carry me on in the intended
prosecution of my adventures." The young ladies, who
had read many romances, could not help concluding that
they had met with some Quixote or Amadis de Gaul, who

was saluting them in the strains of knight-errantry. "Sir knight," said one of the most jocular of the company, " we heartily commiserate your condition, and are very much troubled that we cannot contribute towards your support ; for we have nothing about us but a sacred *depositum,* which the laws of your order will not suffer you to violate." The captain was much pleased at having met with such a pleasant lady, and was much inclined to have permitted them to proceed; but his necessities were at this time very urgent. "May I, bright ladies, be favoured with the knowledge of what this sacred depositum, which you speak of, is, that so I may employ my utmost abilities in its defence, as the laws of knight-errantry require." The lady who had spoken before told him, that the depositum she had spoken of was 3000*l.* the portion of one of the company, who was going to bestow it upon the knight who had won her good-will by his many past services. " Present my humble duty to the knight," said he, " and be pleased to tell him that my name is Captain Hind ; that out of mere necessity I have made bold to borrow part of what, for his sake, I wish were twice as much ; that I promise to expend the sum in defence of injured lovers, and in the support of gentlemen who profess knight-errantry." Upon the name of Captain Hind, the fair ones were sufficiently alarmed, as his name was well known all over England. He, however, requested them not to be affrighted, for he would not do them the least injury, and only requested 1000*l.* of the 3000*l.* As the money was bound up in several parcels, the request was instantly complied with, and our adventurer wished them a prosperous journey, and many happy days to the bride.

Taking leave of the captain for a little, we shall inform our readers of the consequences of this extorted loan of the captain's. When the bride arrived at the dwelling of her intended husband, she faithfully recounted to him her adventures upon the road. The avaricious and embryo curmudgeon refused to accept her hand until her father should agree to make up the loss. Partly because he detested the request of the lover, and partly because he had sufficiently exhausted his funds, the father refused to comply. The pretended lover, therefore, declined her nand, because it was emptied of the third part of her fortune; and the affectionate and high-spirited lady died of a broken heart. Hind often declared, that this adventure caused him great uneasiness, while it filled him with detestation at the dishonourable and base conduct of the mercenary lover.

The transactions of Hind were now become so numerous, and made him so well known, that he was forced to conceal himself in the country. During this cessation from his usual industrious labours, his funds became so exhausted, that even his horse was sold to maintain his own life. Impelled by necessity, he often resolved to hazard a few movements upon the highway; but he had resided so long in that quarter, that he durst not risk any such adventure. Fortune, however, commiserated the condition of the captain, and provided relief. He was informed that a doctor, who resided in the neighbourhood, had gone to receive a handsome fee for a cure which he had effected. The captain then lived in a small house which he had hired upon the side of a common, and which the doctor had to pass in his journey home. Hind, having long and impatiently waited his arrival, ran up to him, and in the most piteou tone and suppliant language, told the doctor his wife was suddenly seized with illness, and that unless she got some assistance, she would certainly perish, and entreated him just to tarry for a minute or two, and lend her his medical assistance, and he would gratefully pay him for his trouble as soon as it was in his power.

The tender-hearted doctor, moved with compassion, alighted and accompanied him into his house, assuring him that he should be very happy to be of any service in restoring his wife to health. Hind showed the doctor up stairs; but they had no sooner entered the door, than he locked it, presented a pistol, showing, at the same time, his empty purse, saying :—" This is my wife; she has so long been unwell, that there is now nothing at all within her. I know, sir, that you have a sovereigr remedy in your pocket for her distemper, and if you do not apply it without a word, this pistol shall make the day shine into your body!" The doctor would have been content to have lost his fee, upon condition of being delivered from the importunities of his patient; but it required only a small degree of the knowledge of symptoms to be convinced, that obedience was the only thing which remained for him to observe: he therefore emptied his own purse of forty guineas into that of the captain, and thus left our hero's wife in a convalescent state. Hind then informed the doctor, that he would leave him in possession of his whole house, to reimburse him for the money which he had taken from him. So saying, he locked the door upon the doctor, mounted that gentleman's horse, and went in quest of another county, since this had become too hot for him.

Hind has been often celebrated for his generosity to the poor; and the following is a remarkable instance of his virtue in that particular. He was upon one occasion extremely destitute of cash, and had waited long upon the road without receiving any supply. An old man, jogging along upon an ass, at length appeared. He rode up to him, and very politely inquired where he was going. "To the market," said the old man, "at Wantage, to buy me a cow, that I may have some milk for my children." "How many children have you?" The old man answered, "Ten." "And how much do you mean to give for a cow?" said Hind. "I have but forty shillings, master, and that I have been scraping together these two years." Hind's heart ached for the poor man's condition; at the same time he could not help admiring his simplicity; but, being in absolute want himself, he thought of an expedient which would serve both himself and the poor old man. "Father," said he, "the money which you have is necessary for me at this time; but I will not wrong your children of their milk. My name is Hind, and if you will give me your forty shillings quietly, and meet me again this day se'nnight at this place, I promise to make the sum double. The old man reluctantly consented, and Hind enjoined him to "be cautious not to mention a word of the matter to any body between this and that time." The old man came at the appointed time, and received as much as would purchase two cows, and twenty shillings more, that he might thereby have the best in the market.

Though Hind had long frequented the road, yet he carefully avoided shedding blood ; and the following is the only instance of this nature related of him. He had one morning committed several robberies, and among others, had taken more than 70*l.* from Colonel Harrison, the celebrated Parliamentary general. As the Round-heads were Hind's inveterate foes, the colonel immediately raised the hue-and-cry after him, which was circulated in that part of the country before the Captain was aware of it. At last, however, he received intelligence at one of the inns upon the road, and made every possible haste to fly the scene of danger. In this situation the captain was apprehensive of every person he met upon the road. He had reached a place called Knowl Hill, when the servant of a gentleman, who was following his master, came riding at full speed behind him. Hind, supposing that it was one in pursuit of himself, upon his coming up, turned about, and shot him through the head, when the unfortunate man fell dead upon the spot. Fortune favoured the captain at this time, and he got off in safety.

The following adventure closes the narrative of Hind's busy life. After Charles I. was beheaded, the Scots remained loyal, proclaimed his son Charles II., and resolved to maintain his right against the usurper. They suddenly raised an army, and entering England, proceeded as far as Worcester. Multitudes of the English joined the royal army, and among these Captain Hind, who was loyal from principle, and brave by nature. Cromwell was sent by Parliament with an army to intercept the march of the royalists. Both armies met at Worcester, and a desperate and bloody battle ensued. The king's army was routed. Captain Hind had the good fortune to escape and, reaching London, lived in a retired situation. Here however, he had not remained long, when he was betrayed by one of his intimate acquaintances. It will readily be granted that his actions merited death by the law of his country, but the mind recoils with horror from the thought of treachery in an intimate friend.

Hind was carried before the Speaker of the House of Commons, and, after a long examination, was committed to Newgate and loaded with irons; nor was any person allowed to converse with him without a special permission. He was brought to the bar of the Session-house at the Old Bailey, indicted for several crimes, but, for want of sufficient evidence, nothing worthy of death could be proved against him. Not long after this, he was sent down to Reading under a strong guard, and, being arraigned before Judge Warburton, for killing George Symson at Knowl Hill, as formerly mentioned, he was convicted of wilful murder. An act of indemnity for all past offences was issued at this time, and he hoped to have been included; but an order of Council removed him to Worcester gaol, where he was condemned for high treason, and hanged, drawn, and quartered, on the 24th September, 1652, aged thirty-four years. His head was stuck upon the top of the bridge over the Severn, and the other parts of his body placed upon the gates of the city. The head was privately taken down and interred, but the remaining parts of his body remained until consumed by the influence of the weather.

In his last moments he declared that his principal depredations had been committed against the republican party, and that he was sorry for nothing so much as not living to see his royal master restored. The following are a few verses to his memory, which, if not remarkable for poetical merit, are interesting, and not without ingenuity.

TO THE MEMORY OF CAPTAIN HIND.

BY A POET OF HIS OWN TIME.

Whenever death attacks a throne,
Nature through all her parts must groan,
The mighty monarch to bemoan.

He must be wise, and just, and good,
Though nor the state he understood,
Nor ever spar'd a subject's blood.

And shall no friendly poet find
A monumental verse for Hind,—
In fortune less, as great in mind?

Hind made our wealth one common store,
He robb'd the rich to feed the poor,—
What did immortal Cæsar more?

Nay, 'twere not difficult to prove
That meaner views did Cæsar move:
His was ambition, Hind's was love.

Our English hero sought no crown,
Nor that more pleasing bait, renown:
But just to keep off Fortune's frown.

Yet when his country's cause invites,
See him assert a nation's rights!
A robber for a monarch fights!

If in due light his deeds we scan,
As nature points us out the plan,
Hind was an honourable man.

Honour, the virtue of the brave,
To Hind that turn of genius gave,
Which made him scorn to be a slave.

Thus, had his stars conspir'd to raise
His natal hour, this virtue's praise
Had shone with an uncommon blaze.

Some new epoch had begun
From every action he had done;
A city built, a battle won.

If one's a subject, one at helm,
'Tis the same vi'lence, says Anselm
To rob a house, or waste a realm.

Be henceforth, then, for ever join'd,
The names of Cæsar and of Hind;
In fortune different, one in mind.

Capt. James Hind.   Page 135.

THE GOLDEN FARMER.

THIS man's real name was William Davis a native of North Wales, but he obtained the title of *Golden Farmer*, from his custom of paying any considerable sum in gold. He was born in the year 1626. At an early period of life he removed to Sudbury, in Gloucestershire, where he took a farm, married the daughter of a wealthy inn-keeper, by whom he had eighteen children, and followed that industrious employment merely to disguise the real character of a robber, which he sustained without suspicion for the space of forty-two years. He usually robbed alone. One day, meeting some stage coaches, he stopped one of them, full of ladies, all of whom complied with his demands, except a Quaker, who vowed she had no money, nor any thing valuable about her : upon which, fearing lest he should lose the booty of the other coaches, he told her, he would go and see what they could afford him, and return to her again. Having rifled the other three coaches, he was as good as his word; and the Quaker, persisting in her former statement, enraged the Farmer to such a degree, that, seizing her by the shoulder, and employing language which it would be hardly proper here to set down, he so scared the poor Quaker, as to cause her to produce a purse of guineas, a gold watch, and a diamond ring. Whereupon, they parted as good friends as when they were first introduced to each other.

Upon another occasion, our desperado met the Duchess of Albemarle in her coach, as she was riding over Salisbury Plain ; but he encountered greater difficulty in this case than he had contemplated. Before he could assault the lady, he was compelled to engage a postillion, the coachman, and two footmen ; but, having disabled them all by discharging several pistols, he approached his prey, whom he found more refractory than the female Quaker. Perceiving another person of quality's coach approach ing, with a retinue of servants, he was fain to content himself by pulling three diamond rings from her fingers by force, snatching a rich gold watch from her side, and venting a portion of abuse upon her obstinate ladyship.

It was not very long after this exploit, that our adventurer met with Sir Thomas Day, a justice of the peace, living at Bristol. They fell into discourse together, and, riding along, the Golden Farmer informed his new acquaintance, that a little while before, he had narrowly escaped being robbed by a couple of highwaymen, but, luckily, his horse having better heels than theirs, he had got clear of them. "Truly," said Sir Thomas, "that, had been very hard : but, nevertheless, as you would have been robbed between sun and sun, the county, upon suing it, would have been obliged to make your loss good." Thus, chatting together, and coming to a convenient place, the Golden Farmer shot Sir Thomas's man's horse under him, and, compelling him to retire to a distance, presented a pistol to the knight's heart, and demanded his money. " I thought, sir," said Sir Thomas, " that you had been an honest man."   " Your worship is mistaken," cried the Farmer; "and if you had any skill in physiognomy, you might have perceived that my countenance is the very picture of necessity; so deliver presently, for I 'm in haste."   Sir Thomas, therefore, being constrained to give him the money he had about him, which was about 60l. in gold and silver, the other humbly thanked his worship, and told him, that what he had parted with was not lost, because he had been robbed between sun and sun, and could therefore come upon the county

One Mr. Hart, a young gentleman of Enfield, who, it appears, possessed a good estate, but was not overburdened with brains, riding one day over Finchley Common, where the Golden Farmer had been for some hours hunting for prey, was met by him, and saluted with a smart slap with the flat of his drawn hanger upon his shoulders: "A plague on you!" said the farmer; "how slow you are, to make a man wait upon you all the morning come, deliver what you have, and go to the devil for orders!" The young gentleman, rather surprised at this novel greeting, began to make several excuses, saying, he had no money about him: but his incredulous antagonist took the liberty of searching him, and, finding about him above a hundred guineas, he bestowed upon him two or three farther slaps on the shoulders, telling him, at the same time, not to give his mind to lying in future, when an honest gentleman required a small gratuity from him.

Another time, this notorious robber having paid his landlord about 80*l.* for rent, the latter, going home with it, was accosted by his goodly tenant in disguise, who, bidding him stand, said:—" Come, Mr. Gravity, deliver what you have in a trice!" The old gentleman, fetching a deep sigh, to the hazard of displacing several buttons from his waistcoat, told him, that he had not above two shillings about him, and hoped, therefore, he was more a gentleman than to take so small a matter from a poor man. "I have no faith," replied the Farmer; "for you seem, by your habit, to be a man of better circumstances than you pretend; therefore, open your budget, or I shall fall foul of you." "Dear sir," cried the landlord, "you can't be so barbarous to an old man? What! have you no religion, pity, or compassion in you? Have you no conscience? Have you no respect for your body or soul?" "Don't talk of age or barbarity to me," said the tenant, "for I show neither pity nor compassion to any body. Talk of conscience to me! I have no more of that dull commodity than you have; therefore, deliver every thing you have about you, before this pistol makes you repent your obstinacy." The landlord being thus threatened, delivered his money, without receiving a receipt for it, although he had given one to the Farmer.

An old grazier at Putney Heath was the next victim to the avaricious farmer. Having accosted him on the road, he informed him, that there were some suspicious persons behind them, whom he suspected to be highwaymen; and, if that should be the case, he begged that he would conceal ten guineas for him, which would be safer with him, from the meanness of his apparel. He accepted the charge, and said, that as he himself had fifty guineas bound in the lappet of his shirt, he would deposit them along with his own. In a short time, the Farmer said :—" It does not appear that any person will run the risk of his neck by robbing you to-day; it will, therefore, be as well that I do so myself." Without any farther preamble, therefore, he demanded of him, instead of delivering up his purse, to cut off the lappet of his shirt ; but, declining to comply with his request, the Farmer put himself to the trouble of lightening the fore-garment of the grazier.

Squire Broughton, a gentleman of the Middle Temple, was the succeeding prey of the Golden Farmer. Happening to meet at an inn upon the road, the Farmer pretended to be on his way to the capital, concerning an offence that a neighbouring farmer had committed against him, by allowing his cattle to break into his grounds. Meanwhile, he requested that Squire Broughton would recommend him to an expert and faithful agent to conduct his cause. Like every other lawyer, Broughton was desirous to have him for a client, and proceeded to explain the nature of his cause. Having spent the night at the inn, they proceeded next morning on their journey, when the Farmer addressed the counsellor, saying, " Pray, sir, what is meant by trover and conversion in the law of England ?" He replied, that it signified, in our common law, an action which one man has against another, who, having found any of his goods, refuses to deliver them up on demand, and perhaps converts them to his own use.

The Golden Farmer, being now at a place convenient for his purpose, " Very well, then, sir," said he, " should I find any money about you, and convert it to my use, it is only actionable, I find." " That is a robbery," said the barrister, " which requires no less a satisfaction than a man's life." " A robbery !" replied the Golden Farmer ; " why, then, I must commit *one* in my time ;" and presenting his pistol, he instantly demanded his money or his life. Surprised at his client's rough behaviour, the lawyer began to remonstrate in strong terms upon the impropriety of his conduct, urging, that it was both con trary to law and to conscience. His eloquent pleading, however, made no impression upon the mind of the Farmer, who, putting a pistol to his breast, compelled the lawyer to deliver his money, amounting to the sum of 40*l.* some large pieces of gold, and a gold watch.

One day, accosting a tinker upon the road, whom he knew to have 7*l.* or 8*l.* upon him, he said, " Well, brother tinker, you seem to be very decent, for your life is a continual pilgrimage, and, in humility, you go almost barefooted, making necessity a virtue." " Ay, master," replied the tinker, " necessity compels when the devil drives, and, had you no more than I, you would do the same." " That might be," replied the Farmer, " and I suppose you march all over England." " Yes," said the tinker, " I go a great deal of ground, but not so much as you ride." " Be this as it will, I suppose that your conversation is unblameable, because you are continually mending." " I wish," replied the tinker, " that as much could be said in commendation of your character." The Farmer replied, that he was not like him, who would rather steal than beg, in defiance of whips or imprisonment. Determined to have the last word of the Farmer, the tinker rejoined, " I would have you to know, that I take a great deal of pains for a livelihood." The Farmer, equally loquacious, replied, " I know that you are such an enemy to idleness, that, rather than want work, you will make three holes in mending one." " That may be," said the honest tinker, " but I begin to wish that there were a greater distance between us, as I do neither love your conversation nor appearance." " I am equally ready to say the same of you ; for, though you are entertained in every place, yet you are seldom permitted to enter the door of any dwelling." The tinker repeated his strong suspicions of the Farmer. " Nor shall it be without cause !" exclaimed he ; " therefore, open your wallet, and deliver the money that is there." Here their dialogue being about to close, the tinker entreated, that he would not rob him, as he was above a hundred miles from home : but the Golden Farmer, being indifferent to all the consequences of the loss of the other's property

seized both his wallet and his money, and left the poor
tinker to renew his journey and his toils.

This famous highwayman had only a few more acts of
violence to perform.   His actions and character being
now universally known, many a hue-and-cry was sent
after him, and conspired to his overthrow.   He was
seized and imprisoned, tried and condemned.   He spent
his time in prison in the same merry way in which his
former life had been passed, and a violent death termina
ted his wicked course on the 20th December 1689.

NAN HERFORD.

THE natural interest which we take in the history and
character of the female sex, renders their actions more
an object of curiosity when out of the common path.
Nan was descended of honest parents, who both died
when she was about seventeen years old. She then came
to London, and served in a family for six months.   It
was her misfortune to fall in with bad company, who se-
duced her from the path of sobriety and honesty, and led
her to that course of life which has been fatal to many,
and was in the end destructive to herself.

One instance of her cunning and address may suffice
for an example.   Her ingenuity enabled her to devise
means by which she always appeared genteelly dressed,
and so saved appearances.   She took lodgings in King's
street, and entertained an old woman as her accomplice,
because she could not execute her plans herself.   After
mature reflection, they directed their attack upon a rich
apothecary in the neighbourhood.   Nan remained close
at home, while the old woman was sent on many an errand to the apothecary's shop.   Being a constant cus-
tomer, out of civility, he became familiar with the good
woman.

One day, in a pleasing accent, she asked him, " Why
he did not marry?"   The miser replied, " That the times
were hard, trading dead, and house-keeping expensive."

That's true, man; but a rich wife, man, would make amends for all this." " A good one, and a rich one, too !" cried he, " would be a brave thing indeed. I must confess, I should be glad to embrace such an opportunity of changing my condition." She insinuated, that such a fortune might be procured. Curiosity being excited, she left him, eager to embrace the first opportunity of a farther conversation. At her own time, she informed him, that there was a niece of a wealthy citizen, who had 2000*l.* in her uncle's hands, to be paid at her marriage, and that, as she was once a nurse in the family, the young lady occasionally called upon her, and that every time the poor girl called, she was lamenting the harsh usage of her uncle, and wished that some good gentleman would free her from his unpleasant hands. The apothecary was charmed with her narrative, and engaged her to do all in her power for him.

To proceed with certainty and caution, he took a note of the names of the uncle and niece, and, upon inquiry, found that she had given a true representation. He was now all anxiety, and, to heighten his impatience, the woman did not visit his shop for some days. She at length appeared, and, with no small degree of seeming reluctance, promised to introduce him. Nan was all modesty, all blushes, all diffidence ; insomuch that she would have imposed upon one whose senses were not confounded and whose eyes were less dazzled with the contemplation of 2000*l.* Their interview was short, lest her uncle should discover that she had been from home.

The cold apothecary was now all flame, and ready to kneel before the old woman and the young heiress, in order to gain his object : but the former now ventured a hint, that as she was poor, it was reasonable she should have some return for her trouble. A hint was only necessary in such an hour, and a bond was immediately executed, agreeing to give her 100*l.* on the happy day he was married to the rich heiress.

He was soon favoured with another meeting, and to both parties it seemed better not to delay matters too long. The young lady consented to marry him, and, as she had been always kept so short of money and clothes by her uncle, and could not, on the present occasion, request an advance, lest it should create suspicion, she therefore hinted, it would be necessary to have money, that she might appear like his wife. " My fortune may be demanded," said she, " when we are married; and it is best not to trouble the old man until all is secure." Her scheme succeeded, and 250*l.* were instantly brought, and more offered.

Both the old and young lady changed their lodging, and, after three days' matrimony, the apothecary dressed himself as he was appareled, upon his wedding-day, and hastened to the uncle, to demand his wife and her fortune. The coach drove to the door, and, being introduced to the uncle, he, in an imperious tone, said, " He was come to demand his wife." " I know nothing of your wife, nor you either, and desire, therefore, you would explain your meaning." " I mean your niece, sir, who is my lawful wife." " Your wife, man! since how long, pray?" The apothecary mentioned the day and the circumstances, in order to convince him of the truth of his statement. The uncle told him, that his niece was not out of his house upon that day, and he could not comprehend his meaning. They came to high words, and the apothecary continuing positive and serious, the old man at last suspected that he was imposed upon. Accordingly, he asked him, if he would know his wife when he saw her? " I should be glad if you would try me." The niece came. " This is none of my wife." " But this is my niece, though, and all the nieces I have in the world, too." They were both astonished, and the young lady equally so, to hear herself named a wife without any previous knowledge of the why or wherefore.

The uncle then said, " Sir, I perceive that there has been some deception in this matter: relate the whole circumstances, that we may be able to judge of the case." It was done, and the conspiracy disclosed. It only remained to exercise patience, and, either by parsimony, or by laying an additional price upon his medicines, to redeem his losses.

After this, Nan became enamoured of a player, who consented to reside with her. To support their extravagances, she visited the shops, and he the highways. It was fortunate for society that his first robbery proved his last : he was apprehended and hanged. Nan, however, continued her business during the space of six years, in which time it was supposed that she stole goods to the amount of 4000*l.* But while Nan visited a linendraper's in a chair, with two or three footmen attending, he was so uncivil as to detect her in removing a piece of muslin from his shop. Before her trial, she offered a hundred guineas to her adversary not to appear against her : but he remained determined in his resolution. During her confinement, she attempted to set fire to Newgate, but, being unsuccessful, was fettered and handcuffed. She was executed before the prison on the 22d December 1690 and her body was afterwards given to the surgeons.

JACK BIRD.

Jack Bird was born of industrious and honest parents, and received an education suitable to their circumstances. He was bound an apprentice to a baker, served three years, then ran away from his master, went to London, and enlisted in the Foot Guards. While in the army, he served at the memorable siege of Maestricht, under the command of the Duke of Monmouth, the general of the English forces in the Low Countries.

His natural avarice and restless disposition excited him to desert his colours, and, flying to Amsterdam, he began his career by stealing a piece of silk. He was detected in the act, and carried before a magistrate. The evidence against him being unquestionable, he was committed to the rasp-house, and doomed to hard labour, such as rasping log-wood, and other drudgeries, during the space of twelve months. Unaccustomed to hard labour, Jack fainted under the punishment, but to no purpose, as his taskmaster imputed it to indolence. To cure this distemper, he chained him to the bottom of a cistern by one foot, and several cocks at once beginning to pour in their streams upon him, he was obliged to pump for his life. The cistern was much higher than he, so that if the water had not been quickly discharged, he would have been drowned, without either relief or pity. This discipline being limited to the space of one hour, Jack vanquished the various floods which threatened to overwhelm him, and was accordingly relieved. The experience, however, of that hour rendered his labour sweet during the remainder of the year.

Upon the expiration of that period, he took leave of a country where he had been so speedily detected and so severely punished, and returned to England to prosecute his adventures upon the highway. Disdaining the mean employment of a footpad, he stole a horse, provided himself with six good pistols and a broad sword, and, in the dress and character of a gentleman, commenced his campaign. In three or four robberies fortune was auspicious, and seemed to offer a plentiful harvest to gratify his avarice, and to nourish his extravagance : but, like many before him, he soon experienced her fluctuating disposition. On the road between Gravesend and Chatham, Bird met with one Joseph Pinnis, a pilot at Dover, who had been to London receiving 10*l.* or 12*l.* for conducting a Dutch ship up the river. He had lost both his hands in an engagement, so that when Bird accosted him in the common language of his profession, the old tar replied, " You see, sir, that I have never a hand, so that I am not able to take my money out of my pocket myself. Be so kind, therefore, as to take the trouble of searching me." Jack complied with his reasonable demand, and began to examine the contents of the pilot's purse. Meanwhile, the furious tar suddenly clasped his arms about Jack, and spurring his own horse, drew our adventurer off his, ther falling directly upon him, he kept him down, beating him most unmercifully with his shod stumps. During the scuffle, some passengers approached, and, inquiring the cause, Pinnis related the particulars, and requested them to supply his place, and give the ruffian a little more of the same oil to his bones, adding, that he was almost out of breath with what he had done already. Informed of the whole matter, the passengers apprehended him, and carried him before a magistrate, who committed him to Maidstone gaol, where he continued until the assizes, and then was tried and condemned.

He, however, had the good fortune to obtain a pardon, and afterwards his liberty. The affront of being so completely buffeted by a man without hands, made such an impression upon Bird's mind, that he resolved to abandon an employment which had been so dangerous and so disgraceful to him. But the want of an occupation by which to supply his necessities, again compelled him to the highway.

The first that he encountered was a Welsh drover. The fellow, being equal in strength and courage to the pilot, began to lay about him with a large quarter-staff. Jack, perceiving the boldness of the Welshman, fled out of the reach of his staff, and said, " I have been taken in once by a villain of a tar without hands, and for that trick, I shall not venture my carcase within the reach of one that has hands, for fear of something worse. Meanwhile, he pulled out a pistol, and shot him through the head. In examining his purse, he found only eighteen pence. Jack, with laconic indifference, observed, " This is a price worth killing a man for at any time," and rode off without the least remorse.

At another time, Bird met with Poor Robin, the almanack maker ; and, as he exacted contributions from the poor when the rich were not at hand, the poor astrologer was commanded to halt and surrender. As this was the first time that Robin had heard such language, and he had received no intelligence of the arrival of Bird from the stars, he stood and stared as if he had been planet-struck. Informed that Bird was in real earnest, Robin pleaded his poverty. " That," said Jack, " is a common, thread-bare excuse, and will not save your bacon." " But," said the star-gazer, " my name is Poor Robin ; I am the author of those almanacks that come out yearly

in my name, and I have canonized a great many gentle
men of your profession : look in my calender for their
names, and let this be my protection." But all in vain,
Bird ransacked his pocket, and from thence extracted the
large sum of fifteen shillings, took a new hat from his
head, and requested him, since he had now given him
cause, to canonize him likewise, which Robin engaged to
do as soon as he had suffered martyrdom at Tyburn.

Emboldened by success, Jack procured a good horse,
and resolved to perform something worthy of the honour
that awaited him ; and fortune soon presented a favourable opportunity. The Earl of ———— and his chaplain
were riding along in a coach, attended by two servants.
Bird advanced ; " Stand and deliver !" was his laconic
address. His lordship informed him, that he was very
little anxious about the small sum he had upon him ;
" But then," said he, " I hope that you will fight for it."
Jack then pulled out a brace of pistols, and let fly a
volley of imprecations. " Don't put yourself into any
passion, friend," said the Earl, " but lay down your
pistols, and I will beat you fairly for all the money I
have, against nothing." " That's an honourable chal-
lenge, my Lord," exclaimed Jack, " provided that none
of your servants be near us." His Lordship then commanded them to keep at a distance. The chaplain, however, could not endure the thought of the Earl fighting
while he was an idle spectator, and requested the honour
of espousing his master's cause. Matters were arranged :
the divine in a minute went to blows with Jack ; but the
latter, who once had the misfortune to be deprived of his
liberty, and exposed to the danger of his neck, by an old
tar without hands, was now determined to retrieve his
lost honour ; and in less than a quarter of an hour, he
beat the chaplain in such a manner, that he had only
breath remaining to utter the words, " I 'll fight no more."
Emboldened by victory, Jack said to his Lordship, " that
now, if he pleased, he would take a turn with him." " By
no means," cried the Earl, " for if you beat my chaplain
you will beat me, he and I having tried our manhood before." Then giving our hero a reward of twenty guineas

he rode off with his vanquished chaplain, well pleased that his own hide was safe.

Continuing his wicked courses, Bird one day, in company with a woman of easy virtue, knocked down and robbed a man between Drury-lane and the Strand. Bird escaped, but the woman was seized, and committed to Newgate. Bird went to visit her in prison, in the hope of accommodating matters with the prosecutor, but was seized upon suspicion of being an accomplice, and tried for that crime. Upon his trial he confessed the fact; the woman was liberated, and he suffered the just punishment of his deeds on the 12th of March 1690, being at that time forty-two years of age.

THE LIFE OF OLD MOB.

Thomas Simpson, or as he was usually called, Old Mob, was born at Ramsay in Hampshire, and continued to reside there as his only home until he had five children and some grandchildren. As there is no record of his education, which appears to have been greatly neglected, his adventures upon the road shall be related in order of time.

One day, near Exeter, he met with Sir Bartholomew Shower, whom he immediately required to deliver his money. Sir Bartholomew obeyed. Old Mob, however, examining his prey, told him that this was not sufficient to answer his present pressing necessities: "therefore, sir," said he, "as you are my banker in general, you must instantly draw a bill upon some one in Exeter for a hundred and fifty pounds, and remain in the next field as security for the payment, until I have received it." The good knight wished to be excused, professing that he knew no one in Exeter who would pay such a sum on demand. But excuses were vain: Old Mob held a pistol to his breast until he complied, and drew upon a rich goldsmith.

Having received the note, he made the knight dis
mount, cut the bridle and girths of the horse, and turned
him off, while he bound Sir Bartholomew hand and foot,
and left him under a hedge. The goldsmith knew the
handwriting, and paid the money. Old Mob, having received the sum, returned to the knight, saying, " Sir, I am
come with a habeas corpus to remove you out of your
present captivity;" which he did, leaving him to walk
home, a distance of three miles.

One day Old Mob quarrelled with a woman in the
neighbourhood, and, in a rage, questioned her virtue.
Her husband resented the affront; and an action commenced in a spiritual court against Old Mob, which cost
him a considerable sum. They who have enjoyed the
experience well know that spiritual courts are not less
litigious and expensive than civil courts.

Not long after, however, Mob met with the proctor who
had agented the plea against him, and had extracted from
his purse a considerable sum. He instantly knew him;
but, being well disguised, Mob was not recognized by the
the other. He demanded his purse : the lawyer began
to be eloquent in framing excuses ; but Mob reiterated his
threatenings, and the purse appeared, laden with fifteen
guineas. As the proctor was about to draw them from
thence, Mob insisted upon having the fine silk purse also.
The proctor told him it was given him by a particular
friend, and that he promised to keep it all his life ; upon
which Old Mob replied, " Suppose that you had a process
against me, and were to come to me for your fees ; if I
had no money, or anything of value but what was given
to me by a friend, would you take it for payment, if I told
you that I had promised to keep it as long as I lived ?"—
" No, sir."—" Stay there ; I love that people should do
as they would be done unto. What business had you to
promise a thing you were not sure of performing ? Am
I to be accountable for your vows ?" The poor lawyer
saw that if he insisted upon dividing the purse and the
gold, his own body and soul might be separated, presented
them to Old Mob.

John Gadbury had also the misfortune to fall in with

Old Mob. Though this man was an astrologer, yet his knowledge of the stars could not prevent his own misfortune. Poor John trembled when his money was demanded, and turned as pale as death, pretending that he had none. Old Mob, after bantering him, and telling him that he could never want money, as he had the twelve constellations always rented to stationers, informed him that his pistol would have his money, in spite of all the stars in the firmament. Dreading that the effect of the pistol would be more violent and sudden than any of the disastrous stars, he surrendered a bag containing about nine pounds in gold and silver.

The next adventure of Old Mob was an attack on the stage-coach from Bath, in which only one lady was passenger. When he stopped the coachman, approached the coach, and demanded the lady's money, she replied that she was a poor widow who had just lost her husband, and hoped that he would have compassion upon her. " And is the losing of your husband any argument why I should lose my booty? Your tears, madam, cannot move me; for I remember the old proverb—' The end of a husband is a widow's tears, and the end of those tears another husband.' "

The disconsolate widow made strong encomiums upon the virtues of her departed husband, with strong asseverations that none should ever succeed him in her affections. Old Mob did not believe one half consistent with truth, and, unwilling to be detained from another adventure, became positive with her; upon which she pulled out a purse with forty guineas, and presented it to him.

Scarcely had he departed from this widow, when he met with the famous Lincoln's-inn-fields mountebank, Cornelius a Tilburgh, going to a stage at Wells. Mob demanded his money in a very rough tone. The poor quack pretended that he himself was a son of necessity. Mob told him he had more wit than to believe a mountebank, whose occupation was lying: " You get your money as easy as I get mine, and it is only fulfilling the proverb, ' lightly come, lightly go;' besides, doctor, the next market-day will refund all; and you may excite compassion by informing them that you were robbed of your all in coming to exercise your benevolence towards them."

The doctor could scarce refrain from laughing at the smart strictures of Mob upon his profession; but unwilling to part with the bird he had in hand, he began to read him a lecture on morality, and to remonstrate upon the iniquity of his conduct, reminding him, that the money he thus took, might be the ruin of whole families, and constrain many to employ improper means to regain what they had lost in this manner; "therefore," said he, "you are answerable for their sin." "What," replied Old Mob, "this is the devil reproving sin, with a witness! Can I ruin more people than you, dear Mr. Theophrastus Bombasustus! You are scrupulously conscientious, indeed, to tell me of ruining people! I only take their money, you their lives! You with impunity, I at the risk of my own! You have made more blind than the small-pox, more deaf than the cataracts of the Nile, and destroyed more than the pestilence! Unless, doctor, you have a specific against the influence of powder and lead, it is in vain to trifle with me; deliver your money." The quack still delaying, Old Mob seized a portmanteau from his horse, and putting it upon his own, took his leave. Arriving at a convenient place to examine the contents, he found fifty-two pounds in money, and a large golden medal, besides all the doctor's instruments and implements of quackery. For the last, however, Mob could find but few buyers.

At another time, Old Mob met with the Duchess of Portsmouth, between Newmarket and London. He stopped the coach, and demanded her money. Accustomed to command a monarch, she could not conceive how a mean-looking fellow should talk in this style. Upon this, she briskly demanded if he knew who she was? "Yes, madam, I know you to be the greatest harlot in the kingdom, and maintained at the public expense! I know that all the courtiers depend upon your smiles, and that even the king is your slave! But what of all that? A gentleman collector upon the road is a greater

man, and more absolute than his majesty is at court.
You may now say, madam, that a single highwayman
has exercised his authority where Charles II. of England
has often begged a favour."

Her grace continued to gaze at him with a lofty air,
and told him that he was a very insolent fellow; that she
would give him nothing; and that he should certainly
suffer for his insolence; adding, "touch me if you dare!"
"Madam," answered Mob, "that haughty French spirit
will do you no good here: I am an English freebooter,
and I insist upon it, as my native right, to seize all foreign
commodities. Your money is indeed English, but it is
forfeited, as being the fruit of English folly. All you
have is confiscated, as being bestowed upon one so worth-
less. I am king here, madam! I have use for money as
well as he! The public pay for his follies, and so they
must for mine!" Mob immediately attacked her, but she
cried for quarter, and delivered him two hundred pounds,
a very rich necklace which her royal paramour had lately
given her, a gold watch, and two diamond rings.

Abingdon market was in general well stored with corn,
and Old Mob being one day there, fell into conversation
with a forestaller of grain. Being in possession of a
considerable sum of money, he contrived a plan to have
a share of the profits acquired by that extensive dealer.
He pretended to have come from London to purchase
corn; and desiring to see a sample, seemed satisfied with
the quality, and demanded the price. Old Mob instantly
made a purchase, paid the money, and sent the corn to a
place where he sold it for his own money. Careful to
ascertain the time when the corn-dealer was to leave town,
and the road he was to take, he was scarcely two miles
from the place when Mob approached him, put a pistol to
his breast, demanded the money which he had lent him,
and whatever more he had about him, as interest for the
loan. The countryman was not a little surprised to hear
such language from his late companion, and asked him
if it was just to take away both goods and money.
"Justice!" exclaimed Old Mob, "how have you the impudence to talk of justice, who rob the poor of their food

and rejoice at the misery of your fellow-creatures, because
you acquire your wealth upon the ruins of the nation?
Can any man in the world be more unjust than an en-
grosser of corn, who buys up the produce of the country, and pretends a scarcity in times of plenty, only to
increase his own substance, and leaves behind him abundance of ill-gotten wealth? Such vermin as you are un-
fit to live upon the earth! Talk no more of justice to
me; deliver up your money, or I shall do the world so
much justice as to send you out of it!" The countryman hereupon found it necessary to deliver up the large
sum of money which he had about him; and Old Mob
rode home highly gratified with his exploit.

Sir John Jeffries was the next to supply the wants of
our adventurer; who first disabled two servants, and then
advancing to the coach, demanded his lordship's money.
Jefferies, by his cruelties exhibited in the western assizes,
had rendered himself sufficiently infamous, and supposing
that his name would carry terror, he informed Old Mob
of the quality of the person whom he had accosted in so
rude a manner. "I am happy," said he, "in having an
opportunity of being revenged of you, for lately putting
me in fear of my life. I might," added he, "deliver you
over to trial for putting me in dread of death; but shall
compound the matter with the money you have in your
coach."

The judge began to expostulate with him upon the
danger to which he exposed both soul and body by such
crimes, reminding him, that if he believed there was a
providence which governed the world, he might expect to
meet with justice as the reward of his iniquities. "When
justice has overtaken us both," said Old Mob, "I hope to
stand as good a chance as your lordship, who have written
your name in indelible characters of blood, and deprived
many thousands of their lives for no other reason than
their appearance in defence of their just rights and liber-
ties. It is enough for you to preach morality upon the
bench, when no person can venture to contradict you;
but your lesson can have no effect upon me. I know you
well enough to perceive that they are only lavished upon

me to save your ill-gotten wealth." Then thundering forth
a volley of oaths, and presenting a pistol to his breast,
he threatened the judge with instant death, unless he surrendered his cash. Perceiving that his authority was of
no consequence to him upon the road, Jefferies delivered
his money, amounting to fifty-six guineas.

The only person with whom Old Mob ever acted in
concert, was the Golden Farmer. Two of their adventures may be selected. Having rendered themselves conspicuous upon the highway, and, by their frequent depredations, exposed themselves to the danger of detection,
they resolved to repose themselves in the capital, and to
employ their ingenuity, as they had now no occasion to
exercise their strength. Their first object was to learn
the manners and habits of the citizens, in order to impose
upon them in their own way. They who are acquainted
with London, know that all is hurry and bustle; that the
greater part are employed in business; and that if a man
dresses well, and for a while makes regular payments, he
may obtain credit to a great amount. Even so it was at
the period in which our adventurers flourished. They
accordingly commenced ostensibly as merchants. They
took a large handsome house, hired several servants, and
commenced business upon a large scale. The Golden
Farmer selected that of a chandler, he being in some
measure acquainted with that line of business. Old Mob
took up his residence near the Tower, and commenced
Dutch trader; for having been in that country when a boy,
he had learned a little of the language, and knew the
commodities that were usually exported from that quarter.
These two passed for near relations, of the name of Bryan,
and said that they were north country men.

With singular activity they inquired after goods in their
respective circles, purchased all that came in their way,
either paying ready money, or drawing upon each other
for one or two days, which draughts were always regularly honoured. They disposed of their goods at the
lowest prices, and thus kept a constant tide of ready
money; and their customers being perfectly satisfied, their
characters were completely established.

Perceiving their plan ripe for execution, they ordered an immense quantity of goods upon a certain day, drew upon each other for the payment, immediately sold the goods at reduced prices to their usual purchasers, under the pretence that they had a large sum of money to make up, and the next day left town with the sum of 1630*l.* the produce of three months' business. The reader may easily conceive what were the feelings and chagrin of the different merchants, when, on the day of payment, it was discovered, that the two extensive dealers and punctual payers had both disappeared.

For some time Old Mob and the Golden Farmer had recourse to their former employment upon the highway, until new dangers constrained them to think of another dexterous adventure by which to recruit their stores. There were two wealthy jewellers, brothers, the one living in London, and the other in Bristol. Old Mob and the Golden Farmer were minutely acquainted with the history of both brothers. These deceitful rogues knew that the jewellers were weak and sickly, which would obtain easy credit to a report of their death. Under this conviction they formed their plan, and wrote the following letter to each brother, only varying the name and place, according to circumstances:

"DEAR BROTHER,   *March* 26, 1686.

"This comes to bring you the sorrowful news, that you have lost the best of brothers, and I the kindest of husbands, at a time when we were in hopes of his growing better as the spring advanced, and continuing with us at least one summer longer. He died this morning about eleven o'clock, after he had kept his bed only three days.

"I send so hastily to you, that you may be here before we prepare for the funeral, which was the desire of my dear husband, who informed me that he had made you joint-executor with me. The will is in my hands, and I shall defer opening it until you arrive here. I am too full of grief to add any more; the messenger, who is a very honest man, and a neighbour of mine, shall inform you

of such particulars as are needful. From your sorrowful
sister.   " SEALS."

" P. S.—I employed a friend to write for me, which I
desire you to excuse, for I was not able to do it myself,
nor, indeed, to dictate any more."

These letters being sealed and directed, the one of our
adventurers set off for London, and the other for Bristol,
regulating matters so as to be at their journey's end at
the same time. Being arrived, they delivered their cre-
dentials, were cordially received, and hospitably entertained. Many tears were shed upon the opening of letters
containing such information, while secret joy arose in
each mind, upon the anticipated accession of wealth that
would accrue from the death of a brother. These two
brothers perhaps indulged common affection for each
other, but self-interest rises superior to every other species
of affection.

The evening at the respective places was spent in relating various incidents of the family history, together
with the narration of what the departed brother said in
his last moments. Next morning each of the villains was
dispatched to inform the sisters-in-law, that as soon as
mourning was got ready, they would hasten to perform
their last sorrowful duties. Old Mob went to Bristol, the
Golden Farmer to London. The first, in the evening,
secured jewels to the value of two hundred pounds. The
second, having taken his aim better, brought away jewels
and other goods to a much greater amount.

In the morning, both set out from their respective places,
and met at a spot previously determined. Meanwhile,
the brothers were both hastening to set out upon their
journey. In the family hurry of both, the shops were
neglected, so that the robbers were not discovered. The
brothers happened to take up their lodgings at the same
inn at Newbury. He from London came in first, and
went to bed before the other arrived. The Bristol brother, along with a companion who accompanied him,
passed through the chamber of his relative, and slept in
an adjoining room. It happened that their conversation

disturbed the repose of the London brother, who recognised the voice of the dead relative whom he was going to inter. In a short time, the latter was under the necessity of again passing through the room of his brother, who, by the moonlight, was more fully convinced that he had not been deceived in the voice. Upon this he cried out; the other brother was equally astonished, and ran back to his room overpowered with fear. They continued both of them sweating and trembling for dread until morning, when dressing themselves in their morning apparel, they mutually shunned each other, until they attracted the notice of the people in the house. They were at last with difficulty brought together, and detected the imposition, but remained ignorant of the cause. After spending two days at the inn, they returned home, and the plot was discovered.

Old Mob was at last apprehended in Tothill Street, Westminster, presented with thirty-six indictments, of which thirty-two were proved, and was executed at Tyburn on the 30th of May 1690.

TOM COX.

THOMAS Cox was born at Blandford, in Dorsetshire. He was the youngest son of a gentleman, so that having but a small patrimony, he soon consumed it in riotous living. Upon the decay of his fortune, he came up to London, where he fell in with a gang of highwaymen, and easily complied with their measures, in order to support himself in his dissolute course of life. He was three times tried for his life, before the last fatal trial, and had, after all these imputations, a prospect once more of making himself a gentleman, so indulgent was Providence to him. A young lady fell in love with him at Worcester, he being a very handsome man; and she went so far as to communicate her passion, and almost make him a direct offer of herself and 1500*l.* Cox married her; but, instead of settling himself in the world, and improving her fortune, he spent it all in less than two years, broke the poor creature's heart by his ill usage, and then took to his old courses again.

The robberies he committed after this were almost innumerable; we shall briefly mention a few, without dwelling on particulars that are not material. One day, he met with Killigrew, who had been jester to King Charles II., and ordered him to deliver. "Are you in earnest friend?" said the buffoon. Tom replied, "Yes, by G—d am I! for though you live by jesting, I can't." Killigrew found he spoke truth; for well as he loved jesting, he could not conceive that to be a jest which cost him twenty-five guineas; for so much Tom took from him.

Another time he robbed Mr. Hitchcock, an attorney of New Inn, of three hundred and fifty guineas, on the road between Midhurst and Tetworth, in the county of Sussex, giving him in return a lesson on the corruption of his practice, and throwing him a single guinea to bear his charges. Mr. Hitchcock was a little surprised at the highwayman's generosity, but more at his morality, imagining the world must needs be near its end, when the devil undertook to reform it.

Tom Cox was as great a libertine in his sentiments as he was in his practice; for he professed a belief that the *summum bonum* of man consisted in sensual pleasures, as Epicurus is said to have thought formerly, whose disciple he called himself. It is a common thing to call persons Epicureans who fall into these notions; and we do not know whether, in a work of this nature, it may be worth while to prove that the word is falsely applied, since the dea is all that we are to regard. Let Epicurean signify what it will, they are no followers of Epicurus who are not lovers of virtue, and who do not place their supreme happiness in the most exalted pleasures of the mind, as that great philosopher certainly did.

Our offender was at last apprehended for a robbery on the highway, committed near Chard, in Somersetshire: but he had not been long confined in Ilchester gaol before he found an opportunity of escaping. He broke out of

his ward into the keeper's apartment, who, as good luck
would have it, had been drunk over night, and was now
in a profound sleep. It was a moonlight night, and Cox
could see a silver tankard on the table in the room, which
he secured, and then let himself out with authority into
the street, by the help of the keys, leaving the doors all
unlocked as he passed. The tankard he had stolen was
worth 10*l.*; besides which, he got into a stable hard by,
and took a good horse, with proper furniture to carry
him off.

It is reported of Tom Cox, that he more than once
robbed persons of his own trade, and that he sometimes
robbed in company. One time in particular, he had accomplices, and had formed a project of robbing a nobleman, well attended, who was travelling the kingdom. Tom
associated himself with this nobleman on the road, and
talked to him, as they passed along, of the adventures he
had met with in such an agreeable manner, as ingratiated
him very much in his companion's esteem. They had
not ridden many miles together, before two of Tom's com
panions came up, and bade them stand, but immediately
fled upon Tom's pulling out a pistol, and making a seem
ing bluster. The nobleman attributed his delivery to the
generosity and bravery of this new companion, putting
still more confidence in him, and desiring his company
as long as possible. They were to stay a whole day at
the next great town, in order to take a ride round the
country, and see what was to be seen, according to the
custom which this noble friend of Tom's had practised
all the way. In the morning, the saddle-horses were got
ready, and our two fellow-travellers set out for the tour
of the day, the person of quality refusing to take a footman with him, as usual, that he might the more freely
converse with his new acquaintance.

We shall not trouble the reader with what they saw on
the way, and how much they were pleased, because that
is little to our story. About noon they came to a convenient place, when Cox suddenly threw off the mask,
and commanded his companion to deliver his money.
" Why, ay," said the nobleman, " such a thing might be

done here, for it's a devilish lonesome country: but I can fear no danger while you are with me,—you, whose courage I have so lately experienced." "Such a thing might be done?" replied Cox: "why, in the name of Satan, I hope you don't think I have kept you company all this time to play with you at last? If you do, sir, let me tell you, you are mistaken." Upon which, he pulled out a pistol, and presented it to his breast, swearing and cursing like a madman, till he had given sufficient proof that he was in earnest. Filled with astonishment and confusion, our nobleman delivered a diamond ring, a gold watch, and near a hundred guineas in money, staring all the while in Tom's face with much gravity. To prevent a sudden pursuit, Tom then dismounted his companion, bound him hand and foot, and killed his horse, according to the custom of experienced highwaymen, taking his leave with a sneer, and " Good bye, fellow-traveller, till I meet you again."

After this, Tom Cox committed two other robberies that were known. One of them was on a grazier, who had been at Smithfield, and received about 300*l.* for cattle, a great part of which was in silver, and, consequently, was sufficiently bulky. When he had got the money, he fell to caning the poor sufferer in an unmerciful manner, who desired to know the reason of such usage after he had taken all. " Sirrah," said Tom, " 'tis for loading my horse at this rate ; that you may remember another time to get your money changed into gold before you come out of town,—for who the plague must be your porter !" We may reasonably suppose the grazier chose rather to pay for the return of his money for the future, than carry so much about him.

Tom's last robbery was on a farmer, from whom he took about 20*l.* It was not above a week after the fact, before the farmer had occasion to proceed to London about business, and saw Tom coming out of his lodgings in Essex street, in the Strand, when, upon crying out " Stop thief !" he was immediately apprehended in St. Clement's Church-yard, and committed by a neighbouring magistrate to Newgate, where he lived till the sessions in an extra-

14 *

vagant manner, being very full of money. Receiving
sentence of death on the farmer's deposition at Justice
Hall, on Wednesday the 3d of June 1691, he was hanged
at Tyburn, in the twenty-sixth year of his age. He was
so resolute to the last, that when Mr. Smith, the ordinary,
asked him, a few moments before he was turned off,
whether he would join with his fellow-sufferers in prayer?
"D——n you—no!" said he, and kicked both ordinary and
executioner out of the cart.

COLONEL JACK.

THE account of the life of Colonel Jack, written by
himself, naturally excites reflections upon the blessings
of education, and the misery and ruin of thousands of
the poorer orders who have been unfortunately deprived
of it.

It cannot, we think, but be apparent, in the auto
biography of Colonel Jack, that the writer, although circumstances and the want of education we have been
lamenting, caused him to become a thief, was naturally
disposed, and had a yearning, towards virtue. A certain
rectitude of principle, strangely at variance with his calling, remained with him constantly, causing him to abhor
the worst parts of his trade, and at last to lay it off altogether.

We have chosen to give the ensuing narrative almost
without the alteration of a word: the spirit of the story
must inevitably evaporate during a process of transfusion :—

" Seeing that my life has been such a chequerwork of
Nature, and that I am able now to look back upon it from
a safer distance than is ordinary to the fate of the clan to
which I once belonged, I think my history may find a
place in the world, as well as that of some, which, I see,
are every day read with pleasure, though they have in

them nothing so diverting or instructing as I believe mine will appear to be.

"My origin may be as high as any body's, for ought I know; for my mother kept very good company:—but that part belongs to her story more than to mine. All I know of it is by oral tradition, thus:—my nurse told me my mother was a gentlewoman, that my father was a man of quality, and that she (my nurse) had a good piece of money given her to take me off his hands, and deliver him and my mother from the importunities that usually attend the misfortune of having a child to keep that should not be seen or heard of.

"My father, it seems, gave my nurse something more than was agreed for, at my mother's request, upon her solemn promise, that she would use me well, and let me be put to school; and he charged her, that if I lived to come to any bigness, capable to understand the meaning of it, she should always take care to bid me remember that I was a gentleman; and this, he said, was all the education he would desire of her for me; for he did not doubt but that some time or other, the very hint would inspire me with thoughts suitable to my birth; and that I would certainly act like a gentleman, if I believed myself to be so.

"My nurse was as honest to the engagement she had entered into as could be expected from one of her employment, and particularly as honest as her circumstances would give her leave to be; for she bred me up very carefully with her own son, and with another son of shame, like me, whom she had taken upon the same terms.

"My name was John, as she told me; but neither she nor I knew any thing of a sirname that belonged to me; so that I was left to call myself Mr. Anything that I pleased, as fortune and better circumstances should give occasion. It happened that her own son, (for she had a little boy about one year older than I,) was called John too; and about two years after, she took another son of shame, as I called it above, to keep as she did me, and his name was John too. But my nurse, who may be allowed to distinguish her own son a little from the rest! would have him called captain, because, forsooth, he was the eldest.

"I was provoked at having this boy called captain, and cried, and told my nurse I would be called captain, for she told me I was a gentleman, and I would be a captain, that I would. The good woman, to keep the peace, told me, 'Ay, ay, I was a gentleman, and therefore I should be above a captain, for I should be a colonel, and that was a great deal better than a captain.' Well, I was hushed indeed with this for the present, but not thoroughly pleased, till, a little while after, I heard her tell her own boy, that I was a gentleman, and therefore he must call me colonel; at which her boy fell a-crying, and he would be called colonel too; so then I was satisfied that it was above a captain. So universally is ambition seated in the minds of men, that not a beggar-boy but has his share of it. Before I tell you much more of our story, it would be very proper to give something of our several characters, as I have gathered them up in my memory, as far back as I can recover things either of myself or my brother Jacks; and they shall be brief and impartial.

"Captain Jack, the eldest of us all by a whole year, was a squat, big, strong-made boy, and promised to be stout when grown up to be a man, but not tall. He was an original rogue; for he would do the foulest and most villanous things even by his own inclination; he had no taste or sense of being honest, no not even to his brother rogues, which is what other thieves make a point of honour of,—I mean that of being honest to one another.

"Major Jack was a merry, facetious, pleasant boy, and had something of a gentleman in him. He had a true manly courage, feared nothing, and yet, if he had the advantage, was the most compassionate creature alive, and wanted nothing but honesty to have made him an excellent man. He had learn to write and read very well, as you will find in the process of this story.

"As to myself, I passed among my comrades for a bold resolute boy; but I had a different opinion of myself; and therefore shunned fighting as much as I could

I was wary and dexterous at my trade, and was not so often caught as my fellow-rogues; I mean while I was a boy, and never after I came to be a man, no, not once for twenty-six years, being so old in the trade, and still unhanged.

"I was almost ten years old, the captain eleven, and the major eight, when our good old nurse died; her husband was drowned a little before in the Gloucester frigate, which was cast away going to Scotland with the Duke of York, in the reign of King Charles II. and the honest woman dying very poor, the parish was obliged to bury her. The good woman being dead, we were turned loose to the world,—rambling about all three together, and the people in Rosemary-lane and Radcliffe knowing us pretty well, we got victuals easy enough; as for lodging, we lay in the summer-time on bulk-heads and at shop-doors; as for bed, we knew nothing that belonged to it for many years after my nurse died; but in winter got into the ash-holes, and annealing-arches in the glass-houses, where we were accompanied by several youngsters like ourselves; some of whom persuaded the captain to go a kidnapping with them, a trade at that time much followed: the gang used to catch children in the evening, stop their mouths, and carry them to such houses, where they had rogues ready to receive them, who put them on board ships bound to Virginia, and when they arrived there, they were sold. This wicked gang were at last taken, and sent to Newgate; and Captain Jack, among the rest, though he was not then much above thirteen years old, and being but a lad, was ordered to be three times whipped at Bridwell, the Recorder telling him, it was done in order to keep him from the gallows. We did what we could to comfort him; but he was scourged so severely, that he lay sick for a good while; but as soon as he regained his liberty, he went to his old gang, and kept among them as long as that trade lasted, for it ceased a few years afterwards.

"The major and I, though very young, had sensible impressions made on us for some time by the severe usage of the captain; but it was within the year, that the

major, a good-conditioned easy body, was wheedled away
by a couple of young rogues to take a walk with them.
The gentlemen were very well matched, for the oldest
of them was not above fourteen; the business was to go
to Bartholomew fair, and the end of going there was to
pick pockets.

"The major knew nothing of the trade, and therefore
was to do nothing; but they promised him a share with
them, for all that, as if he had been as expert as' themselves; so away they went. The two dexterous rogues
managed it so well, that by about eight o'clock at night,
they came back to our dusty quarters at the glass-house,
and sitting them down in a corner, they began to share
their spoil by the light of the glass-house fire. The major
lugged out the goods, for as fast as they made any
purchase, they unloaded themselves, and gave all to him,
that if they had been taken, nothing might be found about
them. It was a lucky day for them; the devil certainly
assisting them to find their prey, that he might draw in a
young gamester, and encourage him to the undertaking,
who had been made backward before by the misfortune
of the captain.

"For such a cargo to be brought home clear in one
afternoon, or evening rather, and by only two little rogues
so young, was, it must be confessed, extraordinary; and
the major was elevated the next day to a strange degree;
for he came to me very early, and called me out into a
narrow lane, and showed me his little hand almost full
of money. I was surprised at the sight, when he put it
up again, and bringing his hand out, " Here," said he,
" you shall have some of it," and gave me a sixpence
and a shilling's worth of the small silver pieces. This
was very welcome to me, who never had a shilling of
money together before in all my life, that I could call my
own. I was very earnest to know how he came by this
wealth; he quickly told me the story; and that he had
for his share seven shillings and sixpence in money, the
silver-thimble, and a silk-handkerchief.

"We went to Rag-Fair, and bought each of us a pair
of shoes and stockings, and afterwards went to a boiling

cook's in Rosemary-lane, where we treated ourselves nobly; for we had boiled beef, pudding, a penny-brick, and a pint of strong-beer, which cost us sevenpence in all. That night the major triumphed in our new enjoyment, and slept in the usual place, with an undisturbed repose. The next day, the major and his comrades went abroad again, and were still successful, nor did any disaster attend them for many months; and by frequent imitation and direction, Major Jack became as dexterous a pickpocket as any of them, and went through a long variety of fortune, too long to enter upon now, because I am hastening to my own story, which at present is the main thing I have to set down.

"Overcome by the persuasions of the major, I entered myself into his society, and went down to Billingsgate with one of them, which was crowded with masters of coal-ships, fishmongers, and oyster-women. It was the first of these people my comrade had his eye upon: so he gave me my orders, which were thus: 'Go you,' said he, 'into all the ale-houses as we go along, and observe where any people are telling money, and when you find any, come and tell me.' So he stood at the door, and I went into the houses. As the collier-masters generally sell their coals at the Gate, as they call it, so they generally receive their money in those ale-houses, and it was not long before I brought him word of several. Upon this, he went in and made his observations, but found nothing to his purpose. At length, I brought word that there was a man in such a house, who had received a great deal of money of somebody, or, I believed, of several people; and that it lay all upon the table in heaps, and he was very busy writing down the sums, and putting it up in several bags. 'Is he?' said he: 'I'll warrant him, I will have some of it;' and in he went, walked up and down the house, which had several open tables and boxes in it, and listened to hear if he could learn what the man's name was, and he heard somebody call him Cullum, or some such name; then he watched his opportunity, and stepped up to him, and told him a long story, 'That there were two gentlemen at the Gun-tavern sent him to enquire for him, and to tell him, they desired to speak with him.'

" 'The collier-master had got his money before him just as I had told him, and had two or three small payments of money, which he had put up in little black dirty bags, and laid by themselves ; and as it was hardly broad day, the major found means, in delivering his message, to lay his hand upon one of those bags, and carry it off perfectly undiscovered. When he had got it, he came out to me, who stood at the door, and pulling me by the sleeve, ' Run Jack,' said he, ' for our lives ;' and away he scowered, and I after him, never resting, or scarce looking about me, till we got quite into Moorfields. But not thinking ourselves safe there, we ran on till we got into the fields, and finding a by-place, we sat down, and he pulled out the bag. ' Thou art a lucky boy, Jack,' said he, ' thou deservest a good share of this job, truly; for 'tis all along of thy lucky news.' So he poured it all out into my hat.

" How he did to whip away such a bag from any man who was awake and in his senses, I cannot tell. There were about seventeen or eighteen pounds in the bag, and he parted the money, giving me one-third, with which I was very well contented. As we were now so rich, he would not let me lie any longer about the glass-house, or go naked and ragged as I had done ; but obliged me to buy two shirts, a waistcoat, and a great coat ; for a great coat was more proper for our business than any other. So I clothed myself, as he directed, and we lodged together in a little garret.

" Soon after this, we walked out again, and then tried our fortune in the places by the Exchange a second time. Here we began to act separately, and I undertook to walk by myself; and the first thing I did accurately, was a trick I played that argued some skill for a new beginner ; for I had never seen any business of that kind done before. I saw two gentlemen mighty eager in talk, and one pulled out a pocket-book two or three times, and then slipped it into his coat-pocket again, and then out it came again, and papers were taken out, and others put in, and

then in it went again; and so several times, the man
being still warmly engaged with another man, and two
or three others standing hard by them the last time he
put his pocket-book into his pocket with his hand, when
the book lay endway, resting upon some other book, or
something else in his pocket, so that it did not go quite
down, but one corner of it was seen above his pocket.
Having seen the book thus pass and repass, I brushed
smoothly, but closely, by the man, and took it clean
away, and went directly into Moorfields, where my fel-
low-rogue was to meet me. It was not long before he
came: I had no occasion to tell him my success; for he
had heard of the action among the crowd. We searched
the book, and found several goldsmiths' and other notes;
but the best of the booty was in one of the folds of the
cover of the book: there was a paper full of loose diamonds. The man, as we understood afterwards, was a
Jew, and dealt in those glittering commodities.

"We agreed that Will (which was my comrade's name)
should return to the Change to hear what news was stirring, and there he heard of a reward of one hundred
pounds for returning the things. The next day he went
to the gentleman, and told him he had got some scent of
his book, and the person who took it, and who, he believed, would restore it, for the sake of the reward, provided he was assured that he should not be punished for
the fact. After many preliminaries, it was concluded,
that Will should bring the book, and the things lost in it,
and receive the reward, which on the third day he did,
and faithfully paid me my share of it.

"Not long after this, it fell out, we were strolling about
in Smithfield on a Friday: there happened to be an old
country gentleman in the market, selling some very large
bullocks; it seems they came out of Sussex, for we heard
him say, there were no such bullocks in the whole county
of Sussex. His worship, for so they called him, had received the money for these bullocks at a tavern, the sign
of which I have forgotten now, and having some of it in
a bag, and the bag in his hand, he was taken with a sudden fit of coughing, and stood to cough, resting his hand

with the bag of money in it upon a bulk-head of a shop,
just by the cloister-gate in Smithfield; that is to say,
within three or four doors of it: we were both just behind him, when Will said to me, 'Stand ready.'   Upon
this he made an artificial stumble, and fell with his head
just against the old gentleman in the very moment when
he was coughing ready to be strangled and quite spent
for want of breath.

"The violence of the blow beat the old gentleman
quite down; the bag of money did not immediately fly
out of his hand, but I ran to get hold of it, and giving it
a quick snatch, pulled it clean away, and ran like the
wind down the cloister with it, till I got to our old rendezvous.   Will in the mean time fell down with the old
gentleman, but soon got up.   The old knight (for such it
seems he was) was frighted with the fall, and his breath
was so stopped with his cough, that he could not recover
himself to speak until some time, during which nimble
Will was got up again, and walked off; nor could he call
out 'stop thief,' or tell anybody he had lost anything for
a good while; but coughing vehemently till he was almost black in the face, he at last brought it out, 'The
rogues have got away my bag of money.'

"All the while the people understood nothing of the
matter; and as for the rogues, indeed, they had time
enough to get clear away, and in about an hour Will
came to the rendezvous: there we sat down on the grass,
and turned out the money, which proved to be eight
guineas, and five pounds eight shillings in silver.   This
we shared upon the spot, and went to work the same day
for more; but whether it was that, being flushed with our
success, we were not so vigilant, or that no other opportunity offered, I know not, but we got nothing more that
night.

"The next adventure was in the dusk of the evening,
in a court which goes out of Gracechurch-street into
Lombard-street, where the Quakers' meeting-house is.
There was a young fellow, who, as we learned afterwards, was a woollen-draper's apprentice in Gracechurch-
street: it seems, he had been receiving a sum of money

which was very considerable, and he came to a goldsmith's in Lombard-street with it, paid in the most of it
there, insomuch that it grew dark, and the goldsmith began to shut up his shop, and to light his candles. We
watched him in there, and stood on the other side of the
way, to see what he did. When he had paid in all the
money he intended, he stayed a little longer to take notes
for what he had paid. At last he came out of the shop
with still a pretty large bag under his arm, and walked
over into the court, which was then very dark. In the
middle of the court is a boarded entry, and at the end of
it a threshold; and as soon as he had set his foot over
the threshold, he was to turn on his left hand into Gracechurch-street.

"'Keep up,' said Will to me; 'be nimble:' and as
soon as he had said so, he flew at the young man, and
gave him such a violent thrust that it pushed him forward
with too great a force for him to stand, and, as he strove
to recover the threshold, Will took hold of his feet, and
he fell forward. I stood ready, and presently fell out the
bag of money, which I heard fall, for it flew out of his
hand. I went forward with the money, and Will, finding
I had it, ran backward, and, as I made along Fenchurch-
street, overtook me, and we scoured home together. The
poor young man was hurt a little with the fall, and reported to his master, as we heard afterwards, that he was
knocked down. His master was glad the rest of the
money was paid in to the banker, and made no great
noise at the loss, only cautioned his apprentice to avoid
such dark places for the future.

"This booty amounted to 14*l.* 18*s.* apiece, and added
extremely to my store, which began to grow too big for
my management; but still I was at a loss with whom to
trust it.

"A little after this, Will brought me into the company
of two more young fellows: we met at the lower part of
Gray's-inn-lane, about an hour before sunset, and went
out into the fields towards a place called the Pindar of
Wakefield, where are abundance of brick-kilns. Here it
was agreed to spread from the field-path to the road-way,

all the way towards Pancras church, to observe any chance game, which, as they called it, they might shoot flying. Upon the path, within the bank on the side of the road going towards Kentish Town, two of our gang, Will and one of the others, met a single gentleman walking apace towards the town, it being almost dark. Will cried, " Mark, ho !" which it seems was the word at which we were all to stand still at a distance, come in if he wanted help, and give a signal if anything appeared that was dangerous.

" Will stepped up to the gentleman, stopped him, and put the question, that is, ' Sir, your money !' The gentleman, seeing he was alone, struck at him with his cane : but Will, a nimble, strong fellow, flew upon him, and with struggling got him down ; then he begged for his life. Will having told him, with an oath, that he would cut his throat in a moment. While this was doing, a hackney-coach came along the road, and the fourth man who was that way cried, " Mark, ho !" which was to intimate that it was a prize, not a surprise ; and, accordingly, the next man went up to assist him, where they stopped the coach, which had a doctor of physic and a surgeon in it, who had been to visit some considerable patient, and I suppose, had considerable fees, for here they got two gold purses, one with eleven or twelve guineas, the other six, with some pocket money, two watches, one diamond ring, and the surgeon's plaster-box, which was most of it full of silver instruments.

" While they were at this work, Will kept the man down, who was under him ; and though he promised not o kill him, unless he offered to make a noise, yet he would not let him stir till he heard the noise of the coach going on again, by which he knew the job was over on that side. Then he carried him a little out of the way, tied his hands behind him, and bade him lie still and make no noise and he would come back in half an hour, and untie him upon his word ; but if he cried out, he would come back and kill him. The poor man promised to lie still, and make no noise, and did so, and had not above 11*s.* 6*d.* in his pocket, which Will took, and came back to the rest. But while they were together, I, who was on the side of the Pindar of Wakefield, cried out, 'Mark, ho!' too.

"What I saw was a couple of poor women—one a kind of a nurse, and the other a maid-servant, going for Kentish Town. As Will knew I was but young at the work, he came flying to me, and seeing how easy a bargain it was, he said, 'Go, Colonel, fall to work!' I wen up to them, and, speaking to the elderly woman, 'Nurse, said I, 'don't be in such haste—I want to speak with you; at which they both stopped, and looked a little frighted. Don't be frighted, sweetheart,' said I to the maid; 'a little of that money in the bottom of your pocket will make all easy, and I'll do you no harm.' By this time Will came up to us, for they had not seen him before; then they began to scream out. 'Hold!' said I, 'make no noise, unless you have a mind to force us to murder you whether we will or no: give me your money presently, and make no words, and we shan't hurt you.' Upon this the poor maid pulled out five shillings and sixpence, and the old woman a guinea and a shilling, crying heartily for her money, and said it was all she had in the world. Well, we took it for all that, though it made my heart bleed to see what agony the poor woman was in at parting with it, and I asked her where she lived? She said her name was Smith, and she lived at Kentish Town. I said nothing to her, but bade them go on about their business, and I gave Will the money. In a few minutes we were all together again. One of the rogues said, 'Come, this is well enough for one road; it's time to be gone. So we jogged away, crossing the field, out of the path, towards Tottenham-court. 'But, hold,' said Will, 'I must go and untie the man, d——n him.' One of them said, 'Let him lie.' 'No,' said Will, 'I will not be worse than my word; I will untie him.' So he went to the place; but the man was gone: either he had untied himself, or somebody had passed by, and he had called for help, and so was untied, for he could not find him, nor make him hear, though he ventured to call twice for him aloud.

"This made us hasten away the faster, and getting into Tottenham-court road, they thought it was a little too near, so they made into the town at St. Giles's, and crossing to Piccadilly, went to Hyde Park gate; here they ventured to rob another coach, that is to say, one of the two other rogues and Will did it between the Park-gate and Knightsbridge. There was in it only a gentleman and a woman whom he had picked up, it seems, at the Spring-garden a little farther: they took the gentleman's money, and his watch, and his silver-hilted sword; but when they came to the woman, she cursed them for robbing the gentleman of his money, and leaving him none for her; as for herself she had not one sixpenny-piece about her, though she was, indeed, well enough dressed too. Having made this adventure, we parted, and went each man to his lodging.

"Two days after this, Will came to my lodging, for I had now got a room by myself, and appointed me to meet him the next evening at such a place. I went, but to my great satisfaction missed him, but met with a gang at another place, who had committed a notorious robbery near Hounslow; where they wounded a gentleman's gardener, so that, I think, he died, and robbed the house of a considerable sum of money and plate. This, however, was not so clean carried, but the neighbours were alarmed, the rogues pursued, and being at London with the booty, one of them was taken; but Will, being a dexterous fellow, made his escape with the money and plate. He knew nothing that one of his comrades was taken, and that they were all so closely pursued that every one was obliged to shift for himself. He happened to come in the evening, as good luck then directed him, just after search had been made for him by the constables; his companion who was taken, having upon promise of favour, and to save himself from the gallows, discovered his confederates, and Will amongst the rest, as the principal party in the whole undertaking. He got notice of it, and left all his booty at my lodging, hiding it in an old coat that lay under my bed, leaving word he had been there, and had left the coat that he had borrowed of me, under my bed. I knew not what to make of it, but went up stairs, and finding the parcel, was surprised to see wrapped up in it, above a hundred pounds in plate and money, and heard nothing of brother Will, as he called himself, for three or four days, when we sold the plate after the rate of two shillings per ounce, to a pawnbroker near Cloth-Fair.

"About two days afterwards, going upon the stroll, whom should I meet but my former brother, Captain Jack! When he saw me, he came close to me in his blunt way, and said, 'Do you hear the news?' I asked him, 'What news?' He told me, 'My old comrade and teacher was taken, and that morning carried to Newgate: that he was charged with a robbery and murder, committed somewhere beyond Brentford; and that the worst was, he was impeached.' I thanked him for his information, and for that time parted; but was the very next morning surprised, when, going across Rag-Fair, I heard one call 'Jack.' I looked behind me, and immediately saw three men, and after them a constable, coming towards me with great fury. I was in a great surprise, and started to run; but one of them clapped in upon me, got hold of me, and in a moment the rest surrounded me, and told me they were to apprehend a known thief, who went by the name of one of the 'Three Jacks of Rag-Fair;' for that he was charged upon oath with having been a party in a notorious robbery, burglary, and murder, committed in such a place and on such a day.

"Not to trouble the reader with an account of the discourse that passed between the justice, before whom I was carried, and myself, I shall in brief inform him, that my brother Captain Jack, who had the forwardness to put it to me whether I was among them or no, when in truth he was there himself, had the only reason to fly, at the same time that he advised me to shift for myself; so that I was discharged, and in about three weeks after, my master and tutor in wickedness, poor Will, was executed for the fact.

"I had nothing to do now but to find out the captain, of whom, though not without some trouble, I at last got

news, and told him the whole story. He presently discovered, by his surprise, that he was guilty, and after a
few words more told me, ' it was all true, that he was in
the robbery, and had the greatest part of the booty in
keeping; but what to do with it, or himself, he did not
know, but thought of flying into Scotland,' asking me,
' if I would go with him?' I consented, and the next day
he showed me twenty-two pounds he had in money. I
honestly produced all the money I had left, which was
upwards of sixteen pounds. We set out from London on
foot, and travelled the first day to Ware; for he had learned so much of the road that our way lay through that
town; from Ware we travelled to Cambridge, though that
was not our direct road. The occasion was this: in our
way through Puckeridge, we baited at an inn, and while
we were there, a countryman came and hung his horse
at the gate, while he went in to drink. We sat in the
gateway; having called for a mug of beer, we drank it
up. We had been talking to the ostler about the way to
Scotland, and he bade us ask the road to Royston : 'But,'
said he, ' there is a turning just here a little farther, you
must not go that way, for that goes to Cambridge.'

" We had paid for our beer, and sat at the door only
to rest us, when on a sudden comes a gentleman's coach
to the door, and three or four horsemen rode into the yard,
and the ostler was obliged to go in with them. Said he
to the captain, ' Young man, pray take hold of the horse,'
meaning the countryman's horse I mentioned above, ' and
take him out of the way that the coach may come up.'
He did so, and beckoned to me to follow him. We walked
together to the turning; said he to me, " Do you step
before, and turn up the lane; I'll overtake you;' so I
went on up the lane, and in a few minutes he got upon
the horse, and was soon at my heels, bidding me get up
and take a lift.

" I made no difficulty of doing so, and away we went
at a good round rate, having a strong horse under us.
We suspected the countryman would follow us to Royston,
because of our directions from the ostler; so that we
went towards Cambridge, and went easier after the firs'

hour's riding; and coming through a town or two, we alighted by turns, and did not then ride double, but by the way picked a couple of good shirts off a hedge; and that evening got safe to Cambridge, where the next day I bought a horse for myself. Thus equipped, we jogged on through several places, till we got to Stamford in Lincolnshire, where it was impossible to restrain my captain from playing his pranks, even at church; where he went, and placed himself so near an old lady, that he got her gold watch from her side unperceived; and the same night we went away by moonlight, after having the satisfaction to hear the watch cried, and ten guineas offered for it again. He would have been glad of the ten guineas instead of the watch, but durst not venture to carry it home. We went through several other places, such as Grantham, Newark, and Nottingham, where we played our tricks; but at last we got safe to Edinburgh, without any accident but one, which was in crossing a ford, where the captain was really in danger of drowning, his horse being driven down by the stream, and falling under him; but the rider had a proverb on his side, and got out of the water.

"At Edinburgh we remained about a month, when, on a sudden, my captain was gone, horse and all, and I knew nothing what was become of him, nor did I ever see or hear of him for eighteen months after; nor did he so much as leave the least notice for me, either where he was gone, or whether he would return to Edinburgh again or no. I took his leaving me very heinously, not knowing what to do with myself, being a stranger in the place, and, on the other hand, my money abated apace too. I had, for the most part of this time, my horse upon my hands to keep; and, as horses yield but a sorry price in Scotland, I found no opportunity to sell him to any advantage: however, at last, I was forced to dispose of him.

"Being thus eased of my horse, and having nothing at all to do, I began to consider with myself what would become of me, and what I could turn my hand to. I had not much diminished my stock of money; for though I was all the way so wary that I would not join with my captain in his desperate attempts, yet I made no scruple to live at his expense. In the next place, I was not so anxious about my money running low, because I had made a reserve, by leaving upwards of 90*l*. in a friend's hands at London; but still I was willing to get into some employment for a livelihood. I was sick of the wandering life I had led, and resolved to be a thief no more, but stuck close to writing and reading for about six months, till I got into the service of an officer of the Customs, who employed me for a time: but, as he had set me to do little but pass and repass between Leith and Edinburgh, leaving me to live at my own expense till my wages should be due, I ran out the little money I had left in clothes and subsistence, and a little before the year's end, when I was to have 12*l*. English money, my master was turned out of his place, and, which was worse, having been charged with some misapplications, was obliged to take shelter in England; so we that were servants—for there were three of us—were left to shift for ourselves. This was a hard case for me, in a strange place, and I was reduced by it to the last extremity. I might have gone for England, an English ship being there: the master proffered to take my word for ten shillings, till I got there; but just as I was upon going, Captain Jack appeared again.

"I have mentioned how he left me, and that I saw him no more for eighteen months. His ramble and adventures were many: in that time he went to Glasgow, playing some very remarkable pranks there; escaped the gallows almost miraculously; got over to Ireland; wandered about there; escaped from Londonderry over to the Highlands, and, about a month before I was left destitute at Leith by my master, noble Captain Jack came in there, on board the ferry-boat from Fife, being, after all his adventures and successes, advanced to the dignity of a foot soldier in a body of recruits, raised in the north for the regiment of Douglas.

After my disaster, being reduced almost as low as Jack, I found no better shift before me, at least not for the present, than to enter myself a soldier too: and thus we were ranked together, with each of us a musket upon our shoulders. I was extremely delighted with the life of a soldier; for I took the exercises naturally, so that the sergeant who taught us to handle our arms, seeing me so ready at it, asked me, if I had never carried arms before? I told him, no. At which he swore, though jesting: 'They call you colonel,' said he, 'and I believe you will be a colonel, or you must be some colonel's bastard, or you would never handle your arms as you do, at once or twice showing.' Whatever was my satisfaction in that respect, yet other circumstances did not equally concur to make this life suit me; for, after we had been about six months in this figure, we were informed, that we were to march for England, and be shipped off at Newcastle, or Hull, to join the regiment in Flanders. Poor Captain Jack's case was particular: he durst not appear publicly at Newcastle, as he must have done had he marched with the recruits. In the next place, I remembered my money in London, which was almost 100*l.*; and if it had been asked all the soldiers in the regiment, which of them would go to Flanders a private sentinel if they had 100*l.* in their pockets, I believe none of them would have answered in the affirmative.

"These two circumstances concurring, I began to be very uneasy, and very unwilling in my thoughts to go over into Flanders a poor musketeer, to be knocked on the head for 3s. 6d. a-week. While I was daily musing on the hardship of being sent away as above, Captain Jack came to me one evening, and asked me to take a walk with him into the fields; for he wanted to speak with me. We walked together here, and talked seriously of the matter, and at last concluded to desert that very night; the moon affording a good light, and Jack having got a comrade with him thoroughly acquainted with the way across the Tweed; when on the other side, we should be on English ground, and safe enough; from thence we proposed to go to Newcastle, and get some collier ship to take us in, and carry us to London.

"About half an hour past eight in the morning, we reached the Tweed; and here we overtook two more of the same regiment, who had deserted from Haddington, where another part of the recruits were quartered. These

were Scotsmen, and very poor, having not one penny in
their pockets; and when they saw us, whom they knew
to be of the same regiment, they took us to be pursuers:
upon which they stood upon their defence, having the
regiment swords on, as we had also, but none of the
mounting or clothing; for we were not to receive the
clothes till we came to the regiment in Flanders. It was
not long before we made them understand that we were
in the same condition with themselves; and so we became
one company. Our money had ebbed very low, and we
contrived to get into Newcastle in the dusk of the evening;
and even then we durst not venture into the public parts
of the place, but made down towards the river below the
town. Here we knew not what to do with ourselves, but,
guided by our fate, we put a good face upon the matter,
went into an ale-house, sat down, and called for a pint of
beer.

" The woman of the house appeared very frank, and
entertained us cheerfully: so we, at last, told her our condition, and asked her if she could not help us to some
kind master of a collier, who would give us a passage to
London by sea. The subtle devil, who immediately found
us proper fish for her hook, gave us the kindest words in
the world, and told us she was heartily sorry she had not
seen us one day sooner; that there was a collier-master
of her particular acquaintance, who went away but with
the morning tide; that the ship was fallen down to
Shields, but, she believed, was hardly over the bar yet,
and she would send to his house, and see if he was gone
on board, (for sometimes the masters do not go away
till a tide after the ship;) and she was sure, if he was not
gone, she could prevail with him to take us all in: but
then she was afraid we must go on board immediately,
the same night.

" We begged of her to send to his house, for we knew
not what to do; for, as we had no money, we had no
lodging, and wanted nothing but to be on board. We
looked upon this as a mighty favour that she sent to the
master's house, and, to our greater joy, she brought us
word, about an hour after, that he was not gone, and was

at a tavern in the town, whither his boy had been to fetch him; and that he had sent word he would call there in his way home. This was all in our favour, and we were extremely pleased with it. In about an hour he came into the room to us. 'Where are these honest gentlemen soldiers,' said he, 'that are in such distress?' We all stood up, and paid our respects to him. 'Well, gentlemen,' said he, 'and is all your money spent?'

"'Indeed it is,' said one of our company, 'and we shall be infinitely obliged to you, sir, if you will give us a passage. We shall be very willing to do any thing we can in the ship, though we are not seamen.'

"'Why,' said he, 'were none of you ever at sea in your lives?'

"'No,' said we, 'not one of us.'

"'You will be able to do me no service, then; for you will all be sick. However, for my good landlady's sake here, I'll do it. But are you all ready to go on board; for I go on board myself this very night.'

"'Yes, sir,' said we again, 'we are ready to go this very minute.'

"'No, no,' said he, very kindly, 'we'll drink together. Come, landlady, make these honest gentlemen a sneaker of punch.'

"We looked at one another, for we knew that we had no money; and he perceived it. 'Come, come,' said he, 'don't be concerned at your having no money: my landlady here, and I, never part with dry lips. Come, good wife, make the punch, as I bid you.'

"We thanked him, and said, 'God bless you, noble captain!' a hundred times over, being overjoyed at our good luck. While we were drinking the punch, he told the landlady he would step home, and order the boat to come at high water, and bade her get something for supper, which she did.

"In less than an hour our captain returned, and came up to us, and blamed us that we had not drunk the punch out. 'Come,' said he, 'don't be bashful; when that's out, we can have another. When I am obliging poor men, I love to do it handsomely.'

"We drank on, and drank the punch out; more was brought up, and he pushed it about apace; then came up a leg of mutton. I need not say we fed heartily, being several times told we should pay nothing. After supper, ne bade my landlady ask if the boat was come; and she brought word, No, it was not high water by a great deal. Then more punch was called for, and, as was afterwards confessed, something more than ordinary was put into it, so that, by the time the punch was drunk out, we were all intoxicated; and as for me, I fell asleep.

"At last I was roused, and told that the boat was come: so I and my drunken comrades tumbled out, almost one over another, into the boat, and away we went with our captain. Most of us, if not all, fell asleep till after some time, though how much, or how far going, we knew not. The boat stopped, and we were awaked, and told we were at the ship's side, which was true, and with much help, and holding us, for fear we should fall overboard, our captain, as we termed him, called us thus:—

Here: boatswain, take care of these gentlemen; give hem good cabins, and let them turn in to sleep, for they are very weary.' And so indeed we were, and very drunk too.

"Care was taken of us, according to order, and we were put into very good cabins, where we were sure to go immediately to sleep. In the mean time, the ship, which was indeed just ready to go, and only on notice given had come to anchor for us at Shields, weighed, stood over the bar, and went off to sea; and when we awaked, and began to peep abroad, which was not till near noon the next day, we found ourselves a great way at sea, the land in sight indeed, but at a great distance, and all going merrily on for London, as I thought. We were very well used, and very well satisfied with our condition, for about three days, when we began to inquire, whether we were not almost in the Channel, and how much longer it would be before we should come into the river? 'What river?' said one of the men. 'Why, the Thames,' said my Captain Jack. 'The Thames!' answered the sailor, 'what d'ye mean by that? What! ha'n't you had time enough to be sober yet?' So Captain Jack said no more, but looked very silly, when, a while after, some other of us asked the same question, and the seamen, who knew nothing of the cheat, began to smell a rat, and turning to the other Englishman who came with us, 'Pray,' said he, 'where do you fancy you are going, that you ask so often about it?' 'Why, to London,' said he; 'where should we be going? We agreed with the captain to carry us to London.'

"'Not with the captain,' said he; 'I dare say, poor men, you are all cheated; and I thought so when I saw you come aboard with that kidnapping rogue Gilliman: you are all betrayed, for the ship is bound to Virginia.' As soon as we heard this news, we were raving men, drew our swords, and swore revenge; but we were soon overpowered, and carried before the captain, who told us, he was sorry for what had happened, but that he had no hand in it, and it was out of his power to help us; and he let us know very plainly what our condition was, namely, that we were put on board his ship as servants to Maryland, to be delivered to a person there; but that, however, if we would be quiet and orderly in his ship, he would use us well in the passage; but if we were unruly, we must be handcuffed, and kept between decks; for it was his business to take care no disturbance happened in the ship.

"'No hand in it! D—n him,' said my Captain Jack aloud, 'do you think he is not a confederate in this villainy? Would any honest man receive innocent people on board his ship, and not inquire of their circumstances, but carry them away, and not speak to them? Why does he not set us on shore again? I tell you he is a villain. Why does he not complete his villainy, and murder us, and then he'll be free from our revenge?"

" All this discourse availed nothing, we were forced to be quiet, and had a very good voyage, no storms all the way; but just before we arrived, one of the Scotchmen asked the captain of the ship, whether he would sell us. 'Yes,' said he. 'Why then, sir,' said the Scotchman the devil will have you at the hinder end of the bargain

' Say you so ?" said the captain, smiling : ' well, well, let the devil and I alone to agree about that ; do you be quiet and behave civilly, as you should do.'

" When we came ashore, which was on the banks of a river they call Potomack, Jack said, ' I have something to say to you, captain ; that is, I have promised to cut your throat, and, depend upon it, I will be as good as my word.' Our captain or kidnapper, call him as you will, made no answer, but delivered us to the merchant to whom we were consigned, who again disposed of us as he thought fit ; and in a few days we were separated.

" As for my Captain Jack, to make short of the story, that desperate rogue had the good luck to have an easy, good master, whom he abused very much ; for he took an opportunity to run away with a boat, with which his master entrusted him and another to carry provisions to a plantation down the river. This boat and provisions they ran away with, and sailed north to the bottom of the bay, as they call it, and there quitting the boat, they wandered through the woods, till they got into Pennsylvania, from whence they made shift to get a passage to New England, and from thence home ; where, falling in among his old companions, and to his old trade, he was at length taken and hanged about a month before I came to London, which was near twenty years afterwards.

" My part was harder at the beginning, though better at the latter end ; I was sold to a rich planter whose name was Smith. During this scene of life I had time to reflect on my past hours ; and though I had no great capacity of making a clear judgment, and very little reflections from conscience, yet it made some impressions upon me. I behaved myself so well, that my master took notice of me, and made me one of his overseers ; and was so kind as to send my note of my friend's hand for the 93*l.* before-mentioned, to his correspondent, who received and returned me the money. My good master a little time after, said to me, ' Colonel, don't flatter me, I love plain dealing : liberty is precious to every body, I give you yours, and will take care you shall be well

used by the country, and will get you a good plantation.'

" I insisted I would not quit his service for the best
plantation in Maryland; that he had been so good to me,
and I believed I was so useful to him, that I could not
think of it; and at last I added, I hoped he could not believe but that I had as much gratitude as a negro.

" He smiled, and said he would not be served upon
these terms; that he did not forget what he had promised, nor what I had done in his plantation; and that
he was resolved in the first place to give me my liberty;
so he pulled out a piece of paper, and threw it to me:
' There,' said he, ' is a certificate of your coming on
shore, and being sold to me for five years, of which you
have lived three with me, and now you are your own
master.'

" I bowed, and told him that I was sure if I was my
own master, I would be his servant as long as he would
accept of my services. He told me he would accept of
my services on these two conditions; first, that he would
give me 30l. per annum and my board, for my managing
the plantation I was then employed in. And secondly,
that at the same time he would procure me a new plantation to begin with upon my own account; ' for Jack,' said
he, smiling, ' though you are but a young man, 'tis time
you were doing something for yourself.'

Not long after, he purchased in my name about 300
acres of land near his own plantation, as he said, that I
might the better take care of his. My master, for such
I must still call him, generously gave it me; ' but Colonel,' said he, ' giving you this plantation is nothing at all,
if I do not assist you to support it, and to carry it on,
and therefore I will give you credit for whatever is needful; such as tools, provisions, and some servants to begin; materials for out-houses, and hogs, cows, horses for
stock, and the like: and I'll take it out of your returns
from abroad, as you can pay it.'

" Thus got to be a planter, and encouraged by a kind
benefactor, that I might not be wholly taken up with my
new plantation, he gave me freely, without any considera-

tion, one of his negroes, named Mouchat, whom I always esteemed.   Besides this, he sent me two servants more, a man and a woman; but these he put to my account as above.   Mouchat and these two fell immediately to work for me; they began with about two acres of land, which had but little timber on it at first, and most of that was cut down by the two carpenters who built my house.   It was a great advantage to me, that I had so bountiful a master who helped me out in every case; for this very first year I received a terrible blow: having sent a large quantity of tobacco to a merchant in London, by my master's direction, which arrived safe there, the merchant was ordered to make the return in a sorted cargo of goods for me, such as would have made a man of me all at once, but to my inexpressible terror and surprise, the ship was lost, and that just at the entrance into the Capes, that is to say, the mouth of the bay; some of the goods were recovered, but spoiled.   In short, nothing but the nails, tools, and iron-work were good for any thing; and though the value of them was very considerable in proportion to the rest; yet my loss was irreparably great, and indeed the greatness of the loss consisted in its being irreparable.

"I was perfectly astonished at the first news of the loss, knowing that I was in debt to my patron or master so much, that it must be several years before I should recover it; and, as he brought me the bad news himself, he perceived my disorder; that is to say, he saw I was in the utmost confusion, and a kind of amazement: and so indeed I was, because I was so much in debt.   But he spoke cheerfully to me, 'Come,' said he, 'do not be so discouraged; you may make up this loss.'   'No, sir,' said I, "that never can be, for it is my all, and I shall never be out of debt.'   'Well,' he answered, 'you have no creditor, however, but me; and, now, remember I once told you, I would make a man of you, and I will not disappoint you.'   For this further proof of his friendship I thanked him with more ceremony and respect than ever, because I thought myself more under the hatches than I was before: but he was as good as his word, for he did

not baulk me in the least of anything I wanted ; and as I
had more iron-work saved out of the ship in proportion
than I wanted, I supplied him with some part of it, and
took up some linen and clothes and other necessaries from
him in exchange. And now I began to increase visibly ;
I had a large quantity of land cured, freed from timber,
and a very good crop of tobacco in view, and I got three
servants more, and one negro ; so that I had five white
servants and two negroes ; and with this my affairs went
very well on ; the first year, indeed, I took my wages or
salary of 30*l.* a-year, because I wanted it very much ;
but the second and third year I resolved not to take it,
but to leave it in my benefactor's hands, to clear off the
debt I had contracted.

" At the same time my thoughts dictated to me, that
though this was the foundation of my new life, yet it was
not the superstructure, and that I might still be born for
greater things than these ; that it is honesty and virtue
alone that made men rich and great, and gave them fame,
as well as figure in the world, and therefore I was to lay
my foundation in these, and expect what might follow in
time. To help these thoughts, as I had learned to read
and write when I was in Scotland, so I began now to love
books, and particularly had an opportunity of reading
some very considerable ones, some of which I bought at
a planter's house who was lately dead and his goods sold,
and others I borrowed. I considered my present state of
life to be my mere youth, though I was now above thirty
years old, because in my youth I had learned nothing ;
and if my daily business, which was now great, would
have permitted, I would have been content to have gone
to school. However, fate, which had something else in
store for me, threw an opportunity into my hand, namely,
a clever fellow that came over a transported felon from
Bristol and fell into my hands for a servant. He had
led a loose life, he acknowledged, and being driven to extremities, took to the highway, for which, had he been
taken, he would have been hanged ; but falling into some
low-prized rogueries afterwards, for want of opportunity

for worse, he was caught, condemned, and transported, and, as he said, was glad he came off so.

"He was an excellent scholar, and I perceiving it, asked him one time if he could give a method how I might learn the Latin tongue; he said, smiling, yes, he could teach it me in three months, if I would let him have books, or even without books if he had time. I told him a book would become his hand better than a hoe, and if he could promise to make me but understand Latin enough to read it and understand other languages by it, I would ease him of the labour which I was now obliged to put him to; especially if I was assured that he was fit to receive that favour of a kind master. In short, I made him to me, what my kind benefactor made me to him: and from him I gained a fund of knowledge infinitely more valuable than the rate of a slave, which was what I paid for it;—but of this hereafter.

"In this posture I went on for twelve years, and was very successful in my plantation, and had gotten by means of my master's favour, whom now I called my friend, a correspondent in London, with whom I traded; shipped over my tobacco to him, and received European goods in return, such as I wanted to carry on my plantation, and sufficient to sell to others also. In this interval, my good friend and benefactor died; and I was left very disconsolate on account of my loss, for it was indeed a great loss to me; he had been a father to me, and I was like a forsaken stranger without him. Though I knew the country, and the trade too, well enough, and had for some time chiefly carried on his whole business for him; yet I seemed greatly at a loss now my counsellor and my chief supporter was gone, and I had no confident to communicate myself to, on all occasions, as formerly; but there was no remedy. I was, however, in a better condition to stand alone than ever: I had a very large plantation, and had near seventy negroes, and other servants.

"I now looked upon myself as one buried alive in a remote part of the world, where I could see nothing at all, and hear but little of what was seen, and that little not till at least half a year after it was done, and sometimes a year or more; and in a word, the old reproach often came in my way, namely, that even this was not yet the life of a gentleman. However, I now began to frame my thoughts for a voyage to England, resolving then to act as I should see cause, but with a secret resolution to see more of the world if possible, and realise those things to my mind, which I had hitherto only entertained remote ideas of by the help of books.

"It was three years after this before I could get things in order fit for my leaving the country: in this time I delivered my tutor from his bondage, and would have given him his liberty, but to my great disappointment I found that I could not empower him to go for England till his time was expired according to the certificate of his transportation, which was registered: so I made him one of my overseers, and thereby raised him gradually to a prospect of living in the same manner, and by the like steps, that my good benefactor raised me, only that I did not assist him to enter upon planting for himself as I was assisted, neither was I upon the. spot to do it; but this man by his diligence and honest application delivered himself, even unassisted any farther than by making him an overseer, which was only a present ease and deliverance from the hard labour and fare which he endured as a servant. However, in this trust he behaved so faithfully, and so diligently, that it recommended him in the country, and, when I came back, I found him in circumstances very different from what I left him in; besides his being my principal manager for near twenty years, as you shall hear in its place.

"I was now making provision for my going to England, after having settled my plantation in such hands as were fully to my satisfaction. My first work was, to furnish myself with such a stock of goods and money as might be sufficient for my occasions abroad, and, particularly, might allow to make large returns to Maryland for the use and supply of all my plantations; but when I came to look nearer into the voyage, it occurred to me that it would not be prudent to put my cargo all on board the same ship that I went in: so I shipped, at several times, five hundred hogsheads of tobacco, in several ships, for England, giving notice to my correspondent in London, that I would embark about such a time to come over myself, and ordering him to insure for a consider able sum proportioned to the value of my cargo.

"About two months after this I left the place, and embarked for England in a stout ship carrying 24 guns, and about 600 hogsheads of tobacco ; and we left the Capes of Virginia on the first of August ———. We had a very sour and rough voyage for the first fortnight, though it was in a season so generally noted for good weather.   We met with a storm, and our ship was greatly damaged, and some leaks we sprung, but not so bad but by the diligence of the seamen they were stopped ; after which we had tolerable weather and a good sea, till we came into the soundings, for so they call the mouth of the British Channel.   In the gray of the morning, a French privateer, of 26 guns, appeared, and crowded after us with all the sail she could make.   Our captain exchanged a broadside or two with her, which was terrible work to me ; for I had never seen such before ; the Frenchman's guns having raked us, and killed and wounded six of our men.   In short, after a fight long enough to show us that if we would not be taken, we must resolve to sink by her side, for there was no room to expect deliverance, and a fight long enough to save the master's credit, we were taken, and the ship carried away for St. Malo's.   I had, however, besides my being taken, the mortification to be detained on board the cruiser, and to see the ship I was in, manned by Frenchmen, set sail from us.   I afterwards heard that she was re-taken by an English man-of-war, and carried into Portsmouth.

"The Rover cruised abroad again, in the mouth of the channel, for some time, and took a ship richly laden, bound homeward from Jamaica.   This was a noble prize for the rogues, and they hastened away with her to St. Malo's ; and from thence I went to Bourdeaux, where the captain asked me if I would be delivered up a state prisoner, get myself exchanged, or pay three hundred crowns.   I desired time to write to my correspondent in

England, who sent me a letter of credit, and in about six weeks I was exchanged for a merchant prisoner in Plymouth. I got passage from hence to Dunkirk, on board a French vessel; and having a certificate of an exchanged prisoner from the intendant of Bourdeaux, I had a passport given me to go into the Spanish Netherlands, and so whither I pleased. I went to Ghent, afterwards to Newport, where I took the packet-boat, and came over to England, landing at Deal instead of Dover, the weather forcing us into the Downs. When I came to London, I was very well received by my friend to whom I had consigned my effects; for all my goods came safe to hand, and the overseers I had left behind had shipped, at several times, four hundred hogsheads of tobacco, to my correspondent, in my absence. So that I had above 1000*l.* in my factor's hands, and two hundred hogsheads besides, left in hand, unsold.

" I had nothing to do now but entirely to conceal myself from all that had any knowledge of me before; and this was the easiest thing in the world to do, for I was grown out of every body's knowledge, and most of those I had known, were grown out of mine.

" My Captain who went with me, or rather who carried me away, I found by inquiring at the proper place, had been rambling about the world, come to London, fallen into his old trade, which he could not forbear, and growing an eminent highwayman, had made his exit at the gallows after a life of fourteen years' most exquisite and successful rogueries; the particulars of which would make, as I observed, an admirable history. My other brother Jack, whom I called Major, followed the like wicked trade; but was a man of more gallantry and generosity, and having committed innumerable depredations upon mankind, had yet always so much dexterity as to bring himself off, till at length he was laid fast in Newgate, and loaded with irons, and would certainly hav gone the same way as the Captain, but he was so dexterous a rogue, that no gaol, no fetters would hold him; and he and two more found means to knock off their irons, worked their way through the wall of the prison, and let

themselves down on the outside, in the night. So escaping, they found means to get into France, where he followed the same trade, and that with so much success,
that the Major grew famous by the name of Anthony,
and had the honour with three of his comrades, whom
he had taught the English way of robbing generously, as
they called it, without murdering, or wounding, or ill-
using those they robbed, to be broken upon the wheel, at
the Grève in Paris.

"All these things I found means to be fully informed
of, and to have a long account of the particulars of their
conduct from some of their comrades, who had the good
fortune to escape, and whom I got the knowledge of, without letting them so much as guess at who I was, or upon
what account I inquired.

"I was now at the height of my good fortune, and got
the name of a great merchant. I lived single, and in
lodgings, and kept a French servant, being very desirous
of improving myself in that language, and received five
or six hundred hogsheads a year from my own plantations, and spent my time in that and supplying my people with necessaries at Maryland, as they wanted them.

"In this private condition I continued about two years
more, when the devil, owing me a spleen ever since I refused being a thief, paid me home with interest, by laying a snare in my way which had almost ruined me.

"There dwelt a lady in the house opposite to the house
I lodged in, who made an extraordinary figure, and was
a most beautiful person. She was well bred, sang admirably fine, and sometimes I could hear distinctly, the
houses being over against one another in a narrow court.
This lady put herself so often in my way, that I could
not in good manners forbear taking notice of her, and
giving the ceremony of my hat when I saw her at her
window, or at the door, or when I passed her in the
court ; so that we became almost acquainted at a distance.
Sometimes she also visited at the house in which I lodged, and it was generally contrived that I should be introduced when she came. And thus, by degrees. we became
more intimately acquainted, and often conversed togethei

in the family, but always in public, at least for a great while. I was a mere boy in the affair of love, and knew the least of what belonged to a woman, of any man in Europe of my age; the thoughts of a wife, much less of a mistress, had never so much as taken the least hold of my head, and I had been, till now, as perfectly unacquainted with the sex, and as unconcerned about them, as I was when I was ten years old, and lay in a heap of ashes at the glass-house.

" She attacked me without ceasing, with the fineness of her conduct, and with arts which were impossible to be ineffectual. She was ever, as it were, in my view, often in my company, and yet kept herself so on the reserve, so surrounded continually with obstructions, that for several months after she could perceive I sought an opportunity to speak to her, she rendered it impossible, nor could I ever break in upon her, she kept her guard so well.

" This rigid behaviour was the greatest mystery that could be, considering, at the same time, that she never declined my seeing her, or conversing with me in public; but she held it on. She took care never to sit next to me, that I might slip no paper into her hand, or speak softly to her. She kept somebody or other always between, that I could never come up to her. And thus, as if she was resolved really to have nothing to do with me, she held me at bay several months. In short, we came nearer and nearer every time we met, and at last gave the world the slip, and were privately married, to avoid ceremony, and the public inconvenience of a wedding.

" No sooner were we married, but she threw off the mask of her gravity and good conduct, and carried it to such an excess, that I could not but be dissatisfied at the expense of it. In about a twelvemonth she was brought to bed of a fine boy, and her lying-in cost me as near as I can now remember, 136*l.* which, she told me, she thought was a trifle. Such jarring continually between us produced a separation; and she demanded 300*l.* per annum for her maintenance. This, however, made me look more closely into her conduct, and, by means of two trusty agents, I was enabled to detect her infidelity, and to sue her before the Ecclesiastical Court, from which I obtained a divorce.

" Things being at this pass, I resolved to go over to France, where I fell into company with some Irish officers of the regiment of Dillon, where I bought a company, and so went into the army directly. Our regiment, after I had been some time in it, was commanded into Italy ; and one of the most considerable actions I was in, was the famous attack upon Cremona, in the Milanese, where the Germans being treacherously let into the town by night, through a kind of common sewer, surprised the town, and took the Duke de Villeroy prisoner, beating the French troops into the citadel, but were in the middle of their victory so boldly attacked by two Irish regiments, that, after a most desperate fight, and not being able to break through us to let in their friends, they were obliged to quit the town, to the eternal honour of those Irish regiments. Having been in several campaigns, I was permitted to sell my company, and got the Chevalier's brevet for a colonel, in case of raising troops for him in Great Britain. I accordingly embarked on board the French fleet for the Frith of Edinburgh ; but they overshot their landing-place ; and this delay gave time to the English fleet, under Sir George Byng, to come to an anchor just as we did.

" Upon this surprise the French admiral set sail, and crowding away to the north, got the start of the English fleet, and escaped, with the loss of one ship only, to Dunkirk ; and glad I was to set my foot on shore again, for all the while we were thus flying for our lives I was under the greatest terror imaginable, and nothing but halters and gibbets ran in my head, concluding that, if I had been taken, I should certainly have been hanged.

' I took post horses for Flanders, and at last got safe once more to London, from which place I embarked for Virginia, and had a tolerable voyage thither, only that we met with a pirate ship, which plundered us of every thing they could come at which was for their turn ; but, to give the rogues their due, though they were the most abandoned wretches that ever were seen, they did not use us ill; and, as to my loss, it was not considerable.

" I found all my affairs in very good order at Virginia, my plantations prodigiously increased; and my manager, who first inspired me with travelling thoughts, and made me master of any knowledge worth naming, received me with a transport of joy, after a ramble of four and twenty years. I was exceedingly satisfied with his management, for he had improved a very large plantation of his own at the same time : however, I had the mortification to see two or three of the Preston gentlemen there, who being prisoners of war, were spared from the public execution, and sent over to that slavery, which, to gentlemen, must be worse than death.

" During my stay here, I married a maid I brought over from England, who behaved herself, for some time, extraordinary well, but at last played the fool and died; and I not liking to stay long in a place where I was so much talked of, sent to one of my correspondents for a copy of the general free pardon then granted, and wherein it was manifest I was fully included.

" After I had settled my affairs, and left the same faithful steward, I again embarked for England, and, after a trading voyage, (for we touched at several places in our way,) I arrived safe, determining to spend the remainder of my life in my native country; for here I enjoy the moments which I had never before known how to employ, and endeavour to atone, as far as possible, for the vices of an ill-spent life.

" Perhaps, when I wrote these things down, I did not foresee that the writings of our own stories would be so much the fashion in England or so agreeable to others to read, as I find custom, and the humour of the times, have caused them to be. If any one that reads my story pleases to make the same just reflections which I acknowledge I ought to have made, he will reap the benefit of my misfortunes, perhaps, more than I have done myself. It is evident, by the long series of changes and turns which have appeared in the narrow compass of one private mean person's life, that the history of men's lives

may be in many ways made useful and instructive to
those who read them, if moral and religious improvement and reflections are made by those who write them."

WHITNEY.

THIS notorious malefactor was born at Stevenage in
Hertfordshire, and served an apprenticeship to a butcher.
He often mentioned that he was happily disappointed in
his first attempt to steal.

He and his master went to Romford to purchase calves,
and there was an excellent one that they would fain have
had in their possession, but the owner and they could not
agree about the price.   As the owner of the calf kept an
alehouse, they went in to taste his ale.   While they were
enjoying themselves, but lamenting the loss of the calf,
Whitney whispered to his master, that it would be foolish
in them to give money for the calf, when they might
have it for nothing.   The good butcher understood his
meaning and entered into his plan.   In the mean while,
they sat still drinking, waiting their opportunity.

Unfortunately for their scheme, a fellow who travelled
the country with a she-bear, had put up at the house
where the butchers were drinking.   The landlord had no
place to put up this bear without removing the calf to
another house, which was accordingly done.   The
butchers continued carousing until it was dark, then hav
ing cheerfully paid their reckoning, in the hope that the
calf would reimburse them, they left the house, and lurked
about the fields until all was quiet.   Approaching the
place where they had seen the calf put up, Whitney was
sent in to fetch it out.   The bear was resting her wearied
limbs when Whitney took hold of them, and was astonished to find the hair of the calf had suddenly grown to such
a length.   Bruin arose upon all-fours, opining, we suppose, that it was her master about to show her in his
usual manner.   But she no sooner discovered that it was
a stranger who thus rudely assailed her, than she seized

him with her two fore-paws and hugged him most love-
ingly to her bosom. The master, surprised that he was
so long in bringing out the calf, began to chide him for
his delay. Whitney cried out, that he could not get
away himself, and he believed that the devil had hold of
him. "If it is the old boy," replied the master, "bring
him out, as I should like to see what kind of an animal
he is." His importunities at length brought the butcher
to his assistance, when they discovered their mistake, and
with no small difficulty disentangled Whitney from the
fraternal hug of honest bruin; which having done, they
proceeded home without their prey, determined to attempt
stealing calves no more.

Our young adventurer now abandoned the business of
buying and slaying animals, and took the George inn at
Cheshunt. In order to make the most of it, he entertained
all sorts of people, whether good or bad. Disappointment
attended him in this as well as his former employment,
and he was constrained to shut up his doors.

He now went up to London, the common haunt of all
profligates, where he lived in the most irregular manner,
giving himself wholly up to villany. After practising
the tricks of sharpers for a time, he at length commenced
business upon the highway. He was one day standing
at the door of a mercer's shop, when two young ladies,
apparently of fashion, passed by, elegantly dressed, one
of whom inquired if he had any silks of the newest pat-
terns. Whitney replied, that he had none at present, but
should soon have some home from the weaver. He then
requested their address, that the goods, when they came
to hand, might be sent to them. They were rather at a
loss; one of them, however, answered, that they were
only lately come to town, and did not remember the name
of their street. They added, that, as it was not far off,
if he would accompany them, they would show him their
habitation.

This was just what he wanted; therefore, going into
the shop, as if to leave orders, he hastened along with
the ladies—they supposing he was the silk-mercer, and
he that they were actually ladies of fortune, whom he

might have an opportunity of robbing, either present.y or at some future period. Upon their arrival, he was introduced into an elegant parlour, and a collation placed upon the table, with some excellent wine, of which he was requested to partake. He was soon left alone with one of the ladies, and discovering his mistake, was resolved to have some more sport at the expense of a silk-mercer, since he had been taken for one.

Whitney went to a mercer, and mentioning the name of a lady of quality in the neighbourhood, said he had been sent by her to request that the mercer would send one of his men with several pieces of his best silks, as the lady was to purchase a gown and petticoat. The shop-keeper readily consented, and one of the apprentices was dispatched along with him. To deceive the young man, and render it impossible for him to discover the place where he should stop, he conducted him through various streets and lanes, until he at last halted at a house which had an entry into another street; here he took the parcel, and desired the lad to stand at the door while he went in to show the ladies the silks. Taking the parcel, he went in, and inquired for some person who he was certain was not there. He then requested liberty to pass through to the next street, which would shorten his way. This being granted, he left the mercer's man to wait for his return.

Having thus fortunately succeeded, and been able to fulfil his promise of giving one of the above-mentioned ladies a silk dress, he hastened to their dwelling where they divided the spoil. For some days he remained there, indulging in all manner of riot and excess, until, satiated, he returned to his labour of seeking new adventures. Determined, however, that no other person but himself should reap the fruits of his ingenuity, he wrote a letter to the mercer, informing him where he would find his silks. Accordingly, having obtained a warrant, the house of the two damsels was searched, the pieces found, and both the ladies were sentenced to Bridewell to undergo whipping, and to submit to hard labour.

When Whitney was confirmed in his business, he met a gentleman on Bagshot heath, whom he commanded to stand and deliver. On which the other remarked, "It is well you spoke first, sir, for I was just going to make a similar demand." "Why then you are a gentleman thief?" Whitney cried. "Yes," said the stranger, "but I have had very bad success to-day, for I have been riding up and down all this morning, without meeting with any prize." Whitney upon this wished him better luck, and took his leave.

At night, Whitney and the above gentleman put up a the same inn, when the latter related to some other travellers by what stratagem he had evaded being robbed upon the road. Whitney having changed his dress, the gentleman did not recognise him. Whitney also heard him whisper to one of the company, that by this contrivance he had saved a hundred pounds. That person informed him, that he had a considerable sum upon him, and that, if agreeable, he would travel next day with him. Our adventurer overheard the conversation, and resolved, without being solicited, to make one of the party. In the morning they commenced their journey, and Whitney followed about a quarter of an hour after. Their conversation turned upon the best means to deceive the highwaymen; and our adventurer's meditations were, how he should be revenged upon his quondam friend for the cheat he had received the day before.

Whitney soon overtook them, and riding before, turned suddenly about, presented his pistols, and commanded them to stand and deliver. "We were going to say the same to you, sir!" "Were you so?" replied our hero, "and are you then of my profession?" "Yes," said they both. "If you are, I suppose you remember the old proverb, that two of a profession cannot agree together, so that you must not expect any favour on that score. But to be plain with you gentlemen, I know you very well, and must have your hundred pounds, sir,—and your considerable sum, sir,"—turning first to the one, and then to the other,—"otherwise I shall be bold to send a brace of bullets through each of your heads. You, Messieurs Highwaymen, should have kept your secret a little longer, and not have boasted so soon of having outwitted a thief

There is now nothing for you but to deliver or die !" These words put them in sad consternation : they were very unwilling to lose their money, but more unwilling to lose their lives; of two evils, therefore, they preferred choosing the least. The one produced his hundred pounds first, and the other gentleman his considerable sum, which was a good deal more.

At another time, our adventurer met with an old miser named Hull, on Hounslow Heath. The word of command being given, he trembled in every joint, and using the most piteous tones and humiliating complaints, said, that he was a very poor man and had a large family, and he would be hard-hearted indeed who would take his money. He added, besides, a great deal more concerning the illegality of such an action, and how dangerous it was to engage in evil courses. Whitney, who knew him well, cried out in a violent passion, " Sirrah, you pretend to preach morality to an honester man than yourself. Is it not more generous to take a man's money from him bravely, than to grind him to death by exacting eight or ten per cent. under cover of serving him ? You make a prey of all mankind, and necessity in an honest man is often the means of his falling into your hands, who are sure to be the means of undoing him. I am a man of more honour than to show any compassion to one whom I esteem an enemy to the whole species. For once, at least, I shall oblige you to lend me what you have, without interest or bond, so make no words !" Old Hull, upon this, reluctantly pulled out eighteen pounds, telling him at the same time that he would see him sometime ride up Holborn Hill backwards. Whitney was retiring until he heard these words, when, returning, he drew Hull off his horse, and putting him on again with his face towards the tail, and tying his legs, " Now," said he, " you old rogue, let me see what a figure a man makes when he rides backwards, and let me have the pleasure at least of seeing you first in that posture ;" so giving the horse a whip, the animal proceeded at a desperate pace until it came to Hounslow Town, where the people untied him, after they had enjoyed themselves at his expense.

Life of Whitney.   Page 200.

In the course of Whitney's rambles, he one day put up at an inn at Doncaster, and lived in a dashing style, as he had then plenty of money. He was informed that the landlord was a complete miser and sharper, and that he would not spare the smallest sum to a poor relation of his, who lived in the neighbourhood. Accordingly, Whitney resolved to exert his ingenuity upon his landlord; and gave out that he had a good estate, and travelled merely for his own amusement. He continued to pay his bills regularly, until he supposed that his credit would be sufficiently established. Then he one day mentioned to his landlord, that as his money was run short, he would be obliged to him for credit until he received remittances. "Oh, dear sir, you need not give yourself any uneasiness about such a thing as this; every thing in my house is at your service; and I shall think myself honoured if you use me as your friend." With abundance of eloquence, our adventurer returned the compliment. He continued to live at his table,—his horse was well fed with corn and hay, while Whitney, almost every day, took a ride to some neighbouring village along with the landlord and some others, who were all proud of the honour he had done them.

It happened that there was an annual fair in that place, and in the morning a box came directed to him; opening it, he took out a letter, and, having read it, locked the box, and delivered it to the landlady, saying, that it would be safer in her custody than in his own. Having gone to see the fair, he returned in great haste in the afternoon, desiring his horse to be instantly dressed, as he had seen a horse in the fair for which he was desirous to exchange his own, adding, that he was determined to have the animal. He then requested the landlady to give him his box; but he was informed that she was gone to the fair. Hereupon he affected to burst out into a violent passion, saying, that he supposed she had locked up what he committed to her keeping :—"If she has," said he, "I had rather have given ten guineas, for I have no money but what is in her possession." Inquiry was made, and it was found to be as he had said, which put him into a still greater rage. This was, however, what he both wished and expected,—the whole being of his own invention. The landlord was informed of his rage, and the cause of it, and entreated that he would be easy, as he would lend him the sum he wanted until his wife came home. Our hero was greatly distressed that he should have to borrow money when he had so much of his own ; but as there was no other method of obtaining cash to purchase his favourite horse, he accepted of the proffered loan : with an imperious and haughty air, demanding that his bill might be prepared for payment forthwith.

With forty guineas he rode to the fair ; but instead of inquiring for any other horse, he spurred his own through the crowd, and hastened to London. The people of the inn waited long for his return that evening; but, as he had frequently stayed two or three days at once in his rambles through the country, they suspected no fraud. After waiting with no small impatience for a whole week, the landlord resolved to break open the box, and went to the magistrates of the place, accompanied by witnesses. It is needless to record his chagrin and mortification, when he found the box filled with sand and stones.

In London, Whitney was apprehended upon the information of one of those abandoned females who live by betraying the simple ones of their own, and by robbing and plundering the profligate of the other sex. He was committed, tried, and condemned at the following sessions. The judge, before passing sentence, made an excellent speech to him and the other malefactors, in strong terms exhibiting the nature of their several crimes ; and in particular addressed himself to Whitney, exhorting him to a sincere repentance, as there could be no hope of a pardon to him after a course of so many villanies.

At the place of execution, Whitney addressed the multitude in nearly the following terms :—" I have been a great offender, both against God and my country, by transgressing all laws, both human and divine. I believe there is not one here present but has often heard my name before my confinement, and seen the long catalogue of my crimes, which have since been made public. Way then should I pretend to vindicate a life stained with so many enormous deeds? The sentence passed upon me is just, and I can see the footsteps of a Providence, which, before, I had profanely laughed at, in my apprehension and conviction. I hope the sense which I have of these things has enabled me to make my peace with Heaven, the only thing which is now of any concern to me. Join in your prayers with me, my dear countrymen, that God would not forsake me in my last moments." Having spent a few minutes in prayer, he suffered, in the 34th year of his age, on the 19th of December 1694.

TIM BUCKELEY.

TIM was reared to the useful occupation of a shoe-maker, but leaving his master, he came to London, and soon found out companions suited to his disposition. He and his associates frequented an ale-house at Wapping; and one day being run short of cash, Tim asked the land-lord for ten shillings, which he refused. Tim was so exasperated, that, along with some of his associates, he broke into his house, and bound him, his wife, and maid. Whilst Tim was about this operation, the landlord conjured him to be favourable. " No, no, you must not expect any favour from my hands, whose prodigality makes you lord it over the people here like a boatswain over a ship's crew; but I shall go to another part of the town, where I will be more civilly used, and spend a little of your money there." Accordingly, Tim and his companions robbed the house of forty pounds, three silver tankards, a silver watch, and three gold rings.

Upon another day Tim was airing in Hyde-park-corner, and met with Dr. Cateby, the famous mountebank. At the words " Stand and deliver!" the doctor went into a long harangue about the honesty of his calling, and of the great difficulty with which he made a living. Tim laughed heartily, saying, " Quacks pretend to honesty!

there is not such a pack of cheating knaves in the nation. Their impudence is intolerable for deceiving honest simple people, and pretending that more men were not slain at the battle of the Boyne, than they have recovered from death, or beckoned their souls back when they have been many leagues from their bodies: therefore, deliver! or this pistol shall put a stop to your further ramblings and deception." The doctor preferring his life to his gold, presented Tim with six guineas, and a watch, to show him how to keep time while spending the money.

Tim was once apprehended by a baker, in the character of a constable, and sent to Flanders as a soldier. He deserted, and returning to London, one day met with the baker's wife. He presented a pistol, and demanded her money; she exclaimed, " Is this justice or conscience, sir !" " Don't tell me of justice, for I hate her as much as your husband can, because her scales are even ! And as for conscience, I have as little of that as any baker in England, who cheats other people's bellies to fill his own! —Nay, a baker is a worse rogue than a tailor; for, whereas the latter commonly pinches his cabbage from the rich, the former, by making his bread too light, robs all without distinction, but chiefly the poor, for which he deserves hanging more than I, or any of my honest fraternity." Then, taking from her eleven shillings and two gold rings, he sent her home to relate her adventure to her husband.

Tim next stealing a good horse, commenced upon the highway, and meeting with a pawnbroker by whom he had lost some articles, he commanded him to stand and deliver. The pawnbroker entreated for favour, saying " that it was a very hard thing that honest people could not go about their lawful business without being robbed." " You talk of honesty, who live by fraud and oppression! —your shop, like the gates of hell, is always open, in which you sit at the receipt of custom, and having got the spoils of the needy, you hang them up in rank and file, like so many trophies of victory. To your shop all sorts of garments resort, as on a pilgrimage. Thou art the treasurer of the Thieves' Exchequer, for which pur pose you keep a private warehouse from whence you ship them off wholesale, or retail, according to pleasure. Nay, the poor and the oppressed have often to pay their own cloth, before they can receive them back by your exorbitant exactions. Come, come, blood-sucker, open your purse-strings, or this pistol shall send you where you are sure to go sooner or later." The poor pawnbroker did not, however, wish to visit his old friend before his time; he therefore ransomed his life at the expence of twenty-eight guineas, a gold watch, a silver box, and two gold rings.

Upon another occasion, Tim fortunately met with a stock-jobber (who had prosecuted him for felony), and robbed him of forty-eight guineas. He requested something to carry him home. Tim refused, saying, "I have no charity for you stock-jobbers, who rise and fall like the ebbing and flowing of the tide, and whose paths are as unfathomable as the ocean. The grasshopper in the Royal Exchange is an emblem of your character. What! give you something to carry you home out of the paltry sum of forty-eight guineas! I won't give you a farthing." He then bade him farewell until next meeting.

Though unexpected and unwished, it was not long before the stock-jobber reconnoitred Tim, and caused him to be apprehended and committed to Newgate. He was tried, and received sentence of death; but obtaining a reprieve, and afterwards a pardon, he was determined to be revenged of the man who would not give him rest to pursue his honest employment; he therefore set fire to a country-house belonging to him. To his no small chagrin, however, it was quenched before much harm was done.

Tim then went to Leicestershire, broke into a house seized eighty pounds, purchased a horse, and renewed his former mode of life. Thus mounted, he attacked a coach in which there were three gentlemen, and two footmen attending. Tim's horse being shot under him, he killed one of the gentlemen and a footman, but being overpowered, was committed to Nottingham gaol, and suffered the due reward of murder and robbery, at the age of twenty-nine, in the year 1701.

TOM JONES.

Tom was a native of Newcastle-upon-Tyne. His father was a clothier, whose business he followed until he was two-and-twenty years of age. In that period, however, the prominent dispositions of his mind were displayed, by extravagance, and running into debt. In order, therefore, to retrieve his circumstances, he went upon the highway.

Out of gratitude for his father's kindness, he commenced by robbing him of eighty pounds and a good horse. Unaccustomed to such work, he rode, under the impression that he was pursued and in danger of being taken, no less than forty miles. Arriving in Staffordshire, he attacked and robbed the stage-coach of a considerable booty. During the scuffle, several shots were fired at the passengers, but no injury was done.

A monkey belonging to one of the passengers, being tied behind the coach, was so frightened with the firing, that he broke his chain, and ran for his life. At night, as a countryman was coming over a gate, pug leaped out of the hedge upon his back, and clung very fast. The poor man, who had never seen such an animal, imagined that it was no less a person than the devil; and when he came home, thundered at the door. His wife looked out at the window, and asked him what he had got. "The devil!" cried he, and entreated that she would go to the parson, and beg his assistance. "Nay," quoth she, "you shall not bring the devil in here. If you belong to him, I don't; so be content to go without my company." Poor Hob was obliged to wait at his door, until one of his neighbours, wiser than the rest, came, and with a few apples and pears, dispossessed him of the devil, and got him for his pains. He accordingly carried him to the owner, and received a suitable reward.

Tom's next adventure was with a Quaker, who formerly kept a button shop, but, being reduced in his circumstances, he was going down to the country to avoid arrest. In this situation he was more afraid of a bailiff than a robber. Therefore, when Tom took hold of him by the coat, broadbrim very gravely said, "At whose suit dost thou detain me?"—"I detain thee on thy own suit, and my demand is for all thy substance." The Quaker having discovered his mistake, added, "Truly friend, I don't know thee, nor can I indeed imagine that thee and I had any dealings together."—"You shall find then," said Jones, "that we shall deal together now." He then presented his pistol. "Pray, neighbour, use no violence, for if thou carriest me to gaol, I am undone. I have fourteen guineas about me, and if that will satisfy thee, thou art welcome to take them. Here they are, and give me leave to assure thee, that I have frequently stopped the mouth of a bailiff with a much less sum, and made him affirm to my creditors that he could not find me." Jones received the money, and replied, "Friend, I am not such a rogue as thou takest me to be: I am no bailiff, but an honest generous highwayman."—"I shall not trouble myself," cried the Quaker, "about the distinction of names; if a man takes my money from me by force, it concerns me but little what he calls himself, or what his pretences may be for so doing."

At another time Tom met with Lord and Lady Wharton, and though they had three men attending, demanded their charity in his usual style. His lordship said, "Do you know me, sir, that you dare be so bold as to stop me upon the road?"—"Not I; I neither know nor care who you are. I am apt to imagine that you are some great man, because you speak so big; but, be as great as you will, sir, I must have you to know, that there is no man upon the road so great as myself; therefore, pray be quick in answering my demands, for delays may prove dangerous." Tom then received two hundred pounds, three diamond rings, and two gold watches.

Upon another day, Tom received intelligence that a gentleman was upon the road with a hundred pounds

He waited upon the top of a hill to welcome his approach. A steward of the gentleman discovered him, and suspecting his character, desired that the money might be given to him, and he would ride off with it, as the robber would not suspect him. This was done; Tom came forward, stopped the coach, and the gentleman gave him ten pounds. He was greatly enraged, and mentioned the sum that he knew the gentleman carried along with him In an instant, however suspecting the stratagem, he rode after the steward with all possible speed; but the latter observing him in pursuit, increased his pace, and reached an inn before Tom could overtake him.

After many similar adventures, Tom was apprehended for robbing a farmer's wife. He was so habituated to vice, that nothing but the gallows could arrest his course, and in the forty-second year of his age, he met with that fate, on the 25th April 1702.

ARTHUR CHAMBERS

ARTHUR CHAMBERS was of low extraction, and destitute of every amiable quality. From his very infancy he was addicted to pilfering; and the low circumstances of his parents being unable to support his extravagances, he had recourse to dishonest practices. It is even reported, that before he was dressed in boy's clothes, he committed several acts of theft.

The first thing which he attempted, was to learn, from an experienced master, all those cant words and phrases current among pickpockets, by which they distinguish one another. Chambers was soon an adept in this new language; and being well dressed, he was introduced to the better sort of company, and took occasion, when such opportunities offered, to rob his companions.

In a short time he was confined in Bridewell, to answer with hard labour for some small offence. Having obtained his liberty, he left the town, where he again began to be suspected, and went to Cornwall. His social turn gained him a reception in genteel companies, and he became a memorable character in the place. Before he left London, he provided himself with a large quantity of base crowns and half-crowns, which he uttered wherever he went. After many had been deceived, strict search was made, and Chambers detected. For this offence he was committed to gaol, where he remained a year and a half.

As he could no longer abide in Cornwall, he returned to London. Upon his arrival he went to an alehouse, and called for a pot of beer and a slice of bread and cheese. Having refreshed himself, he entered into conversation with some persons in a neighbouring box. The conversation turned upon the superior advantages of a country life, but was insensibly directed to that of robbery. Chambers, improving the hint, regretted that no better provision was made for suppressing such villanies; for, added he, death is too scarce a punishment for a man even if he robbed the whole world. "But why do I talk thus?" he continued; "if great offenders are suffered, well may the poor and necessitous say, we must live, and where is the harm of taking a few guineas from those who can spare them, or who, perhaps, have robbed others of them? For my own part, I look upon a pickpocket as a very useful person, as he draws his resources from the purses of those who would spend their money in gaming, or worse. Look ye, gentlemen, I can pick a pocket as well as any man in Britain, and yet, though I say it, I am as honest as the best Englishman breathing. Observe that country gentleman passing by the window there, I will engage to rob him of his watch, though it is scarcely five o'clock."

A wager of ten shillings was instantly taken, and Chambers hastened after the gentleman. He accosted him at the extremity of Long Lane, and pulling off his hat, asked if he could inform him the nearest way to Knave's acre. The stranger replied that he himself wished to know the way to Moorfields, which Chambers pointed out: and while the other kept his eyes fixed upon the places to which he directed him, he embraced an opportunity to rob him of his watch, and hastening back to the alehouse, threw down his plunder, and claimed the wager.

He next exerted his ingenuity upon a plain country-man, newly come to town. This rustic had got into the company of sharpers, and stood gazing at a gaming-table. Our adventurer stepping up, tapped him on the shoulder, and enquired what part of the country he came from, and if he was desirous to find a place as a gentleman's servant. Robin answered that it was his very errand to town, to find such a place. Chambers then said, that he could fit him to a hair. " I believe I can afford you my-self four pounds a-year standing wages, and six shillings a-week board wages, and all cast clothes, which are none of the worst." This was sufficient to make Robin almost leap out of his skin, for never before had such an offer been made to him. Having arranged every thing to his wish, Robin entered upon his new service. He received Chambers' cloak, threw it over his arm, and followed his master. Chambers ordered a coach, and Robin being placed behind, they drove off to an inn. Dinner being ordered, Robin sat down with his master, and made a hearty meal, the former in the meanwhile instructing him in all the tricks of the town, and inculcating the ne-cessity of his being always upon his guard. He informed him, also, that the servants of the inn would be request-ing him to join in play at cards, and that he was in dan-ger of being imposed upon; therefore, if he had any money upon him, it would be proper to give it to him, and he would receive it back when necessary. Robin, accordingly, pulled out his purse, and delivered all that he had, with which Chambers paid his dinner, and went off, leaving Robin to shift for himself, and to lament the loss of his money and his new master.

The next adventure of Chambers was directed against the innkeeper of the Greyhound, St. Alban's. His wife was rather handsome, and exceedingly facetious; and Chambers, being often there, was on terms of the great-est familiarity with the household. Directing his steps thither, and pretending to have been attacked by three

men near the inn, he went in with his clothes all besmeared. The travellers who were in the inn condoled
with him on his misfortune, and gave him a change of
clothes until his own should be cleaned. To make
amends to himself for this sad disaster, he invited six of
his fellow-travellers, with the landlord and his wife to
supper. The glass circulated pretty freely, and the wife
entertained them with several appropriate songs. Chambers was careful that her glass never remained long
empty. In a short time he saw with pleasure that all
his companions, with the solitary exception of the landlord, were sunk in the arms of sleep, and he proposed
that they should be conveyed to bed; whereupon two
or three stout fellows came to perform that office.
Chambers was so obliging as to lend his assistance, but
took care that their money and watches should pay for
his trouble.

Left alone with the landlord, he proposed that they
should have an additional bottle. Another succeeded
before the landlord was in a condition to be conveyed to
rest. In aiding the servants with the corpulent innkeeper, he discovered the geography of his bedroom, and
finding that the door was directly opposite to his own,
he retired, not to rest, but to plot and perfect his villany.

When he was convinced that the wine would work its
full effect upon the deluded pair, he revisited the bed-
chamber, waited some time, and extracted what property
he could most conveniently carry away; by the dawn of
day dressed himself in the best suit of clothes which his
bottle companions could afford, called for the horse of the
person whose clothes he now wore, left two guineas with
the waiter to pay his bill, gave half-a-crown to the ostler,
and rode off for London.

His first enterprise after his arrival was attacking an
Italian merchant upon the Exchange. He took him aside,
eagerly inquired what goods he had to dispose of, and,
entering into conversation, one of Chambers's accomplices
approaching, joined the conversation. Meanwhile, our
adventurer found means to extract from his pocket a

large purse of gold and his gold watch, which he delivered to his accomplice. Not satisfied with his firsi
success, and observing a silk handkerchief suspended
from his pocket, he walked behind him to seize it, bu.
was detected in the act, and kept fast hold of by the
merchant, who cried out lustily, " Thief! thief!"   In
this dilemma, Chambers's accomplice ran to the crier,
and requested him to give public proclamation, that if
any body had lost a purse of gold, upon giving proper
information it would be restored.   With the expectation
of finding his money again, the merchant let go his hold;
and in the crowd, Chambers and his friends retired with
their booty.

But Chambers was now resolved to perform an action
worthy of his talents. He hired the first-floor of a
house, and agreed with the landlord for 14s. a week.
Having, in the first instance, been mistaken for a man
of fortune, both from his appearance and style of living,
a mutual confidence was gradually established. When
his plot was matured, he one day entered, with a very
pensive and sorrowful look, the apartment of his landlord,
who anxiously inquired the cause of his great uneasiness; when Chambers, with tears in his eyes, informed
him, that he had just returned from Hampstead, where
he had witnessed the death of a beloved brother, who had
left him his sole heir, with an express injunction to convey his dear remains to Westminster Abbey. He therefore entreated the favour of being allowed to bring his
brother's remains at a certain hour to his house, that from
thence they might be conveyed to the place of their des-
tination, which very reasonable request was readily
granted by his unsuspecting landlord.

Chambers went off the next morning, leaving word,
that the corpse would be there at six o'clock in the evening. At the appointed hour, the hearse, with six horses,
arrived at the door. An elegant coffin, with six gilded
handles, was carried up-stairs, and placed upon the
dining-room table, and the horses were conveyed by the
men to a stable in the neighbourhood. They informed

the landlord, that Chambers was detained on business and would probably sleep that night in the Strand.

That artful rogue was, however, confined in the coffin, in which air-holes had been made, the screw-nails left unfixed, his clothes all on, with a winding-sheet wrapped over them, and his face blanched with flour. All the family were now gone to bed, except the maid-servant. Chambers arose from his confinement, went down stairs to the kitchen wrapped in his winding-sheet, sat down, and stared the maid in the face, who, overwhelmed with fear, cried out " A ghost! a ghost!" and ran up-stairs to her master's room, who chid her unreasonable fears, and requested her to return to bed, and compose herself. She, however, obstinately refused, and remained in the room.

In a short time, however, in stalked the stately ghost, took his seat, and conferred a complete sweat and a mortal fright upon all three who were present. Retiring from his station when he deemed it convenient, he continued, by the moving of the doors, and the noise raised through the house, to conceal his design : in the meantime, he went down stairs, opened the doors to his accomplices, who assisted in carrying off the plate, and every thing which could be removed, not even sparing the kitchen utensils. The maid was the first to venture from her room in the morning, and to inform her master and mistress of what had happened, who, more than the night before, chid her credulity in believing that a ghost could rob a house, or carry away any article out of it. In a little time, however, the landlord was induced to rise, from his bed, and to move down stairs, and found, to his astonishment and chagrin, that the whole of his plate, and almost the whole of his movables, were gone, for which he had only received in return an empty coffin.

A great many other stories of the like nature are told of Chambers; and it is well known, that for the few years he was permitted by singular good fortune to go at large, he committed as many artful and daring actions as were ever accomplished by one man.

At length, however, one Jack Hall, a chimney-sweeper, being apprehended, to save his own life made himself an evidence against Chambers, who, being cast upon that information, was, with two other notorious offenders, executed at Tyburn, in 1703, in the twenty-eighth year of his age.

RICHARD TURPIN.

THERE never, perhaps, was a man in the particular profession to which this notorious fellow devoted himself whose name was more familiar in the mouths of the common people than that of Richard Turpin. But, since it invariably happens that a certain proportion of curiosity respecting the life and actions of a man is sure to beget a corresponding desire to satisfy it, we cannot wonder if the perplexed biographer should sometimes resort to fiction to supply the deficiencies of fact. Hence it has happened that certain exploits have been attributed to Turpin which do not properly belong to him; amongst others, the unparalleled ride from York to London in an unprecedentedly short period, performed, it is averred, on a single horse. We have never been able to find any authentic account of this feat, nor have we, as yet, discovered any conceivable necessity that should compel him to such a rapid journey. Turpin was never tried but once, and that was, indeed, at York; but the reader will perceive that he had no opportunity of escape, nor did he attempt any thing of the kind after his first apprehension.

Richard Turpin was the son of John Turpin, of Hempstead in Essex, and was put apprentice to a butcher in Whitechapel, where he served his time, during which period he was frequently guilty of misdemeanors, and conducted himself in a loose and disorderly manner.

As soon as his time was up, he married, and set up in

business for himself at Suson in Essex, where, having no credit in the market, and no money in his pocket, he was shortly reduced to the necessity of maintaining himself by indirect practices; and, accordingly, very often used to rob the neighbouring gentry of sheep, lambs, and oxen.

Upon one occasion, he stole a couple of oxen from a farmer at Plaistow, which he caused to be conveyed to his own house and cut up. Two of the men belonging to the farm, having a suspicion of Turpin, went to his house, and seeing an ox slaughtered, were convinced of his guilt; and having traced the sale of the hides, returned to Suson to apprehend him. Turpin, apprized of their intention, left them in the front-room, jumped out of a window and made his escape.

By this time his character had become notorious, and he never could entertain a thought of returning to Suson, or of following the trade of a butcher in that county. He, accordingly, resolved to commence smuggler, and raising as much money as he could scrape together, he betook him to the hundreds of Essex, where he soon became connected with a gang of smugglers. This his new profession he followed for some time with tolerable success; but fortune taking a turn, he lost all that he had acquired; upon which he began to turn his thoughts to another, but by no means a more honest, way of life. In a word, he connected himself with a gang of deer-stealers, who finding him a desperate fellow, and fit for their purpose, admitted him among them. This desperate gang, afterwards known and feared under the title of the Essex Gang, not only robbed the forest of deer, but thinned several gentlemen's parks of them, inasmuch that they obtained a considerable sum of money. They followed deer-stealing only for some time; but not finding the money come in so quickly as they wished, and being narrowly watched by the park-keepers, they, by Turpin's direction, resolved to go round the country at nights, and when they could find a house that had any thing valuable in it, one was to knock at the door, which being opened the rest should rush in and plunder it, not only of plate but of household goods.

The first person attacked in this manner was a Mr. Strype, an old man who kept a chandler's-shop at Watford; from whom they only took the money he had by him; but Turpin informed his companions that he knew an old woman at Loughton, who, he was certain, had seven or eight hundred pounds in her possession. The plan being declared feasible, away they went, and coming to the door, one of them knocked, and Turpin and the rest of the gang rushed in. The first thing they did was to blindfold the old lady and her maid. Turpin then examined the former touching her money, upon which she declared that she had none, being naturally loth to part with it. Some of the gang were inclined to believe her, but Turpin, with an oath, declared that if she remained obstinate he would set her on the fire. The poor old lady imagining that this was a mere threat, suffered herself to be lifted on to the fire, till the anguish she had endured for a long time, compelled her to disclose, and the gang retired with about 400*l.*

They then consulted together who should be their next victim, and agreed to wait upon a farmer, near Ripple Side. The people within not answering the door so soon as they would fain have had it opened, they broke in, and according to their old custom, tied the old man, the old woman, the servant-maid, and the farmer's son-in-law. They then ransacked the house, and robbed the old farmer of about 700*l.* Turpin, seeing so considerable a booty, cried, " Ay, this would do, if it were always so," their share being about 80*l.* a man.

The success the gang met with, made them resolve to p oceed against those who had attempted to detect them. They accordingly agreed to attack the house of Mason, the keeper of Epping Forest. The time was fixed when he house was to be attacked; but Turpin having still a great deal of money in his possession, could not refrain from coming up to London to spend it; and, getting drunk, forgot the appointed time for putting their design into execution: however, the rest, resolving not to be

baulked, set out for Mason's, after having bound themselves by oath not to leave one whole piece of goods in
the house.   Accordingly they went, broke open the door,
beat poor Mason in a cruel manner, and finally killed
him under the dresser.   An old man sitting by the fire-
side, who declared that he knew nothing of them, got off
untouched.   After ransacking the lower part of the house
and doing much mischief, they proceeded up-stairs, and
broke every thing in their way ; at last, espying a punch-
bowl, they broke that, when out dropped a hundred and
twenty guineas, which they seized upon and made off
with.

Turpin, with five others, in January 1735, came to the
door of Mr. Saunders, a wealthy farmer, at Charlton in
Kent, and knocking, inquired if the gentleman of the
house was at home ; he was answered he was, and that
being the signal, they rushed in, and going directly to the
parlour where Mr. Saunders, his wife, and some friends
were amusing themselves at a quiet game of cards, desired them on no account to be alarmed, for that they
would not hurt their persons, if they sat still and made
no disturbance.   A silver snuff-box that lay upon the
table, Turpin at once appropriated to himself, and the rest
having bound the company, obliged Mr. Saunders to accompany them about the house, and open his closets and
boxes, to prevent the necessity of laying violent hands
upon them, and perhaps upon himself.   They then possessed themselves of upwards of a hundred pounds in
money, besides other property, including all the plate in
the house. While this was proceeding, the maid-servant,
a girl of some presence of mind, ran up-stairs, and bar-
ring herself in one of the rooms, called out lustily at the
window for assistance ; but one of the rogues following
her, broke open the door with a poker, and brought her
down again.   In their search for all things of value in
the house, they hit upon some bottles of wine, a bottle of
brandy, and some mince-pies, with which they immedi
ately sat down and regaled themselves, inviting the company to partake, indeed compelling them to drink a dram
of brandy each, to work off the fright.   Mrs. Saunders

however, fainted, and a glass of water with some drops in it was instantly provided, with which they bathed her temples, and were very anxious for her recovery. After staying about two hours in the house, they packed up their plunder, and made off with it, threatening the inmates of the house, that, if they stirred within two hours, they would murder them.

The names of Turpin's principal associates were Fielder, Rose, and Walker; there was another, also, whose name we have not learned. These, made an appointment to rob a gentleman's house at Croydon, and for that purpose, agreed to meet at the Half Moon tavern, which they accordingly did, about six o'clock in the evening. Walker, having some knowledge of the house, went at the head of his companions into the yard, and found the coachman dressing the horses; him they bound, and going from thence met Mr. Sheldon the master, whom they seized and compelled to show them the way to the house. As soon as they entered, they tied Mr. Sheldon's hands behind him with cords, and having served the rest of the family after the same fashion, fell to plundering the house. Eleven guineas, and several pieces of plate, jewels, and other things of value, was the result of this adventure; but before they left the place they returned two guineas, thanked Mr. Sheldon for the very courteous manner with which they had been received, and bade him good night.

Their next design was upon the house of Mr. Lawrence, at Edgeware-bury near Stanmore. About five o'clock they went from the Queen's Head at Stanmore, and proceeded to the destined spot. On their arrival, they left their horses at the outer gate, and climbing over the hatch into the sheep-yard, met with a boy just putting up some sheep. They seized him, and presenting a pistol told him, they would shoot him if he offered to cry out, but if he would inform them truly what servants Mr. Lawrence kept, and who was in the house, they would give him money. The boy, terrified at their threats, told instantly what they desired, and one of them thereupon knocked at the door. When it was opened they all rushed in with pistols in their hands, and seizing Mr. Lawrence,

rifled his pockets, out of which they took one guinea, a
Portugal piece of thirty-six shillings, about fifteen shillings
in silver, and his keys. Dissatisfied with so small a booty,
they then drove him up stairs, and breaking open a closet,
plundered it of money, silver cups and spoons, gold rings,
and many other things of value. A bottle of elder wine
which they found, they divided amongst the servants, lifting it to their mouths, as their hands were pinioned behind
them. A maid-servant who was churning in an outhouse,
hearing a noise, suspected there were thieves in the house,
and put out the candle to secrete herself. One of them,
however, discovered her, and dragging her from her
hiding-place, menaced her with the most horrid threats
if she raised the alarm. All of them, indeed, disappointed and enraged at their ill-success, (for they had calculated upon a rich return for their trouble and hazard,)
practised on this occasion the most savage cruelties. Having stripped the house of every thing of worth, even to
the sheets from the beds, they dragged Mr. Lawrence
down stairs again, and declared with the most dreadful
oaths, they would cut his throat if he hesitated to confess
what money was in the house; and being answered that
there was none excepting that which they had taken, they
beat him barbarously with the butt-ends of their whips,
and inflicted a terrific cut upon his head with a pistol.
One of them took a chopping-bill and swore he would
cleave his legs off; another a kettle of water from the
fire, and flung on him, which happening, however, to
have been recently filled, did no serious injury. In their
search, besides the beforementioned particulars, they met
with a chest belonging to one of Mr. Lawrence's sons,
which they broke open, taking therefrom twenty pounds,
and all his linen. Some of these things were afterwards
traced to a place called Duck-lane, where two of these
fellows were apprehended.

Although in this robbery they got about 26*l*. in money
in the whole, yet they made no fair distribution of it
amongst themselves. The honour mentioned as existing
amongst thieves, was, in this instance, at any rate, something of that character which distinguishes their dealings

with others not of their profession ; for it appeared upon
evidence, that those who were most fortunate in the plunder, on the division of the spoil, could bring their minds
to produce no more than three pounds nine shillings and
sixpence.

These frequent and daring burglaries induced His
Majesty to offer a pardon to any one of the criminals
who had been concerned in entering the house of Mr.
Lawrence, and committing such atrocities on the evening
of the 4th of February ; and further, a reward of 50*l.*
to every person who should be instrumental in the discovery of any of the offenders.

Notwithstanding which, on the 7th of February, the
party again met by appointment, having fixed upon the
White Hart in Drury lane, as the best place whereat to
concert future depredations. Accordingly, they agreed
upon making an attempt to rob Mr. Francis, a large farmer near Mary-le-bone, at whose house they arrived
shortly after seven. The details of this outrage are much
the same as the previous robberies in which they were engaged. They succeeded in obtaining thirty-seven guineas
and ten pounds in silver, a quantity of jewels and linen,
and the unfortunate Mr. Francis's wig, all of which they
carried off; not forgetting the latter, the value of which,
excepting to the owner, we are quite at a loss to conceive.

They also formed a design to rob the house of a country justice, and with that intention met at a public house
near Leigh. Not rightly knowing, however, the way into
the jolly justice's domicle, they concealed themselves
under some furze bushes; but while they were thus lying
perdue there, they heard several persons riding along
together, who happened to be some of the neighbouring
farmers returning from the table of the rustic Rhada-
manthus in a state of noisy mirth, induced, doubtless,
by the genial fumes of the justice's wines ; and by their
conversation it was plain that there were others still remaining there, who, dreading neither riotous spouses, nor
the midnight bottle, might probably have determined with
wine and song to " outwatch the bear ;" they, therefore,
deemed it advisable not to attempt it that night, and ad-

journed accordingly their attack to some more promising
period, which so far proved of advantage to them, that it
thereby prevented their being taken, as otherwise they
unavoidably would have been; for they had been observed by some of the neighbourhood, as being suspected as
smugglers, information was given to the custom-house,
and a party of dragoons sent out after them, whom they
met; when after a strict search, nothing having been
found upon them, they were suffered to pass. Thus the
jolly justice escaped.

The daring robberies of these men at length roused
the country, and one of the King's keepers waited on the
Duke of Newcastle, and obtained His Majesty's promise
of a reward of one hundred pounds to him who should
be fortunate enough to apprehend any of them. This
made them lie a little more concealed; but some of the
keepers and others receiving intelligence that they were
regaling themselves at an ale-house in Westminster, they
pursued them there, and bursting open the door, took
three, after a stout resistance, two of whom, the third
turning evidence against them, were hanged in chains
accordingly. Turpin, however, made his escape by leap-
ing from a window.

The gang thus broke up, and Turpin quite left to himself, made a determination never to command another,
but to go altogether upon his own bottom; and with this
view he set out for Cambridge, as he was not known in
that country.

Notwithstanding this resolve, the following strange
encounter provided him with his best companion (as he
would call him) before he reached his journey's end.
King, the highwayman, who had been towards Cambridge
on professional business, was returning to town. Turpin
seeing him well mounted; and bearing the appearance
of a gentleman, thought it was an excellent opportunity
to recruit his pockets, and accordingly with a loud voice,
commanded King to stand. King, enjoying the joke,
though at the ugly prospect of a bullet through his head
if he carried the jest too far, assumed all the conduct of
a person so unceremoniously addressed. "Deliver!"

shouted Turpin, "or by —— I'll let day-light through
you." "What," said King, laughing heartily, "what!
dog eat dog! Come, come! brother Turpin, if you don't
know me, I know you, and should be glad of your company." After mutual assurances of fidelity to one another, and that nothing should part them till death, they
agreed to go together upon some exploit, and met with a
small booty that very day; after which they continued
together, committing divers robberies for nearly three
years, when King was accidentally shot.

King being very well known about the country, as
likewise was Turpin, insomuch that no house would entertain them, they formed the idea of dwelling in a cave,
and to that end pitched upon a place inclosed with a large
thicket, between Loughton Road and King's-Oak-Road,
here they made a place large enough to receive them and
two horses, and while they lay concealed there, they could
see through several holes, purposely made, what passengers went by on either road, and as they thought proper
sallied out and robbed them. This they did in such a
daring manner, and so frequently, that it was not safe for
any person to travel that way, and the very higglers
were obliged to go armed. In this cave they drank and
lay; Turpin's wife supplied them with food, and frequently remained in the place all night with them.

From the forest, King and Turpin once took a ride to
Bungay in Suffolk, where the latter had seen two young
market-women receive thirteen or fourteen pounds, and
was determined to rob them of it. King attempted to
dissuade him from it, saying, they were pretty girls, and
he would never be engaged in an attempt to deprive two
hardworking women of their little gains. Turpin, however, persisted, and coming up with them relieved them
of the burden of their coin, which exploit occasioned a
dispute between them. ·

As they were returning they robbed a gentleman, who
was taking an airing in his chariot, with his two children.
King first attacked him, but found him so powerful and
determined a person, returning such sound replies in the
shape of blows to poor King's civilities, that he was fain

to call upon his companion for assistance. Their u.iited strength at last overcame him, and they took from him all the money he had about him, and then demanded his watch, which he declined on any account to part with but one of the children became frightened, and persuaded its father to let them have it. They then insisted upon taking a mourning ring which they observed he wore, and an objection was raised on his part, even to that proposition. Finding, however, it was useless to oppose them he at length resigned it, telling them it was not worth eighteen pence, but that he much valued it. Upon which information they returned it to him, saying, they were too much of gentlemen to take any thing which another valued so much.

About this time the reward offered for the apprehension of Turpin had induced several poor, but resolute men, to make an attempt to get him into their power. Among the rest a man, groom to a Mr. Thompson, tempted by the placard setting forth the golden return in the event of success, connected himself with a higgler to ward off suspicion, and commenced his search. Turpin one day standing by himself in the neighbourhood of his cave, observed some one who, he supposed, was poaching for hares, and saluted him with, " No hares near this thicket; it's of no use seeking, you'll not find any."—" Perhaps I shall a *Turpin*, though," replied the fellow, and levelled his piece at him. Seeing his danger, Turpin commenced a parley, retreating at the same time by degrees towards his cave, the groom following him with his gun presented. " I surrender," said Turpin, when he reached the mouth of the cavern, and the man dropping the point of his piece, the former seized his carbine, and shot him dead on the spot. Turpin instantly made off to another part of the country, in search of King, and sent his wife a letter to meet him at a certain public-house, at which, in a few days, enquiring for her under a feigned name, he found she was awaiting his appearance. The kitchen where she was, happened to be at the back through a public room, where some farmers and others were regal-'ng themselves. On passing through, a butcher, to whom he owed five pounds, recognized him, and taking him aside said, " I know you have money now, Dick ; if you'd pay me it would be of great service."—" My wife has certainly money to some amount," replied Turpin. with a most unmoved countenance ; " she is in the next place ; I 'll get it of her, and pay you presently." When Turpin was gone, the butcher apprized the company who he was, and added, " I'll just get my five pounds of him, and then we'll take him." Turpin, however, was not to be so caught, and instead of going to his wife, leaped out of the next window, took horse, and was off in an instant, much to the discomfiture of the knight of the cleaver and the assembled company, who doubtless had calculated most correctly the proportion of the reward that would be due to each by virtue of the king's signet.

Having discovered King, and one of his associates whose name was Potter, they determined to set out at once for London ; and coming over the forest about three hundred yards from the Green Man, Turpin found that his horse, having undergone great fatigue, began to tire. On such an occasion it was no question with Turpin how he should provide himself with another, for, overtaking a gentleman, the owner of several race-horses, he at once appropriated his steed and a handsome whip to his own peculiar use, and recommending his own broken-down jade to the kind consideration of the party, speaking highly of his points, left him to mount the sorry courser, and urge the wretched quadruped forward in the best way he could.

This robbery was committed on a Saturday night, and on the Monday following the gentleman received intelligence, that such a horse as he had lost and described was left at an inn in White-chapel ; he accordingly went there, and found it to be the same. Nobody came for it at the time appointed, but about eleven o'clock at night, King's brother called for the horse, and was seized immediately. The whip he carried in his hand, the gentleman instantly identified as that stolen from him, although the button upon which his name had been engraved was half broken off; the latter letters of his name, however, were plainly

distinguishable upon the remaining part. They charged
a constable with him, but he becoming frightened, and on
the assurance that if he spoke the truth he should be released, confessed, that there was a lusty man in a white
duffel coat waiting for it in a street adjoining. One Mr.
Bayes immediately went out, and finding the man as
directed, perceived it was King. Coming round upon
him, Mr. Bayes (the then active landlord of the Green
Man, to whom the gentleman at the time had related the
robbery,) attacked him. King immediately drew a pistol,
which he pointed to Mr. Bayes's breast, but it luckily
flashed in the pan. A struggle then ensued, for King was
a powerful man, and Turpin hearing the skirmish, came
up, when King cried out, " Dick, shoot him, or we are
taken, by —— !" at which instant Turpin fired his pistol,
but it missed Mr. Bayes, and shot King in two places.
" Dick, you have killed me, make off," were King's words
as he fell, and Turpin, seeing what he had done, clapped
spurs to his horse, and made his escape. King lived for
a week afterwards, and gave Turpin the character of a
coward; telling Mr. Bayes that if he pleased to take him,
he was to be found at a certain house near Hackney
Marsh, and that when he rode away, he had three brace
of pistols about him, and a carbine slung. Upon inquiry,
it was found that Turpin had actually been at the house
which King mentioned, and made use of something like
the following expressions to the man. " What shall I
do? where shall I go? Dick Bayes, I'll be the death of
you; for I have lost the best fellow-man I ever had in
my life; I shot poor King in endeavouring to kill that
dog." The same resolution of revenge he retained to the
last, though without the power of effecting it.

After this, he still kept about the forest, till he was
harassed almost to death; for he had lost his place of
safety, the cave, which was discovered upon his shooting
Mr. Thompson's groom. When they found the cave,
there were in it two shirts in a bag, two pair of stockings,
part of a bottle of wine, and some ham. Turpin was
very nearly taken while hiding in these woods by a Mr.
Ives, the king's huntsman, who, thinking he was secreted

there, took out two dry-footed hounds; but Turpin perceiving them coming, climbed up a tree, and saw them stop beneath it several times, as though they scented him, which so terrified Turpin, that as soon as they were gone, he made a resolution of retiring that instant to Yorkshire.

Soon after this, a person came out of Lincolnshire to Brough, near Market-Cave, in Yorkshire, and stayed for some time at the Ferry-house. He said his name was John Palmer; and he went from thence sometimes to live at North Cave, and sometimes at Welton, continuing in these places about fifteen or sixteen months, except such part of the time as he went to Lincolnshire to see his friends, which he frequently did, and as often brought three or four horses back with him, which he used to sell or exchange in Yorkshire. While he so lived at Brough, Cave, and Welton, he very often went out hunting and shooting with the gentlemen in the neighbourhood. As he was returning one day from shooting, he saw one of his landlord's cocks in the street, and raising his gun, shot it dead. A man, his neighbour, witnessing so wanton an act, complained of such conduct, asking him by what authority he shot another man's property. "Wait one moment," said Mr. Palmer, "just stay till I have charged my piece, and I'll shoot you too." The landlord being informed of the loss he had sustained by the death of his favourite bird, and the man who saw the act, being enraged at the threat Palmer had used towards him, they both obtained a warrant against him, and he was brought up at the General Quarter Sessions, where he was examined. Sureties for his good behaviour in future were the penalty alone exacted from him, which, however, refusing to find, he was committed to the House of Correction. His conduct thus excited great suspicion; for it was strange that a man who was in the habit of bringing from his friends in Lincolnshire half-a-dozen horses at a time, and plenty of money, should be so forsaken as not to be able o provide sureties; and still stranger, that on so trivial occasion as the present, if he could find them at all, he did not produce them. A man's pride under other circumstances might be concerned, or a consciousness of innocence that excluded the possibility, or the benefit of release, under other conditions than free acquittal; but on a charge of this nature, which might have been made up even by the purchase of the fowl, or a simple excuse, his refusal was very suspicious. Inquiries were set on foot in all quarters; and the magistrate, not contented with the accounts he gave of himself of having been a grazier in Lincolnshire, despatched officers to learn how far that statement was consistent with truth. The result was a confirmation of Palmer's account, so far as the fact of his having lived in Lincolnshire, and having been a grazier there; that is, that there he had something to do with sheep, confined principally, however, to the expert practice of stealing them. Mr. Palmer, upon the receipt of this information, was removed from the Beverley house of correction to York castle, and accommodated on the way with the use of hand-cuffs, and a guard of honour. When he arrived at his new abode, two persons from Lincolnshire challenged a mare and a foal which he had sold to a gentleman, and also the horse on which he rode when he came to Beverley, to be stolen from them off the fens in Lincolnshire. We need not add that Mr. Palmer was one and the same person with Dick Turpin, the notorious highwayman.

Turpin at one time, with another fellow, laid a scheme for seizing the Government money, ordered to be paid to the ships at Portsmouth. Both of them were to have attacked the guard in a narrow pass, with sword and pistol in hand; but Turpin's courage failed him, and the enterprise dropped. Gordon, his accomplice in this design, was afterwards taken on a charge in which he alone was concerned; and while in Newgate he declared that "after that, Turpin would be guilty of any cowardly action, and die like a dog."

Turpin was tried and convicted of stealing the horse and the foal and the mare from the fens, and was executed on Saturday, April 7th, 1739. He behaved himself with remarkable assurance, and bowed to the spectators as he passed. It was observed that as he mounted the ladder his right leg trembled, on which he stamped it down with violence, and with undaunted fortitude looked around him. After speaking to the executioner for nearly half an hour, he threw himself off the ladder, and expired in about five minutes.

His corpse was brought back from the gallows and buried in a neat coffin in St. George's church-yard. The grave was dug deep, and the persons he appointed to follow him (mourners we hesitate to call them, for we cannot imagine anybody to mourn upon the death of such an unprecedented ruffian,) those persons whoever they were, however, took all possible care to secure the corpse; notwithstanding which, some men were discovered to be moving off the body, which they had taken up; and the mob having got information where it might be found, went to a garden in which it was deposited, and brought it away in a sort of triumph, and buried it in the same grave, having first filled the coffin with slacked lime.

CLAUDE DU VALL.

IT might very naturally be objected to us by some, that we should introduce into our work the life of any highwayman, however celebrated, whose fortune it was to have been born in France ; but, without insisting upon the celebrity of the person whose life we are about to narrate, it will be sufficient to inform the objecting reader, that many of the adventures achieved by Claude du Vall were performed in England, and that he is accordingly, to all intents and purposes, although a Frenchman by birth, an English highwayman.

This noted person was born at Domfront, in Normandy.* His father was a miller, and his mother was de-

---

* We find, by reference to an old Life of Du Vall, published in 1670, that Domfront was a place by no means unlikely to have produced our adventurer. Indeed, it appears that common honesty was a most uncommon ingredient in the moral economy of the place, as the following curious extract from the work in question will abundantly testify :—

" In the days of Charles IX. the curate of Domfront, (for so the

scended from a worshipful race of tailors. He was brought up in the Catholic faith, and received an education suited to the profession for which he was intended,—namely, that of a footman. But, although his father was

French name him whom we call parson, and vicar,) out of his own head began a strange innovation and oppression in that parish; that is, he absolutely denied to baptize any of their children, if they would not, at the same time, pay him his funeral fees : and what was worse, he would give them no reason for this alteration, but only promised to enter bond for himself and successors, that hereafter, all persons paying so at their christening should be buried *gratis.* What think ye the poor people did in this case? They did not pull his surplice over his ears, nor tear his mass-book, nor throw crickets at his head : no, they humbly desired him to alter his resolutions, and amicably reasoned with him; but he, being a capricious fellow, gave them no other answer, but 'What I have done, I have done; take your remedy where you can find it; it is not for men of my coat to give an account of my actions to the laity ;' which was a surly and quarrelsome answer, and unbefitting a priest. Yet this did not provoke his parishioners to speak one ill word against his person or function, or to do any illegal act. They only took the regular way of complaining of him to his ordinary, the Archbishop of Rouen. Upon summons, he appears : the Arch bishop takes him up roundly, tells him he deserves deprivation, if that can be proved which is objected against him, and asked him, what he had to say for himself? After his due reverence, he answers, that he acknowledges the fact, to save the time of examining witnesses; but desires his grace to hear his reasons, and then do unto him as he shall see cause. 'I have,' says he, 'been curate of this parish seven years; in that time I have, one year with another, baptized a hundred children, and buried not one. At first I rejoiced at my good fortune to be placed in so good an air; but, looking into the register-book, I found, for a hundred years back, near the same number yearly baptized, and no one above five years old buried; and which did more amaze me, I find the number of communicants to be no greater *now* than they were *then.* This seemed to me a great mystery; but, upon farther inquiry, I found out the true cause of it; for all that were *born* at Domfront were *hanged* at Rouen. I did this to keep my parishioners from hanging, encouraging them to die at home, the burial duties being already paid.'

"The Archbishop demanded of the parishioners, whether this was true or not? They answered, that too many of them came to that unlucky end at Rouen. 'Well, then,' says he, 'I approve of what the curate has done, and will cause my secretary, in *perpetuam rei memoriam,* to make an act of it ;' which act the curate carried home with him, and the parish cheerfully submitted to it, and have found much good by it; for within less than twenty years, there died *fifteen* of natural deaths, and now there die three or four yearly."

careful to train up his son in the religion of his ancestors, he was himself utterly without religion. He talked more of good cheer than of the church; of sumptuous feasts than of the ardent faith; of good wine than of good works.

Du Vall's parents were exempted from the trouble and expense of rearing their son at the age of thirteen. We first find him at Rouen, the principal city of Normandy, in the character of a stable-boy. Here he fortunately found retour horses going to Paris: upon one of these he was permitted to ride, on condition of assisting to dress them at night. His expenses were likewise defrayed by some English travellers whom he met upon the road.

Arrived at Paris, he continued at the same inn where the Englishmen put up, and by running messages, or performing the meanest offices, subsisted for a while. He continued in this humble station until the Restoration of Charles II., when multitudes from the Continent resorted to England. In the character of a footman to a person of quality, Du Vall also repaired to this country. The universal joy which seized the nation upon that happy event contaminated the morals of all; riot, dissipation, and every species of profligacy abounded. The young and sprightly French footman entered keenly into these amusements. His funds, however, being soon exhausted, he deemed it no great crime for a Frenchman to exact contributions from the English. In a short time, he became so dexterous in his new employment, that he had the honour of being first named in an advertisement issued for the apprehending of some notorious robbers.

One day Du Vall and some others espied a knight and his lady travelling along in their coach. Seeing themselves in danger of being attacked, the lady resorted to a flageolet, and commenced playing, which she did very dexterously. Du Vall taking the hint, pulled one out of his pocket, began to play, and in this posture approached the coach. "Sir," said he to the knight, "your lady performs excellently, and I make no doubt she dances well; will you step out of the coach, and let us have the

honour to dance a courant with her upon the heath?"
" I dare not deny any thing, sir," replied the knight readily, " to a gentleman of your quality and good behaviour;
you seem a man of generosity, and your request is perfectly reasonable." Immediately the footman opened the
door, and the knight came out. Du Vall leaped lightly
off his horse, and handed the lady down. It was surprising to see how gracefully he moved upon the grass:
scarcely a dancing-master in London but would have
been proud to have shown such agility in a pair of pumps,
as Du Vall evinced in a pair of French riding-boots. As
soon as the dance was over, he handed the lady to the
coach, but just as the knight was stepping in, " Sir," said
he, " you forget to pay the music." His worship replied, that he never forgot such things, and instantly put
his hand under the seat of the coach, pulled out 100*l.* in
a bag, which he delivered to Du Vall, who received it
with a very good grace, and courteously answered, " Sir,
you are liberal, and shall have no cause to regret your
generosity; this 100*l.*, given so handsomely, is better
than ten times the sum taken by force. Your noble behaviour has excused you the other 300*l.* which you have
in the coach with you." After this, he gave him his
word that he might pass undisturbed, if he met any
other of his crew, and then wished them a good journey.

At another time, Du Vall and scme of his associates
met a coach upon Blackheath, full of ladies, and a child
with them. One of the gang rode up to the coach, and
in a rude manner robbed the ladies of their watches and
rings, and even seized a silver sucking-bottle of the
child's. The infant cried bitterly for its bottle, and the
ladies earnestly entreated he would only return that article to the child, which he barbarously refused. Du Vall
went forward to discover what detained his accomplice,
and, the ladies renewing their entreaties to him, he
instantly threatened to shoot his companion, unless he
returned that article, saying, " Sirrah, can't you behave
like a gentleman, and raise a contribution without strip-
ping people; but, perhaps, you had some occasion for

the sucking-bottle, for, by your actions, one would ima·
gine you were hardly weaned." This smart reproof had
the desired effect, and Du Vall, in a courteous manner,
took his leave of the ladies.

One day Du Vall met Roper, master of the hounds to
Charles II., who was hunting in Windsor Forest ; and,
taking the advantage of a thicket, demanded his money,
or he would instantly take his life. Roper, without hesi-
tation, gave him his purse, containing at least fifty
guineas : in return for which Du Vall bound him neck
and heel, tied his horse to a tree beside him, and rode
across the country.

It was a considerable time before the huntsmen discovered their master. The squire, being at length released, made all possible haste to Windsor, unwilling to
venture himself into any more thickets for that day, whatever might be the fortune of the hunt. Entering the town,
he was accosted by Sir Stephen Fox, who inquired if he
had had any sport. " Sport !" replied Roper, in a great
passion, " yes, sir, I have had sport enough from a vil·
lain who made me pay full dear for it; he bound me neck
and heels contrary to my desire, and then took fifty
guineas from me to pay him for his labour, which I had
much rather he had omitted."

England now became too contracted a sphere for the
talents of our adventurer ; and, in consequence of a pro·
clamation issued for his detection, and his notoriety in
the kingdom, Du Vall retired to his native country. At
Paris he lived in a very extravagant style, and carried
on war with rich travellers and fair ladies, and proudly
boasted that he was equally successful with both ; but his
warfare with the latter was infinitely more agreeable,
though much less profitable, than with the former.

There is one adventure of Du Vall at Paris, which we
shall lay before our readers. There was in that city a
learned Jesuit, confessor to the French King, who had
rendered himself eminent both by his politics and his
avarice. His thirst for money was insatiable, and
increased with his riches. Du Vall devised the following

plan to obtain a share of the immense wealth of this pious father

To facilitate his admittance into the Jesuit's company, he dressed himself as a scholar, and, waiting a favourable opportunity, went up to him very confidently, and addressed him as follows: " May it please your reverence, I am a poor scholar, who have been several years travelling over strange countries, to learn experience in the sciences, principally to serve mine own country, for whose advantage I am determined to apply my knowledge, if I may be favoured with the patronage of a man so eminent as yourself." " And what may this knowledge of yours be?" replied the father very much pleased. " If you will communicate any thing to me that may be beneficial to France, I assure you no proper encouragement shall be wanting on my side." Du Vall, upon this growing bolder, proceeded : " Sir, I have spent most of my time in the study of alchymy, or the transmutation of metals, and have profited so much at Rome and Venice, from great men learned in that science, that I can change several metals into gold, by the help of a philosophical powder which I can prepare very speedily."

The father confessor was more elated with this communication than all the discoveries he had obtained in the way of his profession, and his knowledge even of his royal penitent's most private secrets gave him less delight than the prospect of immense riches which now burst upon his avaricious mind. " Friend," said he " such a thing as this will be serviceable to the whole state, and particularly grateful to the king, who, as his affairs go at present, stands in great need of such a curious invention. But you must let me see some proof of your skill, before I credit what you say, so far as to communicate it to his majesty, who will sufficiently reward you, if what you promise be demonstrated. Upon this the confessor conducted Du Vall to his house, and furnished him with money to erect a laboratory, and to purchase such other materials as were requisite, in order to proceed in this invaluable operation, charging him to keep the secret

from every living soul. Utensils being fixed, and every
thing in readiness, the Jesuit came to witness the wonderful operation. Du Vall took several metals and mine-
rals of the basest sort, and put them in a crucible, his
reverence viewing every one as he put them in. Our
alchymist had prepared a hollow tube, into which he conveyed several sprigs of real gold ; with this seeming
stick, he stirred the operation, which, with its heat, melted the gold, and the tube at the same time, so that it sank
imperceptibly into the vessel. When the excessive fire
had consumed all the different materials which he had
put in, the gold remained pure, to the quantity of an
ounce and a half. This the Jesuit ordered to be examined, and ascertaining that it was actually pure gold, he
became devoted to Du Vall, and, blinded with the prospect of future advantage, credited every thing our im-
postor said, furnishing him with whatever he demanded,
in hopes of being made master of this extraordinary secret. Thus were our alchymist and Jesuit, according to
the old saying, as " great as two pickpockets." Du Vall
was a professed robber ; and what is a court favourite but
a picker of the people's pockets ? So that it was two sharpers endeavouring to outsharp one another. The confessor was as candid as Du Vall could wish ; he showed
him all his treasures, and several rich jewels which he
had received from the king ; hoping, by these obligations,
to incline him to discover his wonderful secrets with more
alacrity. In short, he became so importunate, that Du
Vall was apprehensive of too minute an inquiry, if he denied the request any longer : he therefore appointed a
day when the whole was to be disclosed. In the meantime, he took an opportunity of stealing into the chamber
where the riches were deposited, and where his reverence
generally slept after dinner ; finding him in deep repose,
he gently bound him, then took his keys, and unhoarded
as much of his wealth as he could carry off unsus-
pected ; after which he quickly took leave of him and
France.

It is uncertain how long Du Vall continued his depredations after his return to England ; but we are informed,

that in a fit of intoxication, he was detected at the Hole-in-the-Wall, in Chandos street, committed to Newgate, convicted, condemned, and executed at Tyburn, in the twenty-seventh year of his age, on the 1st of January, 1669: and so much had his gallantries and handsome figure rendered him the favourite of the fair sex, that many a bright eye was dimmed at his funeral; his corpse was bedewed with the tears of beauty, and his actions and death were celebrated by the immortal author of the inimitable Hudibras. He was buried with many flambeaux, amidst a numerous train of mourners, (most of them ladies,) in the middle aisle of the church in Covent Garden.

JAMES MACLAINE.

James Maclaine, called in his own time by the distinguished title of "The gentleman highwayman," seemed at his birth to be far removed from the common temptations which too frequently lead to an infamous death. Until the decease of his father, which took place when he was about eighteen years of age, a fair prospect of prosperity was presented to him; but, unhappily, being conscious of his birth, which entitled him, by a slight straining of courtesy, to the designation of a gentleman, he imbibed, together with an inordinate vanity, an aversion from business, and an immoderate desire to appear a gay young fellow.

Lauchlin Maclaine, the father of our adventurer, was a Presbyterian divine, and pastor of a congregation of that communion at Monaghan, in the North of Ireland. He designed James, his second son, for a merchant, and bestowed upon him a sound education, but died before he could put his intentions into effect of sending him to Rotterdam to be placed in the counting-house of a Scotch merchant of his acquaintance.

Young Maclaine, the instant his father's breath was out of his body, proceeded to take possession and to dispose of his father's substance; and treated with perfect contempt the remonstrances of his friends and relations, and the exhortations of his aunt, who, finding all her entreaties ineffectual, took his only sister into her charge, and left him to pursue what course he pleased.

Thus left to himself, Maclaine forgot altogether the projected Dutch counting-house, and equipping himself in the gayest apparel that part of the country could afford, and purchasing a gelding, set up fine gentleman at once, and in a twelvemonth dissipated almost the whole of his property. During his extravagances, however, his ear had been frequently troubled with the remonstrances of his aunt and his other relations, which at length he found so disagreeable, that he was fain to set out for Dublin without communicating his intention to any one. It was here, it appears, that he first conceived the notion of making his fortune by marriage; and having no disagreeable person, he gratuitously gave himself credit for many more excellencies than, unfortunately, other people could discover in him. The demands for the maintenance of such an appearance as would realize his hopes of a rich marriage, soon swept away the small remainder of his property; and he had now full time to reflect on his folly and vanity, and to regret not a little having despised the advice of his relations, who had for some time turned a deaf ear to his entreaties by letter for a supply of money. But upon them, nevertheless, he felt was now his sole dependance. He had long spent his all—he was an entire stranger to a single individual of worth or substance in the place, and his credit and clothes, even to the last shirt, were gone. Selling his sword, therefore, the last piece of splendour that remained to him, he raised as much as would bear his charges on foot, and with a heavy heart set out to return to Monaghan, his native place.

Not a hand was outstretched to welcome the prodigal home again; his aunt refused to see him, all his other relations followed her example, and the companions of his former riots not only refused him relief, but rendered him

the sport and ridicule of the town. His sister, however,
sometimes contrived to see him by stealth to give him her
pocket-money, but that could not long support him. Here,
then, he must inevitably have starved, had not a gentleman on his way to England, passing through the town,
compassionately offered him the place of a servant who
had recently died. Want, and the dread of starving, had
by this time entirely banished all unnecessary or super-
fluous pride, and our young gentleman accepted the offer
with joy. But, unhappily, the extreme pressure of want
once removed, old thoughts return, old vanities are renewed; and so it was with Mr. Maclaine. His master's
commands, though uniformly softened by good-nature
and benevolence, appeared to him as so many insults offered to his birth and breeding; it is no wonder, therefore, that in a few months he was discharged from his
service. Depending on his sister, who was about to be
married to a man of some wealth, he set out once more
for Ireland, to endeavour to obtain enough from his relations to fit him out for America or the West Indies; but
here again he was doomed to disappointment. His sister's marriage had been broken off—she was unable to do
any thing for him;—and his other relations, deeming
themselves scandalized by his having been a footman,
were even less tractable than before, treated him with
great indignity, and finally refused all manner of assistance.

Again reduced to starvation, he was obliged to think
of service as his only resource. With much difficulty
he obtained a situation as butler to a gentleman near
Cork, with whom he did not live long, being discharged
for some breach of trust. Here he remained for many
months out of place, wandering about, without any settled abode or means of subsistence, except occasional remittances from his elder brother, a pastor of the English
congregation at the Hague, whose friendly assistance
was less relished, because it was accompanied by warm
remonstrances on the past, and wholesome advice on the
future conduct of his life.

Fortune was at length favourable; his old master

though he refused him a character to another family, generously paid his passage to England, and allowed him, for a limited period after his landing, a shilling a day for subsistence.

Once again on this side of the water, his notions of gentility returned; he scorned being a menial servant; and valuing the *minimum* of his ambition at a pair of colours, he actually had the impudence to attempt to borrow the purchase money on the bond he had obtained from his master. This absurd scheme failing, he threw up his shilling a-day in disgust, and heroically cast himself for support on a celebrated courtesan, a countrywoman of his own, who maintained him for some months in great magnificence, and enabled him to attend the public places with something like splendour.

But having disgusted this lady by his pusillanimous conduct in a rencontre with a certain peer,—who bestowed upon him a severe castigation, and very nearly ran him through the body, though he was much stronger, and as well armed as the nobleman,—he was once more without resources. His grandeur now suffered an eclipse for two or three months, and his last suit had been laid by in lavender, or, in other words, pawned, when he inspired the regard of a lady of quality, the consequence of which was that for five or six months longer he flourished away as an idle fellow in all the public places.

But Maclaine inwardly was not idle. He was extremely anxious for an independent settlement, and the thought of inveigling some woman of fortune by the charms of his person was still uppermost in his mind. Among other schemes to this end, there was none he built so much upon as a very hopeful and grateful plot he had laid for the daughter of his patroness and benefactress, who had a considerable fortune. But the young lady's waiting-maid, who had either more honesty than abigails in general are furnished with, or had not received the price with which they are usually rewarded, discovered the affair to the old lady, who forthwith dismissed Maclaine from her services, but when, in a few months after, he was much reduced, she privately bestowed upon him fifty pounds in order to fit him out for Jamaica, where he had proposed to go and seek his fortune, and where the lady was willing enough that he should retire, that she might be free from fears on her daughter's account.

But Maclaine was no sooner possessed of this sum than he forgot his Jamaica expedition, and returned to his favourite scheme of fortune-hunting; for he never could rid himself of the idea that one day or other he should succeed in the main object of his existence. He released, therefore, his best clothes from the durance vile in which they had been plunged, and after various treaties with match-makers and chambermaids, relating to ladies of great reputed fortune, all which treaties ended in disappointment, he reluctantly contracted his ambition, and made suit to the daughter of a considerable inn-keeper and dealer in horses, with whom he was fortunate enough to succeed, and whom he married with her parents' consent and five hundred pounds.

Here it would seem that Maclaine had laid aside all thoughts of the fine gentleman, and had really determined to make the most of his wife's fortune by industry and diligence. He took a house in Welbeck street, and set up a grocer's and chandler's shop; was very obliging to his customers, punctual in his dealings, and, while his wife lived, was esteemed by his neighbours a careful and industrious man. However, though at times, and while he was in his shop, he appeared to like his business, yet in parties of pleasure, which he made but too often, and on holidays, he affected the dress of a gentleman, and thus created expenses which only a gradual encroachment on his capital enabled him to meet; insomuch, that when his wife died, which was about three years after their marriage, he resolved to leave off business, and converted his furniture and goods into the miserable sum of eighty-five pounds, which, perhaps, with frugality, might have supported him in business, but which was at all times too small a sum for Mr. Maclaine.

His mother-in-law consenting to take charge of his only daughter, and once more in a manner a single man, with

his eighty-five pounds in his pocket, again did the desire
of appearing the gay fine gentleman obtrude itself upon
his mind, and his old project of marrying a rich fortune
engrossed all his faculties. For this purpose, Mr. Maclaine, who, but a few weeks before was not ashamed to
appear in a patched coat, or to carry a halfpennyworth
of coal or sand to his customers, now hired handsome
apartments near Soho-square, and resume his laced
clothes, and a hat and feather.

But, however unreasonable to others this sudden transition from the grub to the butterfly might appear, Mr.
Maclaine had very good private reasons for his actions.
It appears that during his wife's last illness, she had been
attended by one Plunket, as a surgeon and apothecary;
this Plunket, after the decease of the poor woman, opened
his mind to Maclaine, saying, that though the latter had
lost a good wife, yet, seeing that she was gone, it was of
no use to despond or to repine, particularly as it might
eventually turn out the most lucky circumstance in his
life. He added at the same time, that if Maclaine would
agree to share the fortune with him, he could help him to
a lady with ten thousand pounds at least in her own right.

This motion was too agreeable to Mr. Maclaine to be
rejected. It is hardly necessary to detail with what zeal
this affair was followed up, or how often they flattered
themselves with the deceitful prospects of success. The
young lady having been taken to the Wells, Maclaine followed her, passing for a man of fortune, and in every
part of his dress and equipage appearing in that character.
Plunket acted as his partner, and was a sort of under
agent, while Maclaine himself was ogling, dancing, and
flirting with the young lady. But an ill-timed quarrel
with an apothecary, one evening in the public room, placed
a quietus upon his hopes for ever; for the disciple of Galen
enlisting a " gallant son of Mars" in his quarrel, the latter had the effrontery to kick our adventurer down stairs,
declaring publicly that he knew the rascal a footman a
few years ago. This statement, which was believed by
every body present, among whom was his mistress, whose
credulity he had ascertained before, and was therefore

not in a situation to doubt, compelled him and his footman
Plunket to decamp without the ceremony of leave-taking
and, indeed, without any ceremony at all.

Returning to town from this woeful expedition, and examining the state of their cash, these faithful friends dis
covered that five guineas were the whole that remained,—
a sum too little to support them, or to enter into any new
project, or to keep up their assumed grandeur. Maclaine
now found himself in a worse plight than he had brought
himself to for some years past, without any visible hope
of a supply, and yet engaged in a mode of life highly
expensive, which it went to his heart either to retrench
or relinquish. He now thought seriously of embarking
for Jamaica, where he hoped to find employment as an
accountant, and flattered himself that his person might
be turned to account amongst the rich planters' daughters
or widows. But no money was forthcoming for this purpose, nor could he think of any possible scheme whereby
it might be raised.

Certainly, never had a man less cause to complain of
fortune than Maclaine, and it would seem throughout his
life, that she had determined to make his ruin entirely the
work of his own hand, and leave him at last utterly without excuse or palliation; for meeting on 'Change with a
gentleman, a countryman of his own, to whom he had
formerly related his hopes of making a fortune in the
manner we have related, he told him his situation at the
present moment, adding that he was now undone, that
he had spent his all in that unhappy project, and had not
wherewithal to subsist here, or to carry him from a place
in which he felt he was cutting a very ridiculous figure.
Hereupon the gentleman spoke in his behalf to some
others of his countrymen; and as his conduct heretofore,
according to the notions of the age, had been rather im-
prudent than vicious, they actually raised sixty guineas
to fit him out for Jamaica, which they gave him, promising
him letters of recommendation from some merchants of
respectability to their own correspondents. Here, then,
was a prospect at once opened to him, of future happiness
and prosperity. Let us see how it terminated.

He had agreed for the passage, paid part of the money in advance, and bespoken some necessaries fitted for the climate, when, unhappily for the infatuated man, he was prompted to go to a masquerade, to take leave, as he said, for the last time, of the bewitching pleasures of London, and to bid a final farewell to this species of enjoyment, which he should have no hope of partaking in the West Indies. He went with the whole of his money in his pocket. The strange appearance of the place and of the company amused him for a while, but the noise of the gamesters drew his attention to the gaming-table, where the quick transition of large sums from one hand to another awakened his avarice, and lulled his prudence asleep. In short, he ventured, and in half an hour had possessed himself of a hundred guineas, with which he resolved, according to their phrase, " to tie up ;" but avarice had now attacked him ; and after taking a turn or two round the room, he again returned, and in a few minutes was stripped to the last guinea.

It is needless to describe his agony on this occasion. His money gone, his expedition utterly disconcerted, and his friends lost past redemption ! What was now to be done ?

In this extremity his evil genius, now in the ascendant, prompted him to send for Plunket to advise with, and from that moment his ruin commenced. This was the favourable moment for Plunket. Himself a man of no honour, an utter stranger to all ties or principles of re- ligion or honesty, an old sharper, and a daring fellow into the bargain, this was an opportunity, when his friend was agitated almost to madness, to propose, at first by distant hints, and at last in plain English, going on the highway.

Had he approached him in a calm hour, it is more than probable that his proposal had been rejected with horror; but the former strongly represented the necessity of a speedy supply before his friends could discover that his money was gone, which he said, would expose him to universal scorn and contempt. A strange infatuation, the dread of shame—the shame of appearing a fool di minished the horror of being a villain, and decided him to recruit his losses by means the most hazardous and wicked.

Having agreed upon a plan of co-partnership, and hired two horses, Plunket furnishing the pistols; for this was not his first entrance upon business of that nature, they set out on the evening after the masquerade, to lie in wait for passengers coming from Smithfield market They met on Hounslowheath with a grazier, next morning about four o'clock, from whom they took, without opposition, between sixty and seventy pounds.

In this, and other expeditions of the same kind, they wore Venetian masks; but this covering could not stifle conscience in Maclaine, nor animate him into courage. He accompanied Plunket, it is true, and was by at the robbery, but strictly speaking, had no hand in it; for his fears were so great that he had no power to utter a word, or to draw a pistol. The least resistance on the part of the countryman would have given wings to his heels, and have caused him to leave his more daring accomplice in the lurch.

Even when the robbery was over, and the countryman out of sight, Maclaine's fears were intolerable. He followed Plunket for some miles without speaking a word; and when they put up at an inn, nearly ten miles from the place of the robbery, he called for a private room, fearful of every shadow, and terrified at every sound. His agonies of mind were so great, that Plunket was fearful that his folly would raise suspicion in the house, and he would fain have persuaded him to return immediately to London; but he would not stir till it was dusk, and then would not appear at the stables from which they had hired the horses, but left the care of them to Plunket.

He was now, by his share of this ill-acquired booty, very nearly reimbursed his losses at the masquerade, and might have easily undertaken his voyage; but he had lost all peace of mind, and was become entirely void of prudence. So great was his dread of a discovery, though Plunket represented the impossibility of it, that he would not stir out of his room for some days, and even then did

not think himself safe, but proposed going down to the
country for a week or two. Plunket did not oppose his
departure, especially as he was to direct the route, and
had gotten some intimation of a prize coming that day
from St. Alban's, towards which place they set out.
When they had gone a few miles, Plunket imparted to
him his design, which Maclaine promised to second with
a great deal of reluctance. When they came within sight
of the coach, in which was their expected booty, Maclaine
would have persuaded Plunket to desist; but the other,
turning his qualms of conscience into ridicule, and dropping some hints of cowardice, Maclaine prepared for the
attack, crying, " He needs must whom the devil drives.
I am over shoes and must over boots ;" but notwithstanding, conducted himself in so distracted a manner as went
nigh to lose them their prey. They took, however, from
a gentleman and a lady in the coach, two gold watches,
and about twenty pounds in money, with which they got
clear off; but did not think fit to keep that road any
longer, but turned off, and before morning put up at an
inn at Richmond, where Maclaine was as much in the
horrors as in London; had no rest, no peace of mind,
and stayed there two or three days, sulky, sullen, and
perplexed as to what course he was to pursue. His wish,
however, to be in town in time for the ship's departure
for Jamaica, determined him to return to London in a
fortnight, when he found that the ship had sailed two
days before,—a disappointment that added to his former
perplexity. Nevertheless, having money in his pocket,
he contrived to excuse himself to his friends for his un-
oward absence, and promised, and seriously designed, to
set out on the very next opportunity.

But the expensive company he kept in the interim, and
further losses at play, once more stripped him of his
money; and his evil genius, Plunket, was ever at his
elbow, ready to suggest the former method of supply,
with which he now complied much less reluctantly than
before. The bounds of honour once overstepped, especially when success and security attend the villany, the habit
of vice grows strong; and the checks of conscience

gradually less regarded, at length pass without notice.
In a word, Maclaine hardened himself by degrees to villany, left the company of his city acquaintance that they
might not tease him about his voyage to Jamaica, and
took lodgings in St. James-street, a place excellently suited to his purpose, for his appearance glanced off all
suspicion, and he had a favourable opportunity, when
gentlemen came to town, of knowing and watching their
motions, and consequently of following and waylaying
them on the road.

In the space of six months, he and Plunket, sometimes
in company and sometimes separately, committed fifteen
or sixteen robberies in Hyde Park, and within twenty
miles of London, and obtained some large prizes. But
still the money went as it came, for Plunket loved his
bottle and intrigue, and Maclaine was doatingly fond of
fine clothes, balls, and masquerades, at all which places
he made a conspicuous figure. As he still had fortune-
hunting in view, he was very assiduous in his attentions
to women, and was not altogether unsuccessful ; but, we
imagine, made sincere return to none but such as had
money in their own hands, or could be useful in helping
him to an introduction to such as had.

And here it were needless and not productive of much
interest to recount several intrigues in which Maclaine
was engaged, and it were not a little painful to narrate
two instances of wanton seduction on his part, which,
were there no other counts in the moral indictment
against him, would be sufficient to consign him to eternal
infamy.

Mr. Maclaine applied himself also to his old profession
f fortune-hunting, and in company with his old and
worthy coadjutor Plunket, made several attempts to entrap
heiresses, all of which proved abortive. While he was
intent upon these schemes, he had no opportunity of making excursions on the road, and to defray his expenses
had borrowed from a citizen's wife, with whom he had
an intrigue, about twenty pounds, which he promised
faithfully to repay before her husband should return from
he country. The time of the citizen's arrival being at

hand, the good wife became exceedingly curious about the coin; and as a similar favour might be wanted by him at a future time, Mr. Maclaine made it a point of conscience to keep his word with her, and appointed her to come to him at his country lodgings at Chelsea, where he paid her the money. He, however, took care that his friend Plunket should ease her of the trouble of carrying it home, by waylaying her in the Five-fields.

Soon after this a supply of cash being wanted, Plunket and he prepared for an expedition, and took the road to Chester; and in three days committed five robberies between Stony Stratford and Whitchurch, one of which was upon an intimate acquaintance, by whom Maclaine had been handsomely entertained but two days before. However, the booty in the whole five robberies did not amount to thirty pounds in cash, but they had watches, rings, &c. to a much greater amount. On the very evening of their return to town, they obtained information that an officer in the East India Company's service had received a large sum of money with which he was about to return to Greenwich. They waylaid and robbed him of a very considerable sum, and it would seem that on this occasion they were under some dread of a discovery; for, in a few days after the commission of it, Maclaine set out for the Hague, and Plunket for Ireland.

On the arrival of the former at the Hague, he pretended a friendly visit to his brother, who received him with cordiality and affection, and as honesty is never suspicious, he was easily induced to give credit to the specious tale which his brother related to him. He told him that he had got a considerable fortune by his late wife, and that her father who died some few months before, had left him a valuable legacy, with which he designed to purchase a company in the army. Upon that and the interest of his other friends, he said, he hoped to live at ease for the remainder of his life. His worthy brother, rejoicing in his prosperity, introduced him to his acquaintance and friends, amongst whom Mr. Maclaine behaved with great politeness, giving balls and large par ties ; to pay for which, it is surmised, he had the art to extract the gold watches and purses of his guests without suspicion.

However, upon his arrival in London, to which place he had been induced to return by a letter from Plunket, informing him of another rich matrimonial prize, which was, as usual, beyond his reach or ingenuity to ensnare; —he again appears to have taken up his old thoughts of preparing for Jamaica, as a last resource. But these thoughts did not long possess him; for though by the sale of his horses and furniture, he might have fitted himself for the West Indies in a very genteel manner, and had still reputation enough left to have procured sufficient recommendations from home; yet he was prevailed upon to try his fate on the road once more, and was but too successful, making several rich prizes. Among the rest he and Plunket robbed Horace Walpole,* and on a

---

* In the very amusing Letters of Horace Walpole to Sir Horace Mann, recently published, we find the following spirited and lively sketch of Maclaine.

" I have been in town for a day or two, and heard no conversation but about M'Lane, a fashionable highwayman, who is just taken, and who robbed me among others; as Lord Eglinton, Sir Thomas Robinson of Vienna, Mrs. Talbot, &c. He took an odd booty from the Scotch Earl, a blunderbuss, which lies very formidable upon the justice's table. He was taken by selling a laced waistcoat to a pawnbroker, who happened to carry it to the very man who had just sold the lace. His history is very particular, for he confesses every thing, and is so little of a hero, that he cries and begs, and I believe, if Lord Eglinton had been in any luck, might have been robbed of his own blunderbuss. His father was an Irish Dean; his brother is a Calvinist minister in great esteem at the Hague. He himself was a grocer, but losing a wife that he loved extremely about two years ago, and by whom he has one little girl, he quitted his business with 200l. in his pocket, which he soon spent, and then took to the road with only one companion, Plunket, a journeyman apothecary, my other friend, whom he has impeached, but who is not taken. M'Lane had a lodging in St. James's-street over against White's, and another at Chelsea; Plunket one in Jermyn-street; and their faces are as known about St. James's as any gentleman's who lives in that quarter, and who perhaps goes upon the road too. M'Lane had a quarrel at Putney bowling-green two months ago with an officer, whom he challenged for disputing his crank; but the Captain declined, till M'Lane should produce a certificate of his

reward being advertised for the watch which they had taken from him, Plunket had the impudence to go and receive it himself, choosing to run the risk rather than trust a third person with their hazardous secret. But all human prudence is in vain to stop the hand of justice, when once the measure of our iniquity is full; our closest secrets take wind, we know not how; and our own folly acts the part of an informer to awaken offended justice. The crisis of Maclaine's fate was at hand. It was he who proposed his last excursion to Plunket, who was ill at the time, and was very unwilling to turn out; but Maclaine, impelled by some uncommon impulse, urged him so earnestly, that he at length complied. They came up, about two o'clock in the morning, near Turnham Green, with the Salisbury stage-coach, in which five men and a woman were passengers. Though this was Maclaine's expedition, yet Plunket was the acting man, and obliged all the men to come out of the coach one by one, and rifled them; and then, putting his pistol in his pocket, lest he should frighten the lady, without forcing her out of the coach, he took what she offered without further search. Plunket would now have gone off; but Maclaine, full of his fate, demanded the cloak-bags out of the boot of the coach; each of them took one before him and rode

---

nobility, which he has just received. If he had escaped a month longer, he might have heard of Mr. Chute's genealogic expertness, and come hither to the College of Arms for a certificate. There was a wardrobe of clothes, three-and-twenty purses, and the celebrated blunderbuss found at his lodging, besides a famous kept mistress. As I conclude he will suffer, and wish him no ill, I don't care to have his idea, and am almost single in not having been to see him. Lord Mountford, at the head of half White's, went the first day: his aunt was crying over him: as soon as they were withdrawn, she said to him, knowing they were of White's, 'My dear, what did the Lords say to you? have you ever been concerned with any of them?' Was not it admirable? what a favourable idea people must have of White's!—and what if White's should not deserve a much better! But the chief personages who have been to comfort and weep over this fallen hero are Lady Caroline Petersham and Miss Ashe: I call them Polly and Lucy, and asked them if he did not sing—'Thus I stand like the Turk with his doxies around.' "

off, bidding a polite adieu to the passengers, and riding as deliberately as though they had been performing some signal service.

On the same morning they met and robbed Lord Eglinton, who was the prize for whom they originally went out. They effected this by a stratagem, as his lordship was armed with a blunderbuss. One of them screened himself behind the post-boy, so that if his lordship fired, he must shoot his servant, while the other with a pistol cocked demanded his money, and ordered him to throw his blunderbuss on the ground. But it appears the prize obtained at this hazard was but seven guineas, with which, and the cloak-bags, they returned to Maclaine's lodgings before the family were up, and divided their spoil.

But though the clothes were described in the public papers, yet so infatuated was Maclaine, that he sold his share of the booty to a salesman, who instantly recognized them as belonging to a Mr. Higden, and the latter immediately had Maclaine taken into custody.

On his first examination he denied the fact, but after wards, that he might leave himself no room to escape, he formed a design of saving his life by impeaching his accomplice Plunket, foolishly imagining that justice would promise life to a villain she had in custody, for impeaching another that was out of her reach. But " Quem Deus vult perdere priùs dementat," or to express a similar sentiment in the words of Massinger—

> " Here is a precedent to teach wicked men,
>   That when they leave religion and turn atheists,
>   Their own abilities leave 'em."

For though he was forewarned that a confession, without impeaching a number of accomplices, would not avail him, he still insisted upon taking that step, not from compunction or remorse, but with the base design of saving his own life at the expense of that of his quondam friend.

On his second examination he delivered his confession .n writing, and behaved in a most dastardly manner whimpering and crying like a whipped school-boy. This conduct, degrading as it was, drew sympathetic tears from, and opened the purses of his fair audience, whose bounty supported him in great affluence while he remained in the Gatehouse, and whose kind offers of intercession gave him hopes of a free pardon.

On his trial, he thought fit to retract his confession, pretending that he was flurried, and in some measure delirious when he made it, and that he had received the clothes from Plunket in payment of a debt. But this evasion had no weight with the jury, who brought him in guilty without going out of court.

On receiving sentence, guilt, shame, and dread deprived him of the power of speech, and disabled him from reading a prayer, pathetically enough composed, in which he prayed for mercy.

In Newgate, ample time was permitted him to make his peace with his offended Maker, and there is every evidence to believe from the testimony of the Rev. Dr. Allen, who attended him constantly to the last moment of his life, that his remorse and contrition were unaffected, sincere, and strong.

He was carried to Tyburn in a cart, like the rest of the criminals, and not, as was expected, in a coach; he stood the gaze of the multitude (which was on this occasion almost infinite), without the least concern; his thoughts were steadfast in his devotion, and when he was about to be turned off, he said, " O God, forgive my enemies, bless my friends, and receive my soul!" His execution took place on Wednesday, October 3, 1750.

THE ABBE DE VATTEVILLE.

ALL my readers will remember that there has been a doubt expressed, whether or not a dignitary of the English Church had not been in early life a Buccaneer and a robber. I say all will remember it, because Lord Byron alluded to the circumstance in a note to "The Corsair," one of the finest of his poems.

As, however, the passage is short as it is curious, I will quote it here.

"In Noble's continuation of Granger's Biographical History there is a singular passage in his account of Archbishop Blackbourne; and as in some measure connected with the profession of the hero of the foregoing poem, I cannot resist the temptation of extracting it.— ' There is something mysterious in the history and character of Dr. Blackbourne. The former is but imperfectly known; and report has even asserted he was a Buccaneer; and that one of his brethren in that profession having asked, on his arrival in England, what had become of his old chum, Blackbourne, was answered, he is Archbishop of York. We are informed, that Blackbourne was installed sub-dean of Exeter in 1694, which office he resigned in 1702; but after his successor Lewis Barnet's death, in 1704, he regained it. In the following year he became dean; and in 1714 held with it the archdeanery of Cornwall. He was consecrated bishop of Exeter, February 24, 1716; and translated to York, November 28, 1724, as a reward, according to court scandal, for uniting George I. to the Duchess of Munster. This, however, appears to nave been an unfounded calumny. As archbishop he behaved with great prudence, and was equally respectable as the guardian of the revenues of the see. Rumour whispered he retained the vices of his youth, and that a passion for the fair sex formed an item in the list of his weaknesses; but so far from being convicted by seventy witnesses, he does not appear to have been directly criminated by one. In

short, I look upon these aspersions as the effects of mere
malice. How is it possible a Buccaneer should have been
so good a scholar as Blackbourne certainly was? He
who had so perfect a knowledge of the classics (particularly of the Greek tragedians,) as to be able to read them
with the same ease as he could Shakspeare, must have
taken great pains to acquire the learned languages, and
have had both leisure and good masters. But he was un-
doubtedly educated at Christ-church College, Oxford.*
He is allowed to have been a pleasant man; this, however, was turned against him, by its being said, ' he gained
more hearts than souls.' "

If the identification cannot be established in the case
of our countryman Archbishop Blackbourne, the French
Church offers a most remarkable and well-authenticated
instance of a murderer, a renegado, and a worse than
robber, who attained eminence in the Catholic Hierarchy.

I translate the wonderful history of this successful and
remorseless villain as it is given in that rich mine of contemporary biography and history, the Memoires of the
Duke of St. Simond.

" The death of the Abbé de Vatteville made less noise
(in the year 1702,) but the prodigy of his life merits to be
mentioned. He was the brother of the Baron de Vatteville, ambassador of Spain in England, who, at London
in October 1661, offered a sort of insult to the Count,
since Maréchal d'Estrade, ambassador of France, touching the etiquette of precedence.

---

* These arguments do not appear to me to be very conclusive
Dampier, Lionel Wafer, and Sharp, and others of the Buccaneers,
were men of considerable education. From their acquirements to
the classical accomplishments of Blackbourne is indeed a step, but
still it is only a question of degree, and in associations where there
were such civilized men as they, there might be one still more cultivated, like Blackbourne. I have no anxiety to prove the identity
of a robber and a bishop, but think there can be nothing so very im-
probable in the story, that a wild youth, even though educated at
" Christ-church College, Oxford," should have been a Buccaneer in
the West Indies, and then have returned, and, after a dubious reformation of his morals, have attained high church preferment, by
his talents, his intrigues, or by a fortunate patronage.

" These Vattevilles are people of quality of the Franche Comté. This youngest son became a monk of the Order of the Carthusians in very early life, and after his profession was ordained as priest. He had a deal of wit and spirit; but a spirit free and impetuous, which soon became impatient of the monastic yoke to which he had submitted. Incapable of remaining any longer in subjection to such annoying observances, he deliberated on the means of liberating himself from them. He found means to procure private clothes to wear instead of his monkish garb; and, moreover, some money, pistols, and a horse that was to be in waiting for him at a short distance from the monastery. He had not been able to do all this without exciting some suspicion. His superior, indeed, suspected him, when one night, as he was between sleep and awake, Vatteville stole into his room. The prior feigned to be fast asleep, and the monk retreated from his bedside with a key that opened one of the outer gates of the monastery. Shortly after the prior went with a *passe-par-tout*, and opened the door of his cell, when he found Vatteville dressed in his secular clothes on a rope-ladder, with which he was going to climb the walls. Hereupon the prior begins to cry out aloud, and Vatteville shoots him dead with a pistol, and escapes. Two or three days after, he stops to dine at a mean public-house, situated alone in a solitary part of the country, for he had avoided as much as he could stopping at inhabited places; he dismounts, and asks what there is in the larder? The host replies, a leg of mutton and a capon. 'Bah!' answers my unfrocked monk, 'put them both on the spit. The host would represent to him that a leg of mutton and a capon are too much for one man, and that these gone, there is nothing else in the house. The monk becomes angry, and tells him that when a man can pay, the least he can expect is to have what he wishes, and that his appetite is good enough to eat both. The host does not dare reply, and puts the leg of mutton and the capon down to the fire. As these two roasts were done, there comes another man on horseback, and also alone, to dine at the cabaret. He asks what there is to eat, and is told there is nothing but what he sees just ready to be taken from the spit. He then inquires how many persons is this ordered for, and is very much aston-ished that it should be all for one man. He proposes in paying his portion to partake of this dinner, and he is still more surprised at the answer of the host, who assures him he doubts whether this will be allowed, judging from the air of the person who had first ordered the dinner. On this the traveller goes up-stairs, civilly addresses Vatteville, and begs he will condescend to let him dine with him, paying of course his share, as there is nothing in the house except what he has ordered. Vatteville will not consent to this: a dispute begins—becomes warm; brief, the monk deals with him as he had done with his superior, and kills his man with a pistol-shot. He then tranquilly goes down-stairs, and in the midst of the af-fright of the host, and of all the people about the inn, orders up his leg of mutton and his capon, which he eats to the very bones, pays his bill, mounts his horse, and is off.

"Not knowing what to do with himself, he goes to the Turks; and to be short, he gets himself circumcised, puts on the turban, and enters their army. His renegation advances him; his wit and his valour distinguish him, and he becomes a Pasha, and a confidential man in the Morea, where the Turks were carrying on war against the Venetians. He took several fortified places, and con-ducted himself so well with the Turks, that he believed himself in a position to take advantage of his circum-stances, in which he could not be comfortable. He found the means of addressing the Government of the Republic, and of making his bargain with them. He promised verbally to give up several fortresses, and to make them acquainted with numerous secrets of the Turks, on con-dition that they should procure and bring him in all and its best forms the absolution of His Holiness the Pope for the sundry misdeeds of his life, his murders, his apos-tasy—an entire security against the Carthusians; an as-surance that he should not be given over to any other monastic order, but fully restored to the secular condition,

with all the rights of those who never quitted it, and fully
reinstated in the exercise of his order of priesthood, with
a faculty of possessing all sorts of benefices. The Venetians too well found their account in this to attempt to
spare themselves, and the Pope believed the interest of
the Church great enough to favour the Christians against
the Turks ; with a good grace he granted all the demands
of the Pasha. When Vatteville was well assured that all
these representations had reached the Government in the
best form, he took his measures so well that he perfectly
executed all that he had engaged to do for the Venetians.
As soon as he had done this, he went over to the Venetian army, then embarked on board of one of their ships,
which carried him to Italy. He went to Rome, the Pope
received him well; and fully reassured, he returned to
Franche Comté to the bosom of his family, where he
amused himself by spiting the Carthusians.

"These singular events of his life made him much
known at the first conquest of the Franche Comté: he
was thought a man of address and intrigue; he closely
connected himself with the Queen-mother, then with
Ministers, who adroitly made use of him at the second
conquest of the same province. He rendered great services, but not for nothing. He had stipulated for the Arch-
bishopric of Bésancon, and in effect, after the second
conquest, he was named to it. The Pope could not make
up his mind to the giving Vatteville the necessary Bulls,
but exclaimed against the atrocity of his murders, his
apostasy, and circumcision. The King entered into the
reasons of the Pope, and he capitulated with the Abbé de
Vatteville, who contented himself with the Abbey of
Beaume, the half of Franche Comté, an intermediate
property in Picardy, and sundry other advantages. He
afterwards lived in his Abbey of Beaume, part of his
time on his estates, sometimes at Bésançon, but rarely at
Paris and the Court, where he was always received with
distinction.

" He had wherever he went, numerous equipages and
attendants, a splendid establishment, fine packs of hounds,
a sumptuous table, and good company. He put himself

under no restraint as regarded women and lived not only
en grand Seigneur, much feared, and much respected
but, after the ancient fashion, tyrannising over the people
on his estates, those about his Abbey, and sometimes over
his neighbours; above all, he was very absolute in his
own house. The Intendants of the Province bent their
shoulders, and by express orders of the Government, as
long as he lived, let him do as he chose, and dared not
oppose him in anything; neither as to the taxes, which
he regulated as he thought fit in all the territories depending on him, nor as to any of his enterprises, which were
frequently most violent ones. With these morals and
with this comportment, that made him be feared and respected, he delighted, at times, to go and see the Carthusians, in order that he might glorify himself on having
thrown off their hood. He was a rare good player at
the game of ombre, and so frequently gained *codille*, that
he was nicknamed from that circumstance L'Abbé Codille.
He lived in this style, and always with the same license,
and in the same high consideration, nearly to the age of
ninety. The grandson of Vatteville's brother, after an
interval of many years, married a half-sister of Monsieur
du Maurepas."

CHINESE PIRATES.

THE Celestial Empire, spite of the boasted wisdom of its government, and the virtue and order that have been supposed to reign there for so many centuries, is no more free from robbers than countries of less ancient date and inferior pretension. On the contrary, if we except India, no part of the world, has, in our time, witnessed such formidable and numerous associations of freebooters. These Chinese robbers were pirates, and I am disposed to give a sketch of them and their adventures, as a striking *pendant* to the former chapter on the Buccaneers of South America; and this, because I am not only in possession of a most curious account of the suppression or pacification of the rovers, translated from the original Chinese, but of a corroboration written by an Englishman, who was so unfortunate as to fall into their hands, and to see his comrades (English sailors) obliged to take part in their marauding and murderous expeditions.

For the translation of *Yuen Tsze's* "History of the Pirates who infested the China Sea from 1807 to 1810," we are indebted to that excellent institution the Oriental Translation Fund, and to the labours of the distinguished Orientalist Mr. Charles Fried Neumann; and for the Narrative of his captivity and treatment amongst the Ladrones, (pirates,) to Richard Glasspoole, Esq. of the Hon. East India Company's service, a gentleman who is still living. I shall make out my account of the Chinese pirates from either of these two authorities, without copying them both, or quoting from them in any other order than what suits the convenience of the narrative.

The Ladrones, as they were christened by the Portuguese of Macao, were originally a disaffected set of Chinese, that revolted against the oppression of the Mandarines. The first scene of their depredations was the Western coast, about Cochin-China, where they began by attacking small trading vessels in row-boats, carrying from thirty to forty men each. They continued this system of piracy, and thrived and increased in numbers under it, for several years. At length the fame of their successes, and the oppression and horrid poverty and want that many of the lower order of Chinese laboured under, had the effect of augmenting their bands with astonishing rapidity. Fishermen and other destitute classes flocked by hundreds to their standard, and their audacity growing with their numbers, they not merely swept the coast, but blockaded all the principal rivers, and attacked and took several large government war junks, mounting from ten to fifteen guns each.

These junks being added to their shoals of boats, the pirates formed a tremendous fleet, which was always along shore, so that no small vessel could safely trade on the coast. When they lacked prey on the sea, they laid the land under tribute. They were at first accustomed to go on shore and attack the maritime villages, but becoming bolder, they, like the Buccaneers, made long inland journeys, and surprised and plundered even large towns.

An energetic attempt made by the Chinese government to destroy them, only increased their strength; for in their very first rencounter with the pirates, twenty-eight of the Imperial junks struck, and the remaining twelve saved themselves by a precipitate retreat.

The captured junks, fully equipped for war, were a great acquisition to the robbers, whose numbers now increased more rapidly than ever. They were in their plenitude of power in the year 1809, when Mr. Glasspoole had the misfortune to fall into their hands, at which time, that gentleman supposed their force to consist of 70,000 men, navigating eight hundred large vessels, and one thousand small ones, including row-boats. They were divided into six large squadrons, under different flags ;—the red, the yellow, the green, the blue, the black, and the white. " These wasps of the ocean," as the Chinese historian pertinently calls them, were further distinguished by the names of their respective commanders. Of these commanders a certain *Ching-yih* had been

"They began by attacking vessels in rowboats, carrying from Thirty to Forty men each."   Page 257.

the most distinguished by his valour and conduct. By degrees Ching obtained almost a supremacy of command over the whole united fleet; and so confident was this robber in his strength and daily augmenting means, that he aspired to the dignity of a great political character, and went so far as openly to declare his patriotic intention of hurling the present Tartar family from the throne of China, and of restoring the ancient native Chinese dynasty.

But unfortunately for this ambitious pirate, "it happened that on the seventeenth day of the tenth .moon, in the twentieth year of Këa-King," he perished in a heavy gale, and instead of placing a sovereign on the Chinese throne, he and his lofty aspirations were buried in the sea of China. And now comes the most remarkable passage in the history of these pirates—remarkable with any class of men, but doubly so among the Chinese, who entertain more than the general oriental opinion of the inferiority, or nothingness, of the fair sex.

On the death of *Ching-yih*, his legitimate wife had sufficient influence over the freebooters to induce them to recognize her authority in the place of her deceased husband's; and she appointed one *Paou* as her lieutenant and prime minister, and provided that she should be considered the mistress or the commander-in-chief of the united squadrons.

This *Paou* had been a poor fisher-boy, picked up with his father at sea, while fishing, by *Ching-yih*, whose good will and favour he had the fortune to captivate, and by whom, before that pirate's death, he had been made a headman or captain. The grave Chinese historian does not descend into such domestic particulars, but we may presume, from her appointing him to be her lieutenant, that *Paou* had been equally successful in securing the good graces of *Mistress Ching*, as the worthy translator somewhat irreverently styles our Chinese heroine.

Instead of declining under the rule of a woman, the pirates became more enterprising than ever. Ching's widow was clever as well as brave, and so was her lieu-

tenant Paou. Between them they drew up a code of laws
for the better regulation of their freebooters.

In this it was decreed, that if any man went privately
on shore, or did what they called " transgressing the
bars," he should have his ears slit in the presence of the
whole fleet; a repetition of the same unlawful act, was
death! No one article, however trifling in value, was to
be privately subtracted from the booty or plundered goods.
Every thing they took was regularly entered on the
register of their stores. The pirates were to receive in
due proportion, out of this common fund, their shares, or
what they stood in need of, and any one of them purloin-
ing any thing from this general fund, was to be punished
with death. (These regulations of the Chinese pirates
correspond with those in force among the Buccaneers;
when the latter robbers had taken a prize, each man held
up his hand, and swore he had secreted nothing for his
private advantage. Similar arrangements will be found
to have existed among all predatory associations, and
only prove how soon even the most lawless bodies of men
must feel the necessity of something like law among
themselves.) The following clause of Mistress Ching's
code is still more delicate.

"No person shall debauch at his pleasure captive
women, taken in the villages and open places, and brought
on board a ship; he must first request the ship's purser
for permission, and then go aside in the ship's hold. To
use violence against any woman, or to wed her, without
permission, shall be punished with death."

That the pirates might never feel the want of provisions and other supplies, it was ordered by Ching-yih's
widow, that every thing should be done to gain the common country people to their interest. Wine, rice, and all
other goods were to be paid for, as the villagers delivered
them: capital punishment was pronounced on every pirate
who should take any thing of this kind by force, or without paying for it. And not only were these laws well
calculated for their object, but the she-commander-in-
chief and her lieutenant *Paou* were vigilant in seeing
them observed, and strict in every transaction.

By these means an admirable discipline was maintain
ed on board the ships, and the peasantry on shore nevei
let the pirates want for gunpowder, provisions, or any
other necessary. On a piratical expedition, either to ad
vance or to retreat without orders, was a capital offence.

Under these philosophical institutions, and the guidance
of a woman, the robbers continued to scour the China
sea, plundering every vessel they came near; but it is to
be remarked, in their delicate phraseology, the robbing
of a ship's cargo was not called by any such vulgar term
—it was merely styled " a transhipping of goods."

According to our Chinese historian *Yuen Tsze*, who
shows throughout an inclination to treat *Paou* as Homer
did some of his doughtier heroes, the herculean lieutenant gained an increase of reputation by lifting up him
self, in the Temple dedicated to the " Three Old Women,"
on the sea-coast,—a heavy image, which all the men
together who accompanied him could not so much as
move from its base. By the lieutenant's orders, this
cumbrous statue was carried aboard ship, where the
superstitious pirates dreaded from the wrath of the idol,
or the Three Old Women, an inevitable and general death
in the next storm or next fight. It did not, however, so
turn out; for a few months after, when the great war
Mandarin, Kwolang-lin, sailed from the Bocca Tigris into
the sea to fight the pirates, Paou, the idol-lifter and lieutenant of Ching-yih's widow, gave him a tremendous
drubbing, and gained a splendid victory. In this battle,
which lasted from morning till night, the Mandarin
Kwolang-lin, a desperate fellow himself, levelled a gun
at Paou, who fell on his neck as the piece went off; his
disheartened crew concluded it was all over with him,
and that the " Three Old Women" had their spite. But
Paou was quick-eyed as he was strong-limbed; he had
seen the unfriendly intention of the Mandarin, and
thrown himself down; but no sooner had the shot gone
over him, than he " stood up again, firm and upright, so
that all thought he was a spirit." The great Mandarin
who had meant him this ugly compliment, was soon after
with fifteen of his junks (three others had been sunk)

taken prisoner.   The pirate lieutenant-chief would have
dealt mercifully with him, but the fierce old man suddenly seized him by the hair on the crown of his head, and
grinned at him, so that he might provoke him to slay
him.   But even then Paou was moderate, speaking kindly to the old Mandarin, and trying to soothe him.   Upon
this, " Kwolang-lin, seeing himself deceived in his expectation, and that he could not attain death by such
means, committed suicide—being then a man of seventy
years of age."

" There were in this battle," continues the Chinese
historian, "three of my friends ; the lieutenant Tao-tae-
lin, Tsaco-tang-hoo, and Ying-hwang, serving under the
former.   Lin and Hoo were killed, but Hwang escaped
when all was surrounded with smoke, and he it was who
told me the whole affair."

Not long after, another great Mandarin, called Lin-fa,
who went out to wage war against the pirates, was
equally unsuccessful.   He no sooner came in sight of
those he was looking for, than his fleet, panic-struck at
their numbers and martial appearance, changed their
track, and tried to run back to port.   But the fleet of
Mistress Ching and her bold lieutenant were too quick
for the Imperial forces.   They came up with them near
a place called Olang-pae, and there, their vessels being
rendered motionless by the dead calm, the daring pirates
threw themselves into the sea, and swimming to the Mandarin's ships, boarded and took six of them.   The Mandarin was killed.

In the next adventure on record, a party of the pirates
sustained a rude check from a lofty argoisie, laden with
goods from Cochin-China and Tung King, and were
obliged to retire to their boats ; " a circumstance," saith
the historian, " which never happened before."

In the action after this, they were still more severely
handled.   The great Admiral Tsnen-Maw-Sun, proceeded with a hundred vessels to attack the pirates, who did
not retreat, but drew up in a line of battle, and made a
tremendous attack on the imperial fleet, where an immense number fell, between killed and wounded.   The

ropes and sails* having been set on fire by the guns of the Emperor's ships, the pirates became exceedingly afraid, and took them away. The Admiral directed his fire against their steerage, that they might not be able to steer their vessels. Being very close one to the other, the pirates were exposed to the fire of all the four lines of the Admiral's fleet at once.

The pirates opened their eyes in astonishment, and fell down ; the Chinese commander advanced courageously, laid hold of their vessels, killed an immense number of men, and took about two hundred prisoners. " There was a pirate's wife in one of the boats, holding so fast by the helm, that she could scarcely be taken away. Having two cutlasses, she desperately defended herself, and wounded some soldiers ; but on being wounded by a match-lock ball, she fell back into the vessel, and was taken prisoner."

But the tarnished laurels of the pirates were soon brightened ; for when the said Tsuen-mow-Sun went to attack them in the bay of Kwang-chow, the widow of Ching-yih, remaining quiet with part of her ships, sent her bold lieutenant Paou to make an attack on the front of the Admiral's line. When the fight was well begun, the rest of the pirate's ships, that had been lying *perdu,* came upon the Admiral's rear, and presently surrounded him.—" Then," saith the historian, " our squadron was scattered, thrown into disorder, and consequently cut to pieces : there was a noise which rent the sky ; every man fought in his own defence, and scarcely a hundred remained together. The squadron of the wife of Ching-yih, overpowered us by numbers : our commander was not able to protect his lines, they were broken, and we lost fourteen ships."

The next fight being very characteristically described, must be given entire in the words of our Chinese historian.

" Our men-of-war escorting some merchant ships, in the fourth moon of the same year, happened to meet the

---

* It must be remembered that the Chinese sails are nothing more than mats.

pirate chief nicknamed ' The Jewel of the Crew,' cruising at sea. The traders became exceedingly frightened, but our commander said : ' This not being the flag of the widow Ching-yih, we are a match for them, therefore we will attack and conquer them.' Then ensued a battle ; they attacked each other with guns and stones, and many people were killed and wounded. The fighting ceased towards the evening, and began again next morning. The pirates and the men-of-war were very close to each other, and they boasted mutually about their strength and valour. It was a very hard fight ; the sound of cannon, and the cries of the combatants, were heard some *le*** distant. The traders remained at some distance ; they saw the pirates mixing gunpowder in their beverage,— they looked instantly red about the face and eyes, and then fought desperately. This fighting continued three days and nights incessantly ; at last, becoming tired on both sides, they separated."

To understand this inglorious bulletin, the reader must remember that many of the combatants only handled bows and arrows, and pelted stones, and that Chinese powder and guns are both exceedingly bad. The pathos of the conclusion does somewhat remind one of the Irishman's despatch during the American war—" It was a bloody battle while it lasted ; and the serjeant of marines lost his cartouche-box."

The pirates continuing their depredations, plundered and burned a number of towns and villages on the coast, and carried off a number of prisoners of both sexes. From one place alone, they carried off fifty-three women.

The Admiral Ting Kwei was then sent to sea against them. This man was surprised at anchor by the ever vigilant and active Paou, to whom many fishermen, and other people on the coast, must have acted as friendly spies. Seeing escape impossible, and that his officers stood pale and inactive by the flag-staff, the Admiral conjured them, by their fathers and mothers, their wives and children, and by hopes of brilliant reward if they suc-

---

" Le, a Chinese mile.—" I compute," says Bell, " five of their miles to be about two and a half English."

ceeded, and of vengeance if they perished, to do their duty, and the combat began. The Admiral had the good fortune, at the onset, of killing with one of his great guns the pirate captain, " the Jewel of the Crew ;" but the robbers swarmed thicker and thicker around him, and when the dreaded Paou lay him by the board, without help or hope, the Mandarin killed himself. An immense number of his men perished in the sea, and twenty-five vessels were lost.

After this defeat it was resolved by the Chinese Government to cut off all their supplies of provision, and, if possible, starve the pirates. All vessels that were in port, of whatsoever kind they might be, were ordered to remain there, and those at sea, or on the coast, speedily to return. The Government officers, for once, seem to have done their duty, and been very vigilant ; but the pirates, full of confidence, now resolved to attack the harbours themselves, and to ascend the rivers, which are navigable for many miles up the country, and on which the most prosperous towns and villages are generally situated.

The Canton river discharges itself into the sea by many channels, through three of which the robbers forced their passage. Hitherto they had robbed in the open sea outside the Canton river, and when the Chinese thus saw them venturing above the Government forts, and threatening the defenceless inland country, their consternation was greater than ever.

The pirates separated : Mistress Ching plundering in one place ; Paou, in another ; O-po-tae, in another, &c.

It was at this time that Mr. Glasspoole had the ill fortune to fall into their power. This gentleman, then an officer in the East India Company's ship the Marquis of Ely, which was anchored under an island, about twelve miles from Macao, was ordered to proceed to the latter place with a boat to procure a pilot. He left the ship in one of the cutters with seven British seamen well armed, on the 17th September, 1809. He reached Macao in safety, and having done his business there and procured a pilot, returned towards the ship the following day. But, unfortunately, the ship had weighed anchor and was un-

der sail, and in consequence of squally weather, accom
panied with thick fogs, the boat could not reach her, and
Mr. Glasspoole and his men and the pilot were left at
sea, in an open boat. " Our situation," says that gentleman, " was truly distressing—night closing fast, with
a threatening appearance, blowing fresh with hard rain
and a heavy sea; our boat very leaky, without a compass, anchor, or provisions, and drifting fast on a lee-
shore, surrounded with dangerous rocks, and inhabited
by the most barbarous pirates."

After suffering dreadfully for three whole days, Mr.
Glasspoole, by the advice of the pilot, made for a narrow
channel, where he presently discovered three large boats
at anchor, which, on seeing the English boat, weighed
and made sail towards it. The pilot told Mr. Glasspoole
they were Ladrones, and that if they captured the boat,
they would certainly put them all to death ! After rowing tremendously for six hours, they escaped these boats,
but on the following morning falling in with a large fleet
of the pirates, which the English mistook for fishing-boats,
they were captured.

" About twenty savage-looking villains," says Mr.
Glasspoole, " who were stowed at the bottom of a boat,
leaped on board us. They were armed with a short
sword in either hand, one of which they laid upon our
necks, and pointed the other to our breasts, keeping their
eyes fixed upon their officer, waiting his signal to cut or
desist. Seeing we were incapable of making any resistance, the officer sheathed his sword, and the others
immediately followed his example. They then dragged
us into their boat, and carried us on board one of their
junks, with the most savage demonstrations of joy,
and, as we supposed, to torture, and put us to a cruel
death."

When on board the junk they rifled the Englishmen, and brought heavy chains to chain them to the
deck.

" At this time a boat came and took me, with one of
my men and the interpreter, on board the chief's vessel. I
was then taken before the chief. He was seated on deck,

in a large chair, dressed in purple silk, with a black turban on. He appeared to be about thirty years of age, a
stout commanding-looking man. He took me by the
coat, and drew me close to him ; then questioned the interpreter very strictly, asking who we were, and what
was our business in that part of the country. I told him
to say we were Englishmen in distress, having been four
days at sea without provisions. This he would not credit,
but said we were bad men, and that he would put us all
to death ; and then ordered some men to put the interpreter to the torture until he confessed the truth. Upon
this occasion, a Ladrone, who had been once to England
and spoke a few words of English, came to the chief, and
told him we were really Englishmen, and that we had
plenty of money, adding that the buttons on my coat
were gold. The chief then ordered us some coarse brown
rice, of which we made a tolerable meal, having eaten
nothing for nearly four days, except a few green oranges.
During our repast, a number of Ladrones crowded round
us, examining our clothes and hair, and giving us every
possible annoyance. Several of them brought swords,
and laid them on our necks, making signs that they
would soon take us on shore, and cut us in pieces, which
I am sorry to say was the fate of some hundreds during
my captivity. I was now summoned before the chief,
who had been conversing with the interpreter ; he said I
must write to my captain, and tell him if he did not send
an hundred thousand dollars for our ransom, in ten days
he would put us all to death."

    After vainly expostulating to lessen the ransom, Mr.
Glasspoole wrote the letter, and a small boat came alongside and took it to Macao.

    " About six o'clock in the evening they gave us some
rice and a little salt fish, which we ate, and they made
signs for us to lie down on the deck to sleep ; but such
numbers of Ladrones were constantly coming from different vessels to see us, and examine our clothes and hair,
 hey would not allow us a moment's quiet. They were
particularly anxious for the buttons of my coat, which
were new, and as they supposed gold. I took it off, and

laid it on the deck to avoid being disturbed by them; it was taken away in the night, and I saw it on the next day stripped of its buttons."

Early in the night the fleet sailed and anchored about one o'clock the following day in a bay under the island of Lantow, where the head admiral of Ladrones (our acquaintance Paou) was lying at anchor, with about two hundred vessels and a Portuguese brig they had captured a few days before, and the captain and part of the crew of which they had murdered. Early the next morning, a fishing-boat came to inquire if they had captured an European boat: they came to the vessel the English were in.

"One of the boatmen spoke a few words of English, and told me he had a Ladrone-pass, and was sent by our captain in search of us; I was rather surprised to find he had no letter. He appeared to be well acquainted with the chief, and remained in his cabin, smoking opium and playing cards, all the day. In the evening, I was summoned with the interpreter before the chief. He questioned us in a much milder tone, saying, he now believed we were Englishmen, a people he wished to be friendly with; and that if our captain would lend him seventy thousand dollars till he returned from his cruise up the river, he would repay him, and send us all to Macao. I assured him that it was useless writing on those terms, and unless our ransom was speedily settled, the English fleet would sail, and render our enlargement altogether ineffectual. He remained determined, and said if it were not sent, he would keep us, and make us fight, or put us to death. I accordingly wrote, and gave my letter to the man belonging to the boat before-mentioned. He said he could not return with an answer in less than five days. The chief now gave me the letter I wrote when first taken. I have never been able to ascertain his reasons for detaining it, but suppose he dared not negotiate for our ransom without orders from the head admiral, who, I understood, was sorry at our being captured. He said the English ships would join the Mandarins and attack them."

While the fleet lay here, one night the Portuguese who were left in the captured brig murdered the Ladrones that were on board of her, cut the cables, and fortunately escaped through the darkness of the night.

"At day-light the next morning, the fleet, amounting to above five hundred sail of different sizes, weighed, to proceed on their intended cruize up the rivers, to levy contributions on the towns and villages. It is impossible to describe what were my feeelings at this critical time, having received no answers to my letters, and the fleet under-way to sail—hundreds of miles up a country never visited by Europeans, there to remain probably for many months, which would render all opportunities of nego-tiating for our enlargement totally ineffectual; as the only method of communication is by boats that have a pass from the Ladrones, and they dare not venture above twenty miles from Macao, being obliged to come and go in the night, to avoid the Mandarins; and if these boats should be detected in having any intercourse with the Ladrones, they are immediately put to death, and all their relations, though they had not joined in the crime,* share in the punishment, in order that not a single person of their families should be left to imitate their crimes or re-venge their death."

The following is a very touching incident in Mr. Glass-poole's narrative.

" Wednesday the 26th of September, at day-light, we passed in sight of our own ships, at anchor under the island of Chun Po. The chief then called me, pointed to the ships, and told the interpreter to tell us to look at them, for we should never see them again! About noon we entered a river to the westward of the Bogue,† three or four miles from the entrance. We passed a large town situated on the side of a beautiful hill, which is tributary to the Ladrones; the inhabitants saluted them with songs as they passed."

---

* That the whole family must suffer for the crime of one individual, seems to be the most cruel and foolish law of the whole Chinese criminal code.

† The Hoo-mun, or Bocca Tigris.

After committing numerous minor robberies; "The Ladrones now prepared to attack a town with a formidable force, collected in row-boats from the different vessels They sent a messenger to the town, demanding a tribute of ten thousand dollars annually, saying, if these terms were not complied with, they would land, destroy the town, and murder all the inhabitants: which they would certainly have done, had the town laid in a more advantageous situation for their purpose; but being placed out of the reach of their shot, they allowed them to come to terms. The inhabitants agreed to pay six thousand dollars, which they were to collect by the time of our return down the river. This finesse had the desired effect, for during our absence they mounted a few guns on a hill, which commanded the passage, and gave us in lieu of the dollars a warm salute on our return.

"October the 1st, the fleet weighed in the night, dropped by the tide up the river, and anchored very quietly before a town surrounded by a thick wood. Early in the morning the Ladrones assembled in row-boats, and landed; then gave a shout, and rushed into the town, sword in hand. The inhabitants fled to the adjacent hills, in numbers apparently superior to the Ladrones. We may easily imagine to ourselves the horror with which these miserable people must be seized, on being obliged to leave their homes, and every thing dear to them. It was a most melancholy thing to see women in tears, clasping their infants in their arms, and imploring mercy for them from those brutal robbers! The old and the sick, who were unable to fly, or to make resistance, were either made prisoners or most inhumanly butchered! The boats continued passing and repassing from the junks to the shore, in quick succession, laden with booty, and the men besmeared with blood! Two hundred and fifty women and several children, were made prisoners, and sent on board different vessels. They were unable to escape with the men, owing to that abominable practice of cramping their feet: several of them were not able to move without assistance, in fact, they might all be said to totter, rather than walk. Twenty of these poor women were sent on board the vessel I was in; they were hauled on board by the hair, and treated in a most savage manner. When the chief came on board he questioned them respecting the circumstances of their friends, and demanded ransoms accordingly, from six thousand to six hundred dollars each. He ordered them a berth on deck, at the after part of the vessel, where they had nothing to shelter them from the weather, which at this time was very variable—the days excessively hot, and the nights cold with heavy rains. The town being plundered of every thing valuable, it was set on fire, and reduced to ashes by the morning. The fleet remained here three days, negotiating for the ransom of the prisoners, and plundering the fish-tanks and gardens. During all this time, the Chinese never ventured from the hills, though there were frequently not more than a hundred Ladrones on shore at a time, and I am sure the people on the hills exceeded ten times that number.*

"October the 5th, the fleet proceeded up another branch of the river, stopping at several small villages to receive tribute, which was generally paid in dollars, sugar and rice, with a few large pigs roasted whole, as presents for their Joss (the idol they worship.†) Every person, on being ransomed, is obliged to present him with a pig, or some fowls, which the priest offers him with prayers; it remains before him a few hours, and is then divided amongst the crew. Nothing particular occurred till the 10th, except frequent skirmishes on shore between small parties of Ladrones and Chinese soldiers. They frequently obliged my men to go on shore, and fight with the muskets we had when taken, which did great execution, the Chinese principally using bows and arrows. They have match-locks, but use them very unskilfully.

"On the 10th, we formed a junction with the black-squadron, and proceeded many miles up a wide and beau-

* The following is the character of the Chinese of Canton, as given in the ancient Chinese books :—"People of Canton are silly, light, weak in body, and weak in mind, without any ability to fight on land."—The Indo-Chinese Gleaner, No. 19.

† Joss is a Chinese corruption of the Portuguese Dios, God.

tiful river, passing several ruins of villages that had been destroyed by the Black-squadron. On the 17th, the fleet anchored abreast four mud batteries, which defended a town, so entirely surrounded with wood that it was im. possible to form any idea of its size. The weather was very hazy, with hard squalls of rain. The Ladrones remained perfectly quiet for two days. On the third day the forts commenced a brisk fire for several hours: the Ladrones did not return a single shot, but weighed in the night and dropped down the river. The reasons they gave for not attacking the town, or returning the fire, were, that Joss had not promised them success. They are very superstitious, and consult their idol on all occasions. If his omens are good, they will undertake the most daring enterprises. The fleet now anchored opposite the ruins of the town where the women had been made prisoners. Here we remained five or six days, during which time about an hundred of the women were ransomed; the remainder were offered for sale amongst the Ladrones, for forty dollars each. The woman is considered the law. ful wife of the purchaser, who would be put to death if he discarded her. Several of them leaped overboard and drowned themselves, rather than submit to such infamous degradation."

Our friend Yuen-tsze, the native Chinese historian of the pirates, from whom I have quoted so copiously, agrees very closely, in all this river warfare and carrying off women, with Mr. Glasspoole's account. At this particular part of the warfare he introduces the following story :—

" Mei-ying, the wife of Ke-choo-yang, was very beautiful, and a pirate being about to seize her by the head, she abused him exceedingly. The pirate bound her to the yard-arm; but on abusing him yet more, the pirate dragged her down and broke two of her teeth, which filled her mouth and jaws with blood. The pirate sprang up again to bind her. Ying allowed him to approach, but as soon as he came near her, she laid hold of his gar- ments with her bleeding mouth, and threw both him and herself into the river, where they were drowned. The remaining captives of both sexes were after some months liberated, on having paid a ransom of fifteen thousand leang or ounces of silver."

So much was the sage historian affected by this event, that he became poetical. "I was affected," he says, "by the virtuous behaviour of Mei-ying, and all generous men will, as I suppose, be moved by the same feelings. I, therefore, composed a song, mourning her fate :—

"Cease fighting now for awhile!
  Let us call back the flowing waves!
  Who opposed the enemy in time?
  A single wife could overpower him
  Streaming with blood, she grasped the mad offspring of
      guilt,
  She held fast the man and threw him into the meandering
      stream.
  The spirit of water, wandering up and down on the waves,
  Was astonished at the virtue of Ying.
            My song is at an end!
  Waves meet each other continually.
  I see the water green as mountáin Peih
  But the brilliant fire returns no more!
  How long did we mourn and cry!

"I am compelled," says the ingenious translator, M. Neumann, "to give a free translation of this verse, and confess myself not quite certain of the signification of the poetical figures used by our author."

We in our town must *confess* that we cannot make much sense of his version.

"The fleet then weighed," continues Mr. Glasspoole, "and made sail down the river, to receive the ransom from the town before-mentioned. As we passed the hill, they fired several shot at us, but without effect. The Ladrones were much exasperated, and determined to revenge themselves; they dropped out of reach of their shot, and anchored. Every junk sent about a hundred men each on shore, to cut paddy, and destroy their orange-groves, which was most effectually performed for several miles down the river. During our stay here, they received information of nine boats lying up a creek, laden with paddy; boats were immediately dispatched after them. Next morning these boats were brought to the fleet; ten or twelve men were taken in them. As these had made no resistance, the chief said he would allow them to become Ladrones, if they agreed to take the usual oaths before Joss. Three or four of them refused to comply, for which they were punished in the following cruel manner: their hands were tied behind their backs, a rope from the mast-head rove through their arms, and hoisted three or four feet from the deck, and five or six men flogged them with three rattans twisted together till they were apparently dead; then hoisted them up to the mast-head, and left them hanging nearly an hour, then lowered them down, and repeated the punishment, till they died or complied with the oath.

" October the 20th, in the night, an express-boat came with the information that a large Mandarin fleet was proceeding up the river to attack us. The pirate chief immediately weighed, with fifty of the largest vessels, and sailed down the river to meet them. About one in the morning they commenced a heavy fire till day-light, when an express was sent for the remainder of the fleet to join them: about an hour after a counter order to anchor came, the Mandarin fleet having run. Two or three hours afterwards the chief returned with three captured vessels in tow, having sunk two, and eighty-three sail made their escape. The admiral of the Mandarins blew his vessel up, by throwing a lighted match into the magazine as the Ladrones were boarding her; she ran on shore, and they succeeded in getting twenty of her guns. In this action very few prisoners were taken: the men belonging to the captured vessels drowned themselves, as they were sure of suffering a lingering and cruel death if taken after making resistance."

Passing over some personal concerns of the unfortunate English captives, we come to the following disagreeable dilemma, and adventures.

" On the 28th of October, I received a letter from Captain Kay, brought by a fisherman, who had told him he would get us all back for three thousand dollars. He advised me to offer three thousand, and if not accepted, extend it to four; but not farther, as it was bad policy to offer much at first: at the same time assuring me we should be liberated, let the ransom be what it would. I offered the chief the three thousand, which he disdainfully refused, saying he was not to be played with; and unless they sent ten thousand dollars, and two large guns, with several casks of gurpowder, he would soon put us all to death. I wrote to Captain Kay, and informed him of the chief's determination, requesting, if an opportunity offer ed, to send us a shift of clothes, for which it may be easily imagined we were much distressed, having been seven weeks without a change of clothes; although constantly exposed to the weather, and of course frequently wet.

" On the first of November, the fleet sailed up a narrow river, and anchored at night within two miles of a town called Little Whampoa. In front of it was a small fort, and several Mandarin vessels lying in the harbour. The chief sent the interpreter to me, saying, I must order my men to make cartridges and clean their muskets, ready to go on shore in the morning. I assured the interpreter I should give the men no such orders, that they must please themselves. Soon after the chief came on board, threatening to put us all to a cruel death if we refused to obey his orders. For my own part I remained determined, and advised the men not to comply, as I thought by making ourselves useful we should be accounted too valuable. A few hours afterwards he sent to me again, saying, that if myself and the quarter-master would assist them at the great guns, that if also the rest of the men went on shore and succeeded in taking the place, he would then take the money offered for our ransom, and give them twenty dollars for every Chinaman's head they cut off. To these proposals we cheerfully acceded, in hopes of facilitating our deliverance."

Preferring the killing of Chinese to the living with pirates, our English tars therefore landed next day with about 3000 ruffians. Once in the fight they seem to have done their work *con amore!* and to have battled it as if they had been pirates themselves. Our friend, the Chinese historian, indeed, mentions a foreigner engaged in battle and doing great execution with a little musket, and set him down, naturally enough, as " a foreign pirate !"

" The Mandarin vessels continued firing, having block-ed up the entrance of the harbour to prevent the Ladrone boats entering. At this the Ladrones were much exas-perated, and about three hundred of them swam on shore, with a short sword lashed close under each arm ; they then ran along the banks of the river till they came abreast of the vessels, and then swam off again and boarded them. The Chinese thus attacked, leaped over-board, and endeavoured to reach the opposite shore ; the Ladrones followed, and cut the greater number of them to pieces in the water. They next towed the vessels out of the harbour, and attacked the town with increased fury. The inhabitants fought about a quarter of an hour, and then retreated to an adjacent hill, from which they were soon driven with great slaughter. After this the Ladrones returned, and plundered the town, every boat leaving it when laden. The Chinese on the hills per-ceiving most of the boats were off, rallied, and retook the town, after killing near two hundred Ladrones. One of my men was unfortunately lost in this dreadful massa-cre ! The Ladrones landed a second time, drove the Chi-nese out of the town, then reduced it to ashes, and put all their prisoners to death, without regarding either age or sex ! I must not omit to mention a most horrid (though ludicrous) circumstance which happened at this place. The Ladrones were paid by their chief ten dollars for every Chinaman's head they produced. One of my men turning the corner of a street was met by a Ladrone run-ning furiously after a Chinese ; he had a drawn sword in his hand, and two Chinaman's heads which he had cut off, tied by their tails, and slung round his neck. I was witness myself to some of them producing five or six to obtain payment !

" On the 4th of November an order arrived from the admiral for the fleet to proceed immediately to Lantow, where he was lying with only two vessels, and three Por-tuguese ships and a brig constantly annoying him ; seve-ral sail of Mandarin vessels were daily expected. The

PIRATES AND ROBBERS.

CHINESE PIRATE.

fleet weighed and proceeded towards Lantow. On pass·
ing the island of Lintin, three ships and a brig gave
chase to us. The Ladrones prepared to board; but night
closing we lost sight of them: I am convinced they al-
tered their course and stood from us. These vessels were
in the pay of the Chinese Government, and styled themselves the Invincible Squadron, cruising in the river
Tigris to annihilate the Ladrones!

" On the fifth, in the morning, the red squadron anchored in a bay under Lantow; the black squadron stood to
the eastward. In the afternoon of the 8th of November,
four ships, a brig, and a schooner came off the mouth of
the bay. At first the pirates were much alarmed, supposing them to be English vessels come to rescue us.
Some of them threatened to hang us to the mast-head for
them to fire at; and with much difficulty we persuaded
them that they were Portuguese. The Ladrones had only
seven junks in a fit state for action; these they hauled
outside, and moored them head and stern across the bay,
and manned all the boats belonging to the repairing vessels ready for boarding. The Portuguese observing these
manœuvres hove to, and communicated by boats. Soon
afterwards they made sail, each ship firing her broadside
as she passed, but without effect, the shot falling far
short. The Ladrones did not return a single shot, but
waved their colours, and threw up rockets, to induce them
to come further in, which they might easily have done,
the outside junks lying in four fathoms water, which I
sounded myself: though the Portuguese in their letters
to Macao lamented there was not sufficient water for
them to engage closer, but that they would certainly prevent their escaping before the Mandarin fleet arrived!

" On the 20th of November, early in the morning, discovered an immense fleet of Mandarin vessels standing
for the bay. On nearing us, they formed a line, and
stood close in; each vessel, as she discharged her guns,
tacked to join the rear and reload. They kept up a con
stant fire for about two hours, when one of their largest
vessels was blown up by a firebrand thrown from a Ladrone junk; after which they kept at a more respectful
distance, but continued firing without intermission till the

21st at night, when it fell calm.   The Ladrones towed
out seven large vessels, with about two hundred row-
boats to board them; but a breeze springing up, they
made sail and escaped.   The Ladrones returned into the
bay, and anchored.   The Portuguese and Mandarins followed, and continued a heavy cannonading during that
night and the next day.   The vessel I was in had her
foremast shot away, which they supplied very expedi-
tiously by taking a mainmast from a smaller vessel.

"On the 23d, in the evening, it again fell calm; the
Ladrones towed out fifteen junks in two divisions, with
the intention of surrounding them, which was nearly effected, having come up with and boarded one, when a
breeze suddenly sprang up.   The captured vessel mounted twenty-two guns. Most of her crew leaped overboard;
sixty or seventy were taken, immediately cut to pieces,
and thrown into the river.   Early in the morning the
Ladrones returned into the bay, and anchored in the same
situation as before.   The Portuguese and Mandarins followed, keeping up a constant fire.   The Ladrones never
returned a single shot, but always kept in readiness to
board, and the Portuguese were careful never to allow
them an opportunity.

"On the 28th, at night, they sent in eight fire-vessels,
which if properly constructed must have done great
execution, having every advantage they could wish for to
effect their purpose ; a strong breeze and tide directly into
the bay, and the vessels lying so close together, that it
was impossible to miss them.   On their first appearance,
the Ladrones gave a general shout, supposing them to be
Mandarin vessels on fire, but were very soon convinced
of their mistake.   They came very regularly into the
centre of the fleet, two and two, burning furiously; one
of them came alongside of the vessel I was in, but they
succeeded in booming her off.   She appeared to be a vessel of about thirty tons ; her hold was filled with straw
and wood, and there were a few small boxes of com-
bustibles on her deck, which exploded alongside of us
without doing any damage.   The Ladrones, however,
towed them all on shore, extinguished the fire, and broke
them up for fire-wood.   The Portuguese claim the credit

of constructing these destructive machines, and actually
sent a dispatch to the Governor of Macao, saying they
had destroyed at least one-third of the Ladrones' fleet,
and hoped soon to effect their purpose by totally annihi-
lating them !

"On the 29th of November, the Ladrones being all
ready for sea, they weighed and stood boldly out, bidding
defiance to the invincible squadron and imperial fleet, consisting of ninety-three war-junks, six Portuguese ships,
a brig, and a schooner. Immediately the Ladrones
weighed, they made all sail. The Ladrones chased them
two or three hours, keeping up a constant fire; finding
they did not come up with them, they hauled their wind,
and stood to the eastward. Thus terminated the boasted
blockade, which lasted nine days, during which time the
Ladrones completed all their repairs. In this action not
a single Ladrone vessel was destroyed, and their loss
about thirty or forty men. An American was also killed,
one of three that remained out of eight taken in a
schooner. I had two very narrow escapes : the first, a
twelve-pounder shot fell within three or four feet of me ;
another took a piece out of a small brass-swivel on which
I was standing. The chief's wife frequently sprinkled
me with garlic-water, which they considered an effectual
charm against shot. The fleet continued under sail all
night, steering towards the eastward. In the morning
they anchored in a large bay surrounded by lofty and
barren mountains.

"On the 2d of December I received a letter from
Lieutenant Maughn, commander of the Honourable Company's cruiser Antelope, saying that he had the ransom
on board, and had been three days cruising after us, and
wished me to settle with the chief on the securest method
of delivering it. The chief agreed to send us in a small
gun-boat till we came within sight of the Antelope ; then
the compradore's boat was to bring the ransom and receive us. I was so agitated at receiving this joyful news,
that it was with considerable difficulty I could scrawl
about two or three lines to inform Lieutenant Maughn of
the arrangements I had made. We were all so deeply
affected by the gratifying tidings, that we seldom closed

our eyes, but continued watching day and night for the boat.

"On the 6th she returned with Lieutenant Maughn's answer, saying, he would respect any single boat; but would not allow the fleet to approach him. The chief then, according to his first proposal, ordered a gun-boat to take us, and with no small degree of pleasure we left the Ladrone fleet about four o'clock in the afternoon. At one P. M. saw the Antelope under all sail, standing towards us. The Ladrone boat immediately anchored, and dispatched the compradore's boat for the ransom, saying, that if she approached nearer, they would return to the fleet; and they were just weighing when she shortened sail, and anchored about two miles from us. The boat did not reach her till late in the afternoon, owing to the tide's being strong against her. She received the ransom and left the Antelope just before dark. A Mandarin boat that had been lying concealed under the land, and watching their manœuvres, gave chase to her, and was within a few fathoms of taking her, when she saw a light, which the Ladrones answered, and the Mandarin hauled off. Our situation was now a most critical one; the ransom was in the hands of the Ladrones, and the compradore dare not return with us for fear of a second attack from the Mandarin boat. The Ladrones would not remain till morning, so we were obliged to return with them to the fleet. In the morning the chief inspected the ransom, which consisted of the following articles: two bales of superfine scarlet cloth; two chests of opium; two casks of gunpowder; and a telescope; the rest in dollars. He objected to the telescope not being new; and said he should detain one of us till another was sent, or a hundred dollars in lieu of it. The compradore, however, agreed with him for the hundred dollars. Every thing being at length settled, the chief ordered two gun-boats to convey us near the Antelope; we saw her just before dusk, when the Ladrone boats left us. We had the inexpressible pleasure of arriving on board the Antelope at seven P. M., where we were most cordially received, and heartily congratulated on our safe and happy deliverance from a miserable captivity, which we had endured for eleven weeks and three days.

(Signed)   RICHARD GLASSPOOLE.
" CHINA, December 8th, 1809."

The following notes added to Mr. Glasspoole's very interesting account of these eastern pirates, will show how ill he fared during his detention among them, and that with all their impunity of plundering, their lives were but wretched and beastly.

" The Ladrones have no settled residence on shore, but live constantly in their vessels. The after-part is appropriated to the captain and his wives; he generally has five or six. With respect to conjugal rights they are religiously strict; no person is allowed to have a woman on board, unless married to her according to their laws. Every man is allowed a small berth, about four feet square, where he stows with his wife and family. From the number of souls crowded in so small a space, it must naturally be supposed they are horridly dirty, which is evidently the case, and their vessels swarm with all kinds of vermin. Rats in particular, which they encourage to breed, and eat them as great delicacies; in fact, there are very few creatures they will not eat. During our captivity we lived three weeks on caterpillars boiled with rice. They are much addicted to gambling, and spend all their leisure hours at cards and smoking opium."

At the time of Mr. Glasspoole's liberation, the pirates were at the height of their power; after such repeated victories over the Mandarin ships, they had set at nought the Imperial allies—the Portuguese; and not only the coast, but the rivers of the celestial empire seemed to be at their discretion—and yet their formidable association did not many months survive this event. It was not, however, defeat, that reduced it to the obedience of the laws. On the contrary, that extraordinary woman, the widow of Ching-yih, and the daring Paou, were victorious and more powerful than ever, when dissensions broke out among the pirates themselves. Ever since the favour of the chieftainess had elevated Paou to the general command, there had been enmity and altercations between him and the chief O-po-tae, who commanded one of the flags or divisions of the fleet; and it was only by the deference and respect they both owed to Ching-yih's widow, that they had been prevented from turning their arms against each other long before.

At length, when the brave Paou was surprised and cooped up by a strong blockading force of the Emperor's ships, O-po-tae showed all his deadly spite, and refused to obey the orders of Paou, and even of the chieftainess, which were, that he should sail to the relief of his rival.

Paou, with his bravery and usual good fortune, broke through the blockade, but when he came in contact with O-po-tae, his rage was too violent to be restrained.

O-po-tae at first pleaded that his means and strength had been insufficient to do what had been expected of him, but concluded by saying,—" Am I bound to come and join the forces of Paou ?"

" Would you then separate from us !" cried Paou, more enraged than ever.

O-po-tae answered : " I will not separate myself."

Paou :—" Why then do you not obey the orders of the wife of Ching-yih and my own ? What is this else than separation, that you do not come to assist me, when I am surrounded by the enemy ? I have sworn it that I will destroy thee, wicked man, that I may do away with this soreness on my back."

The summons of Paou, when blockaded, to O-po-tae was in language equally figurative :—" I am harassed by the Government's officers outside in the sea ; lips and teeth must help one another, if the lips are cut away the teeth will feel cold. How shall I alone be able to fight the Government forces ? You should therefore come at the head of your crew, to attack the Government squadron in the rear, I will then come out of my station and make an attack in front ; the enemy being so taken in the front and rear, will, even supposing we cannot master him, certainly be thrown into disorder."

The angry words of Paou were followed by others and then by blows. Paou, though at the moment far inferior in force, first began the fight, and ultimately sustained a sanguinary defeat, and the loss of sixteen ves

sels. Our loathing for this cruel, detestable race, must
be increased by the fact, that the victors massacred all
their prisoners—or three hundred men !

This was the death-blow to the confederacy which had
so long defied the Emperor's power, and which might
have effected his dethronement. O-po-tae, dreading the
vengeance of Paou and his mistress, Ching-yih's widow,
whose united forces would have quintupled his own, gained over his men to his views, and proffered a submission
to Government, on condition of free pardon, and a proper
provision for all.

The Government that had made so many lamentable
displays of its weakness, was glad to make an unreal pa-
rade of its mercy. It was but too happy to grant all the
conditions instantly, and, in the fulsome language of its
historians, " feeling that compassion is the way to heaven—that it is the right way to govern by righteousness
—it therefore redeemed these pirates from destruction,
and pardoned their former crimes."

O-po-tae, however, had hardly struck his free flag, and
the pirates were hardly in the power of the Chinese, when
it was proposed by many that they should all be treacherously murdered. The governor happened to be more
honourable and humane, or probably, only more politic
than those who made this foul proposal—he knew that
such a bloody breach of faith would for ever prevent the
pirates still in arms from voluntarily submitting; he knew
equally well, even weakened as they were by O-po-tae's
defection, that the Government could not reduce them by
force, and he thought by keeping his faith with them, he
might turn the force of those who had submitted against
those who still held out, and so destroy the pirates with
the pirates. Consequently the eight thousand men, it
had been proposed to cut off in cold blood, were allowed
to remain uninjured, and their leader, O-po-tae, having
changed his name to that of Heo-bëen, or " The Lustre
of Instruction," was elevated to the rank of an Imperial
Officer.

The widow of Ching-yih, and her favourite Paou, continued for some months to pillage the coast, and to beat

the Chinese and the Mandarins' troops and ships, and seemed almost as strong as before the separation of O-po-tae's flag. But that example was probably ope-rating in the minds of many of the outlaws, and finally the lawless heroine herself, who was the spirit that kept the complicate body together, seeing that O-po-tae had been made a government officer, and that he continued to prosper, began also to think of making her submis sion.

A rumour of her intentions having reached shore, the Mandarins sent off a certain Chow, a doctor of Macao, " Who," says the historian, " being already well acquaint-ed with the pirates, did not need any introduction," to enter on preliminaries with them.

When that worthy practitioner presented himself to Paou, that friend concluded he had been committing some crime, and had come for safety to that general *refugium peccatorum*, the pirate fleet.

The Doctor explained, and assured the chief, that if he would submit, Government was inclined to treat him and his far more favourably and more honourably than O-po-tae. But if he continued to resist, not only a general arming of all the coast and the rivers, but O-po-tae was to proceed against him.

Paou was puzzled, but after being closeted for some time with his mistress, Ching-yih's widow, who gave her high permission for him to make arrangements with Doc-tor Chow, he said he would repair with his fleet to the Bocca Tigris, and there communicate personally with the organs of government.

After two visits had been paid to the pirate fleets by two inferior Mandarins, who carried the Imperial procla-mation of free pardon, and who, at the order of Ching-yih's widow, were treated to a sumptuous banquet by Paou, the Governor-general of the province went himself in one vessel to the pirates' ships, that occupied a line of en *le*, off the mouth of the river.

As the governor approached, the pirates hoisted their flags, played on their instruments, and fired their guns, so that the smoke rose in clouds, and then bent sail to meet him. On this the dense population that were ranged thousands after thousands along the shore, to witness the important reconciliation, became sorely alarmed, and the Governor-general seems to have had a strong inclination to run away. But in brief space of time, the long dreaded widow of Ching-yih, supported by her Lieutenant Paou, and followed by three other of her principal commanders, mounted the side of the governor's ship, and rushed through the smoke to the spot where his excellency was stationed; where they fell on their hands and knees, shed tears, knocked their heads on the deck before him, and received his gracious pardon, and promises for future kind treatment. They then withdrew satisfied, having promised to give in a list of their ships, and of all else they possessed, within three days.

But the sudden apparition of some large Portuguese ships, and some Government war-junks, made the pirates suspect treachery. They immediately set sail, and the negotiations were interrupted for several days.

Matters were in this state of indecision, when the two inferior Mandarins who had before visited the pirates, ventured out to repeat their visit. These officers protested no treachery had been intended, and pledged themselves, that if the widow of Ching-yih would repair to the Governor, she would be kindly received, and every thing settled to their hearts' satisfaction.

With this, in the language of our old ballads, upspoke Mistress Ching. "You say well, gentlemen! and I will go myself to Canton with some other of our ladies, accompanied by you!" And accordingly, she and a number of the pirates' wives with their children, went fearlessly to Canton, arranged every thing, and found they had not been deceived. The fleet soon followed. On its arrival every vessel was supplied with pork and with wine, and every man (in lieu, it may be supposed, of his share of the vessels, and plundered property he resigned) received at the same time a bill for a certain quantity of money. Those who wished it, could join the military force of Government for pursuing the remaining pirates; and those who objected dispersed and withdrew into the country. "This is the manner in which the great red squadron of the pirates was pacified."

The valiant Paou, following the example of his rival O-po-tae, entered into the service of Government, and proceeded against such of his former associates and friends as would not accept the pardon offered them. There was some hard fighting, but the two renegadoes successively took the chief Shih Url, forced the redoubtable captain styled "The scourge of the Eastern ocean" to surrender himself, drove "Frog's Meal," another dreadful pirate, to Manilla, and finally, and within a few months destroyed or dissipated the "wasps of the ocean" altogether.

"From that period," saith our Chinese historian, in conclusion, "ships began to pass and repass in tranquillity. All became quiet on the rivers, and tranquil on the four seas. People lived in peace and plenty. The country began to assume a new appearance. Men sold their arms and bought oxen to plough their fields ; they burned sacrifices, said prayers on the tops of the hills, and rejoiced themselves by singing behind screens during day-time"—and, (grand climax to all !) the Governor of the province, in consideration of his valuable services in the pacification of the pirates, was allowed by an edict of the "Son of Heaven," to wear peacocks' feathers with two eyes!

THE END.